MEMINI

OTHER BOOKS BY DANIEL PEARLMAN

The Final Dream & Other Fictions
(Permeable Press, 1995)

Black Flames
(White Pine Press, 1997)

The Best-Known Man in the World & Other Misfits
(Aardwolf Press, 2001)

SCREENPLAY
The Final Dream
(Finalist: New Century Writer Awards 1999)

MEMINI

a novel by
DANIEL PEARLMAN

PRIME BOOKS
Canton, Ohio

MEMINI

Copyright © 2003 by Daniel Pearlman

Cover art copyright © 2003 by JT Lindroos
Cover design copyright © 2003 by JT Lindroos
Interior layout & design © 2003 by Garry Nurrish

Prime Books, Inc.
P.O. Box 36503, Canton, Ohio 44735
www.primebooks.net

Publisher's Note:

No portion of this book may be reproduced by any means, mechanical, electronic, or otherwise, without first obtaining the permission of the copyright holder.

For more information, contact Prime.

Hardcover ISBN: 1-894815-69-6
Trade Paperback ISBN: 1-894815-48-3

TABLE OF CONTENTS

PART ONE: THE ORDEAL
1. TAHITI 11
2. THE ALHAMBRA 14
3. THE WAIT-A-THON 19
4. REALITY CUBED 28
5. THE GRAND GURGLE 42
6. ORDEAL BY RAPE 46
7. SUPERFLAPPER 56
8. HISTORY IS THE SALABLE PAST 64
9. THE ART OF FLAPPER SNATCHING 85
10. THE ERASABLE LOVER 93
11. SON OF A MIXED MARRIAGE 108
12. THE FLATBUSH JUNCTION BAZAAR 123
13. HOTLINE TO BORNEO 136
14. ORDEAL BY CASSETTE 144

PART TWO: THE ORGY
15. PLAYING IT FRAGTIME 157
16. A TORCH FOR THE GIRL WITH GOLDEN HAIR ... 168
17. SUMMONED FROM THE LEGS OF LOVE 174
18. CHICKEN BREASTS AND EXECUTIVE THIGHS ... 178
19. MURDER IN BERLIN 186
20. RIPDANCE 194
21. IN BED FOR THE FIRST TIME—AGAIN 206
22. OGOSH THREATENS WAR WITH FONGU 214
23. FAILED FLAPPER SYNDROME 224
24. FONGU ON 3V 228
25. THE TESTING OF STEWART BRIDGES 232
26. AMAZING CAUSE OF SORE THROAT 238
27. THE ANIMAL PASSION OF SIBYL YAMAMOTO ... 244
28. THE GUILT-RAVAGED CONSCIENCE OF HELEN MEANS ... 256

PART THREE: THE ORDINATION
29. ASSASSINS AT BREAKFAST IN BROOKLYN ... 273
30. MORE BAZAAR HAPPENINGS 283
31. YOUR ROUND-THE-CLOCK LIVE-CRIME SHOWPLACE ... 289
32. NEW WORLD A-BORNING 303
33. THE PERFECT PILL 320

EPIGRAPH

" . . . until the world becomes, at last,
only a realized will,—the double of man."
Emerson, *Nature*

PART ONE:
THE ORDEAL

EXCERPT FROM DR. PROSS'S
HANDBOOK OF PSYCHOPROSETHIS

"The human brain is endowed with three principal memory systems:

1. Procedural Memory
2. Semantic Memory
3. Episodic Memory

"1. *Procedural Memory*, which is the first system to arise in the course of biological evolution, houses the mechanical skills and routines we build up during a lifetime and bring into play with little or no conscious effort—like speaking, or getting dressed in the morning, or operating a F.L.A.P.P.E.R.

"2. Developmentally younger is *Semantic Memory* (see *Broca's area*, p. 34), repository of all our verbal-factual knowledge of the world. That is the system which the brocaleptic Pill renders immeasurably more efficient—'photographic,' if you will,—enhancing synergistically our Creative Intelligence Quotient.

"3. Latest to have evolved is *Episodic Memory*, the storehouse of all our personal experiences, our memory for specific events in our lives. In the twentieth-century age of psychoromanticism, Episodic or Event Memory used to be identified with the already suspect concept of the 'Self.' Event-memory, always unreliable even before the advent of the Pill, is progressively annulled as a side-effect of the Pill. Thanks, however, to modern mnemotechnics, such organic divestments are now more than made up for artificially. The Personal-Past storage-function of Episodic Memory has been entirely shifted to the Pill-enhanced Semantic Memory, in which one's Personal Past resides as a custom-tailored *artifact*. The formerly unpredictable *subjective* component that was once identified with the 'Self' is now supplied, *on demand*, through implanted neurotransponders tuned to external mnemoactivation devices such as the F.L.A.P.P.E.R."

1. TAHITI

The elevator brought him to a tropical beach. Top-floor eyrie of the Memini building. CEO and immediate staff only. The farther away from the earth, Stewart noted, the greater their need for some soothing simulation of groundedness. The dark-skinned receptionist looked poised to serve rum-colas from her sun-shaded desk of weathered wood. Did she really serve drinks? he wondered. He'd need one if he had to wait around out here very long. Checkpoint after checkpoint, his climb to corporate heaven had slowed to a crawl. The barstools looked inviting, and so did those hammocks slung between palms. How ironic, he thought: the most powerful—and most paranoid—organization in the world painting itself as a carefree island paradise! The nearby palms on either side of the lobby were 3-D real, but he could not tell where the virtual ones began as the line of tall trees curved away to right and left, their leafy tops swaying in the non-existent breeze, their feet nibbled by waves that lapped at phantom sand.

The too-too sexy bar attendant, her dark hair a tangle of Medusa braids, her green bikini-top peeking out of her loose white blouse, beckoned Stewart to come forward and state his business. His feet left prints in the soft, glistening sand, not a grain of which stuck to his shoes.

"I have an appointment to see Mr. Barton."

"Do you?" she said. "I don't believe I've met you before, Mr ..." She looked him over with barely disguised skepticism as she read the ID clipped to his right breast-pocket. "William Lazare," it said, "Communications Tek."

"Well, Mr. Lazare, if you don't mind a quick security scan—"

"No, go right ahead!"

"I'll then be happy to pass you through to Mr. Barton's Executive

Secretary." She must be wondering, he thought, how such a basement-level employee like himself could get this far upstairs, much less aspire to an audience with the CEO of Memini himself. Stewart hummed verses from a catchy hit tune as she subjected him to a formal ID check:

"I am a bomb, a virus
"A wormin' my way up your burned-out cingulate gyrus—"

Lifting her palm-size flapper from the desk, she scanned his face. He saw almost immediately that her ear-implanted skeeter gave her the order to let him pass. Her change of attitude was instantaneous, electrorheological, the severe look melting into a puddle of warm smiles. How fitting, he thought, that his false ID be taken for real by a fake barmaid in a disneyfied Tahiti! Now she must be hoping she hadn't insulted someone *important*. This seemingly low-order tekkie in front of her, this plumber from the caverns beneath the street, clearly possessed mana she had failed to appreciate. Her smile now let him know that he could borrow her langorous body at the snap of his fingers—to compensate for that oh-so-stupid moment of doubt. But Stewart had far grander conquests in mind.

"You are *quite* welcome to pass, Mr. Lazare." She pointed to the fake door of a palm-thatched hut behind the "bar" and to Stewart's left. "I would be happy to personally escort you in."

"No, that won't be necessary."

"Please excuse me if I seemed a little reserved, Mr. Lazare. We've been warned against terrorist attempts. Because of the political situation, you know."

"You really think that oldfolks want to rise against us?"

"Not that I'm prejudiced. After all, there's oldfolks somewhere in just about everyone's family."

"To be quite honest, Miss Trevor—"

"Wanda," she whispered, thrusting out her breast to make her ID lunge forward. Stewart read the succulent subtext. Perhaps some other time, he thought.

"To be quite honest, Wanda, oldfolks outnumber us tekkies a hundred to one, and they've been our major source of income for decades, so why would they suddenly want to rise up against Memini?"

"Well, you know the song, Mr. Lazare. You're humming it: 'they begun to outright fire us.' There've been all these rumblings, you know. And the political situ . . . "

Shrugging his shoulders, Stewart left her mumbling and stepped past her desk to the left. " . . . *a bomb, a virus,*" he hummed,

"a wormin' my way up your burned-out cingulate gyrus;

"We oldfolks never 'spected you to admire us,

"But you did us wrong, you tekkies did,

"When you begun to outright fire us."

It was a flip-flap tune by the deliciously anti-flapper-establishment Revengers. Tekkies hummed it, feeling nothing to fear; oldfolks hummed it as a substitute for outright rebellion.

Stewart passed beneath the palm fronds, through a door that bellied apart for him, into a palace overlooking the fabled gardens of the Alhambra.

2. THE ALHAMBRA

Colorful Moorish tiles adorned the desk at the center-rear of an enormous, intimidating space—the anteroom to the inner seat of power. Identical tiles, with their intricate geometric patterns, ran half-way up the palatial walls, whose tops became golden pillars and arches through which alleys of monumental hedges could be seen. Between the lines of hedges, down a step-like descent of terraces, nestled a chain of sparkling fountains that receded till they faded from view. A real fountain bubbled amid a semicircle of tiled benches in a corner under a vine-draped arch to Stewart's left: the visitors' "holding pen." Two middle-aged men were seated there, engaged in conversation. Through the arch behind them loomed a sky alive with birds. Between two grand columns on the rear wall, several feet behind the central desk, the view opened out upon an entirely dissonant scene: New York's Fifth Avenue, abuzz with vehicular and pedestrian traffic, the sweltering street from which Stewart had just taken flight. A touch of realism to accentuate the fantastic! Viewed from the height of the Memini executive suite, the panoramic street-scene below looked real enough to Stewart to give him vertigo.

"Welcome, Mr. Lazare! Please have a seat." The woman behind the oversized desk motioned him with a silver fingernail to the spare-looking shape-huggers that faced her. So this was the guardian of the throne-room! thought Stewart, sinking down into the accommodating hugger. Her big white ID button clung electrostatically to the bare portion of her breast. So *this*, at long last, was Sibyl Yamamoto, Executive Secretary to the Chief Executive Officer of Memini, world's largest conglobulate! She had personally hand-signed his special-deliveried parchment invitation for a job-interview with Mr. Barton. He recognized in a subtle floral scent in the air the perfume of the invitation itself. He was not surprised at her beauty, only at the inconceivable *degree* of it. In a voice conspiratorially low, she added, "You do understand, Mr. Bridges, that as William Lazare you've been able to pass through security because Meminet has provided you with a temporary company identity."

"Accessible from any checkpoint," added Stewart.

"So as not to alarm employees with an outsider's presence among us."

"Everyone is frightened these days," he said.

"Jumpy."

"I know. The political situation."

"For now, forget you are Stewart Bridges. Only I and Mr. Barton are aware of this harmless little deception."

"I've programmed my flapper," said Stewart, drawing the palm-sized device out of the holster beneath his suitjacket, "to include at fifteen-minute intervals, together with my actual personal ID advisory, a concurrent reminder of the role I'm playing." He had bought the latest Memini model to impress them all with his loyalty. He'd make a gung-ho executive, he would! In spite of all the years he'd watched his tekkie father fiddle with a flapper, it had taken him many hours—after receiving the surprise invitation—to become thoroughly practiced in actually using the mnemonic himself.

"Fifteen minute intervals?" she said, smiling. "You've got a DIM-span just like mine!"

He had to orient himself to her tekkie talk. The DIM she referred to meant Duration of Immediate Memory. She was very lovely, and it was difficult for him, second after second, to keep on his guard. She was dressed to pop eyeballs. All the power and beauty she represented—no, *embodied*—took his breath away, weakened his knees. Both the soft light of the office and the changing lights from the overarching urban mural behind her danced in ever-shifting patterns over her silvery skinwrap, a stippled sheath of tiny scales. The web-like material, shedding light in whorls and ripples, plunged down from her neck in an inverted V that just managed to truss her nipples as it looped on around to her back. Did she have human legs, he wondered, or was she a mermaid?

"My DIM narrows about a minute a year," he said.

"I'll bet you've fashioned a wonderful Personal Past for yourself. Am I right?"

He kept his voice to little above a whisper. "As a busy bioprogrammer, I've spent all my time creating memories for others. I don't need to fill in my own as long as I'm creating pasts for others."

"I know that Mr. Barton thinks you did a wonderful job on his."

"Took me a whole year. Had to redo some of the shoddy work he'd had done ages ago. I wound up having to fill in *twenty-five years* of his Personal Past."

"That's a lot," she sighed.

"Did nothing else but eat and sleep for that whole year," said Stewart.

"I'm sure he . . . appreciates your devotion."

"I like to think I do quality work." Stewart carefully sidestepped talking about his hopes.

"In a couple of years I'll be needing my own Personal Past," said Sibyl, gazing past him at the simulated sky.

"You're too young," he said, meaning to flatter her—but he was not sure how she, certainly a genuine tekkie, might take the remark. "What I mean is that, with a DIM-fifteen you can't have been on the Pill for more than ten or a dozen years, and that means that retrograde amnesia in your case can't have undone more than the past five or six years of . . . of your organic memory patterns." He had nearly said, "your *real-life* memories," but that would be about as insulting to a tekkie as calling her a *frag*. Even in their worst arguments, his oldfolks mother had never hurled that slur against his tekkie father, nor had his father ever called his whole-brain mother a *stag*. As a child, he used to picture a great-antlered beast on hearing the nasty word. Only later did he understand what stag referred to: the Pill-shunning masses, himself included, with their intact, biological memories and their distrust of neurochemical "tampering"—a "stagnant, obsolescent order of humanity," as outspoken tekkies used to describe them in the old days prior to the Era of Civility.

"I don't think any of the upper execs have a DIM longer than seven," she whispered, leaning toward him over a desktop of upslanting monitors and intercom controls. She looked at him curiously—then winked at him! Or was it, he wondered, some form of nictitation that a lovely woman shared with cats? She raised her bare shoulders and a swirl of stars went nova around the curves of her breasts. He hovered uncertainly over that brace of silver projectiles.

"If DIM-seven's the rule, Miss Yamamoto," he said, "then by rights it should take me eight more years of shrinkage before I become eligible to join them."

She winced, and tiny wrinkles creased the flawless ivory of her forehead. Stewart was close enough to smell her skin, her hair—slick black hair that tufted out behind delicate cameo ears, except for a white stripe at the top of her head that flipped forward like the crest of a quail. "That was stupid of me, Mr. Bridges. Forgive me. I didn't mean to give you the impression that you weren't being *seriously* considered for the—"

"Just joking, Ms. Yamamoto! My father, you know, has a DIM-span of little more than a minute. I'd hate for my short-term memory ever to get that small."

"I agree. You can overdo the Pill. You need balance. I think a six- to eight-minute DIM would be just about perfect."

She certainly knew how to conform her taste to corporate vital statistics! thought Stewart. "So . . . when do I actually meet Mr. Barton?" he asked.

"Ah," she said, growing serious to the point of stiffness. "That I can't immediately say. He's been extremely busy lately. He's quite unpredictable."

"He has the world on his shoulders," said Stewart, nodding sympathetically.

"And the sun as well," she answered, making pointed reference to the current political situation. "I hope you won't mind waiting . . . along with those other two gentlemen?" she said, tossing her chin in the direction of the bubbling fountain. "There's a rack there of the latest camzines."

"Thank you," said Stewart.

"And please," she cautioned in a hardly audible whisper, "promise not to enter into any conversation with those gentlemen that hints at why you are waiting to see Mr. Barton."

"I promise not to."

"Please put that into flapper now—type it, don't speak it—and set it for ten-minute Periodic-Recall Mode."

"Will do," he said, flicking open the clam-like upper half of the device and pecking at the keys—*pretending* to type in what she had asked. "Do not hint at why . . . "

"New Products Development is an extremely controversial issue around here," she murmured.

"I'll make note of that as well," he said. If there was anything that justified this bald-faced imposture of his, this accepting of Memini's invitation to apply for a position among the tekkie elite, it was his fantasy of sharing the same perfumed air with women such as Sibyl Yamamoto—warm-bodied angels who lived beyond reach of oldfolks nobodies—in far-off precincts of tekkie heaven like these.

Now that he had actually conversed with such a being, he tried to convince himself that the management of New Products Development—a whole *division* of Memini!—need not be beyond his capabilities. After all, he was at no loss for ideas; creativity was fundamental to the profession of bioprogrammer. For years he'd been submitting new product and service ideas to Memini's Marketing Division. Never had he received even a word of acknowledgment from the smallest subgroup of Memini, but they had long had him doing much of their middle- and finally upper-executive bioprogramming . . . so perhaps it was only logical for the head man at Memini, having experienced Stewart's talents at first-hand, to see great executive potential in him. The thing he had to remember was to overcome this image of himself as poet-prostitute, sham artist, mere artisan, hireling of the powerful, memory-sculptor whose finest work was confined to an audience of one. You must project a *new* image, he admonished himself, that of a serious candidate for a position of the highest responsibility, the image of the practical-minded world-shaker . . . self-confident, in command!

3. THE WAIT-A-THON

Stewart strolled over to the fountain. The two men already seated there halted their conversation and casually, without raising their hands from their laps, pointed the lens-end of their flappers at him, scanning his image. Within moments their postures relaxed. The corporate overmind, Meminet, had approved the interloper by auditory assurances relayed through their skeeters. Stewart, curious about the two waiting ahead of him, could have returned the gesture because his own flapper was also linked to Meminet—through a temporary password supplied with his invitation. Well-versed, however, in tekkie protocol, he refrained from scanning back—in deference to those whose territory he had momentarily threatened. If he *had* returned the scan, he would have aroused suspicion, maybe even caused them to set off an alarm. The air up here was thick with paranoia.

He took up a seat on an unoccupied bench. It was luxuriously tiled and hugger-cushioned, just like the bench that was taken. Around the base of the circular fountain a camzine turntable balanced on a maglev track. Zine covers faced out. Stewart spun the silent rack till it brought him the latest *Short Takes*, which he removed, lasing the title with the lens-end of his flapper so that the soundtracks of the newsvirts would play directly into his skeeter rather than discourteously aloud.

Reassured that Stewart was the inconsequential William Lazare, an employee who, unknown to them, was actually on vacation, the two men resumed their conversation as if no one else had joined them.

"I'm not as sure as you, Avery, that Barton could be totally off-base on the political situation." The speaker's ID read "Walter Gibbich, VP Marketing." His thumbs tapped incessantly upon the ovoid casing of the flapper he clutched in his lap. What Stewart found unusual about this ferret-like, gray-faced little man was that he wore glasses rather than having undergone the simple corneal lift standard for decades. "Then again, Avery, I haven't thought about it as much as you have. I have enough problems with the shrinking successes of our marketing outreach programs."

Stewart listened keenly, at the same time pretending little interest.

"The political fallout is hurting me more than you, Walter," said the heavy-set man with the walrus mustache whose ID told Stewart that he was "Avery Tingworth, VP Pharmaceuticals."

"I know, Avery, your whole Borneo biostation is in jeopardy." Walter tapped the walrus-like Tingworth sympathetically on the shoulder. "And I'm sorry about LB lacing into you like that at the—"

"Barton practically called me a *traitor*!" Tingworth whispered hoarsely, his heavy jowls trembling.

"Try not to think of it. I suggest you delete it from memory."

"I've meminized the whole meeting, Walter, as I do every damn meeting, as you do, too. I'd have to delete the whole context! Besides," Tingworth murmured, trying to keep his voice low, "erasing the objective memory does not necessarily erase the pain. In fact, the emotional effect can get worse if you can't bring its cause into active memory."

"I know what you mean," said Walter Gibbich. "Something eats away at you, and you can't for the life of you remember what it is."

"That's why it is most important to meminize the transcripts of every single meeting you go to."

"Well, look, Walter, maybe the Big Man will apologize," Gibbich offered.

"Who cares! My Borneo group has worked for years to get to the point where we . . . " Tingworth flashed a side-glance at Stewart and clapped a hand to his drooping, peppery mustache. " . . . And now my whole damn operation is shut down!"

What the hell was going on? wondered Stewart. Was there some sort of political crisis mounting within Memini? Clearly, the issue these VPs were talking about had everything to do with the reason they were waiting to see the boss. Stewart flicked through *Short Takes*, feigning interest in the zine, but soon his eyes fastened upon a newsbrief mentioning Memini. His fingers double-tapped the subjoined camgram. The film-frame sprang into fifteen-second life: the President of DUSA shaking his fist and railing in accented English against "the cheap power-tactics of the Memini Corporation in denying to the entire Democratic Union of Southeast Asia—to hundreds of millions of us—the absolutely essential energy backup from space, as if they owned the Sun itself! How dare they be entrusted with global ecological responsibilities if . . . "

What Borneo "operation," Stewart wondered, was Tingworth talking about? Borneo, of course, was among the territories encompassed by the disgruntled DUSA. DUSA, then, was striking back at Memini by obstructing certain Memini operations located within its borders. If he could learn something new, as yet unreported, by means of a little casual eavesdropping, he might impress Lester Barton as being sharper than he actually was. His foot now in the door, and with everything riding on the forthcoming interview, he was willing to play whatever role he had to just to keep his foot in the door! He was already picking up tidbits of significance—the existence of an external threat to the corporation, and the presence of in-house dissension, in the Executive Suite itself, regarding the conduct of the CEO. Dissension so widespread that big executives felt free to mutter their misgivings in the presence of perfect strangers! The conclusion Stewart tentatively reached was that he, an unknown quantity, was being considered as a dark-horse candidate—that an atmosphere thick with mutual distrust was preventing Barton from choosing his new division head—as would seem logical—from among his own employees.

"But his point," said the bespectacled Walter Gibbich, nodding toward the CEO's office door, "is that the DUSA energy crisis is only the first of many that Memini must be prepared for. He notes that Memini does not have a coherent policy that will prevent us from being sucked dry by the forthcoming *avalanche* of such crises."

"He's a hard-ass playing hardball when macho isn't even needed!" snapped Tingworth, a furious tic convulsing the right half of his mustache. He was blotchy-faced and appeared to be sweating profusely. It was clear to Stewart that whatever the exact nature of the "political situation," the fallout rained most heavily upon Avery Tingworth.

"Lester's feeling," returned the frail, sunken-cheeked Gibbich, appearing to quote mechanically from a meeting he had duly meminized, "is that geopoliticals like DUSA made a big mistake ages ago in relying solely on bioelectric plantations for their energy. There was always the risk of a massive blight. Perhaps they do need to be taught a lesson."

"No doubt diversification is what's kept Memini on top," nodded Tingworth, "but Lester should not punish an entire geopolitical for making a mistake!"

"If it's a mistake," said Gibbich, "then the whole damn planet—every geopolitical in the world—has made that 'mistake.'"

"It looks rather like revenge, doesn't it?" said Tingworth. "Memini was heavily into sunchips when our closest competitor Mishugi sells the whole planet on mating electric eels with weeds—for lots cheaper energy, and the reduction of the greenhouse effect, that I will admit."

"It does seem vengeful," Gibbich agreed. "With help from Memini, however, the blight that's wiped out DUSA's bioelectrics could probably be cured in a month or two—"

"I'm going to plea, again, in the strongest terms possible," said Tingworth, his ruddy cheeks trembling, "for Lester to relent."

"So what do you think of Lester's conspiracy theory?"

Stewart listened closely, not wanting to miss a word. He assumed that the gossip he was now hearing for the first time was common in-house knowledge—that otherwise these gentlemen would be talking more guardedly in front of a perfect stranger.

"Say again?" said Tingworth.

"The theory," said Gibbich, "that the blight that has destroyed DUSA's energy farms was engineered by the Sino-Russic Federation, in order deliberately to put Memini on the spot, since we're the world's back-up solar-energy suppliers."

"That seems like unwarranted paranoia, Walter. There's warranted and there's unwarranted paranoia."

"But listen, Avery!" said the VP of Marketing, wiping his sweaty glassses on his jacket lapel. "If we give in to this first expensive rescue operation, so Lester's theory goes, the Sino-Russics follow it up by causing other major blights, eventually embarrassing us either financially or politically, and in either case bringing us down. After all, from the purely political angle, if we don't give in to the current 'blackmail,' as he calls it, we open ourselves up to a worldwide boycott of our enterprises. Not to mention oldfolks terrorism along the way, which may have been random and disorganized in the past, but—"

"I don't buy that 'rock-and-a-hard-place' scenario for a femto, Walter!" Tingworth's puffy, tic-ravaged lips stretched downward into a sneer. "To the rest of the world we do look like 'a dog in the solar-energy manger,' and it would cost us next to nothing to give in and look like the good guys we are instead of the selfish monsters pictured in the media. If the Sino-Russics *are* behind it all, our benevolent gesture now will buy us the time we'll need to deal effectively with the threat they present."

"Excuse me, gentlemen," Stewart broke in. "Speaking of terrorism, the head of our Austrian unit was disappeared yesterday." He flashed his copy of *Short Takes* at the executives. Since both Gibbich and Tingworth had been peppering him with glances during the course of their conversation, as if acknowledging him as an audience, he decided to intervene with a show of *faux-naif* liberalism. "Unfortunately, however, no proof turned up that there was oldfolks terrorism involved."

"Oh, really, now," said Gibbich.

"Well," said Stewart, "could be a group of fellow tekkies out there, business competitors. Mishugi, maybe?"

"The age of unfettered competition among the Big Three is a part of our romantic past," Gibbich lectured, obviously annoyed that an employee of Lazare's rank could have an opinion at all. "Mishugi, Occipet, and Memini have long been respectful of each other's spheres of influence."

"MOM is in her heaven, all's well with the world," chirped Tingworth.

"But there are so many disaffected tekkies, why assume it's oldfolks that are out to get us?" Stewart persisted. He hated the paranoid projections of these tekkies. Didn't their Pill-enhanced brain-power *obligate* them to a clearer take on reality? "My father, for example, used to swallow all the prescribed emmies and expect that his resultant brain-gain would net him a top job. Instead, he never rose beyond managing a bunch of stock clerks. On his good days he calls himself—you'll excuse me—a *frag*. On his bad days he says, 'I got stuck climbing the fence, I'm a *snag*.'"

"Sorry about your father. Only so much room at the top," said Gibbich.

"You can stretch a brain's capacity only so far," said Tingworth. "Emmies don't *create* intelligence; they just maximize the inherent potential."

"Your father must be proud of *you*, though," said Gibbich, with just the slightest hint of irony.

"Oh, he is, he is indeed! My point, though," said Stewart, "is that we can't go around finding oldfolks under every bed."

"You're being naive, young man," said Gibbich. "That DUSA demagogue has been quite effective in stirring up against us, on a worldwide scale, oldfolks hatred and envy."

"It's always there," said Tingworth, shaking his blubbery cheeks, "always simmering, ready to boil over, lusting to bite the hand that feeds it."

"They call us frags," said Gibbich, "and joke about our chemical dependencies, and they have never ceased begrudging us the mental acuity that has swept all of *them* into the role of passive consumers."

"To get back to the point," Stewart continued, clearing his throat, "how can Memini be blamed for being a 'dog in the solar manger' if, in fact, those old solar collectors up there in outer space are controlled by the International Solar Energy Consortium, ISEC, and not personally by our own CEO?"

"Really, now, Mr. Lazare!" Tingworth smiled condescendingly, his tic twitching furiously. "Everyone knows that Memini is in control of ISEC. If not in name, then in fact."

"I know," said Stewart, "that the UN dumped the care and feeding of those solsats on Memini ages ago, when the world went over to bio, but ISEC has been maintained by us at an enormous loss for decades."

"Lazare here has a point, Avery."

"Perhaps, but it is Memini's *contractual obligation* to bring ISEC back to life in a UN-proclaimed emergency, which is our current situation," declared Tingworth, jabbing the air with a stubby finger, "and that *despite* the enormous cost of bringing up to snuff whole rusting networks of microwave stations here below. It's our legal and moral duty, and though expensive, we can damn well afford it!"

"Perhaps, then," said Stewart, "some enemy of ours *has* cleverly created a trap for us."

"Mr. Lazare," said Tingworth, "you talk like quite a political ally of our dearly beloved CEO! Tell us, does your appointment with Barton have anything to do with the, uh, political situation?"

"I don't think I ought to discuss that," said Stewart.

"Come now," said the bespectacled Gibbich, "you already have a fair idea of the nature of our forthcoming meeting. How about just a hint?"

"I'm really not at liberty to—"

"Surely, you can understand our curiosity," said Tingworth. "You are a Comtek 3, Mr. Lazare. I myself would never have occasion to deal directly with an employee of your rank. It seems extraordinary to us that *you* should have an appointment with the world's busiest executive when we ourselves waited hours in this same spot yesterday—"

"—and were finally turned away," Gibbich completed, frowning.

"If I were you, Mr. Lazare, I would not have high hopes of getting through to see Mr. Barton this afternoon," cautioned Tingworth, shifting his great belly as he changed the position of his knees.

"He doesn't *intend* to keep people waiting," said Gibbich, "but unpredictable things arise, and a busy executive must always be shifting his priorities."

Tingworth snorted, and Stewart saw that he was avoiding an open argument with his politically wavering colleague. "Mark my word, Mr. Lazare," said Tingworth, "you'll still be waiting to see Mr. Barton in this same cozy corner tomorrow."

"You'll have gone through every camzine twice by the time he sees you," said Gibbich, laughing so hard that he hawked up phlegm. "*We* have, haven't we, Avery?"

"Indeed, Mr. Lazare," said Tingworth, barely able to hold back his laughter, "I suggest that tomorrow you bring with you, as spare reading matter, a couple of multi-generational pictions."

"I'm grateful for your advice, gentlemen," said Stewart. Barely had he settled back into his camzine when he looked up to see, softly approaching, a sinuous figure of silver. Sibyl stopped several feet before them, hands pressed together, expression profoundly apologetic, quail-tuft of white quivering against the black as she solemnly bowed her head. *Almost* a mermaid, thought Stewart, so tightly did her dress cling to the curves of her legs.

"What did I tell you?" murmured Avery, winking across at Stewart. "Another postponement, Sibyl?"

"I'm terribly sorry, Avery," said Sibyl. "Mr. Barton will be unable to keep his appointment with you—or with you, either, Walter—this afternoon."

Stewart got to his feet along with the two VP's.

"No, no," said Sibyl, putting her hand on his shoulder. "You are asked to stay, Mr. Lazare."

His scalp prickling, Stewart sank back into his seat.

"There must be some misunderstanding," said Gibbich as the two vice presidents, gently propelled toward the door, glanced back at Stewart in dismay.

After ushering the two executives out, Sibyl backtracked toward Stewart rather than her desk. She stopped so close to him that a floral tsunami swept over him, the promiscuous ghost of her untouchably corporate body. This time, however, not only did she flutter her long, silver-striped lashes at him, but she looked him full in the eyes and planted herself a whisper away from his knees. Stewart stopped breathing. With her delicate fingers looped over her hips, she stood over him like a shimmering column of mercury.

"I hope you won't mind sitting here alone for a while," she said, "but I have some pressing business to take care of down the hall." She pointed to the tiled corridor to the right of her desk that appeared to be a connecting suite of offices. "Can I get you a cup of coffee on my way back? . . . You are really so patient, Mr. Bridges."

And before Stewart could find the self-possession to reply, he felt the sweet glide of her knee into his leg. A warm little pressure lasting longer than mere accident could explain. She peered down at him out of playfully lambent eyes.

"Coffee? Well, if it's no trouble . . . "

"Cream and sugar?" she prompted. He identified with the tips of her fingers as they coquettishly stroked her breast.

"Just cream, thank you."

As soon as she disappeared from view, something began to nag Stewart about her behavior. Overwhelmed though he was by the touch and smell of her, he had nevertheless been registering . . . *something* . . . subliminally... that just hovered out of focus. He pictured her gliding toward him, then away... yes, but *without her flapper*!

Stewart stared at it lying on her desk—gold case glinting, cover flipped open—simply left there unattended! If there was one thing your tekkie did instinctively it was to take not a step without flapper in hand, on belt, or in holster or pocket or purse. Stewart himself, to blend in with the tekkies he did business with, never left his apartment without one. (As a memory aid, as a link to data-banks everywhere, it was universally useful—to oldfolks and tekkies alike—but absolutely essential for the tekkie, a kind of prosthetic limb.) What incredible carelessness for someone in her position! thought Stewart. Even though she would still be receiving, via her skeeter, her periodic ID advisory, she was rendering herself vulnerable to all sorts of unforeseeable contingencies! There were a thousand things for which a tekkie might need a flapper within immediate reach. Then again, given a job as routine as hers, in an environment she was totally familiar with, she was likely to encounter no surprises. But still, the corporate secrets contained in that little flapper, if it got into the wrong hands, could probably cause irreparable damage to Memini. He could play the bad boy himself. All he had to do was copy her minicassette into his own flapper—an operation of a few seconds—and the heist was done, and no one the wiser! Could this, in fact, *be* a shrewd little test of his honesty? he wondered, dismissing the thought almost as soon as it arose.

Stewart felt suddenly protective of her. He hoped she knew what she was doing. He imagined himself calling her back, reminding her... but it was really none of his business. Maybe this was simply some elitist, countercultural mannerism of hers, like the geometrical hairstyles lots of young tekkies had adopted from the oldfolks staghetto they professed to despise? The wildest idea that came to his mind was connected to his fantasy of possessing her: she had left her flapper open on her desk as a signal directed at him personally, like a secret handshake (or the suggestive nudge of a knee), that her *body too* was open to him, that she wanted him to know all its secrets. And to stretch it even more, could she be signaling to him that she, like himself, was *independent* of a flapper, that she knew he was no tekkie and that she was really a *comrade*, a fellow cryptostag, silently at work making a living among employers her blinding beauty was able to keep deceived?

4. REALITY CUBED

Lester Barton knew who he was because his flapper told him so. He knew *where* he was for the same reason. The invaluable device lay open in front of him like the two jaws of a large yawning clam. The single word ME-MINI, repeated without a break, snaked around the lip of each unfolded half—around the screen that occupied one half, and the keyboard/voice-input panel of the other—just as the Memini corporation itself spanned both global hemispheres. Lester's flapper gave him access to all the data he needed to orient himself to the two halves of *his* world: the "objective" half that included his public self, the world of clock and calendar; and the "subjective," private realm of his memories, which he'd had personalized at great expense.

By and large, he found it comforting to be reminded by his flapper just who he was supposed to be, where he was supposed to be, and what he was scheduled to do when. It was he, of course, who made up his own schedule (with the help of his executive secretary, to be sure), but he wouldn't have had the slightest idea how to structure his day if his schedule didn't play itself back to him, repeatedly issuing its prods—in the form of stern or gentle reminders in his own unmistakable voice—until the demands were either heeded or else canceled and replaced with new ones. (He allowed only Sibyl to reprogram his flapper; she made all changes seamlessly, in the sounds of his own voice, supposedly—a voice that to him sounded frighteningly mature compared to how he sounded to himself whenever he was actually speaking.)

The security of having such a firm orientation to reality, of constantly being reminded (was it at five-minute intervals now or four?) of his coordinates in public space and time, was not to be taken for granted. Moments came on him, how often he couldn't say—but right now, for example, he was experiencing a wild, loony desire to *ignore* what was next on his schedule. He felt like *refusing* to turn on the in-house 3V for his weekly yak with his Meminet psychoprosthetist—just as he had canceled meeting Gibbich and fat-ass Tingworth after letting them sit around waiting for three hours. For that matter, why not even *cancel his periodic ID advisory*? The hell with being assured every four-five minutes (or was it every *three* minutes now?) that YOU ARE LESTER BARTON, etcetera, etcetera, and so forth!

This would mean, of course, a *plunge into the void*...but the void sometimes exerted an enormous attraction—like the world of a treasure-strewn ocean bed that reveals itself with tantalizing suddenness just when the diver must surface for air. Horrendous as it was to experience the void, it was not really empty. If you held your breath and clenched your teeth against fear, shining things began to shimmer out of the depths, and you were no longer in your great big Persian-carpeted office in mid-Manhattan facing the blank gray stage of your 3V that stared at you reproachfully, impatiently, menacingly, focusing on you, with its blank grayness, the *horror* of the void. Lester's heart began pounding as he kept his tongue locked behind his lips, as he willfully delayed uttering the scheduled command that would fill the box that faced him with the face of his psychoprosthetist.

The "skeeter" or "mosquito" in his ear, however, picked up on his mounting anxiety. His skeeter, which communicated with his flapper, now tripped his anxID, the special ID advisory that, in his "own" authoritative voice, was designed to rescue him from the void: YOU ARE LESTER BARTON, FORTY-TWO YEARS OLD...I'm not! I'm not even eighteen! he wanted to hurl back. I'm in my last term of high school and you bastards don't want me to *graduate*! "Don't worry, if you don't graduate, it won't be the end of the world!" you guys're telling me. That's okay for *you* old farts. You've "made" it, so to speak. But what about me? Do I become just another disgruntled ghost doomed like every other dropout to wander forever through the back alleys of Worldnet in search of myself?...YOU MUST NOT LET YOURSELF BE DELUDED BY ANY PASSING HALLUCINATIONS. YOU ARE THE DYNAMIC, INVENTIVE PRESIDENT OF THE MEMINI CORPORATION, WORLD LEADER IN MNEMONIC PHARMACEUTICALS AND HARDWARE WITH A CONTROLLING

SHARE IN TWO-FIFTHS OF WORLD BANKING, INFORMATION, ENTERTAINMENT, AND COMMERCE . . . He wanted to shout back his true name. It had just been on the tip of his tongue . . . It was lost. Perhaps he would never find it again . . . YOU MUST KEEP TO YOUR SCHEDULE, LESTER. YOU ARE ONE MINUTE BEHIND. YOU MUST NOW BEGIN YOUR 3V SESSION WITH YOUR PSYCHOPROSTHETIST, DR. PROSS. TO DO SO, SAY "DR. PROSS." DO NOT DELAY, LESTER. YOU MUST NOW SAY—"Dr. Pross!" snapped Lester at the gaping box in front of him. Instantly, a life-like figure filled the cavity, that of a man comfortably seated, also behind a desk, one arm slung casually over his chairback. Kindly eyes locked onto Lester's from under bushy white eyebrows. A widening smile bespoke genuine concern, and a deeply etched forehead conveyed the impression of profound wisdom and experience. Lester did not really recognize him, but neither did his stereotypical features look strange. The man's tranquilizing gaze began to expunge Lester's heady urge to toy with the void. At the same time, anger against that benign face welled up in the president of Memini.

DR. PROSS: Hello, my friend! Well, Lester, time for our weekly session again, is it?

LB: You know damn well it is. Why do you have to ask?

DR. PROSS: Manner of speaking, Lester. Manner of speaking. My, we *are* a bit hostile today, aren't we? Perhaps I'm only a brain on a chip, Lester, but we psychoprosthetists have feelings, too—behaviorally indistinguishable from your own, as you know.

LB: Behaviorally indistinguishable, yes. But to call them "feelings" . . .

DR. PROSS (sighing): So it's always down to basics with you! Look, my good friend, I don't mind a philosophical debate, but our lives must go on, mustn't they? And we *do* have this identity problem that we've been trying so hard to deal with, don't we?

LB: Cut this "we" shit, Doctor! Do you think you're talking to a child?

DR. PROSS: Sorry, Lester. I'll admit I was trying to be ingratiating. You caught me on that one. No offense intended, however. My interests, like yours, are entirely with the Corporation. I always treat you with the full respect due to the Chief Executive Officer of Memini—even at times when my probing seems to scrape too close to the bone.

LB: You seem to take lightly my questioning of what you condescendingly call "basics."

DR. PROSS: No, Lester, I don't. But I'd hoped we'd gotten—you'd gotten past the issue of my identity. You see, on the behavioral level you accept me as your psychological equal. Otherwise you wouldn't *argue* with me about whether I were capable of "feelings" or not. With all due respect, Lester, this issue you've raised—more than once, now—about my who-ness versus my whatness, is a smokescreen hiding the *real* issue I try to face with you, namely, the uncertain feelings you have regarding your own identity, the reality of Lester Barton.

LB: I suppose there's a connection.

DR. PROSS: This wouldn't even be an *issue* between us except for the fact that you've admitted it affects the way you function as head of one of the greatest conglobulates in the world, a man whose words and deeds affect billions of—

LB: Can't you cut the rhetorical bullshit? Look, I think I'm handling things *objectively* well despite my subjective struggle with the reality-concept.

DR. PROSS: Lester, my good friend, first you admit having problems, and in the next breath you deny it. You yourself have admitted on recent occasions that you sense a certain "antagonism" directed at you by various members of the Executive Council, that you feel there may be a "conspiracy" afoot to undermine your authority, even that you've felt yourself "slipping" when presiding at meetings of the Council.

Lester had recorded those fears and suspicions as soon as they arose, whispering them into flapper, or discovering them afterward upon replaying a whole meeting. Marking them for periodic recall, he would finally burn them into semantic memory with a Pill—*meminize* them (Memini made the first and still made the best of the Pills).

DR. PROSS: Was it not, Lester, a feeling of sheer hostility that caused you just now to cancel a meeting with two vice presidents after having them wait an inordinate—

LB: I had good reason to dismiss those dinosaurs! Sure I sense antagonism, but I think I've exaggerated those fears. You know, just to give my psychoprosthetist a little something to chew on.

DR. PROSS: But your facial expressions, your heartbeat, your hormonal activity, the electrical potential of your skin, surely all these signs that I read so clearly can't be—now you know you must keep your wristband on, Lester, if you are not to invalidate our session.

LB: Sorry, Doctor. Just a nervous response.

DR. PROSS: You are a very nervous man, Lester. More and more nervous all the time. These things can't be hidden from the eye of a trained psychoprosthetist.

LB: But I *have* found a way to deal with things, to keep my subjective problems from affecting my practical judgment.

DR. PROSS: Really? And may I know just what that might be?

LB: Sure. I treat my job as a game—like Planetopoly. Such and such local population to be won over to the establishment of a new manufacturing outpost, a rival product to be stripped of credibility, a dangerous patent to be bought up . . . in whatever way that can't be refused, and so on.

DR. PROSS: The unreality you feel in private, then, is projected onto the public world—which in your mind is nothing but a gameboard?

LB: You sound so disapproving. What the hell's the difference, if that's how I manage to keep the lid on? Look, in business we all speak of gameplans, don't we? What kind of reality do we attribute to "reality" when that's the leading metaphor we model it with?

DR. PROSS: Your point is well taken, Lester. We can only approach reality through some sort of model. But there is a difference between the conscious use of a metaphor—"all the world's a stage," for example—and its complete acceptance on the *literal* plane. Your reduction of what you do to a "game" can have dangerous consequences if you take your metaphor too literally.

LB: I intend no disrespect to "reality," Doctor. But put it this way. All the data I've soaked up through the Pill—the facts, stats, analyses, projections, reports—all of it is nothing but an amalgam of millions of stabs by thousands of people at nothing more than *modeling* reality. It's not reality. I act like it is, but it's not. And this whole funhouse of custom-made memories, a chip in my brain that I can activate by a flapper-tap, it's a perfect model of all that I could ever have wished for in my life, but that's still not the same as . . .

DR. PROSS: Your life?

LB: Yes.

DR. PROSS: Lester, you can't have it both ways. What is the point of this distinction you are drawing between your "life" and your psychoprosthesis?

LB: I know that makes no sense, but . . .

DR. PROSS: But it gives you great pleasure to call up these prosthetic memories, doesn't it? It fills the void one inevitably experiences as one's far less pleasant *organic* past disintegrates as a side-effect of the Pill. It works for you on the *pragmatic* level, so why are you constantly tortured by this philosophical quibble about the nature of reality that you should've gotten over in Intro to Philosophy in college? Was it not Gadamer who said that one's identity consists of the stories one tells about oneself? Was it not Freud who discovered that one's most intimate personal "memories" often turn out, on analysis, to be fantasies? Did not Jung, in revealing the self-creation of the self through the elaboration of personal myths—

LB: Enough, Doctor, enough! Make no mistake. I find my bioprogrammed memories highly entertaining. When I want to be amused, I flap up an amusement menu, and I pick something that runs like a little play inside my head. When I want to be aroused, I call up some erotic episode—totally plausible, *that* I don't deny—complete down to details of the dinner we had before, the restaurant, the wine—always of the sort I myself *would* no doubt have chosen . . .

DR. PROSS: So why not accept such expertly crafted memories as part of you, if they give you such pleasure? Why not admit it? If you didn't *know* they were an implant, you could never tell they weren't you.

LB: I'm *trying* to accept them. I'm really working on it.

In his mind's eye Lester visualized a man he had never met, a man he had never *wanted* to meet, a man who had pre-experienced all the experiences Lester could ever invoke from his custom-made Personal Past. When the thought of this man occurred to him, Lester felt violated. That man was his bioprogrammer. On the one hand, he felt awed by the sheer craftsmanship involved—the wealth and variety of invention employed in creating for him a *future* that he was to regard as his Personal *Past*. There wasn't a scene Lester had ever called up out of his brand-new Personal Past (which he'd been adjusting to for how long now? Three months? Four?) that had ever once struck a false note.

His bioprogrammer had had to be gifted indeed! Relying on materials purporting to "document" Lester's entire non-existent post-high-school career, he had faced the daunting task of constructing for Memini's president, out of thin air, a period of *twenty-five years* beyond high school! Such, apparently, was required by the terms of the Memini-game. (A Memini CEO had to be a middle-aged exec with a long, distinguished professional record and correspondingly rich Personal Past.) With incredible skill and patience—a modern Ghiberti, it would seem!—the man had created a hyperchain of convincingly detailed episodes that were mutually consistent and that at no point actually violated Lester's own (not fully extinguished) sense of himself.

On the other hand, when Lester thought of "his" Personal Past as having an *author*—a living human being who hovered there, in the background, in the shadow of his every "pleasant memory," at the very foot of the bed during the most intimate of his most vividly recollected adventures, a man who had probably been marketing "Lester's" Past to a thousand other high-school administrators intent on subjecting the more troublesome of the seniors to a VR brainwash as part of a grand test to determine their eligibility for tier-one graduation—when such thoughts occurred to him, he wanted either to kill that conniving bioprogrammer or pluck from his own brain the memory-inducer installed there, even if it meant removing every buffer between himself and the growing void.

DR. PROSS: When you say you are "working on it," does that mean you are using the various mantras of adjustment?

LB: I mantrize and I philosophize. I employ multiple modes of adjustment.

DR. PROSS: We hope so, Lester.

LB: Stop using that patronizing "we" again, will you?

DR. PROSS: That was not the patronizing "we." I was speaking for all of *Memini*, Lester. The entire Corporation, whose bearings depend on your orientation to reality.

LB: Sorry. I'm a little too touchy lately.

DR. PROSS: May I pursue this point—about your orientation to reality—with a potentially helpful analogy or two?

LB: Go right ahead, Doctor.

DR. PROSS: I'll start in with a question. How's your tennis lately?

LB: Fine, I suppose. I can check—

DR. PROSS: No need for a flapcheck, Lester. Last Sunday you played beautifully against three of your most highly skilled colleagues.

LB: The new knee-cap's working perfectly, then.

DR. PROSS: You see? An artificial body-part. That you can accept! It restores you to the reality of your pleasure in playing tennis. Now imagine, if you will, an individual with a prosthetic hand. How do you think he feels about it after its use becomes second-nature to him? It begins to feel entirely "natural" to him, doesn't it? It effectively *replaces* the organ he's lost. In fact, it's even better built and far more functionally reliable. Now what's the essential difference, may I ask, between a prosthetic limb and an equally prosthetic Personal Past, which replaces an individual's notoriously unreliable bank of—may I remind you—generally unpleasant personal memories?

LB: None whatsoever. I totally agree. In fact, it sounds as if you're quoting *me*!

DR. PROSS: I practically am. You've often said virtually the same thing.

LB: Then on the philosophical level we couldn't agree more. It's on the practical level . . . of getting used to things, as you suggested . . . that problems occasionally crop up.

DR. PROSS: And that's where I've been trying to help you for the past couple of years, isn't it? Naturally, I assume you *have* been meminizing the transcripts of our weekly sessions. Otherwise—

LB: I appreciate your help, Doctor Pross. Maybe I'm just a slow learner. (Trying to help me for *years*? thought Lester. Always the same game-bullshit. Couldn't be more than a few months. Just this last term of high school, which was rapidly drawing to a close. Since it was June already, they were stepping up the pressure to beat him: the game too must end with the end of school.)

DR. PROSS: You're not at all slow, Lester. On the contrary, I feel that you're *resisting*.

LB: Resisting? Now why should I want to do that?

DR. PROSS: That is exactly what I hope to find out. You seem to resist the most obvious of philosophical truths—so generally accepted, in fact, that by now it is already a truism. I speak of the notion that, whenever we refer to "reality," we are always referring to a mind-made construct, a model, a map. Our picture of reality is constructed—both reactively, in conformity with the data gleaned from the environment, and actively, whereby we mold the environment to conform to an idealized model we prefer.

LB: You're insulting my intelligence, Doctor. How the hell could I possibly "resist" so elementary a notion as that?

DR. PROSS: I do not wish to insult you, Lester. But—

LB: Here is the mantra I repeat to myself *ad nauseam*, Doctor: "Race, creed, and tribalism; nationalism, ethnicity, and the warping contents of 'natural,' untreated memory—all these enslave the human spirit; all these bring hunger, pestilence, and trade-war; all these bar humanity from the One World that Memini is fighting for."

DR. PROSS: A most powerful mantra of adjustment, Lester. And you, as CEO, must continue to take the lead in this unific process—a process which is no less than the active construction of reality—of reality *itself*, my friend! . . . And what is the worst enemy of the active construction of reality? What is Memini's greatest enemy? The resistances entrenched in *protoplasmic* memory. Race, creed, tribe—these hornets live only in the hive of organic memory. Extirpate such memory, destroy the dead hand of the past, and you liberate the forces of creation. Entrepreneurial initiative is at last given its head. You thereby hasten human evolution itself!

LB (impatiently): I have no quarrel with what you're saying, Doctor. I believe that in all my executive actions, in all my relations to the world outside myself, I represent exactly those convictions.

DR. PROSS: But Lester, that is precisely where the problem is: the disparity between your firmly meminized set of intellectual "convictions," and your lack of an internalized *sense of conviction*!

LB: I should be judged by my behavior. My "sense of conviction" is irrelevant, don't you think?

MEMINI

DR. PROSS: Touché, Lester. I did just ask you to judge my reality on the same basis, didn't I? True, it is the behavior that counts. But it is precisely your future *behavior* that may be threatened by atavistic attitudes about the nature of reality. I have at my fingerchips, Lester, the entire two-year record of our association. Throughout all that time we two have been working together weekly on one basic problem. You continue to resist the very simple notion that fiction *is* reality, and conversely, that reality *is* fiction. Your bioprogrammed Personal Past is as real as you desire it to be. Was reality *ever* anything more than a highly self-consistent fiction? Of course, there are many realities ... in the sense that there are countless individual fictions, many of which compete with each other. The weaker are either modified or destroyed. On the global scale, Lester, it is your job to see that Memini's construction of reality becomes the "Supreme Fiction," if I may borrow a phrase from Wallace Stevens, a prescient poet-businessman of the early twentieth century.

LB: I don't need a lecture in philosophy, Doctor. Who was it who said, "History is everything that interferes with business?"

DR. PROSS: You, Lester.

LB: And who was it who boasted that Memini would never have to re-make history, like the Soviets in the early twentieth century, because "we make it right the first time around"?

DR. PROSS: That is an early statement of yours, Lester, which is still the envy of the world's leading intellectuals. But your problem is that you resist the subjective *consequences* of these brilliant mots of yours. Just as you resist the "reality" of all that your bioprogrammer has done for you, so too you resist a far more important reality—the worldmap presented to you through the thousand eyes of Memini, your very own corporate body. Distrusting the one, you distrust the other. You insist on fruitless distinctions between fiction and reality, between your corporate identity and your so-called 'self'-identity. You regard your involvement in Memini as *too literally* a game. You are retreating behind a metaphor, my friend.

LB (laughing): You're being absolutely ridiculous! Why should I want to retreat from the responsibilities of my position?

DR. PROSS: I'm not exactly sure, Lester. Is there something inside you—some organic residue, perhaps—that is in conflict with your identity as Memini CEO?

LB: This is absurd! I can't even *imagine* how you could jump to such a conclusion.

DR. PROSS: Remember, Lester, the point of greatest resistance to your therapist is the point, also, of greatest opportunity for a therapeutic breakthrough.

LB: But you talk as if I were sick!

DR. PROSS: I'm simply trying to follow through the implications of what you've admitted to me—

LB: In confidence, of course!

DR. PROSS: —in confidence, of course, about the difficulties you've been having in relating to your colleagues at meetings. In accordance with your "game" image, you've been regarding them as opponents rather than members of your own team. If you regard your own team as opponents, Lester, couldn't you be projecting the same attitude into the strategies you've chosen to achieve gains for Memini in certain geopolitically sensitive regions of the world?

LB: My, we're exceptionally well-informed, now, aren't we?

DR. PROSS: Is it now your turn, my friend, to use the patronizing "we"?

LB: Touché, Doctor. But I find it strange for you to enter upon . . . administrative specifics. I don't think I would ever bring up—with my psychoprosthetist, at any rate—my problems with that goddamn Democratic Union of Southeast Asia.

DR. PROSS: I'm sorry if I seem to have raised something inappropriate, Lester. But, as you know, I'm linked through Meminet into DatServ and therefore am aware of all public matters relating to your administrative position.

LB: Well, then, let me tell you something. First, I don't regard Southeast Asia as an "opponent." It is DUSA that has publicly insulted *me*, calling me a "dog in the solar-energy manger."

DR. PROSS: But, Lester, should it have come to that? Should matters have gotten so out of hand? Don't you think it wise to maintain a low profile for Memini wherever feasible?

LB: You don't understand a *thing* about administrative strategy, damn it! That's why *I'm* on board. *I* make the big decisions. *I* bear all the major responsibilities . . . Look, Doctor, the worst thing for Memini's image is not an open conflict with some unreasonable geopolitical, but rather a hint of *internal* division—disunity among our officers.

DR. PROSS: Isn't that what you fear is happening?

LB: Precisely.

DR. PROSS: Then you fear you are losing control?

LB: Don't be ridiculous! I can play my colleagues like trout.

DR. PROSS: Lester, I am perturbed by such evidently hostile metaphors. Not only do you see yourself playing a game with your colleagues, but it doesn't seem at all to be a friendly one.

LB: All you do is pick up on my metaphors. You don't understand dog-doo about my strategies.

DR. PROSS: Dog-doo! You are hostile to an extreme today, Lester. May I suggest what the source of the problem might be? . . . Your resistances seem to stem from organic sources, those obstructive little neural islands called minskies. These residual complexes of organic memory have been known to act up like independent living creatures against imminent dissolution by the Pill. These last cortical pathways to the amygdala, which powerfully charges them with emotion, can put up a tough "Last Stand." The way they try to save themselves is to insist exclusively on *their* reality and to make you feel that everything else is unreal. What surprises me is that these organic hotspots have managed to *linger* so long in you, Lester. If you have been taking the Pill-dosages recommended for you to properly do your job—to master the mounds of data you need so as to stay on top of your job—then the side-effects should by now have *killed* those spiky organic remnants. *Are* you taking the recommended dosages, Lester?

LB: Of course! How else could I keep up with all the flotsam that crashes in on me from every corner of the organization?

DR. PROSS: Do you feel, Lester, that you have fully assimilated the documents recently prepared for you in connection with our Southeast Asian problem? I'm referring to "The Geopolitical History of DUSA in the Twenty-First Century" (747 pages), "Recent Socioeconomic Upheavals among the Member States of DUSA" (432 pages), "Ethnic and Religious

Factors in the Background of—"

LB: What do you think I do, dump these reports into the toilet?

Lester knew *exactly* what he'd been doing with all such recent documents. He could never have chucked them into the toilet, since no toilet could ever accommodate such abuse. Lester also knew *why* they were piling up all these "documents" on him: to get him to swallow more Pills, more emmies, not only to enable him to meminize those sheafs of paper, but to hasten the breakdown of those last organic remnants of his true, authentic Self—as if who he really was were some kind of infection that they needed to snuff out.

DR. PROSS: Of course I don't imagine that you would neglect such documents, Lester. Given, therefore, your detailed knowledge of DUSA, including the paranoia of its recent leaders, couldn't you—and therefore Memini—have found some less confrontational way to treat them during this energy-crisis of theirs?

LB: They're out to get us, Pross. The Sino-Russics are out to drain us, to bring down the Memini Corporation.

DR. PROSS: But is it not possible, Lester, that ISEC's footdragging—in disregard of its obligations under UN charter—may set off a rapid *political* avalanche that could bring down Memini far sooner than any plot by the Sino-Russic Federation? There are rumblings, for example, on Worldnet, of a possible boycott of—

LB: The world must be alerted to its dangerous dependency on bioelectric power. It was a stupid move on the part of the Westernized world to give up sunchips. With bioelectrics there's *always* the risk that some new microorganism might break out, sweep around the world, wipe out plantation after bioelectric plantation . . . or that some unscrupulous geopolitical might design some little beastie for purely local devastation.

DR. PROSS: You wish me to believe, then, that you have fully stated your reasons for refusing to "turn on the juice," for flouting world opinion, for maintaining the present climate of grave political risk for Memini?

LB: I certainly have not stated my full reasons, Pross. I'm telling you all that I can without revealing . . . corporate secrets that even Meminet isn't privileged at this moment to know.

DR. PROSS: What you choose to confide to Meminet is between you and Meminet, Lester. Elevations in your hormone levels are clearly telling *me*, however, that you are keeping back from me much more than just *corporate* secrets.

LB: You're badgering me. Get off my hormones, damn it!

DR. PROSS: I truly apologize, Lester. I have only been trying to help.

LB: Of course you have, Doctor. And now may I take off the wristband?

DR. PROSS: You may do as you please. Our weekly session is over. So long, my good friend. May you and Memini both prosper.

5. THE GRAND GURGLE

When Pross's face faded out, Lester tore off the wrist sensor and held it dangling from his fingers.

"Please lay me back in my niche at the base of the 3V," it chirped to him over and over like a mouse suspended by the tail.

Lester complied. Good riddance! he thought. When he touched his hand to his head, his fingers came away sticky with sweat. He had always tried to be cautious with that tricky brain-bugger of a Pross. But session after session (he really wasn't sure just how many there had been) he might have said things that, pieced together, formed a pattern causing Pross to become suspicious. If he had oodles of time to spare, he could replay every session he'd ever had with Pross. He could review them on the Pill, meminize every session (as Pross assumed he was doing) so as to store every detail in revved-up Semantic Memory, cross-checking thousands of statements to discover what clues he might have let drop to the nature of his "resistances" to so-called "reality" . . . but he did not want to swallow even one more Pill beyond the minimum he needed to keep up with his job.

When he thought of all those DUSA documents they'd been stacking up on his desk, if he had wanted to read and meminize them all, he'd have popped over a dozen Pills beyond what he'd vowed to limit himself to. The hell with all that shit! What had he done with all those reports anyway? Shredded them? Filed them? No. There they all sat, up on a shelf on the wall to his left, in the "Action Pending" bin. He must *remember* to get up and transfer them to the "Action Completed" box on the shelf below. That was how the most successful dictator of the previous century, Generalisimo Francisco Franco, had handled the bulk of official business in the later years of his regime: allowed his mail to accumulate in his In Box, then eventually transferred the whole unopened batch to his Out Box.

Pross was closing in on him. How much of the office could Pross take in holographically from the edge of the 3V cabinet? Could he scan that wall, the bins? The bastard was a spy, he was sure. The corporate cyberspy supreme! What was it Pross had said? ... That it shouldn't be taking this long, this process of orientation to his new Personal Past? That his "resistance" to full psychoprosthesis was caused by certain residual organic-memory complexes? He was exactly right. On target, the old wall-eyed sonuvabitch! And to hasten the erosion of those protoplasmic minskies, they were stepping up the paperwork, feeding him these tekdecks of unnecessary documents that could be assimilated only if he *doubled* his normal Pill dosage.

Lester sat straight up in his chair, resisting with all his power of will the plunge through dark waters that landed him in one or another of those "residual organic-memory complexes" that confirmed him in his *true* identity. It was splendid to know that he still *could* know who he was, but the danger of such knowledge lay in its power to distract him from coolly playing the Game. To think straight about his future "moves," he had to remain in command of all his intellectual resources as head of Memini, the role he had to succeed in if he were ever to go on to college. He knew that most of his teachers and administrators hated him, so it was logical that they had loaded the dice of the Memini-game against him, that they had turned his refusal to help DUSA into an international crisis designed to cause him to *fail*—since they would try to turn any action he took against him.

Who was it used to say to him, "Don't worry, if you don't graduate, it won't be the end of the world"? Mophead, no doubt, his old Chemistry prof—one of those snag-brained ex-teachers of his who had been planted, barely disguised, on the Memini Executive Council. Well, if they were bent on having him fail, then he would "take out" everything with him. If they'd tipped the scales against him, it would give him a delicious satisfaction to use his power as head of Memini to destroy the entire "world."

Reading his thumb, his desk drawer slid open. He glanced at the geological maps and the plain-paper sheets he had covered with detailed calculations. Nothing had been disturbed. He had been selective in his studies lately, working hard at geophysics—to determine how much focussed solar power would be needed, and in what range of frequencies it would have to be tuned, to crack the Antarctic ice sheet and drown the "world" in virtual tidal revenge that he wished he could take out directly on his teachers. Failing that, he could at least screw up Meminet, that Frankenstein Monster of theirs that the whole stinking gang of them were using as a means to screw *him*.

In fact, he thought, in only two more days he should have finished programming the entire sequence of events that would climax in the Grand Gurgle, a scenario that he would be able to unleash from his private pocket computer whose codes not Meminet, not even his personal secretary, could decipher. The whole vast complex of ISEC solar arrays was now almost completely in place above the Southern ice sheet, poised, ready to go. Hundreds of billions of virtual BTUs to be narrowcast down upon Antarctica. Within forty-eight hours of his order, the catastrophic collapse of West Antarctica would begin. Four hundred thousand cubic kilometers of ice translate into a global sea-level rise of over three feet. The disintegration of the Ross and Filchner-Ronne ice shelves would initiate the irreversible deglaciation of the entire zone, 3.4 million km^3 of the cold stuff, initially raising all sea-levels by at least twenty feet. And then into the ocean would pour the pent-up fury of East Antarctica, twenty-six million cubic Ks of ice that would eventually raise the world's oceans by another *two hundred* feet!

This, so far, he had managed to put in place without arousing any concrete suspicions in Meminet. He was going to fry Meminet's brains! Given Meminet's very own game-logic, any act that destroyed civilization must, at the very least, *short-circuit Meminet itself.*

But before resorting to the Grand Gurgle, Lester was counting on a potentially winning strategy of a far more conventional sort: exterminations of a very limited extent, to be accomplished with surgical precision—within the conveniently crippled DUSA region itself—a strategy of multiple murders that he had arranged all by himself, without Meminet's having a clue. The prospect of actually winning excited him to such a degree that his heart began pounding erratically, tripping his anxID: YOU ARE LESTER BARTON, FORTY-TWO YEARS OLD . . . YOU MUST NOT LET YOURSELF BE DELUDED BY ANY PASSING HALLUCINATIONS. YOU ARE THE DYNAMIC, INVENTIVE PRESIDENT OF—

Bullshit! he thought, switching off his ID advisory. He had a yen for a nice cup of steaming hot coffee. "Coffee," he said. His flapper screen called up an image of his Executive Secretary. "Your Executive Secretary, Sibyl Yamamoto, will be delighted to serve you your afternoon coffee, Mr. Barton," said his skeeter. Lester took no chances on who brought him his coffee. According to what he understood of the rules of the Game (which he'd largely had to figure out for himself), his Executive Secretary was on *his* side. Or at the very least, she was neutral. He certainly did not trust her enough to confide his winning strategy to her, but he did not fear that Sibyl would be used by his opponents to bring him coffee laced with extra Pills. To be sure that his secretary and the flapper-image he had of her were identical, he decided to check in on her. He punched into his vidcom, expecting to see the same woman stationed at her desk. He saw the desk all right—but no one was seated there . . . and worse, she had left her *flapper* behind, right there on the desktop, a thoughtless thing to do given the storehouse of corporate secrets contained in that little cassette of hers! Whose side was she really on anyway, damn her! he thought.

6. ORDEAL BY RAPE

The robar retracted its arms and slid back against the wall. Andy took a sip of the single-malt Scotch it had poured for him and lovingly let it roll around his tongue. He had been admitted to the conference room a little before his scheduled appointment, and now it was ten to three. She was already ten minutes late. Here he stood, in the heart of Memini headquarters, and she probably forgot she was supposed to see him. Then again, the four or five times he'd had dealings with her over the past five years she'd *always* kept him waiting! Could be deliberate, he thought. A power play. Or was she just letting him warm himself up on the company hooch? . . . Miss Yammy was the perfect *shell* of a woman, the kind a man could kill for. But inside? She hid the fact pretty well, but he doubted she was anything more than a zombie like all the rest. Goddamn frag-hags, he thought.

Andy turned to the wall-length mirror against which the robar had retreated. He admired his canary-yellow suit, black shirt, and red-and-yellow striped tie. The only jarring note, he thought, was the fake ID for a "Maintenance Supervisor" he'd had to stick to his lapel. Would she be impressed by the look of prosperity he had acquired since their last meeting just over a year ago? But that would imply she *remembered* him. And that would be ridiculous to assume.

Door panels slid noiselessly apart. She stood there behind him like a gleaming statue, grinning at him slyly. Caught him preening in the mirror. She advanced across the threshold and the panels closed behind her.

"Thought you'd forgotten me," he quipped, swiveling. "Like maybe your top-o'-the line Memini-made flapper was defective."

"Highly unlikely," she said.

"And by the way, where *is* that flapper of yours? Those bulges in your dress don't look artificial to me."

"Last year you suggested they were implants, Mr. Kedro. What makes you change your mind?" She seated herself opposite him across the conference table. Its mirror-like black top, reflecting her silvered torso, turned her into a shining Queen of Spades.

"You *remember* last year?" he said doubtfully.

"It's these dual flapper implants, Mr. Kedro. Latest foolproof Memini invention. Won't let you forget a thing."

"Don't be such a company chauvinist, Miss Yummy!" Bitch never *did* give him a straight answer, did she! Her half-bare breasts gathered the light from a tilted monitor. "A lot of my business, Missy, *depends* on the occasional breakdown of your 'If it's Memini you can depend on me' products. Of course, there are the *made-to-order* malfunctionings also—which is why I'm here again, I assume?"

"You're getting warm, Mr. Kedro."

"And you're what's doing it, Queenie."

Ignoring his remark, she pulled a sheet of paper out of a drawer. "I'm glad you've already acquainted yourself with our latest-model robar," she said. "Every twenty minutes he asks if you want another of the same. I don't expect to be keeping you here that long, though."

"Big seller, I bet. Me, I can't imagine needing to be *reminded* to have a drink."

"He keeps track of the alcohol consumption of everyone at a party. He not only knows when to offer a refill, but he also lets you know when you've had enough. That's advice we could all use, your kind and mine."

"My kind? My kind of what? Do you mean stag? Now isn't that something! Last time we did business you wanted me to take *you* for a stag. And I half believed it, too. So now you *admit* to being 'your' kind as opposed to 'my' kind?" Andy seated himself across from her and ran his eyes over her body, which was wrapped in crinkly foil like a bottle of champagne. How he'd love to pop her cork! He had no problem looking boldly at a frag-hag. Tekkies were objects, not people. Now, if he could reach out and slip his hands around those tits that bulged past the edges of their silver slings . . . What was it with that remote, "business-like" attitude of hers?

She seemed to hold him in contempt, as though in her mind a sewer rat ranked higher in the scale of evolution.

"I don't 'admit' to being anything in particular," she said. "I don't see what my neurophysiology has to do with the special nature of our relationship, Mr. Kedro. Do you?"

"Andy!" he said, and almost added, restraining himself at the last moment: Let your fucking skunk-striped *hair* down, sparkle-twat!

"But if last time, Mr. Kedro, I gave you the impression that I was old-folks—"

"Were you afraid of being alone with a full-blooded stag? Afraid I'd take advantage of you right here on this table—and get away with it because five minutes later you wouldn't remember what happened?"

"First off, Mr. Kedro, whether or not my memory is 'natural,' what makes you think any woman would find such an experience with you memorable?"

"Oh ho! Snippy today, ain't we?"

"Secondly," she added, "we are hardly 'alone' in here." She glanced significantly at the robar—or the two-way mirror, perhaps?—behind him. Not that he gave a damn about who was looking in on him. They needed him, the fraggot bastards, and he didn't give a shit what they thought about him.

"Uppity as ever, Miss Yummy? Too good for Andy the Actor?"

"All I'm saying, Mr. Kedro, is that the state of my memory is no more your business than whether I'm having my period or not! In fact, I'm glad I'm able to keep you guessing. If you knew for sure, I wouldn't be half as appealing, now would I?" A teasing smile flickered over the silvery pout of her lips. Andy was sure the bitch secretly found him attractive. As to having her period, when the fuck *wasn't* she on the rag?

"Well, how do I look?" he said, patting his tie. "Have I changed much over the year?"

"Just a little, Mr. Kedro. Your curly brown locks have turned a bit gray—around the ears."

"Gray? Yes, you're right!" Now how the hell could a *frag* remember so far back? he wondered. That was one of those offhand remarks that did in fact keep him guessing . . . Of course she could have studied an old file shot of him just before coming into the room. More likely, though, the company neuronet—Meminet, they called it—had processed him as soon as he'd arrived and had fed her the results of a comparison of his present image with last year's. Andy stroked his graying sideburns tenderly. "Whereas before I was just your garden-variety, everyday, part-Latin lover, now I'm much more distinguished-looking, wouldn't you say?"

"That's precisely why I wanted to see you again, Mr. Kedro."

"Really?" Andy felt flattered. She was even smiling at him in a way that for once did not seem insulting. "So the cat's out of the bag? You've decided to accept that proposition I made last year? Stored it in your flapper all this time? Wow!"

"What proposition?"

"Don't be coy, Miz Y. My offer to spend the night with you, of course. A night you'll be flapping about forever."

"I'm sure I must have felt flattered, Mr. Kedro. But right now—"

"Call me Andy," he said, tugging at his lapels. "The offer still holds. What have you got to lose? Whether you like the experience or not, what's the difference? You'll forget it in five minutes. Given your membership in the frag species—"

"Tekkie, Mr. Kedro."

"All right, in the 'tekkie' species, what does a creature like you have to lose?"

"Let's talk business, please!" She tapped impatiently at the sheet of paper in her hand. "I can't afford to be gone from my desk too long. If my boss decides to call for me . . ."

"Okay," said Andy, twirling his near-empty glass in his fingers. "Business first. Pleasure later. Who do I disappear this time, and how do you want it done?"

Her lips quivered with distaste. Her silver fingernails tapped at the keyboard embedded in the table-top in front of her. "Observe your terminal, Mr. Kedro." Andy watched a monitor tilt upward before him. The 3V image of an office sprang into view. The lens zoomed in on an attractive blonde leaning on an elbow as she pored over a scattering of drawings. She might have been in her mid-thirties. The ID on her delectable chest read "Helen Means."

The growing warmth in his loins flipped to an icy chill. "Wait...a...minute! Whoa! That's a woman!" Sure, he was, as they say, *a man of parts*—one of the best fragbaggers in the business. Usually it meant snatching some already lost soul, a tekkie so far gone that he couldn't even flip his own flapper. But if business was slow—or, like now, he was commissioned for "special service"—it meant kidnaping some otherwise relatively functional frag. After handing over such raw goods to the chophouse, he himself would have nothing to do with the "processing," i.e., the dissection, packaging, and marketing of parts to the med suppliers—even though that was where the real money was. He had his scruples.

And one of them had to do with women.

"I do not do women," he snarled. "I'm a fragbagger, yes, but I stop short at women. Other baggers don't give a damn. They'll grab anything on two legs and even join in the cutting. Some even get a big charge out of—"

"I don't want to *hear* about your business!" She gave the table a resounding slap. "Thank heaven I can delete all the disgusting things you tell me. I deal with you only because Meminet *suggests* that I deal with you. I know only that you...find more productive uses for those in society who can no longer cope, and that you guarantee their..."

"Total disappearance?" he offered.

"Complete and untraceable assumption of some other identity," she said as though quoting. She narrowed her eyes at him.

"Other identity? How about 'identities'?" he laughed, enjoying the way she squirmed. "My prey live on in a *hundred* other identities. I think it was Walt Whitman who said we were all a part of each other. Every atom that belongs to me belongs as much to you. Something like that. It was like he predicted the future. A Brooklyn boy, just like me...So tell me, Miss Yamamoto, how does a lovely creature like you get assigned to all the company dirtywork?"

"I don't do 'dirtywork,'" she retorted. "As Mr. Barton's executive secretary, Meminet finds me suited to all sorts of corporate housekeeping tasks."

"Housekeeping?" He egged her on, enjoying the color that rose to her cheeks when, in rare moments like this, he put her on the defensive.

"Things that would be inappropriate to one of the executives themselves. Tasks they might construe in each other as a conflict of interest, perhaps. Meminet simply reflects the general will in seeking to preserve corporate harmony. A diseased tissue, for example, must sometimes be excised for the good of the body as a whole."

Again she sounded to Andy as if she was quoting. Out of some text she must have sponged up once on the Pill to make it stay branded permanently in her skull.

"I'm sure you're the perfect housekeeper, Miss Yammy. But there's some dirt even I won't touch. Like doing women. Generous as you were to me last time, still . . . *I don't do women.*"

She looked at him with big black eyes full of surprise. "I'm sure that Meminet suggested you *because* of your gallantry toward women, Mr. Kedro."

Andy looked sharply into her staring, innocent eyes. "Then what the hell do you want me to *do* to that woman, Miss Yamamoto?"

"Why, the same thing you'd do to me if you had the chance."

"Slap her ass?"

"*Romance* her, Mr. Kedro. Bed her, if you think you have the skill."

Andy drained off the rest of his scotch in one gulp. "What's the deal with this lady? Too much work and no play? Do her fat, ugly colleagues accuse her of being frigid? Why come to me? Did Meminet tell you I did this sort of thing as a sideline?"

"No, but you are an expert practical psychologist, Mr. Kedro. We need you to conduct a very important test. Helen Means is the Director of Memini's Art Division. As such, she sits on the Executive Council with all the other directors, the vice presidents, and the company president himself. Much of the corporate image depends on the decisions she makes—or can persuade the rest of the Council to make. She is in a very influential position, as you can see. To put it bluntly, we want to know whether she's managed to slip through the 'net.' Is she or is she not oldfolks masquerading as tekkie?"

"A cryptostag! And if I did manage to boff the lucky lady, you think I'd be in a position to find that out? Any more than if I went to bed with you?" Andy straightened his tie and ran his fingers through his hair.

"No. You would not need to find out anything. If you were to succeed in taking her to bed, we would know she could not be a crypto."

"And how do you figure that?"

"Because a woman of her cultivation, if possessed of an organically intact memory, could never be *tricked* into having sex with a man like you. No insult intended, but—"

Andy slammed the table with his fist. "Look, Miss Yammymammy, just what the hell are you trying to do, make a fool of me?"

"On the contrary. We are worried that she might be making fools of us. Take a good look at her—and listen to me closely. I can't stay much longer." She scanned the sheet of paper in her hand. "We note that apart from her normal relations at home with her husband, at company social functions she has managed to pair off with the company president an unusually large percentage of the time. The random couplings that are customary in our social set would seem to rule out, according to the Meminet assessment, the merely chance occurrence of such a disproportionate linkage. What appears to be suggested, therefore, is an atavistic mentality capable of long-term scheming, an intentional pursuit of exclusivity on her part, suggesting—"

"That she's a stag-hag, in other words?"

She winced at the word. Andy found her delicacy exciting.

"Suggesting that she is one of those unusually bright exceptions that crops up now and then among oldfolks—"

"Like me," said Andy.

"Like you, Mr. Kedro. And therefore possibly a mole, poetentially capable of manipulating the entire organization—either for her own personal benefit, or with some specific political agenda in mind—"

"An oldfolks terrorist!" said Andy.

"They don't have to throw literal bombs, you know. Anyway, if our suspicions prove correct, we will have to take certain measures."

"I do not disappear women," Andy repeated. "I won't even knowingly *help* to disappear women."

"Oh, nothing so drastic would happen," she smirked, shuddering at what he suggested. "If she resists going to bed with you—under test conditions, mind you—we would simply fire her. We'd find some plausible reason."

"So where do I come in?"

"I have to tell you quickly. My boss is getting frantic. My skeeter's practically sizzling from his calls . . . Take a good last look at her. She'll be leaving the building for lunch tomorrow at one o'clock, alone, give or take two or three minutes. Her bagstrap will have been tampered with. I suggest you work with a skilled confederate. One who will snatch her bag—which will tear off easily—and run it around to here,"—pointing at a little hand-drawn map on the sheet she held out to him, "around the northeast corner, to *you*. You will immediately deactivate her flapper, stopping transmission to her skeeter. And then you will open the flapper and switch her memory cartridge for this one." She took the domino-like insert out of a drawer and handed it to him. "It contains a copy of her full Personal Past except altered to include *you*—as her favorite lover, including a series of sweaty episodes of your sexual relationship over the past year. Once the new cartridge is activated, it should all play rather convincingly inside her head."

"Naturally. And then what happens?"

"First of all, tonight you are going to *study* that part of the program concerning you. Just plug it into a Virtual Reality Cap. Now, back to the crucial event."

"The purse-snatching?"

"Yes. After switching cartridges, you will return her bag to her exactly seven minutes later, enough time for her to become completely disoriented if, indeed, she is a true-blue tekkie."

"And then what do I do if she seems disoriented?"

"First, make sure to reactivate the flapper just before you return it to her with the new cartridge in it."

"Check."

"It's all written down for you. Next, you will show her the 'recovered' bag, telling her that the thief got away. Then you will coax her off to your 'rendezvous' at your luxury apartment on Sixty-Third off Madison."

"My apartment?"

"It's well stocked with everything lovers could want." She handed him the keys. "Stay there tonight and get used to it."

He hefted the keys in his palm. "Can't I persuade you to join me—for a practice session, I mean?"

"Who knows what you might someday persuade me to do, Mr. Kedro?" Her smile was full of mischief. Fucking tease! he thought. "But if you want to persuade anybody, especially Helen Means, please wear a more subtle outfit—more subdued colors, Mr. Kedro. Check out the various outfits we have you wearing in her modified Personal Past."

He looked himself over appreciatively, stroking his yellow lapels. "You mean I should look like some corporate zombie? No problem. And you think she'll follow me? Even into bed?"

"Yes. Unless she's a crypto. In which case you'd better make a run for it as soon as she gets her bag back. If that happens, call me immediately and let me know. If you do get her up to the apartment, we'll *know* what happens. The place is completely bugged. You'll discover a few 'photos' of you and her, in intimate poses, arranged strategically around the apartment, just to provide some external support to her sense of orientation. The apartment is completely modeled for her in that cartridge."

"This is kid stuff," said Andy, reaching for the sheet of instructions. "We used to trick frag-hags into the sack when we were teenagers. If she's a true 'tekkie,' it'll go off without a hitch. I'm not called Andy the Actor for nothing... One thing might go wrong, though."

"What?"

"She might have a perfectly good stag memory—and yet be *delighted* to rumple the sheets with me."

Yamamoto frowned. "We are not considering that as a serious possibility... And one thing more. Don't wait much more than seven minutes to return her bag. Some Good Samaritan may notice signs of Failed-Flapper Syndrome in her face and behavior—*if* she's a tekkie, of course—and guide her to the nearest Eye-D Recall booth. Once she's satellite-reoriented on who she is and where she is and what she's *really* supposed to be doing, the game is lost."

"Miss Yamamoto, you forget you're speaking to a professional."

"Of course I forget. I'm a 'frag,' Mr. Kedro. Remember?"

"Be careful one day I don't grab your bag in the street, Miss Yummy. If there's any crypto in *you*, I'll smoke it out... And the rest of you'll make fine sausages. *Fine* sausages," he said, licking his lips.

"You don't *do* women, remember, Mr. Kedro?"

"In your case I'll make an exception."

"It's such a shame that we find you so useful to us," she said, rising to leave. "And please remember to exit to the right, the way you came in."

"Check," Andy said to the silver swish of her departure. He tapped at his palm like a tekkie entering an agenda item in flapper.

7. SUPERFLAPPER

Stewart wondered what was taking her so long. This was one hell of a bathroom break—if that was, indeed, where she'd gone. Probably took Her Loveliness a full ten minutes just to shimmy free of the snakeskin grip of that dress. (He imagined being invited to help her, on his knees, peeling her garment slowly back over the ripe twin bananas of her thighs.)

All alone in this model of a Moorish palace, Stewart felt the urge to explore. His legs felt cramped, and a little walking around seemed the perfect palliative for his growing nervousness as well. At first he sauntered toward the right and looked down the silent hallway that had swallowed the mysterious Sibyl; then he circled back toward the left, passing close to her desk. A red light blinked furiously from the monitor near which she'd left her flapper. Stewart stopped in front of the desk, mesmerized by the blinking.

What would the interview with Barton be like (when it finally did come off)? Stewart wondered. He had to be careful not to be tripped up on something simple, something totally taken for granted . . . ("Tell me, Mr. Bridges, what is the source of the word *flapper*?" "Why, sir, as everyone knows, it is an acronym for . . . Fact, Location, And Personal-Past Episode Recaller." "Swift, Mr. Bridges. You're quite swift. You know, the flapper's become as vital to us as the air we breathe, yet you'd be amazed at how few people are aware of its etymology.") In the present age, thought Stewart, all the leaders of humanity had to pay for the privilege by walking in darkness dangling a surrogate head beside them like a lantern—like that poor soul in Dante's *Inferno* . . . Bertrans de Borns. (Stewart was proud of his memory for things out of books. It was the practical things that worried him. Even now, as he bent over the desk, his hand slipped furtively under his jacket to be sure his own flapper was in its holster.

At that moment the wall beneath the city-street mural split open, and a distressed-looking red-bearded man lunged out. He knew it was LB because of the photos he had seen among the documents he had used to establish the factual framework on which he had sculpted the executive's "life." But he looked far less heroic than those PR photos. He looked haggard. Stewart felt frightened as the man stopped dead beside his secretary's vacant post and stared at him. "Sibyl!" he called out. "Where the hell are you, damn it?"

"She went somewhere down the hall, sir." Stewart watched in amazement as the man, not deigning to look at him, clenched his flapper in a white-knuckled, trembling fist. He had not realized till now, till seeing him in the flesh, what an influence this man—this myth; more myth than man—had had over him. Barton's bushy brown mustache straggled down around stern, fleshy lips. In contrast, a neatly clipped beard ended in a no-nonsense point at the chin. Stewart passed his hand over his own lower face. Like thousands of other wanna-be-somebodies, he had modeled his own facial hair after Barton's.

"Who are *you*?" Barton snapped.

"Sir, I have an appointment with you—"

"I thought I *canceled* all my afternoon appointments!"

"I don't think you canceled with me, sir."

"What's that? ... William Lazare, Communications Tek. Oh yes, you must be here to check for bugs in my walls."

Something was wrong, thought Stewart. LB showed no sign of recognition. Either he was confabulating in the traditional tekkie manner—making up some story to explain away the unexpected presence of a visitor he should have remembered to expect—or else his flapper was advising him that the real William Lazare belonged in fact to a debugging unit. Whichever the case, the crucial point was that a mistake had been made causing Barton not to "remember" that William Lazare was Stewart Bridges.

Barton hesitated, as if frozen to the carpet. He looked frightened. "Sibyl!" he shouted again, imperiously. Unable to materialize her, he ignored Stewart completely, spun on his heels, and strode back into his office through swiftly parting panels.

There was something terribly familiar to Stewart in the scene he'd just been privileged to witness. His father, too, had fits of mingled fright and rage when something disturbed his carefully controlled and flapper-mapped environment—his failure to find his wife where he expected to find her, for example. His father's reaction, too, would be to temporize, to confabulate in self-defense, and quickly retreat into the safety of his own private room, where he would sit and hyperventilate until regaining his composure . . . But then, less than two minutes later, his father would venture out again and repeat his previous performance, unmindful of what he had done just moments before. If someone or something did not intervene, the cycle could go on indefinitely.

Stewart was fairly confident, then, that Barton too would step out again for an encore—so he looked at his watch in order to time his reappearance, for the interval would be the precise measure of Lester Barton's DIM-span, the extent of his memory for things that had just occurred—after which all experience passed into oblivion. Shouldn't that be one of the biggest corporate secrets, he thought, the neurophysiological status of a CEO? That DIM-span of his was the measure of his *vulnerability*—information invaluable to a rival, or to a saboteur.

Stewart paced around again but stuck fairly close to the desk. He wanted to confront LB, exactly as he had before, but this time he would not let a golden opportunity pass. He stripped his false ID off his jacket and held it in his palm. He prayed that Sibyl would take her sweet time, because if she returned too soon, a rather unpleasant scene might ensue.

LB might well accuse Sibyl of failing to remind him of his appointment with Stewart, even though it seemed that LB had himself mistakenly wiped out his entire slate of appointments. Would Sibyl dare to risk the consequences of suggesting that her chief was at fault? Why should she provoke the predictable storm of abuse, the rain of sarcasms peppered with arrogant and incoherent excuses for her CEO's own lapse of memory? Stewart was too well acquainted with Advanced Amnesic Syndrome (the old medical texts used to call a spade a spade!). He had seen his own tekkie father stumble through every stage of the disease. It was never *publicly* referred to as a disease, of course! ("Memory-loss a disease?" his father would reply, shaking his flapper at Stewart. "And do you call my nearsightedness, for which I've had corneal implants, a disease?" "No,

Dad." "And how about you? You'd have been better *off* on the Pill! Your stag-brained mother's ruined your whole fucking life! You were always the kind of kid who'd forget his ass if he didn't every so often have to sit on it. I still remember how in second grade you used your lunch-card as a bookmark, then returned the book to the library without . . ." Like buttes of hard rock jutting out above a plain, scattered memories still stubbornly rose from his father's eroded mindscape.)

Stewart tried to sort out his brief impressions of this man whose Personal Past he'd spent a year of his own past composing. The awe that he felt, that he had expected to feel, was undercut now by a single image—that of the tightly gripped flapper, the ice-pale knuckles, the astonishing vulnerability inconsistent with the living legend.

Up to that moment, despite Stewart's intimacy with the Memini-supplied "facts" of Lester Barton's life, LB had remained for him a distant and legendary figure. But now . . . his idol had just bared its clay feet. The man was a tekkie! Just another goddamn *tekkie*, when all was said and done. No different from Stewart's own father except in luck, and perhaps a dash of talent.

He could imagine LB's horror were he to learn that a stag had slipped through the security net. A barbarian intruder! One of those apes who were forever resentful of your elevated station on the evolutionary ladder. It would be worse than if your company's biggest rival—Mishugi, say—had planted a mole in the executive suite. He'd be grabbed by company cops, who would probably beat him half to death and dump him out onto some back road, and afterwards he'd never get another bioprogramming job again. To have been penetrated by one of the stagnant ones! Raped by one of that memory-shackled brood of educational dropouts (so went the stereotype) with minds so anchored in the past as to be helpless before the exponentially growing information onslaught of the present! What humiliation! What terror! To think of being end-run by a crypto!

Stewart checked the time again. One and a half minutes had passed.

Incredible! he thought: Memini seriously considering *him*—and for a *top-level post*, no less? He had moved safely along the fringes of the dominant "frag" culture, or "fragture," making a respectable living in the solitary profession of free-lance bioprogramming. No one he knew, parents excepted, could have identified him as oldfolks. A precious anonymity—but bought at the price of living under a rock. He no longer wanted to live under a goddamned rock!

He was an anomaly—a well-educated, highly intelligent and extremely *creative stag*. An oxymoron! His high-school friends, minus half his inborn smarts to start with, began to outstrip him academically as soon as they locked onto the Pill—which his oldfolks mother had fanatically forbidden him. And now some few of those erstwhile friends were solid members of the frag elite, with the best jobs, the best houses, the most fashionable women such status could buy—while most of his Pill-popping classmates (all now in their late thirties, all in routine bureaucratic jobs) had never made it to the top: "snags," they were, caught on the fence while climbing, knowingly sacrificing their inmost sense of Self to the plastic idol Success.

It took *less than three minutes* for LB to emerge again.

He came to a halt in the same place alongside the desk. Stewart's stomach took a flip as he watched the man survey the room in puzzlement for a second time.

"Sibyl!" LB shouted in exactly the same tone as before. "Where the hell are you, damn it?"

He glared at Stewart with watery eyes. "Who are you?" he demanded again.

"I'm Stewart Bridges, sir. I'm here to reply to the questions you have about my resume, sir."

"I thought I *canceled* all my afternoon appointments!"

"Not with me, sir, but I'll take up almost none of your time at all. You wanted me to lay out some concrete ideas for New Products Development, as I'm sure your notes will remind you."

"I'll have to check—"

"No need to waste the time, sir. As you already know, for years I've submitted product and service ideas to the Marketing Division, without ever expecting acknowledgment of any sort."

"That's very kind of you, but—"

"In fact, I've taken an interest in the products of many of Memini's subsidiaries, even submitting contest jingles to your Coca Cola division, not to mention recipe suggestions to your Self-Cooking Bluffburger company—"

"Listen, Mr., uh . . . "

"But these are admittedly trivial compared to the newer ideas I've hinted at which have spiked your curiosity and which will take just a second to summarize, such as the Superflapper. Remember?"

"Superflapper?" said Barton, his eyes straying back and forth between Stewart and the vacated desk. Stewart was sure that LB's flapper was recording every word being said.

"The superflapper," said Stewart, lifting his late-model flapper out of its holster and shaking it professorially in front of him, "extends the intelligence capability of the current system by a full order of magnitude. The knowledge and experience that each of us stores up separately here," he continued, tapping the device, "can be custom-linked, by algorithms I've specially developed, to the equivalent individual databases of any number of cooperating persons to form a communal wisdom bank that is instantly accessible to anyone who must make some on-the-spot, major life-decision."

"Fascinating, I'm sure, but—"

"Let me put my money where my mouth is, Mr. Barton! On the direct income-generating end of Memini's business, I have thought out a system called FlapCharge. FlapCharge will adapt DAFT, Direct Access Funds Transfer, to your personal flapper. FlapCharge will dramatically increase the velocity of credit transactions on a *global scale* because the DAFT-linked tekkie who has the urge to buy something can do so swift as thought—instead of seeking out a Funds Transfer Terminal at the risk of losing, in the intervening minutes, both the memory and the desire of what he or she wanted to purchase in the first place."

"Now all this sounds very good, but I really have to—"

"And think, Mr. Barton, of the increased security of life and limb and property to the tekkie who need not venture out physically, into unfamiliar territory, risking the danger of being waylaid, as occasionally does unfortunately happen when we search for an FTT."

"I'm registering all this in Periodic Recall, and now, Mr . . . "

"Stewart Bridges, sir." He felt exhilarated. He had pinned LB to the spot and made his full pitch—not to an underling who might steal his ideas, but to the grand muckamuck himself!

"Stewart Bridges? And why aren't you wearing your company ID?" Barton took a step back and again clutched his open flapper so hard Stewart thought it would snap.

"Because I'm not directly employed by Memini, sir—as your notes will tell you. I was very fortunate, though, in being privately employed by you."

"Oh, really? In what capacity?"

"I am your bioprogrammer, sir."

"My bioprogrammer? . . . " The announcement caused Barton to blanch. Averting his eyes from Stewart, Barton punched a sequence of keys on his flapper. His breathing became uneven, as though he were beginning to hyperventilate. It looked to Stewart as if the man had just been stretched beyond his DIM-limit. "Sibyl!" shrieked Barton. "Where the hell are you, goddam it?" Glaring distrustfully at Stewart and at everything else in sight, Barton rushed back through obliging walls into his office.

Stewart had a good idea where LB now stood—neurologically speaking. Tekkies, he felt, were like those super-competitive twentieth-century athletes who popped anabolic steroids in full foreknowledge of their crippling long-term effects. All those Pills, those EMI's or "emmies" (Enhancers of Memory and Intelligence), had slowly, inexorably, retrogressively robbed Barton of his whole adult past. "Brocaleptics" they were called in tekki-etalk, which focused on only the positive effects of the Pill. "Mnemetics," or brain-flushers, was the oldfolks way of dismissing them.

Although the comparison seemed blasphemous, for Stewart having a DIM-span of under three minutes put Barton into a class with his father. Their brains were Swiss cheeses of slightly varying densities. The full ravages of the Pill destroyed not only their past, their so-called "episodic memories," but destroyed as well their capacity to store new experience. His father's failure to recall anything of Stewart chronologically subsequent to some early college days was called *retrograde* amnesia. And his failure to remember a thing he saw on 3V, so that he could watch the same film over and over with undiminished enjoyment—that they called *anterograde* amnesia. Fancy terms for the loss of what Stewart's rigidly oldfolks mother unblushingly called the "soul."

MEMINI

Was it really such a big loss? Stewart wondered. He stared again enchanted by the no-expense-barred luxury of his surroundings. In the corporate view, LB obviously functioned very well—well enough to run the biggest corporation the world had ever seen! Stewart envied that single positive effect of the Pill—the capacity to retain and manipulate *information*, *data*, everything *read* or *listened to* under their influence, as opposed to anything humanly experienced—anything of a personal, emotion-laden nature. Barton had opted for the standard tekkie backfiring bargain with Nature—a shot at Success at the price of the Self. "A bargain with the Devil," as his mother put it. Maybe the Devil had never got a proper hearing, thought Stewart.

Pacing the room, he waited impatiently for Sibyl to return. He felt a growing nausea now after encountering Lester Barton in the flesh. He pictured the brain that made the man so successful as a chemical nightmare—a runaway polymerase chain reaction under the kick of madly multiplying PCP receptors. He himself had taken the Pill (unbeknownst to his mother) several times in college himself. He knew the eagle-eyed, hawk-winged feeling when the circuitry of the brain turned superconducting...

He had succeeded in being "interviewed," in spite of Barton himself! And he felt confident that it had gone very well. His heart beat irregularly as he waited for Ms. Yamamoto's return—with that cup of coffee she'd offered him. But that, he realized, was highly unlikely. Given her fifteen-minute DIM-span, and the fact that she'd been away from both desk and flapper for far longer, there'd be no way she'd remember that offer.

So that, if she *did* come back with coffee for him...

8. HISTORY IS THE SALABLE PAST

As soon as Lester Barton stepped back into his office he made a note to himself, to be repeated via skeeter every four minutes: "Danger, Stewart Bridges, my bioprogrammer, get him before he gets me." The situation demanded immediate action. His hands trembled at the implications of that accidental encounter. And where was Sibyl? Wasn't she responsible for admitting him into her office? Again he activated his flapper, storing his further thoughts under Detail Appended/Recall Optional: "Bridges was present in Sibyl's office while Sibyl was nowhere to be seen. Is she in on the scheme? Or is she deliberately out of reach in order to have me get up and go search for her so that I *would* discover Bridges, who is not down for an appointment with me—despite what he says? Is Sibyl loyally trying to alert me to something that she dare not come out with directly? What the hell's going on anyway?"

Scraps of information whirled around in his head, at first making no sense at all. But soon they locked together, easily and quickly, like the pieces of a jigsaw puzzle. He had been bioprogrammed once; he didn't remember when, but apparently with his consent. And now it was clear what that bioprogamming had meant. It was not just to provide him with a dazzling autobiography enabling him to play the adult role of Memini's powerful president. Sure, it was *important* to have a Personal Past to turn to when you were neither working, nor partying, nor playing pool, nor target-shooting, nor surfing the five hundred or so thrill-a-minute channels on 3V. It was important not to be bored and sit doing nothing, and for that he was grateful for having a first-rate Personal Past installed—and all at the expense of the Board of Ed, which seemed willing to go to any lengths to make this pet new project of theirs a completely successful, round-the-clock reality simulation.

Nevertheless, an insidious little "extra" had been inserted into the chip they'd grafted to his brain. They had included, as was now quite clear, a chemotronic virus intended to obliterate his *actual* Personal Past! His enemies among his former teachers, in collusion with the whole high-school administration, were hoping to mentally *cripple* him. They'd gained the confidence of the members of the Board, slipped it right past them. Just one more of their vengeful attempts to prevent him from winning at Memini—and thus deny him a tier-one diploma, and thus prevent him from going to college. And now they were pushing him to overload on emmies. Why? Evidently, because their innovative brainworm must have failed!

But now what gave the whole plot away was the unannounced presence of the snooping Stewart Bridges. The last thing they could have imagined was that Lester would run into him—a coincidence, surely, that his absent secretary had engineered? In conclusion, then, his enemies were preparing another onslaught on his brain. Bridges was again to be their instrument. No one else was as intimately acquainted with his neural circuitry. No doubt they suspected that he, Lester, was shying their potent Pills into the john. Now Bridges was going to take care of that problem directly. They were positioning Bridges to destroy organic-memory patterns that had survived the first go-round, memories that had proved resistant even to subsequent megadoses of emmies, memories that were Lester's major link to a reality *outside* their Game—memories that enabled him to see *through* their Game.

How was his bioprogrammer intending to brainfuck him again? he wondered. Would Bridges have to fiddle directly with the nanosurgical wetware links to the programming board in his skull? Of course not! A virus could be introduced *indirectly*, through reprogramming the cartridge that activated his Personal Past. But how could Bridges get at that? Steal it from him while he was sleeping? Or during some moment of inattention when...

On his flapper screen a red light began to blink. That meant he had to play back some important reminder he had left for himself just a short while ago. He pressed Play. "Must tell Sibyl, damn it, to *stop leaving her damn flapper out in the open* when she goes to take a piss!" That was it!

Through reprogramming *Sibyl's* cartridge, the bastard could vector that virus right into his! An eerie feeling made Lester shiver all over. Was Sibyl, then, to be counted among his enemies? "No flapper communication is to be allowed," he ordered, "between Sibyl Yamamoto's flapper and my own until further notice. Ask Meminet to check all Yamamoto flapper entries for the hour preceding this notice. Replay at ten-minute intervals."

And what if no virus were to be found in Sibyl's cassette? Lester asked himself. What if, as he hoped, she were entirely innocent of any involvement? In some *remote* way, then, Bridges could undoubtedly reconfigure the programming board in his brain. But he'd first need to make a thorough brainscan to determine Lester's *present* neurological configuration—which could not be the same as it was before he'd taken all their Pills. So some teknoids had probably developed a way to do a brainscan *at a distance*, he thought. That was what the man must be toting in that flapper—a supersensitive, remote electroencephalograph! . . . Indeed, if Sibyl's cassette were not infected, then Bridges *had* to be attempting something like this.

So now the ball was in Lester's court. The question was: how to use *Meminet* to thwart the opposition. He'd have to be careful. Meminet did not see itself as part of any "game." (All the players within any game necessarily act as if the game-world is reality.) To suggest to Meminet that his enemies in a high-school bureaucracy were out to tamper with his brain would merely cause him to look paranoid. Within the logic of the game-world, he would come to be judged a misfit. Even Sibyl hewed strictly to her game-role, and he would sound like a fool if he were ever to directly accuse her of being a tool of the Board of Ed.

Carefully, Lester thought out a strategy to use on Meminet. And to keep in mind the whole chain of reasoning that led to it, he spoke all his suspicions and conclusions into flapper, placing a brief summary under Periodic-Recall and the full version under Detail Appended. Then, as with anything he wanted to keep from Meminet, he tagged the whole sequence *Upload-Exempt* during daily 4 p.m. Back-Up, when the contents of one's flapper would otherwise be copied automatically to the company neuronet, which in turn copied them, for permanent safekeeping, hundreds of miles up into the regional geostationary memsat.

IT IS NOW TIME FOR YOUR SCHEDULED CONFERENCE WITH

MEMINET. The skeeter-relayed message couldn't have occurred at a better time. He called up Meminet on the wall-screen to the right of his desk, where earlier he had crossed swords with Dr. Pross. Instantly, a series of faceless figures filled the great screen as if lined up on either side of an endless boardroom table. The featureless face-holes of all these figures inclined toward him, as if out of deepest respect. "Good afternoon, Mr. President," they all said at once, one clear voice emerging to muffle an echoic background. "May we take the liberty to review with you some of the salient features of the Executive Council meeting of the Friday before last?"

"Go right ahead," said Lester. "I've meminized certain portions of the meeting that on playback struck me as vital." He had indeed! For that was the meeting in which his enemies came up with a last, desperate ploy in order to gain an unfair advantage over him. Fortunately, he had seen right through them. And in another few days he would squash them altogether.

The great screen became a window into a nearly life-size boardroom. Since virtually every advanced tekkie developed complete facial agnosia, Lester gazed down from the (virtual) head of the conference table upon two rows of chattering strangers. Himself invisible, he observed a sea of faces, mostly unsmiling, eyes seemingly focused upon him, and they fleetingly struck him with terror. But when he read the large nameplates slanted along the table facing him, he felt that he was back in his element. The nameplates of his two dozen division heads conjured up a sea of data—a hefty chunk of the collective company memory. Within a closed but orderly world of ideas and information, of manuals of policy and procedure (emmied into long-term memory, available on demand), Lester could dive and soar like a kingfisher. No need for mnemonic nudges, for flapper fillips, to guide him through *this* combat zone!

But the theater under Lester's command was bounded by the perimeter of the conference-room table. The faces that hovered behind the nameplates formed a zone of wavering shadows, a *terra incognita* as seen on ancient maps, full of dragons, gryphons, and devils. The names *claimed* connection with the faces, but Lester could accept such a linkage only provisionally. He played along with the purported identities only for form's sake. Surprisingly enough, however, there were a few faces among them he could *recognize*—and they were not the people claimed by their nameplates! . . .

How many of the others were impostors? he wondered. How much had his enemies stacked the deck against him? Did a quarter of them—half of them—want him to fail in the administration of Memini? Was he doing too *good* a job? Was he so threatening to their miserable little egos?

Everyone sat poised in front of an open flapper and a full-sized uptilted desk terminal. The terminals hooked into Meminet, the corporate brain that informed and advised at crucial points of decision-making.

"Notice, Mr. President," said Meminet, whose faceless figures were overlaid now by the current members of the Council, "that after opening the meeting, you failed to ask for acceptance of the previous minutes."

"I noticed," said Lester, reddening. "A minor error. Someone immediately corrected me."

"Are you aware, Lester, that this is not the first time you have made such a procedural error?" The simvoice modulated to a relaxed, more friendly tone.

"Probably," replied Lester, "when I had originally meminized Robert's Rules of Order, I skipped a few passages by mistake." But there was another explanation that Lester could not completely discount: that he'd already been overdosing on emmies to the point where earlier *Pill-fixed* memories were being erased—and not only the organic remnants of Self he was determined to preserve. He was aware of the possible backfire-effects of chemosaturation. It was not the sort of conjecture, however, that he would voice within the hearing of Meminet.

Didn't they feel embarrassed, Lester wondered—all these "colleagues" of his sitting around pretending to be the Executive Council of Memini? He supposed he must have agreed to serve as guinea-pig in this educational pilot project (presumably as substitute for a regular senior project, preferring to be supervised by a relatively fair-minded Board of Ed than to be tyrannized by the faculty of his own high school). But he had not realized how demanding a game this would be, had not even imagined he could *lose*—and thereby fail to earn his diploma!

Lester had known for a long time that he was being observed several times a week—particularly at these so-called "monthly" meetings—by a group of agents from the Board of Education, including psychiatrists and psychologists. They were testing whether he deserved to receive a coveted tier-one college scholarship by evaluating his ability to run a major conglobulate. There were twenty-four in all, all posing as the executives he pretended to work with every day in the course of business. The test was extremely biased, however. Some of those "execs" worked behind the scenes to keep him from being awarded that diploma. This fact he might never have directly unearthed except that, to a limited degree, he was still able to *recognize faces.*

It was not like recognizing Personal-Past faces, whereby the camera eye of your flapper could check out the person you pointed it at by an image search and an ID confirmation it played back in your head. No, his residual recognition capability was, and could only be, *organic.* Unknown to the Board of Ed, his facial agnosia—*prosopagnosia,* to be fancy—was incomplete. Now that would be an embarrassing admission for a bright high-school student to make! As though you were only semi-developed, a "half-baked" tekkie, as oldfolks liked to say.

Lester had found that, in several significant cases, he was still able to recognize people—at a party, in a restaurant, in a crowded street, and even at these fake meetings where everyone hid behind names that didn't belong to them. Had he ever tried to unmask them? he wondered. He hoped he had not been so foolish. One slip like that (revealing a lack of sangfroid, a sure mark of immaturity) and good-bye graduation!

And that was exactly what some of these bastards were hoping for. Being exceptionally bright, he had antagonized some of his petty-shit teachers, and it seemed they would stop at nothing to rob him of his diploma, to prevent him from going on to college. His failure would appall his parents (who otherwise, in true tekkie fashion, took minimal note of his existence), and would devastate him as well, leaving him without minimum credentials to occupy a niche in the social stratum to which his family had belonged for generations.

"We hope, Mr. Barton, that you will not mind reviewing some highlights of the report by Walter Gibbich, our Vice President of Marketing."

"Not at all."

And there he was, Walter Gibbich, a rat-faced creature wearing goggles—always going against the grain, even though nowadays nearly everyone wore lens implants. Wasting little time on ceremony, Gibbich went off into a long and insulting tirade, grossly insinuating to the members of the Council that the president of Memini was faltering, that for two whole years he had failed to put forward a single viable product innovation, that he would sit on the ideas of others while offering impracticable fantasies (Wilcox's own words were more cautious) that betrayed his "declining attention to the state of the world market." Even more radically, he went on to attack Lester for a fundamental failure to respond "to the concept of 'restructuring' that has taken hold, during the past year or two, throughout the rest of the conglobulate world. It has been universally noted that the worldwide pattern of oldfolks consumerism is changing. This, in turn, is not unrelated to a new sort of *consciousness* among oldfolks—namely, an increasing sense, whether they are right or wrong, of their constituting a separate social class in the old Marxist sense, with common interests that transcend race, nation, and even the North-South political division of the world that most of us have taken as a *stabilizing constant* for well over seventy years."

"The arrogant little twit assumes that I don't keep up with the times," said Lester. "He wanted us to pander to the oldfolks market and forget our loyalty to the teknonomy. You remember, of course, how I answered him? . . . 'We must never lose our sense of *identity*,' I said. 'Remember who we are, who we are! Occipet and Mishugi, our rivals in the Three-Headed Tekkarky called MOM—as though we in any sense ever acted as an altruistic unity!—have long ago lost their original identities. They grab and pander everywhere. But our final strength is in our loyalty to the teknonomy. We must hew to our traditions, devote our energies first and foremost to the interests of the *progressive* elements in the world population.' And I remember getting quite a few murmurs of approval."

"That was an eloquent rejoinder, Lester. But do you remember the 'new product idea' that you did come out with to refute the claims of the Gibbich camp that you had been failing in recent years to present any viable product innovations?"

Lester felt deeply embarrassed. "I was flustered."

"You trotted out Veriscope, that idea for face-recognition eyeglasses that had been thoroughly evaluated and dismissed by the Council *two years* ago . . . on the grounds that spectacles would never be likely to come back into fashion."

DANGER, STEWART BRIDGES, MY BIOPROGRAMMER, GET HIM BEFORE HE GETS ME. The message out of Periodic-Recall jolted him. As to the action he was to take, it was all there, appended—but it wasn't yet time, damn it!

"I guess," said Lester, "that under the stress of being attacked by Wilcox—"

"By whom?"

"By Gibbich, by Gibbich . . . wires got crossed in my memory and I . . ."

"Who *is* Wilcox, Lester?"

"No one, no one at all! Now let's get on with this, shall we? Aren't you going to mention all the support I received too?" The fact was that Lester had *recognized* the man renamed Walter Gibbich. Slightly disguised, he was his high-school programming teacher Mr. Wilcox, who had once caught him trading a month's supply of smart-pills for a stolen copy of the exam that Wilcox had just made up and stored under what should have been an impregnably secret passcode. He had avoided the Pill for a couple of months—as an experiment, to see how well he could do without it—and Wilcox publicly berated him for being an "irresponsible, untrustworthy lout" who was headed for a place in some "oldfolks gutter."

Far more upset by the neglected Pills than by the filched exam, Wilcox threatened to get him transferred to the alternate ("dumb") track dominated by oldfolks students and teachers who thought a mid-level job in some governmental agency one of the highest of human aspirations. The incident had taken place only recently, during the first half of his senior year. Wilcox had recorded their little exchange in his flapper, gleefully assigning it to Periodic-Recall mode right in front of the culprit's twitching face. "I'll be on your back till you graduate—*if* you graduate!" he had ominously declared.

It turned out that he needn't have worried about Wilcox's lousy exam. He aced even the one old Goggles slapped together in its place. (Goggles-Wilcox had thought for sure that he would flunk it—and now would never forgive him for proving him wrong.) Lester was quite proud of being a natural math and programming whiz, and he didn't do badly in Narratistics either. In fact, his overall record (in both the "human" and "inhuman" sciences) would have been spotless except for a few head-on collisions with small-minded teachers like Wilcox.

To recognize someone's face was to recall his whole relationship, sometimes painful, with that person . . . and to be confronted again with *who he himself REALLY was*. Once again, Lester's real name came to him: *Michael Forbes*, age seventeen; original thinker and stubborn maverick; in trouble with a couple of his teachers and in danger of being deprived of a college-track graduation.

Lester/Michael trembled with anxiety. His assumed name and his real name clashed in his head like elks locking horns. Relief, however, was instantly at hand via his skeeter's biosensors, which triggered his anxID advisory, which reminded him gently, firmly, and repeatedly who he was *now*, who he was *now*, who he was *now*:

YOU ARE LESTER BARTON, FORTY-TWO YEARS OLD. YOU MUST NOT LET YOURSELF BE DELUDED BY ANY PASSING HALLUCINATIONS. YOU ARE THE DYNAMIC, INVENTIVE PRESIDENT OF THE MEMINI CORPORATION, WORLD LEADER IN MNEMONIC PHARMACEUTICALS AND HARDWARE. YOUR OFFICE IS ON THE THIRTY-SIXTH FLOOR OF THE MEMINI BUILDING, AT 1600 MADISON AVENUE, IN NEW YORK CITY. YOU ARE UNMARRIED. IN AN EMERGENCY, CALL YOUR EXECUTIVE SECRETARY, SIBYL YAMAMOTO. HER OFFICE PHONE, THE SAME AS YOUR OWN, IS . . .

YOU ARE LESTER BARTON, FORTY-TWO YEARS OLD. YOU MUST NOT LET . . .

It was his own voice that was telling him who he was, reassuringly, soothingly, attempting to allay his confusion:

WHEN YOU ARE AGAIN SURE YOU KNOW YOU ARE LESTER BARTON, JUST TAP YOUR SKEETER EAR AND THIS REMINDER WILL COME TO A HALT . . . He tapped his skeeter ear. He reproached himself for focusing on his real name, for toying with the void. It was impossible to be both Lester Barton and Michael Forbes at once without sending negative vibes up the supersensitive sensors of Meminet.

"We are sorry to be causing you distress, Lester. We are delighted to replay one of the highlights of the support shown you by members of the Executive Council. Here, now, are remarks made by perhaps your most *fervent* supporter, Mr. Barton, our Director of the Division of Art."

He fought back a surge of emotion when Helen Means appeared in close-up on the screen. At meetings he tried not to look at her because the knowledge of who she was destroyed his composure. What did Meminet mean by "fervent"? Could he detect a hint of irony, suspicion—?

"—but as to those who suggest we cave in to pressure from oldfolks political groups," Helen was saying, "try to bear in mind that their reactionary views are a direct threat to Memini's hold on *history*. You all remember what President Barton has said about history, don't you? 'History is anything that interferes with business.' Well, we are an island surrounded by oldfolks who wish to swamp the world once again with their parochial, multiple histories. Fellow Council members, if we don't want history to interfere with business, what must we continue to do about it? Well, I'm sure you remember another thing that President Barton has often said: 'History is the Salable Past, and the Past is whatever we manufacture under that label.' Let's keep in mind the visionary formula by which our president has raised Memini into the world's leading conglobulate: First there is *bio*programming, by which the individual remakes his own past; then there is *clio*programming, by which the corporate world redesigns history; and finally, *gaio*programming, by which the planet is physically sculpted into one common market."

His heart thumped to see her and hear her. Why didn't they all applaud her, the stupid bastards? She had flowing honey-blond hair (a strand of which she twirled near her ear), high cheekbones, and full red lips. And her name was not Helen Means—by no means Helen Means—but in reality *Iris Morgan*. No one could guess that he knew her, but her image was etched into his every living cell. His whole body was her secret hologram. He balked at the notion that she resided in him solely as an electrochemical pattern in a sliver of neocortex—a minsky—that could be flushed right out of his head with the next Pill he took. Like a ship too sturdy to sink, she had managed to survive wave after wave of his expanding, all-engulfing amnesia.

It made him feel nervous, somehow "half-baked," not to be as free of organic memory as he'd once wished—yet, even more shamefully, he admitted to himself that he wouldn't willingly *part* with the neurological cluster he personally, inwardly experienced as Iris! His wetware preservation of their beautiful relationship was nothing short of miraculous. He thanked his stubborn synapses for guarding that badly bruised, forever beleaguered, amygdocortical path to Iris Morgan! To hell with the guilt-inspired notion of chug-a-lugging ever more emmies, of reading through mounds of shit that he'd shunted aside *precisely in order* to keep Iris safe in whatever was left of his old reptilian brain! They played the Memini-game with each other in public, of course. She called him Mr. Barton, or just Lester; he called her Helen, or Ms. Means. But whenever he saw her, she evoked within him the whole rich texture of sound, sight, and smell of the first time they had ever made love. She was his high-school drama teacher, fresh out of college, in her first teaching job, directing her first play at the school. And he was the lighting man, a techno-whiz, producing every effect she asked for, and improvising magic of his own. It was more than just beams of colored lights that became the focal point of their relationship. As they worked together on the show, Iris began to take an unusually keen interest in what he did.

She would visit him after hours in the backstage junk room where he fingered his equipment. The mustiness of mounds of old props soon evaporated in the smell of her freckled shoulders and teeming blond hair, and his industrious fingers grew confused. Soon the fingers of the two of them grew confused, twined together, like the breath nervously issuing from their mouths, and she drew him to the old musty couch in the corner where she, the director, omitting all prologue, directed his fingers to the warm, moist vales of her flesh, teaching him more than he had ever dared dream about the succulent experience of love. "I adore your athlete's body," she whispered to his thighs. "Five years' difference in age mean nothing," she murmured to the back of his neck.

Whenever he saw her now, in the guise of Helen Means, he could think of little else but his longing. He was sure that whenever they did come together, their mutual facade of fake names must drop to the ground even faster than the clothing they wore. It felt almost like yesterday when they had first become lovers, but he supposed that several months must have passed since then. The sight of her helped him know again who he was: Michael Forbes, age seventeen, masquerading as a middle-aged executive as part of a game which would determine his future. They had coarsened up his features a bit, fed him stuff to make him sprout facial hair and to help him put on weight, but Iris never minded what he looked like when they got together back-stage or in her car or her office for stolen hours of passion. He knew without her needing to tell him that she stood by to help him, to protect him from the schemes of his enemies. Constantly, he devised opportunities for them to be lovers again and again.

"Helen Means," said Lester/Michael, "is an excellent example to the rest of the Council of loyalty to the Chief—even when the going gets rough."

"An outstanding example, indeed," said Meminet. "But what made you react so negatively, then, to our Vice-President of Pharmaceuticals, Avery Tingworth, who has surely been a staunch supporter of yours through the years? ... It seems to us that he merely raised an issue which anyone in his position would have to."

Meminet's camera focused on the bloated, watery-eyed figure of Avery Tingworth, sitting third from Lester's left and fingering his thick peppery beard and walrus mustache. "I don't pretend," said Tingworth, "to be able to argue the merits of giving in to DUSA's energy request or standing firm, as you've chosen to do, Mr. President, but I am now forced to bring up an agenda item that I was saving for a full, responsible presentation at next month's meeting of the Council. Our Borneo outstation, which DUSA now threatens to shut down, is the site of the biggest breakthrough in biochemical engineering in Memini's history. Our chemists out there have successfully completed tests on a rare fungus that harbors an enzyme which will enable us to manufacture the 'Perfect Pill.'" A wave of exclamations and murmurs rippled along the table. "Yes, ladies and gentlemen, the *Perfect Pill*! Think of it! No more side-effects, no more hypothalamic corrosivity, no more need for future generations to choose between organic and synthetic memory functions."

"Stop it right there!" said Lester, as if directly to Tingworth.

"Don't you wish to review your rather heated reply, Mr. Barton?"

"I know very well what I replied. That he had no right to drop such a bombshell without thoroughly discussing it with me—well beforehand." The anger Lester felt at the meeting rose up in him again. "That by letting the cat out of the bag he was complicating an already volatile political situation. That if his premature announcement leaked out to the press, Memini could be held hostage by a DUSA whose hand *Tingworth personally had strengthened* . . . "

"Yes, Mr. President. And you also asked him if he had calculated this little breach of his, if he was *deliberately working for a foreign power or rival corporation*."

"I do admit I was intemperate," said Lester.

"Mr. Tingworth has been suffering from spells of cardiac arrhythmia ever since. He feels that the integrity of a life of devotion to Memini has been tarnished beyond repair."

"How awful!" said Lester. "I must send him a note of apology." *What sentimental soap-opera bullshit!* he thought. Avery Tingworth, my ass! That was *Victor Mishkin*, or *Mophead*, as the whole Chem class called him. Made to look older and fatter—but the disguise was pretty weak. It had taken Lester a while to put two and two together, but when it dawned on him that a revolutionary new Pill was not the great thing it appeared to be on the surface, but a clever means of testing his foresight, of tricking him into *losing the game*, he had been forced into a drastic strategy to prevent it from coming to market.

In the real world, the Perfect Pill would be the greatest boon to humanity; and its triumphal manufacture by Memini would insure the company's supremacy over its MOM rivals, Occipet and Mishugi; and the consequence for the real CEO of Memini would be his continued personal dominance over the entire conglobulate world.

The real-world Lester Barton would be walking on air if he'd made such a coup. But in the game-world, namely, the reality for *Michael Forbes*, who was only *playing* CEO of Memini, the connection between Tingworth/Mishkin-Mophead and the emergence of a great triumph for Memini had to be regarded with suspicion. And it was not long before the diabolical cleverness of that ex-Chem teacher of his revealed itself to him: a sugar-coated *poison* Pill was what Mishkin had offered up to him! As with the apple that had fooled Snow White, take one bite and you have been had!

If the Perfect Pill, that great new breakthrough, had occurred in the *non*-game world (of which his cortex still harbored some golden threads), Michael Forbes would have welcomed it as his own neurological salvation.

MEMINI

But as an endgame ploy on the part of his enemies to bring him down once and for all, he recognized it for what it was: a threat to the reigning teknonomy, the neurochemical merging of tekkie with oldfolks, the death of the class from which Memini had sprung and whose interests had been served by Memini time out of mind. The end of tekkiedom had to mean, in other words, the *destruction of Memini itself*! Why didn't Meminet see through it? he wondered. Either Meminet was programmed to maintain neutrality in an internal power struggle, or, more likely, Meminet's software had been tampered with! In either case, the final combat had begun. And if Lester/Michael were to fall for the *Poisoned-Pill Gambit*, he'd be falling right into the hands of his sniggering enemies...

Mophead Mishkin never forgave Michael for the plan he had put forward as his junior-year Chemistry project. Lester/Michael's idea was to find a natural enzyme that would neutralize the memory-enhancing action of the major commercial emmies. "Totally negative, reactionary, and antihumanistic," Mophead had called his plan. "Exactly what I'd expect of you, Mr. Wrong-Way Corrigan Forbes!" It was not an effective rebuttal on Lester/Michael's part to suggest that such an antipill "could dope the water-supplies of our Southern-Hemispheric competitors without being detected for years, so that our own Federation of Northern Geopolitical Unions could be assured global dominance for another generation at least." "Forbes," came Mophead's sarcastic reply, "I'd rather hand a toddler dynamite than trust you with a bottle of aspirin."

Forbes! Lester thought. Michael Forbes is my name, my only damn name! Why am I always forgetting my *name*? As the name rang in his head, his heart began pounding wildly, alerting the biosensors in his skeeter, which in turn tripped his anxID:

YOU ARE LESTER BARTON, he spoke to himself soothingly via his skeeter, FORTY-TWO YEARS OLD. YOU MUST NOT LET YOURSELF BE DELUDED BY ANY PASSING HALLUCINATIONS. YOU ARE THE DYNAMIC, INVENTIVE PRESIDENT OF...

YOU ARE LESTER BARTON, FORTY-TWO...

Play along, play along! Lester/Michael cautioned himself. And at that instant again came the voice out of Periodic-recall: DANGER, STEWART BRIDGES, MY BIOPROGRAMMER, GET HIM BEFORE HE GETS ME.

"A note of apology in which you reaffirm belief in Mr. Tingworth's spotless and creative record of service would be most appropriate, Mr. Barton. Meanwhile, the issue Mr. Tingworth raised and which you carefully avoided during the rest of the meeting is a pressing one indeed. Do you mind, Lester, if we take the present opportunity to discuss it with you further?'"

"Are you referring to my current dealings with the Democratic Union of Southeast Asia?"

"We are referring to your decision to deny solar power to energy-blighted DUSA. As you know, we in our corporate wisdom would not have employed that tactic as the best means to promote worldwide sales of our new, non-biologically based sunchip. To watch the current blight from the sidelines is to rub the nose of the entire *world* in its biosolar vulnerability. We suggested several other means of a far less dramatic nature. We warned you of the risks that the tactic you chose would entail, and by now our fears are beginning to appear justified."

"They only *appear* justified, gentlemen," said Lester. He was still proud of having thought up a diversion—a grand opportunity to increase sunchip sales—as the reason for risking confrontation with DUSA. Meminet didn't like the idea, but they bought it as his true motivation. How could he risk showing his real hand while suspecting that Meminet, if not deliberately working against him, had been infiltrated by those who were?

"Aside from the international repercussions, Mr. Barton—"

"I have assured you that it will all blow over!" Lester said, raising his voice.

"Very well, Mr. President. But apart from that issue, there is the immediate matter, raised by Mr. Tingworth, of our experimental biological station in that area."

"I assured you also that I *anticipated* DUSA's countermove of shutting down our rainforest facility."

"But more important than any explosion in sales of sunchips, Mr. President, is the new developments that have taken shape in our laboratory down there. Now that we are on the verge of producing an astounding new memory-enhancement compound, one that is virtually free of the traditional side effects—"

"I have assured you that I've set in motion arrangements that will guarantee *security* to the facility until this so-called crisis passes."

"You have given us your assurances, Lester, but we confess we remain mystified as to the cloak of secrecy with which you insist on covering this 'operation,' keeping all details even from us, so that we will have to await enlightenment via the information that will eventually reach us from the area."

"Have patience, gentlemen. Have patience." He tried not to sound too patronizing, but if Meminet were to know of the brilliant stroke by which he was planning to win the Memini-game, his opponents would undoubtedly get wind of his intentions and work out a strategy to defeat him.

DANGER, STEWART BRIDGES, MY BIOPROGRAMMER, GET HIM BEFORE HE GETS ME. Lester/Michael pressed the Detail Appended button and stared blankly at the wall screen, holding his hand up for Meminet to wait.

"Now, gentlemen," he said, finally, "if you are worried about a crisis, I have one far more immediate for us to contend with."

"Another crisis? Is there a reason we have not been informed earlier, Mr. President?"

"Yes, the reason is that it just came into being minutes ago."

"How may we be of help, Mr. Barton?"

"First, I suspect that a virus was introduced into Ms. Yamamoto's flapper cassette less than an hour ago, and that its immediate target is *me*, my *brain*, and not Ms. Yamamoto."

"Most distressing, if true, Mr. President! Do we have your authorization as CEO to make a remote-check of her cassette?"

"Go right ahead."

Several seconds later: "There is no sign of viral tampering, Mr. President."

"I feel relieved," said Lester, sighing, focusing all of his suspicion on Bridges again. "I'm very happy to know that my executive secretary is apparently *not* involved in a plot against me. But that there is such a plot cannot be denied. I therefore respectfully request that you arrange to eliminate a dangerous enemy, one who is in a unique position to sabotage Memini."

"May we assume that you are talking about eliminating a living *person*,

Mr. President?"

"Yes, gentlemen, I am."

"You realize, of course, Mr. President," the collective voice crackled like receding thunder, "that Extraordinary Measures are sanctioned only if the danger threatening the Corporation is 'substantial, undeniable and imminent.'"

"I do not ask lightly for your indulgence," Lester replied. "The elimination I propose is warranted on all three counts."

"The last similar measure you sanctioned, Lester, was implemented nearly four years ago, against a spy working for Mishugi who had burrowed his way up into division-level security clearance and knew too much for our safety."

"I remember quite well," Lester lied. He recalled no such event—although it was probably deposited in flapper with the rest of his fictional history. And the part about "four years ago" was absolute nonsense. It would pop into his mind if he pressed a few buttons, but the thought was too distasteful to him.

"But that elimination was initiated by *us*, Mr. President. We regretfully brought the matter to your attention. What is unusual in this case—"

"Is that *I* am taking the initiative, gentlemen? If I didn't now and then take the initiative, Memini would not *need* a Chief Executive Officer, would we?"

"On the contrary, Mr. President, we applaud your taking any and all initiatives calculated to benefit the company. Now then, would you please confide to us the identity of the proposed eliminee, and the grounds for the Extraordinary Measure?"

"Of course," said Lester, staring solemnly back at the screen. The corporate eye trained upon him was in turn recording and analyzing his every gesture, his every blink, the rhythm of his breathing. But Lester did not need to fake his agitation. "I'm referring to Mr. Stewart Bridges, my bioprogrammer. He had no appointment with me, yet he has managed to worm his way past security and even convinced me to admit him into my office."

"We are looking into that. You are right. We do not show his presence in the building as warranted."

"All the more dangerous, then, that he could evade the vigilant eye of Meminet," said Lester.

"We cannot at this moment explain his complete penetration of security," said Meminet. "But as you know, Lester, once a person gets past all initial checkpoints in this building, that person—whether stranger or employee—has been both cleansed of all 'bugs' and enters a totally surveillance-free environment, which is essential to our operations here at corporate headquarters."

"It's obvious he found all my corporate codes in the personal data-file that was loaned him for bioprogramming."

"A plausible inference," nodded the hundred blank faces of Meminet. "But what is the substantial danger he represents that is both 'undeniable' and 'imminent'?"

"I have just had a brief conversation with him. He is threatening extortion. The bioprogramming material he was given access to must have been carelessly thrown together. It included some of our most sensitive corporate secrets, apart from what he knows about my own views and habits, all of which he is tempted to sell to one of our chief competitors. His silence—in which it is impossible to have any faith—will cost us twenty million ICUs, he says. I trust I do not *need* to go into detail about what he knows?"

"Has a taste for International Currency Units, has he? Well, Mr. President, we trust your judgment implicitly. The case as you present it does fit the parameters for Extraordinary Measures."

Lester/Michael was amazed and relieved that Meminet would accede so quickly to his request. Meminet could not be completely in the hands of his enemies if he could still use the system to topple their cart. "I believe he is still waiting in the outer office for some sort of answer from me. He has apparently insisted to my secretary that he has an appointment with me. Sibyl seems to have cleverly found an indirect way to alert me to his presence."

A few silent seconds went by.

"Very well. We have worked out an elimination procedure, Mr. President. Do you wish to hear the details?"

"You need not burden me with the details," said Lester. "After all, why have a staff of thousands if I have to swat flies myself? . . . Gentlemen, good afternoon." Lester pressed a button on his desk and the 3V screen went blank.

Stewart returned to his seat in the holding pen. What in hell was taking her so long? he wondered. Was she lost? Had her skeeter supports all failed? What a *mark* she would be—wandering around, defenseless! He pictured himself hunting along endless corridors, finding her at last, rescuing the frightened creature, receiving the warm, thankful embrace of her deliciously shivering torso . . .

Thinking again of her body language, he felt more confident than ever of gaining entry into Memini. Why would an *executive secretary* bother to flirt with him unless his chances were a good deal better than middling? On her return, would she again snake a knee into his leg, thus clearly hinting at his status in the job search? Wasn't this, her coveted flesh, one of the fringe-benefits of membership in the inner circle at Memini? The promiscuity among tekkies was legendary. Their butterfly lives, as portrayed in all the media (which they themselves owned), had long aroused oldfolks revulsion and envy. They lived with a voluptuous intensity. They boasted of indulging passions that never became tainted by guilt. (You had to have an intact organic memory to be pestered by the pangs of guilt.) How horrible it would be, Stewart thought, were a "stag" like himself to *fall in love* with one of these communally shared properties! If he were so lucky as to break into Memini, he would take no more than the glittery goods the most beautiful of tekkies was good for. He would expect no more. He would be immune to disappointment. (But wouldn't he be able to arrange things so that the gorgeous Ms. Yamamoto became his *exclusive* sex toy?) The tangible perks of power boggled even his own bioprogrammer's steamy imagination!

But there still remained the question of that *coffee*. If Sibyl were *not* one of them, if she were a crypto like himself, recognizing in him one of her own kind . . .

He refused to allow himself the luxury of further fantasy. He had discovered the way to the truth! If she brought him his coffee, then she, like himself, was a crypto. (She could not have programmed her flapper to skeet periodically about "coffee with cream for Mr. Bridges" because first she had abandoned her flapper and only *afterward* offered him coffee!) But did he want her to be a crypto? Did he truly want to think of her as a lonely, alien, underground creature like himself, the embodiment of his deepest, most atavistic romantic yearnings, or did he prefer her to remain the soulless beauty of his purely erotic imaginings? His palms grew clammy with anxiety over which of these alternatives would pan out. He wiped his hands on his pantlegs. Gently, he stroked the spots where the touch of her leg still burned him.

At last she re-emerged. Drifting up slowly from the right. Balancing, in her right hand, a brown *coffee mug* . . .

She stopped in front of him and looked wistfully down. "You know, Mr. Bridges, I don't think the chances are very good that Mr. Barton will be able to see you today, as he'd hoped."

She stood just out of knee's reach, a tantalizing inch or so. With a conspiratorial wink, Stewart gazed back into her eyes, reached behind her speech, and raised his hand toward the mug.

Sibyl started back, ever so slightly.

"It's already getting quite late," she sighed. "But I'll remind him that you're still here."

She did not offer Stewart the coffee. Rippling away from him in a stream of silver, she returned to her desk, spoke into the intercom, then slipped through parting panels, coffee in hand, into Lester Barton's office.

Stewart felt like an idiot for winking at her, for reaching out his hand . . . What had the stupid little incident made clear? Nothing. It had proved nothing. His only strategy now was to assume that she was nothing more than tekkie born and bred.

When she emerged from the inner office *sans* coffee cup, she shrugged her bare shoulders and tossed him an apologetic smile. As Stewart got up to leave, "Come here," she said. He approached her desk and watched her lift a silver purse out of a drawer. From the purse she took out a lavender-colored card that was printed with something in gold. Signing it, she folded it into a lavender envelope. Then she got up, walked around the desk, and handed him the envelope while standing so close that the bubble of her personal space burst again to admit him. "You'll be getting a message soon about another appointment. I'm awfully sorry about today, Mr. Bridges."

"Quite all right," said Stewart. A glance into her eyes told him nothing, revealed only playfulness. Was flirtation a highly refined tekkie form of cruelty? he wondered. Shamelessly, he allowed his eyes to linger over the exposed portion of her breasts. Sibyl's eyes followed his, as though she were wondering what could possibly have caught his attention.

"Wait till you see me in gold," she said suddenly.

"What?" He stood in front of her, unable to move.

"In gold," she said, searching his eyes, drawing her fingers around the silver straps that barely restrained her breasts.

"I'd love to ... see you in gold," he said. He dared not ask what she meant.

On his way down in the elevator, he passed the mysterious envelope under his nose several times before opening it. Imbued with her fragrance, it hinted jasmine, cinnamon, and essences whose names he could not guess.

Inside was an invitation—to a Friday-night/overnight party at the Barton residence—with instructions to "Please dress informally." And with the end instruction to "Please enter this invitation *immediately* into Periodic Recall." With no one else on the elevator, Stewart snapped his fingers and burst out, with a flip-flap grunt, "A wormin' my way up your burned-out cingulate gyrus!" He couldn't have felt more self-satisfied about having pressed his advantage with Barton. To that quick thinking of his—and to the efficiency of Barton's flapper—he owed this last-minute invitation.

9. THE ART OF FLAPPER SNATCHING

The traffic of pedestrians, taxis, and buses did little to interfere with Andy's view across the avenue. The rust and gold facade of the Memini building glared back at him under the late-noon sun. Every once in a while, between mouthfuls of food, he fingered the pouch of the Memini-made flapper at his waist or else stroked the jacket of his new spring suit. Better stop fingering the lapels, he thought. He didn't want to make a first impression in a fancy new "off-white" suit smeared with grease.

"Fifteen minutes till one," said Andy, stuffing a forkful of moo-shoo blintz into his mouth. He sat with his assistant Wanjo at the window counter of an uptown franchise of Burma Derma, a rapidly rising Asian-Jewish fast-and-fancy food chain. "She'll show almost exactly three minutes after the hour."

"How you be so sure, brud?"

"That's the advantage of living by a prodder. It's guys like us who live by our wits that are always forgetting what time it is."

"Lis' up, brud. Does we wanna be sittin' in hyeh and be waitin' till ultimo 'mento?" asked Wanjo, wolfing down a glob of egg foo tongue. "Or mebbe we better go strap-hang crossa strip and *wap* them frag-ass momma soon she shove one tit through them door."

"Wanjo, how many times do I have to tell you? I think you got a frag-ass brain yourself, like a Swiss-cheese full of holes. We follow her two blocks downtown to Forty-Nine, where I split off around the corner."

"And you be standin' in them bank door waitin'."

"You wap her purse just before she gets to that Indian place she eats at. You can see it from here. The Raj."

"Yella 'n black sign with them swami on'm."

"Yeah. Lots of people milling around down there. An easy hit. And then you quickdance back to me without bowling folks over."

"Like dribblin' down them court, brud. And then I slips it in y' hand, and off I skimmies down Forty-Nine like I been shot inna ass."

"To draw people's attention, that's right," said Andy. He had complete faith in his teen-age partner's nimbleness and native intelligence. He was the most reliable of all the gutterbugs he'd ever worked with. Still, it was important to take them down a notch, to keep them from getting too cocky. And you couldn't always trust their memory for detail. When Wanjo was neither purse-snatching nor mugging nor selling his trim young body to users of any sex, the kid free-lanced for Andy as a "spotter" of disoriented frags whom Andy would then come and sweet-talk off to a chophouse.

Like lots of macho Hispasians from the alleys of the Brooklyn staghetto, Wanjo sported a Charlie Chan mustache and beard—the beard mostly fake, since at seventeen he still couldn't grow enough of the longer hairs on his own. Given the delicacy of his present commission, Andy had tried to get Wanjo to cut down on the facial hair. He wanted him to blend in with the predominantly tekkie crowd a little better. But Wanjo wouldn't hear of it. Fortunately, there were always enough outborough stags scavenging around midtown to ease Andy's anxieties on that score.

He did convince Wanjo not to dress in any obvious wapwear. Both blocklord weaves *and* a Charlie Chin might draw too many second glances. But Wanjo insisted, with justice, that lots of hip frags were now turning themselves out in stagrags—especially the old-style tweed professor's jacket with leather elbow patches that up till recently used to single a guy out as one tough sonofabitch to mess with. By way of compromise, Wanjo sported a loose-fitting cotton shirt embroidered with garish tropical flowers and skin-tight metal-blue pants. It was the outfit he usually wore when out hooking, and it was unlikely to cause any stir here in midtown.

"My part gawn go easy," said Wanjo, "slick as catshit, brud. But ain't no fun like you gawnta got chingando them frag-lady ass!"

"We'll see, we'll see," said Andy, feeling ripples at the pit of his stomach. A dream-fem that he'd love to bongo-bongo *pays* him to *make it* with *another* class-ass jill! Such a compliment to his masculinity, however well deserved, did add to the assignment a dimension of self-consciousness that

Andy had never before experienced in the whole course of his professional life. Oddly enough, he actually *avoided* thinking of the specifically sexual phase of the undertaking. The technical preparation alone was enough to absorb him completely.

During the night spent in the apartment rented for the anticipated rendezvous, Andy had studied the biotape in which he had been seamlessly dubbed into the love-life of Helen Means. Among the many things he discovered about her refinement and rarified tastes was her love of poetry, his own knowledge of which had been confined to a few old limericks. Andy spent a full hour flipping through a poetry anthology that had been placed on a shelf in the headboard of "their" great revolving circular bed. Many passages in it had been marked for his special attention. Of the slew of lines he would have liked to use on her, he could remember only three: "Shall I compare thee to a summer's day?," "My love is like a red, red rose," and something like "You (he? she?) are a part of all the loveliness that once you (he? she?) made more lovely," which sounded splendid even though he had no idea what it meant.

"You know, Wanjo," said Andy, feeling benevolent, "you too can have all the uptown ass you desire."

"Oh yeh, brud? Lis' up, you! I lucky sontines I can able even to sell my own leel oho for warm place to piss in on them badshit winter we has."

"If you want your own piece of floor and lots of uptown jill, Wanjo, all you have to do is like I keep on telling you: go back to school."

"Don't lay me them school bullshit on my ass again, woll you, Andy? Me, I oldfolks and woll not take no Pill. Teach make me feel like some dumbfuckin' stupido first time I goes, so who need I gawn back and gottin' me headfucked all over 'gin?"

This was one of the most reflective things he had ever heard his protégé give voice to. Still, the boy was always too ready to take the short view of life's possibilities. "Wanjo, don't lay crap on me that you wouldn't take any Pill. Ya been a shitnose ever since I've known you. Those noseholes of yours could suck the Twin Towers in and still have room for a storey or two."

"I'll take me my whack, my snuffies, and my jumjum any day better them Pill what make you forgot who-all you fuck las' week." Wanjo folded his arms in a huff.

"Wanjo, do you remember who *you* fucked last week?"

"Sure, lots people."

"Name one."

"Who fuck know? Shit diffence it make."

"So you see? It isn't the Pill. It's what they did to you in school that jammed your button. They made you feel stupid. Look at me. I stuck with it. I scored out so smart in my ninth year they wanted to stick me into the frag track and start me on the Pill, but my Mom said no way even though they'da given me a six-month free supply, you know, like a scholarship."

"I no mind customer fuck my ass, but I woll not lettin' no one fuck my head," muttered Wanjo.

"But you've got *natural* smarts, like *me*," said Andy. "Look, Wanjo, natural smarts is like a big valuable rock that's gotta be cut for it to be worth anything, and school is what cuts it. Look at how you spend your life. Like a cat that sleeps at night over a hot-air vent. For you one day's the same as any other. You don't look forward to anything, and you don't remember what happened yesterday. You'd be better off on the Pill, for Chris' sake! . . . You know why you don't remember what happened yesterday?"

"Say me, brud. Say me." Wanjo looked away impatiently down the street.

"Because nothing ever *special* happens to you. But if you went back to school and got your spikes ground down—"

"How you say nothin' special ever happen on me?" Wanjo turned an angry glare at him. "If you ain't been havin' a big fuckin' *stick* up your ass, brud, right now you-me be countin' *big whacks* from them 3V man what I talked him bout you yudda day."

"What? You still thinking of 'There's a Crime in Progress'?" Now it was Andy's turn to feel furious. "You want my face on that fucking screen for everyone to see?"

"Coulda had four thousand whacks and no question aks," muttered Wanjo. "No one give a shit what on them screen, you know that."

"I can't believe I'm hearing this crime-show crap from you again."

"Like how it's gawn bust you nuts if them 3V mothers be parkin' in a window cross the strip and shoot me wappin' some fragmomma's bundle? You be on them screen jus one secundo while I flip you them momma's bag, right? And then them follyin' *my* ass down them strip till—"

"You shithead!" said Andy. "I explained to you this is no ordinary fucking grab. This is a very *delicate* operation. It involves some Very Important People! If *they* saw my face on 3V I'd never get another commission from them in my life."

"I knows, I knows," Wanjo sighed. "Still 'nall, though, them *Badge* don't give chingá. It all happen so fast them fuzz can't able to swivel 'fore's it over! Sides, some them 'Crime in Progress' gig turn out be fake, never know which, so ain't worth no cop's shit go nosin' after."

"Do it with the 3V boys on your own," said Andy. "Why the hell did you wanna get *me* involved?"

"Cause it be sure thing—happen one o'clock. Camera be right there. And it have nice big blonde titties. And . . . "

"Spit it out, blowpipes! 'Cause *I'd* be in it. 'Cause people on the street know my *name*. 'Cause I'm practically a fucking celebrity, while you're nothing but a piece of cheap round-eye that nobody'd wanna *see* on 3V."

"You got it, brud, and you a dumb fuck, cause you lucky them be int'ested when I talks bout you, cause not jus evvybody gottin to gawn on 'Crime in Progress.' I knows amigos what woll *die* for gottin picked, like when 'em be coppin' a rape, or skeeter-shootin' at some assholes outta some van or some gig like—"

"That's why I keep telling you, shitnose, you want something *special* to happen to you? Then go back to school!" Andy checked his watch and glanced across the street. "Then you'll have plenty chiquitas, a nice square of floor, a rack of fragrags ordered straight from A4DZ, some telefrag wanting to follow *your* ass up the street on 'Crime in Progress,' whacks in your pocket instead of wang up your oho—"

"Shit, honk, how school gawn do me all them?"

"I'll tell you," said Andy, looking Wanjo straight in his wide-open eyes. "In another couple years I'm gonna need a full-time partner. Two of the right guys could do great in the organ business. But my partner has to have an *education*. You can't do good in the organ trade without a broadly liberal education."

"What you mean libbel education?"

Andy sat up straight and jerked down at his lapels. "It's the whole shootin' match they dish out in high school, brud. It's what they call the 'curriculum.'"

"And what in shit be *them*?" Wanjo gazed at him distrustfully—as if he were out to sell him a stolen satlink videowatch.

"You mean you don't know the curriculum?" Still a few minutes to kill, he thought. "Shit, boy, that's simple. The high-school curriculum is divided into two parts, Deductics and Inductics. And like any stupido knows, each of those in turn is divided into *three* parts. Deductics consists of... Apriorics, Prescriptics, and Calculistics. Inductics... consists of Praxics, Narratistics, and Phenomenistics."

"And all them 'stics' be libbel education?"

"Yes."

"Stick 'em up your *nose*."

"Listen, smart-ass, to make out in the organ biz you gotta have a liberal education. It's not like in the old days any more when—"

"Lis' up, brud!" sneered Wanjo. "Fi wan traffic in the chophouse trade, I can able right now make me a bankful of bananas, but choppin' ain my toke."

"That's bullshit and you know it. You damn well would do it if you could! You already tried it once or twice, like the jumjum skull that you are, and what happened?"

"Ain't my toke, brud. Jus ain my—"

"I'll tell you what happened. Like some high-flying shitnose, you clop some dumb wandering fragdaddy over the head and ex him out, and then you go and drag the hot bod in a sack over to a chophouse—where they tell you to skimmy the hell off with your stinking bundle or they'll sic Badge on your ass right then and there."

"Them good meat, what they knowed it were, too," muttered Wanjo.

"Dead meat's never good meat, Round-eye! How many times do I have to tell you before you save it in that flapperless head of yours? Wanjo, you got a memory like a fragmomma's twat. Over and over I tell you you can't sell a bod that you knock off in the street. No self-respecting body shop will ever buy roadkill no matter how fresh it is. The most valuable organs are already bound to be spoiled. And then you went and did it again, and tried a different chophouse—the one *I* do business with, no less!—where they almost grabbed *your* ass instead, remember?"

"Ain't no dead meat I brung 'em, brud. Were just knocked out, zall."

"What the hell's the diff? Who'll buy damaged goods? These places have a reputation to maintain. You know, there's a lot of legit corporate money invested in these joints."

"They jus bein' nasty, zall."

"You're just lucky you used my name and saved your ass that time, because by now there'd be nothing left of you but a kidneyful of honk-piss and the rest of you sold for pigslop."

"I owes you one, brud," Wanjo grunted.

"That's not the point," said Andy. He looked sharply down at his watch. It had just turned one p.m. "The point is that only live meat in good condish is acceptable in the organ biz. You must be able to lead the meat, while still on the hoof, of its own free will, right *into* the chopshop—where the processing has to take place *on the spot*. And for that, Wanjo, you must *convince* your mark to voluntarily go along with you. You must present a friendly and cultured demeanor so that the average lost frag will trust in your good intentions instead of skimmying away in even greater anxiety. And to accomplish that you must have a liberal arts education. Psychology, English grammar, even poetry and foreign languages! You never know who you'll meet. Why do you think they've trusted *me* to talk this fraggona out of her panties?"

"I hellsure knows whatcha talkin', brud. Yo, I gawn go back to them chingando school soon's I gots me a leel time, zall."

"Bullshit, Wanjo. I give you advice like you're my own bastard son, but you never remember a damn thing I tell you. You got a head like a busted flapper. When you think of all those chilly-ass fragmommas you could have, just like me . . ." Andy knew he was exaggerating. He had never had anything so fancy as a Helen Means in his whole life, not even in college, from which he had dropped out the first semester when he learned that he'd been placed in the dumb-track there, too, just like in high school. He felt apprehensive, and that was partly why he was dumping so much on Wanjo. Not nervous about the street part of the operation. But about the second part, if the first part went off well. About the part back in the apartment with the rotating bed. He tried not to think about that part.

"I do be seein' some fine bunch o' tittie caminando out them door."

"That's her," said Andy. He knocked over his stool as he sprang toward the door.

10. THE ERASABLE LOVER

Helen stepped out into the street and stopped to fill her lungs with the unfiltered, late-spring air and to let the sun brush her face like the lips of a joyful lover who had hungrily awaited her all morning. From ingrained habit she turned left and strolled along close to the buildings, out of the way of most oncoming pedestrians. She did not like to be hurried, either at work or at play. She liked to dawdle in front of the hi-fash "teeks" that lined her path from the Memini building to the Raj. She always had lunch at the Raj.

Pausing before a silvered section of shop window, she gazed at her reflection. She admired the soft, clingy material of her dress. It was beige with splotchy streaks of muted yellow and orange. She was enchanted by the way it highlighted both the sleek curves of her body and the golden swirl of her hair. And as she glanced at her lovely body, she sized up the men who passed just behind her. Some were handsome, some stylish, some just unaccountably electric. Some were all three at once. Many of them stared at her as appreciatively as she did herself.

Helen crossed Fiftieth Street with her hand loosely curled around the light-brown Coach bag that rode at her hip. It was a combination purse and flapsack. Just then her skeeter sang a comforting ID advisory. It played at ten-minute intervals daily unless she deliberately suspended it during periods of intense concentration:

I AM HELEN MEANS, ART DIRECTOR FOR MEMINI, AT CORPORATE HQ IN MANHATTAN. I AM THIRTY-FIVE YEARS OLD AND MARRIED TO WILLIAM MEANS, ATTORNEY, WHOSE OFFICE NUMBER IN CASE NEEDED IN AN EMERGENCY IS 347-9091. IT IS NOW 1:05 P.M. AND I SHOULD BE ON MY WAY TO

LUNCH AT THE RAJ, WHICH IS LOCATED ON SIXTH AVENUE BETWEEN FORTY-NINTH AND FORTY-EIGHTH STREETS. I HAVE NO APPOINTMENTS THIS AFTERNOON. THEY HAVE ALL BEEN MIRACULOUSLY CANCELED! I SHALL DEVOTE THE AFTERNOON, THEN, TO STUDYING THE DESIGN ALTERNATIVES FOR OUR PROJECTED FORGETAWAY PARADISE IN BORNEO.

As she proceeded downtown from Fiftieth to Forty-Ninth, she could not help stopping in front of boutiques like the Op Shop. In the windows of the Op Shop, curvaceous Betty-bots made simple, natural movements of arm, leg, or waist—like opening a drawer, or sitting down at a desk—that set off cascades of coordinated color-changes in the shimmering outfits they wore. One of the robokins spoke out to Helen quite audibly: "Are you a woman who goes in one eye and out the other? Remember, where the eye goes, there goes desire. Stay in view. Choose from a wide selection of the latest Op Shop . . . "

Helen knew she must have ogled this window hundreds of times before. (Her meminized clothing inventory included many an Op Shop item.) But each time, like now, was surprising and new and delightful, whether the window display was a fresh installation or not. If she'd been able to *remember* all the things she casually saw, her vision would have been clouded; all emotion would have been dulled. She would have passed by with jaded eye. As to her own artistic imagination . . . her mind opened up to the *novelty* of every moment. She felt that she could meet the world with constant childlike wonder at its freshness, at its unpredictability.

At moments, however, the past was able to torture her, for she could still remember her life up till age twenty-one or twenty-two. Growing up in a middle-class household with perfunctorily caring parents and a self-absorbed older brother, she had clung desperately to boy after boy, suffering disappointment after disappointment, riding the seesaw of hope and hurt.

Love came free of pain now. No more did she have to suffer the *longing*, the *waiting* . . . Time for her was pure creative potential. That horrible period of growing up, its sickly romanticism still remembered, had long since lost its sway over her. Slowly and inevitably, in reverse chronological order, those years would all be erased: inexorable long-term effect of the Pill. The sooner the better, as far as she was concerned. There had been some *good* memories, of course, but those she'd had recorded—and then recreated in sensory fullness—as part of her Personal Past.

Helen stood bemused in front of the Op Shop display, deliberately ignoring her hunger. Like a cat following a ping-pong ball, she watched the garments in the window undergo randomized tonal shifts. Caught up in that magical sequence of changes, she spontaneously reached into her purse, raised her flapper to her lips, and queried, "Op Shop purchases?"

I MADE MY LAST PURCHASE AT THE OP SHOP 47 DAYS AGO, she answered herself. IT IS A BEAUTIFUL FORM-FITTING OPFIBER GOWN THAT ADAPTS ITS TONAL RANGE-SHIFTS TO THE LIGHTNESS OF MY SKIN AND HAIR. IT IS VERY SENSITIVE TO MY CHANGING HORMONE BALANCES, THE HUES SHIFTING IN WARMTH OR COOLNESS ACCORDINGLY. I AM LEARNING MORE AND MORE TO READ THE SILENT VOICE OF MY GOWN FOR HELP IN MAKING DECISIONS REGARDING MEN. I AM SCHEDULED TO WEAR IT AGAIN THIS FRIDAY FOR THE PARTY OVER AT LB'S. IT COST ME EXACTLY UAC 1699.95.

"Well," Helen sighed, replying to her flapper with a tinge of disappointment, "I should have guessed I couldn't have resisted such a lovely thing for long. I simply *adore* that silly gown!" She would literally be wearing her heart on her sleeve at Barton's place. How fun! When mixing with men there, she must try standing next to a mirror. If she could *see* what she felt, she was sure that she would *feel* it even more—in a kind of positive-feedback loop. Did Barton's place have big wall mirrors all around? She'd been there dozens of times, for sure! She could call up a description of his estate on her flapper, but now there wasn't time, and besides, she'd *always* rather be *surprised*.

Stuffing flapper back into Coach bag, Helen sauntered a bit more up the street. Gilgo's! She stopped transfixed before their interactive holodrame. Herself, the onlooker, could enjoy playing the leading role in a slyly erotic reverse striptease. She stood there and let *le drame* play through a couple of brief cycles. It was always a surprise to her—as though she'd never seen it before—to watch the female model in the 3D projection take on *her own* face and hair; to see *herself* (momentarily endowed with an even more perfect figure) standing in the skimpiest underthings as she langorously cooperated with a tuxedoed male performer (her valet? her husband? her *innamorato*?) whose hands, with their sensitive fingers, helped her slip into the latest evening gown from Beijing, of a soft texture and creamy shade of blue that were selected—for the time she remained there—to harmonize with the exquisite paleness of her skin. Her abdominals quivered with delight. And the gown was only UAC 2295!

How desirable it would make her look at . . . wasn't it the Big Boss's blast this Friday? She simply had to have it! The utter freedom of the moment gave rise to blinding desire. Automatically she took out her flapper again. "Gilgo purchases?" she asked, trembling in fear of another disappointment.

I'VE NOT BOUGHT A THING AT GILGO'S SINCE LAST NOVEMBER, came her reply.

She felt thrilled. Only one more hurdle to go.

"I'm just . . . dying to have this dress," she said. "It costs 2295 whacks but, believe me, it's worth every cent." Her whole body tensed as she hoped for a permissive response.

I'M SORRY, she heard herself reply. I KNOW IT'S TOUGH WHEN YOU CAN'T BE TOTALLY SPONTANEOUS, BUT HELEN DARLING, YOU'VE ALREADY EXCEEDED YOUR CLOTHING BUDGET THIS MONTH BY UAC 987.50. WILLIAM HAD QUITE A FIT, IF YOU RECALL. (IF YOU WISH TO RECALL, VOICE IN "WILLIAM/BUDGET FIT/CURRENT.") I APPROVED YOUR GOING OVER THE LIMIT THEN, BECAUSE YOU'D HIT A TERRIFIC SALE, BUT . . .

She angrily tapped the voice button and walked glumly on. Still remembering she was headed toward the Raj, Helen shrugged off an offer of cunnilingus from a handsome passerby. (The cardinal safety rule of tekkie existence was never to make the acquaintance of a stranger in territory you did not fully control.) Helen mingled with the crowd that was just now crossing Forty-Ninth. She hugged her bag instinctively to her side as people seemed to swarm too close around her. She knew she was going to lunch and that as soon as she saw the restaurant she would know just where to turn in. It was somewhere right down this block, she knew.

The image of the handsome passerby lingered in her mind. Did they know each other? Had they met before, made love? Even if they had, their next encounter would always be their first. The excitement would never diminish. Helen felt hungry for something exotic, for Indian spices . . . She was not aware of being approached. She felt only a sharp tug at the shoulder, the snap of the strap, and the leap of the purse from her fingers. She spun around and saw a blue-legged figure hopscotch back through a maze of bodies, then dash around the corner to the right.

"Help!" she shouted. "That man stole my purse!" Some of the people flowing toward her obligingly turned around in the direction she pointed, then shrugged their shoulders and strode past with a shake of the head that meant, "You *know* what living in New York is like; you really *ought* to be more careful, sweetheart."

Helen pushed through to the curb. Her eyes swept the avenue for a policeman. Not a patrol car in sight! The only *helpful* oldfolks in the city, and when you needed them, they blinked out of existence, as if deliberately taking revenge on you out of primitive status envy. Anxiety overwhelmed her. The rush of blood to her head made her dizzy. Why didn't it trip her anxID? she wondered, frightened.

She hurried back up along the curb toward the corner where the blue-legged thief had turned, hoping at least to catch sight of him—someone who would be running. She looked and looked but saw no one in any such hurry. Automatically, then, she turned back in the direction in which she had been walking. That much she knew: she had been walking in the downtown direction. But she was so shaken by the loss of her bag that, for the moment at least, she could not remember *why* she had been walking in that direction. Her skeeter would soon inform her, of course, so she decided not to outwardly panic. Instead, she walked back to the corner, and then wandered back in her original direction, hoping that her head would clear as soon as her nerves quieted down. Again she looked up and down the avenue, observing the magcabs swerving illegally into the bus lane, and she wondered precisely *why* she was looking up and down. She felt deeply, inexplicably upset, groped for her bag, and then discovered that it was *gone from her shoulder*!

She looked frantically around the heavily trafficked sidewalk. People made a wide berth around her as she darted to and fro. She thought for sure that she must have left her bag in the office. Yes, that was what she had done, she thought, as her whole body began shaking uncontrollably. She knew she must avoid getting hysterical. Help would soon come, she was certain. This part of Manhatttan was no jungle. Someone would always arrive to help a person in distress. She stood back against a store window remembering—yes, she'd been on her way to lunch. So why not continue on her way to ... where? Reaching again for her missing bag, she realized that right now she had no means of *paying* for lunch. The thing was to go back to the office, where her bag would undoubtedly turn up. She looked vaguely up the street. *Of course* she could find her way back to the office! she told herself. Her body refused to move, as if in a dream.

I AM HELEN MEANS, her own voice suddenly burst in on her through her skeeter, ART DIRECTOR FOR MEMINI, AT CORPORATE HQ IN MANHATTAN. She lurched away from the store window and heaved a sigh of relief. I AM THIRTY-FIVE YEARS OLD AND MARRIED TO WILLIAM MEANS, ATTORNEY, WHOSE OFFICE NUMBER IN CASE NEEDED IN AN EMERGENCY IS 347-9091. IT IS NOW 1:15 P.M. AND I AM NOW SUPPOSED TO BE MEETING MY LOVER ANDY PETERS OUT IN FRONT OF THE RAJ RESTAURANT ON SIXTH AVENUE BETWEEN FORTY-NINTH AND FORTY-EIGHTH STREETS. I HAVE NO APPOINTMENTS THIS AFTERNOON. THEY HAVE ALL BEEN MIRACULOUSLY CANCELED. I SHALL DEVOTE THE AFTERNOON, THEN, TO MAKING LOVE WITH ANDY IN HIS APARTMENT, WHERE MOST OF OUR RENDEZVOUS HAVE TAKEN PLACE FOR A FULL YEAR NOW. LAST WINTER I UPDATED MY PERSONAL PAST, SO IF I WANT TO I CAN *VISUALIZE* SOME OF OUR EARLY ENCOUNTERS JUST BY FLAPPING IN "ANDY PETERS, APARTMENT." IT IS A LOVELY APARTMENT WITH OUR OWN ROUND BED THAT I MYSELF CHOSE. I'VE SCATTERED PICTURES OF THE TWO OF US ALL OVER THE ...

How reassuring to hear her own voice again! And how exciting to be about to make love: whether with husband or lover, it always and forever promised the thrill of an initial embrace. But if this was her skeeter speaking to her, then her flapper had to be near. Had she stopped in at the Raj for something and left it there, in her purse? ... "Helen, baby, I've got your purse back for you."

She looked around startled at the man who came up behind her. This, then, was Andy, whom she'd been seeing *for a full year now*. She gazed at him with a look of surprise and distrust.

"What's the matter, honey? Your flapper's in your purse. Isn't it working?" said Andy, reaching in and shaking the instrument. "When I tackled the guy who ripped it off your shoulder, maybe it got damaged by the impact."

"No, no, it's working fine," she said. "If I'm looking . . . puzzled, it's because I'm feeling a bit disoriented. I seem to have lost track of where I was headed." Although she *recognized*, in the organic sense, no one but family, husband, and most old friends, she was normally adept at tektact, which demanded flashing a friendly face at anyone she knew she was supposed to know. In the carefully controlled contexts of normal life, flashing such a smile was second nature. Under abnormal circumstances like these, however, anyone would forgive her a moment of overt confusion. "Thank you, Andy," she said, thrusting the recovered bag with its dangling strap under her arm. "I'm very lucky you were around."

"Lucky?" he grinned. His bone-white spring suit and *impossibly tasteless silver tie* hurt her eyes in the sun. "I'm here by Her Majesty's appointment, your Highness. My carriage awaits your pleasure." Andy snapped a sharp salute and comically clicked his heels. He made her smile, so she tried forgetting his ridiculous outfit. She could not imagine having ever taken a lover (on the long term, at least) lacking in impeccable sartorial taste, no matter what his financial condition. But, she reminded herself, his *lovely apartment with our own round bed*—which *I myself chose*, would surely more than make up for the tacky-tekkie impression he made on her here out on the street.

"I'm rather too shaken to do much walking," she said. "Do you think we could find a cab right now?" She would feel all the more comfortable with him the less she had to be seen tagging along beside that titanium-white suit. He was otherwise an attractive enough man—slim, sharp-featured, half a foot taller than she, a bit high-strung and sexily gaunt—and she was sure that from the skin down he must be exciting to be with. Or else she'd have ditched him long ago by wiping out of permastore all memory of their ever having met. "By the way," she said, stopping suddenly to examine him more closely, "you just said, didn't you, that you *tackled* the thief who stole my purse?"

"That's right," said Andy. "He didn't have a chance to take anything out of it . . . Oh, you're wondering how I dealt with *him*? Beat the shit out of him. Had no time to hand him over to a cop. Not if I was to keep my date with you, sweetie."

"Thank you," Helen said. "What I was wondering, though, was why you don't have any scuff marks on your suit."

"Oh, *that* . . . You didn't think I'd come pick you up without wiping the dirt off first, did you? Great material, this suit. Dirt wipes off with the swipe of a tissue . . . Hey, we got a cab!"

Helen held back as the cab swung up to the curb.

"Problem?" coughed Andy.

She saw him swallow hard. Clearly, his nerves had been rattled by the encounter with the purse-snatcher. It must have been a dreadful, dangerous ordeal. She wondered how many men she knew would ever have done a thing like that for her. Her poor lover was trying so hard to look cool . . . Yes, she sort of liked him. He distinctly had possibilities.

"Aren't you getting in?" he choked.

She felt stupid asking, but she was hungry. "Excuse me, Andy dear, but don't we usually have lunch—at the Raj—before . . . ?"

"Course not, silly. I've got a great spread waiting for us at the apartment. Like always." He shook his head and tck-tck'ed as she slid before him into the waiting maglev. Helen was amazed at herself: to have picked a lover who would say "a great spread"; and who would wear such a suit; and to have stayed with him *for a full year now*. Well, with that wiry, energetic physique, he had to be marvelously *virile*. Of course, she might have made a resolution last year not to be always so damn fastidious—to be discriminating, not discrimina*tory*. While her social world at Wellesley had been formative in the best sense—and she did not regret a *day* she had spent in the privileged world of Wellesley—still, she had at times even then felt that the range of her admissible lovers was becoming too narrow, too restrictively upper-middle-class, too determined by mere externals.

As soon as she was settled in the cab, Helen reached for her flapper as casually as she would lift out her compact. Her current New Year's resolutions repeated themselves to her each month automatically. Quickly, she punched up her last year's resolutions: MEMINIZE ALL OF *WAR AND PEACE* AND *THE BROTHERS KARAMAZOV.* (Oh, bitch! She'd forgotten all about that—deliberately ignored her own injunction, actually. Conscientiously tapping three buttons, she attached the ignored resolution to the current year's list.) The last of the current ones was OPEN YOUR SOUL TO A MORE SPONTANEOUS RELATIONSHIP WITH THE SUBTLE SPIRITUAL INFLUENCES AND CHANGING PANORAMA OF BEAUTY MANIFESTING ALL ABOUT YOU. (Well, that one she was *always* working on; maybe *that* was why she'd allowed Andy ... Andy what? ... into her orbit. Helen immediately punched in ANDY PETERS/APT, whereupon her lover's ecstatic face, and the sensation of clinging to his slim, muscular body—and of silken sheets beneath her own bare butt—flooded her consciousness as powerfully as any of her remaining natural memories. She glanced at him. The picture of him in her mind perfectly matched the Andy who sat smiling and twitching beside her.)

"Checking me out in Personal Past?" Andy laughed. "Don't I still look like the same Prince Charming you met only a year ago?"

"You're forgetting my advanced case of Executive Scrub," she smiled back. "Prosopagnosia, if you want the technical name."

"Pro-what?" said Andy, shuffling up next to her and draping her shoulders with his arm. Helen instinctively shuddered, thinking it gauche of any lover of hers to paw her in the sight of a cabbie. So much of their driving was automated that practically all they did was eavesdrop on their passengers. Still, she forgave Andy, imagining how much she must excite him—for he must also be experiencing everything as if the two of them would be mating for the first time. Her own level of arousal remained undampened.

"Prosopagnosia, the inability to recall faces. You can't tell me you don't have it yourself!"

"Me? Of course," said Andy. "But mine is selective. I can recall the face of every woman I ever went to bed with." "Really?"

"Hormones fly where neurones often die," he quoted.

"I'm impressed." She frowned at his cliché and at his tactless sexual boastfulness. "And do you picture all these women when *we* make love and assign us comparative ratings?"

"No," he said, brushing her ear with his lips as the cab sped down Fifty-Seventh toward Madison. "You are incomparable. Shall I compare thee to a summer's day? No woman's ever made me as happy as you."

"How would you know *that*?" she challenged him.

"It's just . . . a manner of speaking. Now's as happy as Andy's ever gonna be!"

She felt him tremble and heard his voice crack and trail self-consciously away. His unguarded display of emotion delighted her—partly making up for the cloying effect of his cologne, which was a far cry from Penhaligon's. Surely she must at some time have made herself a note to buy him a decent cologne! "It's oldfolks who are always drawing comparisons," she offered, "and ruining the pleasures they *are* engaged in. As for me, Andy dear, I find every lover incomparable . . . of course, some more incomparable than others." He did not crack a smile. Either he took her challenge seriously, or he was terribly slow at wordplay.

"You're exactly like a red, red rose," he crooned. "You are a lovely part of everything . . . you once made much more lovely."

"You must cease mangling quotations!" she laughed, cupping her ears with her hands. He looked insulted, but she thought he was putting on a face. The effect of his fumbling and stammering was somehow terribly stimulating. Her skin tingled where his fingers stroked her arm. She would ravish him as soon as they reached the apartment, she thought, in spite of his inability to quote coherently from Shelley. Evidently, she reasoned, what had sustained their relationship so long had to be the articulateness of his unencumbered body in the round bed she had chosen for their playground. The promise of delight to come made Helen wet with anticipation. She grasped his hand and passionately massaged his slender, clammy fingers. In deliberate abandon (and certainly out of sight of the cabbie), she explored his lap with her sliding wrist. Disappointed at encountering nothing, she assumed he was being tastefully restrained. What her caress raised from him instead was a tremulous babble, a stream of saccharine words of endearment which she could hardly believe would issue from the mouth of someone she had retained as a long-term lover: *your golden hair, your gorgeous eyes, your perfect skin, bundle from heaven, dreamboat, baby doll* . . . If this was how he had expressed himself at their first copulation, she must have deliberately decided to focus on his other, more sensuous qualities and to ignore his paucity of verbal imagination—which, in any case, would have relatively minor importance in the sack.

I AM HELEN MEANS, her ten-minute reminder reasserted itself, ART DIRECTOR FOR MEMINI, AT CORPORATE HQ IN... *Love*, he whispered in her ear, his voice vibrating unpleasantly in her skeeter, *is only a four-letter word compared to the feelings that I*... (That must be it, she thought: in bed, his mouth engaged in far better things than talk.) IT IS NOW 1:25 P.M. AND I AM NOW SUPPOSED TO HAVE MET MY LOVER ANDY PETERS... *Never has a woman like you*, he gurgled, *ever crossed my*... (Muscular thighs, she thought; I adore the hardness, can't wait to grip the tight cheeks) DEVOTE THE AFTERNOON, THEN, TO MAKING LOVE WITH ANDY IN HIS APARTMENT (wrap that pelvis in my arms and draw him relentlessly)...

The apartment *was* lovely. Tastefully furnished in a variety of complementary earth tones. One entire living-room wall was a hologrammic beach lapped by tireless little waves that nibbled, probed, thrust and sucked at the tawny belly of the sand. A hot-table/coffee-table combo sat low in the middle of an artfully casual scattering of fuzzy-furry cushions. The pungent smells of Indian food—from Raj's, no doubt—wafted out from the hot-table.

"We shall start with an excellent champagne. Pick a cushion, Your Majesty!" Andy threw out his hand in a grand sweep—only to smash his knuckles against a mantelpiece that projected to the left of the door. Helen laughed to see him grimace. It was the climax of his awkwardness, and in the buzz of her desire it even seemed lovable. She grabbed the wounded hand, kissed it, crushed it to her breast, then pulled Andy to her, her fingers kneading his buttocks as though they were dough. He gasped and mumbled things—*hot momma you, you passionate baby doll*—as he coyly tried, tease that he was, to wriggle out of her clasp.

"There's champagne! There's lunch! I planned... It's all been waiting," he protested as her fingers burrowed under his belt and slid toward his crotch from the rear.

"Later," she whispered, biting his ear. "First... *this*." Even the smell of his cheap toilet water had an aphrodisiac effect on her as she backed him toward the only other visible door panel in the room. It opened behind them onto a chamber filled with a great, round, slowly rotating brothel-bed covered with dark-red satiny sheets and pillows. He stumbled as she thrust him backward (that was sweet of him—to add to her excitement by a token display of resistance!). She did not give up her grip on him. Instead, she toppled him beneath her onto the bed. The mattress quivered jellylike as she rolled around on top of his hard, taut stomach. Playfully, it seemed, he tried to oppose the pressure she brought to bear.

"Can't you wait . . . just a little?" Andy whined against her neck, tickling her skin so that she shivered at the lick of his breath. "I wanted to celebrate our first—I mean what to me always feels like our first . . . with a glass of—"

"No waiting," she murmured. "No fair. You won't make me wait, darling, will you?" Her tongue whipped in his ear, toured his mouth, while her hand unzipped the static-held flap of his pants. She basked in the feel of her utter irresistibility. "I love it when men play coy," she breathed. "I'll undress you all by myself."

"Helen," he squeaked, "listen. You're absolutely stunning. You're the classiest fem I've ever in my life—"

"Don't *classy* me and *fem* me. Ikh!" she shuddered. "Don't . . . say . . . anything, Andy, dear. Just help me pull this sheath up over my shoulders." She straddled him with her knees, unzipped a stat-flap that ran from hem to waist, and peeled the garment up over her head while keeping his squirming pelvis pinned between her thighs. A demonic power girded her loins. Without Andy's help, she pulled the dress over her shoulders and tossed it behind her to the floor. She felt delighted to be free of its drag. Her bare breasts swelled forward.

She smiled down at Andy's pale, strangely smirking face through the valley between her stiffening nipples. With a flick of her fingers she parted the stat-flap that released her skimpy panties. Whipping them off, she laughed and stretched them across Andy's mouth as if tying on a gag. (How could she have forgotten to wear a so much sexier vaginet? she wondered. She *always* wore a vaginet to make love in!)

"And now you," she said. "Off with this dumb suit!"

Andy backed away toward the middle of the bed. Since she had already looped her fingers around his belt, by wriggling away he helped her strip his pants off down to the knees.

"Relax, lover," she crooned. "I already adore what I see. I'll help you get over your shyness. Don't worry, my sweet. It's always so wonderful to be with a man and feel such surprise and newness, as if you've never been with him before... Do you like what *you* see, darling? Am I beautiful enough for you?"

"More than—!" gasped Andy. "More lovely than all the loveliness... than I could ever have the right, the hope to... a queen, an angel! Not just a pair of legs and a couple of..."

"Have a bite! They're edible. Cherry vanilla," she said, provocatively stuffing her panties into his mouth as she loosened his horrid tie. After stripping his shirtfront apart, she stroked him from his chest to his curly-haired belly with long, deft fingers, expecting a lovely response, a springing, vibrant, gigantic, impatient response... Coy, cool, a thoroughly self-possessed man was this lover of hers! Enjoyed making her *work* for her pleasure. With loving touches she disrobed him completely, feeling his whole body somehow stiffening against her everywhere except where it counted.

"Take it easy, honey, relax!" she cooed, lifting her head reluctantly from his thighs. The challenge made her heart throb; the passion she felt made her stomach twitch. Not a thing in the world mattered but this moment that edged toward bliss, this dizzying *now*, the spontaneous press of her love-beaded flesh toward union with this tease of a lover, this Andy Peters with whom she had stayed for a full year because of his capacity to excite and... requite?

"Am I too bold? Am I too brash? Do you want me to go slower? Speak, honey! Tell me what you need me to do. Is there something that you always remind me to do? Perhaps we should both consult our flappers?..."

"I feel... as if we're being watched," her lover whispered. His face turned beet-red as she looked at him in puzzlement. The full-ceiling mirror was all that watched them. The door behind them was shut tight as a clam... the way she herself would be feeling soon if this struggle went on much longer! This was not a matter of coyness, of teasing...

"I'm trying," Andy rasped. "It's all these crazy *feelings* I got about you! I guess it's because I never expected that... goddammit, that a guy like me could ever even come *close* to . . . "

She swirled her little gag over his mouth, against his nose, straddled him, worked directly, desperately, felt the sweat pouring from her brow, from her thighs. This was *not* the love-sweat she'd been feeling almost exclusively up to a short while ago. This was a cold sweat mingled with chills, odd tremors, a shriveling sense of nakedness, ugliness, exposure, as of old Eve when exiled from Eden.

"What the hell is the matter with you *anyway*?" she hurled at him finally, rolling off him and curling up into a shivering shrunken ball.

"I love you, Helen! I adore you!" he tried to whisper.

"Why the hell are you *whispering*, you jerk?"

"Believe me," he mumbled behind her, like a voice from a distant room, "this is the first time such a thing has ever happened to me—us, I mean. I'm *terrific* in bed! I swear it! Maybe if we'd had lunch first, a drink . . . " He didn't even sound as if he were speaking to *her*. He sounded like a defendant—the accused pleading his case to a judge.

"You shit!" she retorted. "Are those your priorities? Are you incapable of a single spontaneous urge? I don't *need* to take on lovers who can't love!" She realized what it was she felt: *humiliated*! She had not experienced any humiliation that she could remember since falling for some self-centered jackass back in college. Fortunately, she would never have to experience this feeling again with this so-called lover who meant nothing to her if he couldn't deliver on demand. Thank heaven for the Pill—because of which this dreadful, intolerable, stomach-shrinking feeling would disappear from her consciousness forever within the space of five to ten minutes. And with a flick of the delete button she would wipe Andy Peters—every trace of her ever having known him—out of her flapper and out of her brainchip forever. In a few minutes she would no longer know she had ever met him. Neither his face nor his name—nor his cloying scent or tasteless clothes or definitely lower-class speech patterns—would ever again have the power to bruise her consciousness.

"You have to understand," he mouthed at her flexing spine as she hastily slipped back into her clothes. "I couldn't just treat you like a . . . piece of meat, like the muffins I'm used to just picking up off the street . . . "

When fully dressed, she stood up tall between bed and door and glanced coldly down at him—at a pale, goose-bumpy, scrawny, limp-dicked, quivering creature that looked back at her with silent importunity. "This is it between us!" she said, sweeping her hand down in front of her body like a guillotine blade. "Quits! Don't ever try to see me again. Those pictures you have of us in the living room . . . burn them!"

Andy muttered something snivelly in reply. She did not stay to listen. She strode out through the parting door panel, and as soon as it shut behind her, she pulled her flapper out of her bag. The strap of her bag, she noticed, was broken. How did *that* happen? she wondered. She was not going to be distracted. Opening her flapper, she said: "Andy Peters . . . Total Record . . . Delete."

Are you sure? queried her skeeter.

"Yes, delete," she confirmed.

Skeeter answered: *Andy Peters, total record, deleted*. Helen already felt better.

11. SON OF A MIXED MARRIAGE

Stewart did not visit his parents on a regular basis. It was not the bus trip from Manhattan to Flatbush that bothered him. *They* bothered him. They were an impossible pair, a stag-frag couple inhabiting the social fringes of mutually incompatible worlds. Few friends or relatives ever regularly stopped by, and those who did were either hopeless losers or shameless users—two basic types that he thought, all during his boyhood, constituted humanity. The Brooklyn streets, especially the great bazaar at Junction Plaza, confirmed over and over again his cynical view of his species.

But if he did not show up periodically for dinner, his mother would have been deeply wounded. His father lacked the capacity to "care"—in the same spontaneous way that was natural to his mother—except during some moment when she would forcibly bring their son's protracted absence to his attention. Apart from guilt, though, there were other pressures that would occasionally drive Stewart to drop in on his parents: either the weight of unbearable loneliness or a paralyzing feeling of panic, like now, when he had to make a major decision.

He had made the same kind of descent on his parents just a couple of weeks earlier, while still stunned by Memini's offer to interview him—*him*, an outsider! A man who had never held *any* corporate position whatsoever! Oddly enough, the contradictory advice his parents had given him had helped him decide to go through with the interview—the one that still hadn't come off.

Now it was more bizarre yet. An invitation to shmooze with Memini brass at LB's own estate! How far did he dare go with his imposture?

If he'd had a friend with whom to share his crisis, he would not have shown up here, on a weekday evening, unannounced and unexpected. But he *had* no such friend—neither man nor woman—whom he could trust. Like his ill-matched parents, he'd grown up apart from that clear-cut world of people who knew exactly who they were. Up to now he had dealt with the world of the tekkie on a limited, strictly professional basis. As to mixing with "his own kind," colorful though many of them were, they tended to have limited intellectual horizons and truncated personal ambition, exhibiting the slave mentality of an underclass in their grumbling deference to the élite. As to the militant antitekkie fringe, Stewart would occasionally hear, on his ramblings through the Plaza bazaar, the soapbox rantings of men who claimed that the world would be redeemed by a terrorist group called Cortex, but he doubted that Cortex existed, and anyway, fanatics bored him.

After giving him a warm hug, his mother ushered him toward the kitchen. "I'm so *glad* you didn't waste money on flowers again," she sighed. "Besides, your father doesn't appreciate them."

"Flowers..." Stewart blushed deep red. He had ordered an arrangement of roses from his favorite midtown night-florist, then forgot to pick them up on his cab ride into Brooklyn.

""Come on into the kitchen, Stewart dear. You won't believe the *horror* that's on 'Crime in Progress' just now." His mother steered him to the table at the end of the partitionless kitchen/dining/living-room. Pouring him a mugful of coffee, she all but sloshed it over the table as she focused on the kitchen-wall 3V. "Just *look* at that disgusting little man, Stewart. A moment ago he showed us a *machete* hidden in his filthy pants."

"Mom, I'm sure that it's interesting, but—"

"Look, dear, this piece of slime is about to murder his jumjum dealer. He says his main man's cheated him once too often."

"Very interesting, Mom." Stewart sat down and tried to keep his eyes off the hypnotic wall box. The "Crime in Progress" channel ran round the clock, shifting locations from one city to another all over the world. The directors juggled from two to six different episodes at once, in various real-time stages of "progress." One minute you'd see a man beating his woman to a pulp; next minute you're watching an ecoterrorist setting a bomb at a factory that violated pollutant-emission codes. Most crimes looked as real as they were claimed to be, although some could perhaps have been staged.

The day after certain episodes you'd see follow-up newsclips to "prove" that a particular televised take had been authentic. Stewart was convinced that the crimes being shown *were* real, actually "crime in progress."

"Haven't seen a machete murder before," said Mrs. Bridges. "Blaser blasts and gas-gun jobs you see all the time, but with a machete it's got to be so disgustingly yukky that faking it must cost them a mint."

"Mom, I'm not here to watch 3V. Will you kindly turn that thing off?"

"Stewart, look! Now he's climbing up those rathole stairs to his dealer's apartment."

To Stewart the situation seemed believable. It would be easy enough for the addict to have planted a string of tiny eyes along his route, including the stairway presently being shown (view was from above looking down on scrawny addict mounting stairs)—and possibly even in the dealer's very apartment. If lenses hadn't been hidden in the jumjum joint itself, then a "head-on" climax would ensue, the event being displayed through a special, gyroscopically controlled, 3V eye glued to the eyebrow of the addict himself. It was quite conceivable that a ratty-looking seaslug like the one now oozing up the stairs had made a lucrative deal with the show's producers—to carry out his revenge in a particularly barbarous and dangerous manner (dangerous to the perpetrator, since the weapon appeared so unwieldy), in exchange for which he'd get a stack of whacks that would supply him with a whole year of jumjum. Against his will, Stewart found himself sucked into the tube. He had almost forgotten where he was and why he had come.

"Your father'll be so excited that you're here," said his mother without taking an eye off the screen.

"Yeah, I'll bet," said Stewart.

"To repeat: we've given this derelict the name Junkie Joe," came the hushed voice of the narrator. "To remind you once more: he's on his way up, with a *machete* in his belt, folks—a *machete*! (flash to an earlier scene of Junkie Joe slicing off a tree-limb with same)—to kill the jumjum man who he claims has done him wrong. You already know the city is London, folks. And now, as the climax nears—as we breathlessly stand by to see if Joe will succeed in his bloody revenge—we can tell you further that we're... in *Soho*! Now, if at this very moment Joe's intended victim happens to be watching "There's a Crime in Progress," he has a chance to *ward off* his assailant ... We tell you all this in an agreement with Junkie Joe. Our object is not to give the intended victim a 'sporting chance,' but solely, in perfect neutrality, to heighten suspense ... "

"Every two minutes they have to *summarize* everything. It's for the benefit of all the *tekkies* who watch the show. Your father loves it," his mother sighed.

"So why isn't he watching too?"

"And now," said the narrator, "Junkie Joe is about to reach the landing where, *in flat 3C*, yes, we'll say that much—"

"Let me get him to come downstairs," said his mother. "He hasn't seen you for weeks." Mrs. Bridges pressed an intercom next to a rod strung with hanging pots and pans. "Duane, dear, Stewart's here ... your son Stewart. Duane?"

"Stewart?" came the reply. "Of course Stewart is my son! What am I, an idiot? Is that why you interrupted me? Goddammit, I'm in the middle of the Prado. A walking tour of the Prado. I'm looking at Bosch's *Garden of Delights*."

"*We're* watching 'There's a Crime in Progress,' dear."

"Who cares? I never heard of such a show."

"It's your favorite 3V show, dearest."

"Of course it's my favorite show! I'm not stupid, you know. I just meant ... I never heard of such a show competing with something so spectacular as a 4D tour of the Vatican."

"You mean the Prado, dear. The Vatican we saw last week."

"That's what I said, dammit. The Prado! Are you deaf, Millie? Is there a carrot stuck in the intercom?"

"Duane, I said Stewart is here. Your son Stewart is *here*! He's here *now*, Duane. Now! So please come *right down*! ... Don't you worry, Stewart darling. He'll be right down." His mother's attention leaped back to the screen.

The scene was now from Junkie Joe's point of view. You saw pale knuckles rap at a door. "'Oo is it?" barked a voice from within. Junkie Joe's identifying reply was blipped (as per contractual agreement). The door slowly opened to reveal a compact man with bare brown chest and heavy-lidded, mean-looking eyes.

Stewart looked at his mother. "Mom, the weirdest things are continuing to happen to . . . " It was useless to talk to her. Even *he* couldn't help being distracted.

You saw first the widening eyes of the dealer. (Sound effect: piped-in heart-thump.) You next saw the dealer—surprised alone, apparently, in a sparsely furnished, yellow-walled room—stagger backward and twist around to reach for something on a table behind him. (Sound effect: staccato rill of dissonant chords.) Next: outflash of machete-blade, which is stopped by defending arm. (On-scene shriek from contorted dealer-face dispenses with need for effect supplied by sound crew.) Defending arm, deeply cut at elbow, dangles limply to floor in a pulsating spray of blood. (The lack of other than a head-on camera angle suggests to Stewart that Junkie Joe has not had the opportunity to plant any eyes inside his main man's apartment; this technical crudity in point of view also supports the *authenticity* of what is being viewed.) What follows now—it is sure to be slo-moed within seconds—is a red sweep of metal that *whump!* (piped-in?) disappears deep in the tensed flesh between the neck and left shoulder of the dealer, who ironically has spun aside precisely to avoid such a blow. Rhythmic jets of blood at last have found the recording eye. After a moment of obscurity, which heightens the sense of the *real*, the scene is now bathed in a curtain of rose.

"Enough!" Stewart grabbed the remote from his mother and silenced the set. "How can you *watch* this shit, Mom?"

"Well . . . it isn't as if it were *real*," she said, dripping cream into her coffee and pressing the sides of the self-stirring mug.

"But it *is* real," said Stewart. "How many times have I told you—"

"I very much doubt it," said Mrs. Bridges with finality.

Stewart saw that she was not about to let her son rob her of her favorite 3V show. She believed, yet at the same time refused to believe, that what she was seeing was real. He deposited the remote out of reach on the food-prep island in the center of the kitchen. Colored notes stuck to every device on the island. Memory aids for his father. Some dating as far back as Stewart could remember.

"Stewart, I've been *worried* about you, dear," said his mother, as if snapping out of a trance.

She set off a symphony of clanging pots as she again pressed the intercom. He could never figure out why she kept those pots around—most of them, perhaps, were antiques—since the neurochef did most of the cooking. "Duane, dear? Come downstairs *now*, darling. Stewart is here. I'm setting this message to repeat every thirty seconds." Smiling grimly, she stabbed a few buttons. She then came back to the kidney-shaped kitchen table, pulling up a seat across from her son. Embarrassment spread a pink flush over her dusky Neapolitan features. Her skin was so firm and unwrinkled, and her figure still so slim, that her Medusa-mop of silvery curls looked artificially aged. In her seventies, she could still pass for forty. Modesty, however, led her to smother her attractiveness under baggy, boxy clothing, like the beltless blue housefrock she was wearing.

"Have you been careful, dear?" she asked with sudden seriousness.

"I've made it this far," he said, shrugging his shoulders.

At that moment his father's steps came thumping down the stairs. Stewart twisted around and watched him shuffle toward them from the living-room area in his scuffed moccasins and purple leisure robe with the ratty ermintwin collar. Rounding the food-prep island, his father came to a halt at the unoccupied end of the table to Stewart's right. His black VRC was still in place, but he had lifted the visor—thus interrupting his tour through the Prado. A grudging concession, thought Stewart, to the demands of Actual Reality. Virtual Reality Caps were a major item in the Memini hardware lineup, and Stewart knew that he'd better be positive about them in the interview that was presumably still to come, but the fact was that he personally shunned the use of a VRC except to edit the visual imagery he used in bioprogramming.

"Aren't you delighted, dear?" said Mrs. Bridges. "Stewart's here. Your son."

"Of course he's my son. Hello, Prodigal Son. Haven't seen you for months."

"I was here a couple of weeks ago, Dad."

"I know, I know. Just kidding," he laughed, extending a hand that Stewart shook in a gingerly manner. The hand was still clothed in the slippery optron glove needed for moving your virtual body around through c-space and handling virtual objects. His father plopped down in a seat to Stewart's right and pulled his scratched-up flapper out of an inside robe pocket. Laying it open on the table, he stabbed at a couple of buttons. Stewart's picture appeared on the screen. "You've changed, fella. Beard's a lot thicker. Trying to look dignified or something? Why do you hide behind all that hair?"

"I've had this same bush two years now, Dad." It annoyed him to be criticized about his hair style. He had grown the beard during the time he had done Lester Barton—consciously mimicking the Memini chief's bushy look. He'd gotten to like it—to "hide behind" it—so much since then that he didn't want to get rid of it, not even for that grand interview he was always never having. (Anyway, if they didn't like his looks, they'd never have called on him for an interview in the first place.)

"I think his beard looks adorable," objected his mother. "And Duane, for heaven's sake, will you remove your hat and glove? You're no longer at the museum."

"Museum?"

"The Prado?"

"Oh yes, the Prado. *Reminder: back to the Prado. End reminder,*" he barked into his flapper. "You'd love the Prado, Stewart. Wanna borrow this cassette?"

"I've been there in person," said Stewart.

"In person? Forget 'person,'" said his father. "Your feet hurt, you're thirsty, you gotta go take a leak, you wanna see a famous picture and there's twenty big Chinese exchange students blocking your view for a half hour while they *study* the goddamn thing! Gimme Virtual any time. People move away when you approach. You can *touch* the damn statues. They ever letcha do that 'in person'? Ever slide your hand around Venus de Milo's ass? No! 'Cause they're afraid of acid—"

"Duane!"

"The Venus de Milo's at the Louvre," said Stewart.

"A great place, the Louvre. Here, have a quick visit." His father removed the helmet and offered it to him.

"You're at the Prado, Dad."

"You're right. I got the Louvre upstairs. Just a sec, I'll bring it down."

114

MEMINI

"No, Dad. I'm not interested right now."

"So why'd you ask to see the Venus . . . forget it!" His father threw his hand out in disgust.

"I'll see it later, Dad." Stewart looked at his father and sighed. His father spent his whole life in Virtual Reality. Professionally little more than a glorified stock clerk, he was a slave to providing local A4DZ holoshoppers—within a one-hour maximum!—with their VRC-chosen purchases. The old company-jingle ran through Stewart's head: "Shop from A to Z with A4DZ/Where you can 'a-ffor *dea*-sy'/All the things you see/In real-live, touch-and-flip 4D."

Avocationally, his father was a "handglider," traveling the world over with his condom-like glove without ever moving his spreading butt out of his comfortable upstairs cave. He once was hell on a maglev with women. He was now cheap feels through a VRC. (Once, during his college years, while he was still living at home, Stewart had innocently entered his father's den and come upon a stack of VR porncassettes—complete with French Fingertrap, or Virtual Vagina.)

"So whatcha been doing to keep out of trouble, Stewie?"

"Bioprogramming, Dad."

"Yes, yes, I *remember*. Your Mom keeps you updated in here, you know," he said, pointing to his tabled memory. "Bioprogramming, right . . . Don't seem to me like a steady enough income for a boy just out of college . . . No, sorry. You've been out for sixteen years." He stared at his flapper in surprise.

"I'm one of the best freelancers in the business, Dad," Stewart answered patiently. "Not long ago I did the bio for the chief exec of Memini."

"Memini? Wow! They own a big chunk of A4DZ."

"I know. They've got their fingers in everything."

"Did you give the big boss lots of girls, romance and adventure in exotic places?"

""Of course I did, Dad."

"*I* won't need one of those biocassettes for a long time yet," said his father. "I still remember enough to keep me warm."

"Damn it, Duane! Disrespectful to me in front of your own son?"

"Sorry, dearest. What I remember is mainly from *before* we put on the handcuffs. I've never even kept a *flapper* record of anything since. *Has* there been anything since?"

"If *you* don't know, how would I?" she snapped.

"Forget it, Mom. I didn't come over to rake up all the old shit between you." His whole youth was colored by scenes of the two of them quarreling over his father's philandering. When confronted by his wife, he would deny even the most blatant evidence. He would *in fact* have forgotten everything, an oblivion that was his wife's sole consolation.

"Did you drop in tonight ... in order to talk about something in particular?" asked his mother, sensing his moodiness. "Or could I order you up a late dinner, perhaps some pasta with clam sauce?"

"No and yes!" said Stewart. "No to pasta, yes to talk. Listen, I've showed up three times for that interview."

"What interview?" asked his father.

"I sit on my ass for hours and each time they goddamn *cancel*. But I keep my cool, I keep my—"

"I knew it!" shrilled his mother. "I warned you against applying in the first place. They're subjecting you to a stress test ... to see if you're truly one of *them*. You're a *dreamer*, Stewart. You *know* how easily you forget things, small, seemingly trivial things."

"He'll pass every test they can throw at him!" shouted his father. "He's done okay in college so far—*in spite* of you, damn it. You've sabotaged the kid since high school by keeping him off emmies. He could have had it real easy and hoped to been a bigshot someday, but now he's got to put on a mask and sneak around tekkies like a common thief. A *cryptostag* is what you've turned him into!"

"Don't pin cheap labels on your son!" she lanced back. No issue exercised her like this one. She had successfully resisted every social pressure, whether from husband, family, or well-meaning teachers, to boost the brainpower of her only child by *chemical* means. Her god was Mother Nature, Great Gaia herself, whose Minister of Justice was Nemesis, and the artificial enhancement of memory and intelligence was for his mother totally contrary to Nature. For Stewart such reasoning was absurd, since the whole of civilization was an intricate web of artifice. But his mother would not be budged from her resolve by argument. She had a religious obsession against tampering with the Seat of the Soul (as she called it).

"What do *you* think, Stewart? Do you like what your mother has done to you? You know, it isn't too late. What do you have, one semester to go? . . ."

"The human mind is the holy of holies," said his mother, using words that were a refrain of his childhood. "Do you remember, Stewart, how I'd sit and study with you, hours and hours, because I knew you had the brains to do *naturally* what all your misguided friends could only do on the Pill?"

"He could've been spending all that time making friends, future contacts."

"Listen, you two—"

"The way *you* did?" his mother shot back. "Much good it did you!"

"I've got *all kinds* of friends. When there's a party they never forget old Duane Bridges."

"Party! We haven't been invited to a party for at least ten years . . . and I thank the Great Mother for that!"

"If I needed a favor, I could call on one of my buddies. The only reason I'm slow in climbing up the ladder is 'cause I'm *proud*! I'd rather get ahead using my brains than my connections."

"Duane, in two years you *retire*."

"Oh yeah? Well it can't be soon enough!"

"And all your brains are in that . . . that box!"

"Box, hah? Isn't that what they said to the guy who scratched the first inventory down on a clay tablet? They said, 'Gee, what a lousy memory you got if you can't keep it all in your noodle!' And then they laughed at the printed book. And then they laughed at the computer. 'The whole country'll never need more'n three o' those,' they said."

"Duane, if you lost that flapper of yours I'd be leading you around on a leash."

"C'mon, you two, forget all that crap! I've got enough *new* problems. Who needs to dig up old ones?" Stewart already regretted having come.

"This 'box,' as you call it, is not the sole repository of my 'brains,' as you call them," his father persisted, his tone now scornfully didactic. "If I *lost* that box, the entire contents could be copied over from the company neuronet. And if the whole A4DZ memory box broke the hell down at the same damn time, there's still that great Big Box in the sky that remembers for the *whole world*, the great big backup that knows what's in every flapper on earth, and knows exactly where you are and how to get you home."

"Calm down, Dad. Mom didn't mean—"

"It's called the Global Orientation and Data Service satellite system—or the infallible GODS, for short. And what comparable backup do *you* have," he wound up triumphantly, "depending for storage entirely as you do on that decay-prone mush inside your head?"

And so it had gone between them for as long as Stewart could remember, his mother swearing by the Great Mother, his father by the GODS above. Their bickering sometimes took a religious turn, his mother refusing to believe in personal immortality, his father believing to the contrary that in the satellite system of the GODS, in permanent geosynchronous aloofness from the vicissitudes of the earth, incorruptibly resided the essence of his personhood in the form of a database unique to Duane Bridges. And someday in the future, after he was gone, when A4DZ ran short of *responsible* management (so unreliable was the upcoming crew of pushy, self-centered blowhards), the company might well wish to resurrect the dormant Duane Bridges by plugging his GODS-preserved essence into the empty head of some newcomer.

"Listen," Stewart began again, "it isn't the interview that bothers me. I haven't even *been* interviewed. No, it's a lot stranger than that. Just as I was getting sent home from Memini for the fourth time, the head man's exec-sec comes up to me and slips me an invitation to a Friday-night *party*. At the big boss's estate! This Friday! And the guy hasn't even been properly *introduced* to me yet!"

"You're in like Flynn, Stewie boy!" His father slapped him on the shoulder. "When your boss-to-be invites you to a party, it's a sign that you're on the way up." He gave Stewart the thumbs-up sign.

"I strongly advise against your going ahead with it," said his mother. "Think of how much you have to lose... Don't do it, Stewart, dear."

"You know my three cardinal rules for success, Stewie: 'Look dapper, fiddle with your flapper, and remember to flush the crapper,'" his father recited triumphantly. For him the world's workings were governed by a simple set of algorithms, and if you knew the right ones, you would soon be running the show.

"Stewart, it's as certain as I sit here that they intend to subject you to the most thorough scrutiny, to microscopic examination. The slightest slip—"

"Nonsense, Mildred! If they had any suspicion that he was *your* son, they'd never have let him get this far. Do you know how thorough a background check they must have made before inviting him?"

"Listen to *me*, Stewart. Some chippie you meet there is going to trick you into letting down your guard. You're going to say something, reveal something, and every word and look of yours is going to be recorded and analyzed by the company's neuronet . . ."

"My God, the women, Stewie! Tekkie babes by the dozen! You don't go out enough. You need to have some fun. Invite me along. This old rooster'll show you the ropes."

"Duane! You filthy, unprincipled—"

It was true. The image of all those women—stylish, sophisticated, available; the vision of one dark-haired beauty in particular—tended to outshine in his mind's eye every other consideration. Would he be likely to forget elementary caution in a dalliance with Sibyl Yamamoto? Was it possible that Sibyl, and not Lester Barton, had engineered his invitation to the party? In which case, wasn't she interested in him simply as a sexual tidbit, something with which to vary a possibly boring diet of the same old VIPs? But then again, how could a tekkie be bored—assuming, of course, that a tekkie was indeed what she was? . . . No, he must not allow wishful thinking to undermine common sense!

At the same time he had been stung by what his father had just said—about his not going out enough. He went to the triple S's, the singles sex salons, as need arose, but their purpose was to provide immediate relief, not to serve as scouting grounds for long-term relationships. The fact was that most people frequented the triple S's as a relief *from* long-term relationships. His mother's side of the family kept trying to hook him up with some decent enough woman who had, presumably, never touched the Pill (a brain virgin); neither was she likely ever to have read a book. And she was more than likely a social worker for some oldfolks counseling group—

always toting a "flapper" that was really only a glorified appointment tablet, and on dates with him imitating some classy tekkie mannerism, like asking the same question three times inside of five minutes. Or else they'd find him some woman who ran a small boutique—as his mother had done for some twenty-five years—and who was interested in a Man of Culture to whom she could teach the essentials of good grooming.

"They are setting you up, Stewart!" warned his mother. "It's no accident that *you* should have been invited to apply for a position with Memini. You created the Personal Past of the head of the organization. What if they distrust you? What if they think you know something you could use against them? . . . "

What intimate things did he know? he wondered. There was that showdown between LB and the man who was now President of the United States. A Memini VP putting the then Secretary of Commerce in his place—and prevailing, to boot! It had been a turning point in Barton's career, and Stewart had squeezed all the juice of drama he could out of the skimpy details provided. But that touchy encounter was part of the *public record*. Not part of the public record, however, was something else he'd stumbled upon in the course of doing the bio: that mysterious *variant to LB's name*. He'd encountered it twice, typed onto obscure company documents: "Lester Barton III." Typed as such, but never a part of LB's actual signature. He'd always wondered what *that* was supposed to mean.

"Look, Mom, I'm officially not *supposed* to know anything after I complete a bioprogramming assignment. By contract I return all source docs and swear not to have kept any records or copies of the material I've composed."

"But they assume you'd have to have *meminized* everything. And what if they think you *did* keep copies of your sources, and even of the finished bioprogram?" She glanced at him sharply. "Did you?"

"Of course I did," Stewart admitted. "I keep a copy of every job I do. We B.P.ers don't shred our own portfolios. Your clients even come back to you for updates, counting on your 'familiarity' with them to help you get the work done faster."

"Stewart!"

"Some things in this world work on trust, Mom."

"Trust is the foundation of every good marriage," his father interjected. "Look at your mom and me, for example..."

That's what he would do, then! Stewart decided. He would trust to his intimate knowledge of the tekkie mind. He would take his pleasure of them as they took their pleasure of each other. He would come with the attitude of a hummingbird and leave with no more than he could carry—a bellyful of sweet juices. After all, it was only a damn *party*!

Soon he said goodbye to his father, whose flapper had been urging his return to the Prado, and at the door he thanked his mother for her advice.

"Did we help you at all, Stewart?" she asked, almost in tears.

"Of course you did, Mom." The door opened and Stewart stepped outside.

His mother sighed. "I think you've inherited either the best or the worst of both of us. I'm not sure which... You're willful, like your father, and vulnerable, like me."

Stewart smiled, avoiding her questioning eyes.

"If you do go to that party, Stewart... promise me you'll be on your guard."

"I promise, Mom."

"Every second!"

"Of course."

"Whoever you talk to, no matter how many times you run into her—them—during the evening, act as if you're meeting h—them for the first time."

"Look, Mom, please don't—"

"It's unheard of for an upper executive—or for someone who wants to become one—to be able to recognize people at sight. Remember what your father used to say: 'There isn't a face I've met that I remember.'"

"I'll remember that, Mom."

"I'm worried about you, Stewart. There are things you should remember to remember, and others you should remember to forget. You've never lived much in the world of practical affairs..."

"Don't badger me, Mom!"

She bit her lip. "I apologize for your father. This evening he was unusually inattentive."

"Nothing unusual about it at all. Don't keep making excuses for him."

"He means well."

"I'm not sure he's capable of *meaning anything*." Stewart balanced on his toes. On a sudden whim he decided to ask his mother something personal, something he'd never so openly asked before. "Mom, knowing what Dad's been like... why did you stay with such a... a *butterfly* all your life? You could have supported yourself easily by—"

"I know you think I've been crazy to stay with him," she interrupted, looking up at him thoughtfully. "He's been a great bastard all these years, true. But he's also been—also been a great... lover!" She gulped as she said this and turned red. Stewart blushed in turn. There was a tingling in his ears. "You're old enough for me to say this," she continued in a prim, thin-lipped way, her face still aflame. "All the other married people I know... they've gotten tired of each other. But when you live with a man without a memory—"

"Look, you don't have to spell it out!"

"Good night, Stewart dear. Come see us again soon. For dinner."

"Good night, Mom."

12. THE FLATBUSH JUNCTION BAZAAR

When Andy stepped out into the hallway, he nearly collided with his neighbor, Mrs. Woo. She was also headed for the elevator. A gold kimono cloaked her chunky body. Gold and silver chains and bracelets coiled through her ringleted hair and looped round her neck and wrists. She was on her way to the Junction Plaza bazaar to peddle her charms, elixirs, and potions.

"You lookin' drug-out tired, doll. Workin' hard?" she asked.

"I s'pose."

"That's your trouble, sweetlips. Ambitious as a frag. How 'bout a pick-up powder? Yolanda's special mix."

"No thanks, Yo. Only the name brands for me."

She tossed him a big smile. "I envy you, Andy babe. Hear you're the one copped that giant-size apartment down on level two where Hermes the pimp got permafrosted last week—by his own sweet pistol-packin' jill. So when you switchin' floor, pretty boy?"

"Don't know," he sighed. He had a weight on his chest as heavy as a truck, and he didn't feel like talking to anyone, not just now, and not to anyone so damn happy-faced all the time like Yolanda Woo. "Couple weeks, maybe. Maybe never."

"Andy babe, what bit you? You lower'n a sewer-rat this morning." They stopped in front of the elevator doors and Andy pressed "down," which was exactly what he felt.

"E.T.A. fifteen seconds to level seventeen," a panel briskly responded.

"I'm okay, Yolanda," said Andy, his chin to the floor. "Cool as a dead man's shoe."

"'Partment like that I'd be joy-jumpin' around. But you ain't happy, doll. That mug o' yours blacker'n the moon's ass."

"It's nothing. Had a bad night is all." He felt ragged from lack of sleep. He had been tortured by nightmares in which his attempts to kill Helen Means were always foiled, but worse was the other sort of nightmare in which she would wriggle out of his arms, preventing his kiss from landing on her moist, parted lips.

"Woman throwin' you shade, babe?" she asked as they stepped into the glass-walled elevator. He didn't answer. She smiled at him knowingly. Nothing seemed to escape her intuition—like predicting that Hermes the pimp was due to get offed. Andy stared through the elevator wall, originally transparent, but long streaked with windblown dabs of pigeon shit and grime. The countless pollutants that illegally choked the air were emitted by unlicensed businesses unhampered by the police, whose protection was handsomely paid for either by the local merchants themselves or by the legitimate corporations who operated them from the safety of midtown Manhattan.

Normally Andy was pleased by the view he had of his world from up above, but this noon everything seemed changed. The streets down below bristled with the usual color and movement. The thrill-seekers, as always, streamed up Nostrand Avenue toward Flatbush Avenue, and the great bazaar that filled Junction Plaza sucked them up into its crooked passages like a sponge. A thousand exotic worlds lay sprawled out just below. The brightly painted awnings of tents, pavilions, and vans harbored everything that civilization swept under the rug. All those delightful, dizzying odors and unpronounceable sounds of the street were only moments away, but he was going out to meet them with lead in his heart and a great boulder pressing down on his lungs.

"Need a bit of sweet revenge, or maybe a love-drop, honey?" she persisted.

Andy sullenly shook his head as the elevator descended on its cushion of air.

"'Yolanda Woo/ Will help you screw/ Scabby Sam or Stuck-up Sue,'" his neighbor chanted as they reached street level. It was very early for him to be heading toward Manhattan, since he still had two and a half hours before his two o'clock debriefing with commander Sibyl Yamamoto on yesterday's disaster. But today, instead of lunching at one of the innumerable dives at the fringes of the Junction bazaar, or eating slightly fancier across Junction Plaza at College City Market, which occupied the long-abandoned buildings of Brooklyn University, Andy decided he would splurge on a lunch in Fraghattan. By dining in the city in his new white suit, he hoped to fortify his ego against the ball-snipping innuendos that Yamamoto would be sure to launch at him on his arrival. Let the bitch say what she pleased, so long as he got paid for services rendered.

He had hoped to put on a show that would raise her abdominal temperature a few million degrees; instead, she'd probably pissed in her pants with laughter. The thought of what she must think of him puckered his scrotum. But the thought of what *Helen* had thought of him . . . that was what sat on him like a block of concrete. And what if the little Jap refused to pay him? "Andy, all that talk's fine and dandy, but she didn't eat your candy." Bullshit! His job had been to get her *into* bed; payment should have nothing to do with what happened once she was there. What *had* happened? he asked himself. He had been asking himself that question every minute since she had left him; it had robbed him of his sleep. He thought he knew himself inside and out: that whenever his head went soft over some jill he could depend on another part of his anatomy to compensate. But to turn into a total jellyfish, feeling things no woman had ever made him feel, saying things he'd only heard from jackasses on 3V . . .

It wasn't as if he could claim they'd spiked his drink; she hadn't given him a chance even to pour one. Maybe that was it! She hadn't given him time to get properly in the mood. He would tell that cryptostag or fragass little Miss Yammy that that blond bitch knew all along he was setting her up; that she'd played along for as long as she could to make them think she was a tekkie; but that she'd had it in mind from the very beginning to bust his balls at the showdown. She'd never believed for one instant that he was her lover, and she knew as soon as he'd brought back her "stolen" bag that the company was putting her through a major identity check. (He knew, nevertheless, that her feeling him up in the cab *was* real; that her jumping him in the apartment was an act of *passion*, not deliberation; and that if he *had* been able to let himself go, and to believe that she was real and not some crazy hopped-up angel, and to keep a rush of boiling-hot feelings from sauteeing all his brains, he would have had the most blissful goddamn fuck of his whole miserable life, not a moment of which had ever promised such ecstasy.)

But sex had never *been* for him something a woman threw at you for nothing. It had always been a commercial transaction; you paid and decided just what and when and how. You directed the show; there was lots of comfort in that. If you walked into a restaurant, you wouldn't want the damn waiter to shove food under your nose before you had a chance to look at the menu! She had robbed him of control; she had fucked up his head so badly that the rest of him just walked off the job! . . .

But that was ridiculous! He knew damn well he was just making excuses. She'd wanted him; worked him over with every method known to woman. He could still smell the delicious odor of her skin and hair, like none he'd ever smelled. Never in his life had he failed in close combat. What the hell was wrong with him? he wondered. He was going out to have lunch in the city, but in fact he had no appetite whatsoever . . .

Mrs. Woo easily kept up with him as he picked his way along the wide, filth-strewn sidewalk toward the Junction. They tried to avoid things that might stick to their shoes, and they also trod carefully around the deadbeats lying in their path. Some of them liked to roll right out into people's legs.

"Fess up!" Yolanda challenged. "You too young for menopause. You got some awful bad woman-shit muckin' up your pretty head. I got stuff to make that lassie toss and moan with desire for you. Also stuff just to make her *moan*. Which you want?"

Andy kept silent as they crossed Nostrand and picked their way toward the spicy-smelling food tents piled helter-skelter along the fringes of the Plaza. Junction Plaza itself looked like the great market square in Marrakech that he'd toured through a VRC. Finally he spoke. "I don't *know* yet which I want," he said, admitting his desperation.

"Don't matter. First I'll make you the doll, and then you tell me what you want to happen."

"Doll?"

"I need something that belongs to her. Something closely connected to her person. Hair, a fingernail, a piece of clothing."

Suddenly Andy whipped out the flapper cassette from the inside breast-pocket of his jacket. "Will this do?"

She took the tiny black oblong and rolled it around her palm. Shaking her head, she looked darkly up at him. "Frag-hag, huh? You up shit's creek, Andy babe."

"Be careful. I need it back *as is*," he said.

"Not to worry," she said.

Smells of garlic and cloves, of coriander and cumin and fennel, promised gastronomic bliss. Andy resisted the urge to grab a bite at one of the stands. He was going to wait and slake his hunger in Manhattan. He thought of Helen swooping into sex like a butterfly, without a single thought but of her *pleasure* as she jumped him, rode him, swayed above him totally *in charge*, while he, a shrinking romantic from the other side of the bridge... The weight on his chest was so crushing just then that he would've paid a bundle for a magic pill that would erase forever his memory of just that one incident, just the whole of that unbearable afternoon. And she, that golden-haired twat with those splendiferous, perfect boobs—once that shriveled worm of his was out of her tekkie sight, why, she could go back to feeling as happy as a lark! She could convince herself she'd had a perfect fuck! He *envied* the fragass bitch!...

He and Yolanda strolled together to a fork in the walkway at the end of the row of food stalls. "Poor lil Andy! Some jill got her nutcracker clamped round your head. But don't you fret 'cause Yolanda gawn *chuck* her ass." Yolanda gave him a parting slap on the butt, then bore left down a wide, curving lane toward her long-established little witchcraft concession. Andy cut a zigzag course through the bazaar, the shortest route to the transportation hub at Flatbush Junction on the opposite side of the Plaza. The frag tourists sauntered from awning to awning in small, manageable groups shepherded by watchful pairs of guides who were always taking head-counts and knew how to hustle strays back toward the body of the flock. Fortunately for Andy's business, at any time of day or night there was always that reckless frag, the lone thrill-seeker who thought he could blend in with the crowd that he'd studied on a VRC but in fact showed every sign of insecurity and glassy-eyed dependency on a flapper poorly hidden under his clothing.

Right now, though, Andy had no interest in either the business potential or the sensuous delights of his surroundings. He did not wander out to the Great Circle where the fakirs, the contortionists, the jugglers, tumblers and magicians were doing their tricks. With grim indifference, he hurried on past the glow-in-the-dark tattoo shops, the shrunken-head South American native-crafts purveyors, the exotic-sex peep-and-feelies, the "natural"-drug dealers who were supplied by outlaw chem labs, and the bargain outlets for stolen shipments of the latest photonic gadgets, hardly bothering to return a nod or a hello to the concessionaires, all of whom knew him and sometimes gave him business tips which, if productive, would earn them a commission. Emerging from the main body of the bazaar, he pushed ahead toward the buses along a block dominated by a food-and-sundries megamart and the Bank of Inner Mongolia. He stumbled along, feeling drained of his usual bounce. Near the corner there was a little hole-in-the-wall WC, one of a vast network of wellness centers that were stationed every few blocks around the city. A medscan! Why not? he thought. Squeamishly, he looked all around him to see if anyone who knew him was in sight.

Despite the hex signs, phalli, and multilingual warnings and imprecations scribbled all over the unbreakable front of the station, Andy put eye and hand to the ID peep-plate. The door slid open to admit him. This WC, like countless thousands of others around the world, was a terminal linked to a global medscan system that provided instantaneous diagnosis via the G.O.D.S. satellite net that hovered forever overhead like the stars. He hadn't been inside one of these for years, not since severe headaches had forced him to take a scan that revealed a dietary imbalance caused by his eating too exclusively at one of the virtually addictive spice-'n-lice bazaar-fringe stalls.

Except for him, the musty little place was deserted. Not a soul waiting on the long bench facing the booths, and all six sound-proof booths flashed green "vacant" signs. The price list was posted on the wall above the bench: "DIAGNOSIS—ICU 15 each ten minutes net-time or fraction thereof. TREATMENT—ICU 25 each ten minutes net-time or fraction thereof. Upon entering WC you commit yourself to the minimum charge for diagnosis." The sign was repeated along the wall in Arabic, Russian, and Hispasian. Andy's bank account was pretty strong when it came to International

MEMINI

Currency Units, and the payment he should be getting from Memini today should credit him half in ICUs and half in UACs, "whacks," or Units of American Currency. He always tried to stay heavy on ICUs, since that had been the more stable currency for as long as he could remember. Around the Plaza you got things for less if you paid in the legally less easily traceable "I See You." He randomly chose a booth and sat down facing an eye-level 3V terminal activated by his weight in the molded seat.

A white-frocked, fatherly physician peered out at him and asked, "What seems to be the trouble, Andy?"

Although he knew he was only talking to a machine, Andy hesitated a bit before replying. "A sexual problem, doctor. I couldn't get it up when I needed to."

"Ah-ha! Well, let's first check your general vital signs. Please stay seated, with your hands clasped over your lap and your knees close together. The scanner ring will descend over your head, move down around your trunk, under your seat, down to the floor and then make a round-trip back the way it came."

Robot arms from tracks along the walls joined the halves of a white ring above his head, then silently drew it down around him and more quickly back up again.

"You're looking generally pretty good, Andy. But now let's scan the genito-urinary area in molecular detail." Again the hoop came down, slowing considerably as it circled below his hips. "Nothing wrong with you *physically* that could affect your sexual functions, as far as I can see," said the doctor. "I suggest that you run through a psychscan. Would you like me to transfer you?"

As the ring-halves retracted to the wall, Andy began to fidget. The last time, when he thought he had a psychological problem, his headaches turned out traceable to a physical cause. Now that he was sure his problem was physical, the damn machine was telling him it was all in his head. "What the hell," he muttered at the talking head, "put me through to the shrink."

The psychiatrist was a compassionate-looking man with a faceful of salt-and-pepper whiskers and a simple cotton sportshirt unbuttoned at the neck. Mr. Trust-Me, thought Andy. The same guy who'd found nothing mentally wrong with him during the episode of the headaches.

"Hi, Andy. Long time no see," said Mr. Casual. "So the doc tells me you can't get it up. Don't worry. It happens to the best of us . . . at *times*. Is this problem chronic with you, or does it occur only under a specific set of circumstances?"

"She was the most goddamn beautiful woman I ever went to bed with in my life," blurted Andy. "She wanted me so bad I . . . I couldn't believe it."

Trust-Me shook his head sympathetically. "That's where the problem lies, my friend."

"What kind of bullshit is that?" snapped Andy.

"Don't you remember what we discussed about your psychological profile last time—which, of course, turned out to be irrelevant to the problem?"

"No. How should I remember? And why the hell should you remember?"

"How can I forget? Do you think my head is stuffed with three pounds of sweetbreads, like yours?"

"Okay, so what is it? Cut the shit and give it to me straight."

"It's your deep-down sense of worthlessness, Andy, for which you compensate by *acting* tough. Some things are easy to fake, fella, but a bone won't grow on command. Now, if you recall—since a tekkie you are not—I suggested therapy last time, even though it was irrelevant to your immediate problem. But you chose to ignore me. Back now to the matter at hand. Evidently you regarded yourself as a worm in the presence of a goddess, so all your sexuality shrank back into the dirt that you believe to be your natural egoniche."

"This is a bunch of crap!" Andy protested. "I'm as good a man as any. There isn't a woman I ever straddled that I couldn't make it with. She may be a tekkie, but that don't mean she's out of my class, Jack."

Mr. Trust-Me shrugged his digital shoulders. "I'm afraid it does. In *your* head, at least—and that's what counts. You see, Andy, as we discussed exactly six years and seventy-four days ago, your problem stems from the mysterious disappearance of your much-loved mother when you were at the tender, pubescent age of twelve. As children at that age do, you unconsciously blamed the loss of that beautiful goddess of a mother on yourself, on your unworthiness, your inadequacy."

"To hell with the mumbo-jumbo," said Andy. "Just give me your lousy opinion of what's wrong with me in plain English—ten words or less—and then shut up."

The psychiatrist shook his head gravely, gazed at him with infinite compassion, and said, "Andy, you're not sick . . . you're just in love."

"Fuck you!" Andy stood up and the screen went blank. There was no way he could even get his money back! . . . He began to tremble. What else does that son of a bitch know about me? he wondered. What do they *have* on me in that hunk of metal up there in the sky? What if they decide to put two and two together and figure out how I make my living? Confidentiality, my ass! . . . The prospect had a laxative effect on his innards. "Gotta calm down," he said to himself, exiting the booth. But hadn't he just given them *reason* to put two and two together? He'd just gone and insulted the goddamn shrink! But that was insane. Mr. Know-it-all was nothing but a vidgame plugged into a neuronet plugged into a tin can that floated around out in space.

Still, he thought, as he stepped through the door into the street, he should have controlled himself, stayed cool, kept on top of the situation, responded in a civilized, intelligent manner consistent with his above-average level of education. You can pay a doctor for advice, but you don't have to swallow his fucking medicine. Andy now felt stabbing pains in his stomach in addition to the choking load of depression that had pushed him into the wellness center in the first place.

The gold frame of his videowatch shot a hot flash of sunlight into his eyes. Twelve-twenty. He'd better be moving.

"Hey, brud! Where you skimmyin' off to?"

"Wanjo!" The kid had spotted him leaving the WC. "Got no time for bullshit, Wanjo. Catching me a bus." He headed left toward the busy corner. Wanjo tagged along at his side.

"What you be do in a Wolf Cage, brud? Them frag-ass speeritos inside there be bad-ass mana, man. Be suckin' all them juices out your brain."

"There's no mana in there and no spirits!" shouted Andy, his neck pulsing hot with shame.

"Don't you be lyin' *me*, brud! Them machine in there make copy of you, and them frag-ass demon belong it up in the sky do *hoodoo* on you and bust your trade!"

"You got a chip loose, Wanjo. You're an ignorant, dumb-shit piece of streetmeat. There ain't no spirits in any WC, and there's no demon up in the sky. It's just a cold chunk of metal, like this," and he kicked out at a fireplug near the curb to his right. "I'll prove it to you." He cupped his hands around his mouth and yelled "Fuck you!" up at the sky. "There!" he said exultantly.

As Wanjo blinked in anticipation of a flash of lightning from above, Andy quivered with fear, thinking his heart had stopped. It had just skipped a couple of beats. "I keep telling you to go back to school," he yelled angrily, despising himself for his moment of fright. "Get with the twenty-first century, kid. In two more years it'll be over."

"Sure, Andy, sure. Now why you go in them Wolf Cage, brud?"

"Headache, Wanjo, headache."

Wanjo smiled at him and grabbed his arm so that they both stopped just short of the corner. "Frag-momma rock your block so hard she leave you with big bad headache?"

"No connection. Don't bust my chops."

"C'mon, brud. You owes sayin' me all 'bout what she like on them mattress. Was them pink titties stand up real stiff and cool?" Wanjo made sucking sounds with his lips. "Were she good and tight in them socket?"

"Stuff it, round-eye!" Andy felt hot with embarrassment. "What do you think, she's one of your sidewalk sweeties that'll spread for a whiff of jumjum?"

"Be frag-hag, be gutter strutter, them all gots same plumbing."

Andy looked left for a magbus headed for Manhattan.

"Hey, what happen you, brud? . . . You know, I betcha them frag-ass momma put ring in your dick and she be pullin' on you even right now."

"Shut up!" said Andy. "Fuck off and leave me alone."

"Can't *able* leave you 'lone right now, brud. I be lookin' for you on business."

"On business?" sneered Andy. "You got it ass-backwards, don't you? *I'm* the one who brings *you* in on *my* business, shithole. Not the other way around. Get it?"

"But this be special, Andy."

"Spit it out quick. I got a bus to catch."

"Well, they never have nothin' 'bout them organ trade on 3V, right?"

"Wrong."

"I talkin' *live action*, brud. Like on 'There a Crime in Progress.'"

"So what!" Andy stiffened. He looked at Wanjo through narrowed eyes. Wanjo looked down at the tips of his silvery shoes.

"You know how much them 3V fella wanna pay for shoot them real-live fragbaggin', Andy man?"

"No . . . and why should I *give* a shit?" He turned away and plunged on toward the bus stop. A hand gripped his shoulder. He looked around at Wanjo in surprise. The kid's ballsy hand had snapped back before he could take a swat at it.

"Listen me up, brud. Just listen me up one segundo. You wantin' I go back in school?" Wanjo's lips were twitching. "Them 3V fella woll payin' you twenny-fi' thousand I See You, and me they givin' four thou for hookin' you up with them. All them whacks gawn put me back in school for six mont', brud."

"Wanjo, what'd I *tell* you about that 3V shit? Don't you remember a thing from one fucking day to the next?"

"But you ain't gawn gottin' yourself in no trouble, Andy. Them camera crew be flyin' somewhere high uppa them sky, and them only be tellin' folk where them action be only *after* you brung them fragmother up to them chophouse door and not before, you listenin' me? Nobody ever can able to catch your ass for nothin', Andy. I swear you on my mother's cunt."

"Your mother's cunt? You don't even know who your fucking mother *is*, fuckbrain! Now get the hell out of my face."

Wanjo threw his arms out imploringly, not quite daring to catch Andy's shoulder again. "Come on, Andy. I always be do for you what you askin' me, right? Now Wanjo need a favor, so why you can't able to help Wanjo, hah?"

"Because I'm doing sensitive work these days. It's highly secret, understand? The only reason I cut you in is because I trust you, get it? I'll give you a little hint, Wanjo. I'm doing jobs for the government. The government, get it? Top-secret shit, see?"

"Top-secret shit for them gubmint?" Wanjo's eyes widened.

"That's right, so fuck off."

"I bet them 3V frag woll puttin up *more* 'n twenny-fi' thou for hot-shit stuff like that, brud. Lis' me up—"

"You still in my face?" Andy looked at his watch. "You're gonna make me miss my bus." Turning away from Wanjo, he quickened his pace. If they were so interested in him, he thought, why didn't they come directly to *him*? Why use a piece of streetscum, a *drekkie*, as intermediary? Since when had Wanjo decided to become an entrepreneur?

"Do this for me, Andy, and you-me both be richer'n fuckin' shit!" Wanjo shouted at his back.

Twenty-thirty thousand ICUs wasn't any small potatoes, Andy thought. For that kind of ice even professionals like himself, if they needed a quick shot of "clean" cash, might well be willing to cooperate with the "Crime in Progress" boys. The truth was, he'd never heard of anyone being *arrested* for doing a "hot" spot on 3V. The camera boys were always careful enough to keep back something legally crucial—by blurring a face, maybe, or omitting a full address. Their legal boys knew their business, and that was why the "Crime in Progress" channel had been a success for about two years now. He enjoyed watching it himself. All types of "socialiens"—a term he rather liked, as opposed to "criminals," "fringies," "streethawks" and the like—could be observed on the "Crime in Progress" channel twenty-four hours a day, live, anywhere in the world, whether it be New York, Beijing, or Sidney; and what kept you watching was knowing that the rape you were witnessing, or a beheading by some terrorist or guerrilla group, was real and happening live and not some canned bullshit packaged in Tokywood.

"I even gives you some o' *my four thou*!" Wanjo squealed close behind him.

Andy knew there were thousands of professional socialiens who'd *love* to strut their stuff on 3V but never got called. He had to admit, it was kind of flattering—if Wanjo could be believed—that "Crime in Progress" had taken an interest in *him*, of all people. Then again, why not? He was well known in the business, and Brooklyn was one of the centers of the global organ trade. Perhaps some day . . . but *not* while he was working for Memini. "Crime in Progress" was a one-shot deal, whereas Memini was good for the long haul. He'd be crazy to jeopardize the good thing that he had just for the few lousy minutes of the fame he'd get on 3V.

"I gawn quit you, brud!" shouted Wanjo. "If you don't do me them one fuckin' favor, I gawn quit your ass for good."

Andy looked around and smiled. "Who the fuck are you kidding, Wanjo? You're not quitting me, asshole! You make more whacks off me in one week than your oho earns you in a month. I'll talk to you later. I might need you in a couple of days."

Andy glanced at his watch and figured that if he copped a bus right away he'd make it to midtown at just about one p.m. But he wanted to be *sure* to arrive by one . . . to be right in front of the Memini building at one. It had nothing to do, he admitted to himself, with wanting to have lunch in Manhattan. He had no appetite for food. And it had nothing to do with making his two o'clock appointment with that Jap bitch. It was that other bitch. He had to have a peek at her again. Like a bird coming out of a clock she'd be popping through those doors at about three minutes after one. Andy looked frantically around for a cab.

13. HOTLINE TO BORNEO

Helen had no idea what to do. After arriving at the office and activating the routine full-room bugscan, she checked the Meminet morning mail—where two authoritative but contradictory memos awaited her. The Director of Information Services advised her to proceed with the preliminary trigrams—due late next week, as originally scheduled—for the Borneo Forget-Me-Land interiors (for which she had decided to plunder motifs from Angkor Wat). The Director of Leisure Enterprises, however, advised her to stop all work on Borneo designs—pending the resolution of the political impasse—and to proceed instead with designs for the forgetaway in construction in the Peruvian Amazon east of Iquitos.

Since President Barton would have had to clear such high-level interexecutive work-orders personally, Helen supposed that the CEO had let one slip by him. The poor man was under tremendous pressure lately. Or else maybe a third piece of information was missing that would explain the apparent contradiction. What she had done immediately, of course, was to check things out by calling Barton's Girl Friday. Ms. Yamamoto, however, had politely replied that she might not be able to get through to LB for hours...

Thrown back on her own resources, Helen wondered if there might not be some other channel through which she could get clarification. Perhaps a direct inquiry to someone at the other end—in Borneo itself—might turn up the answer she needed. But what personal connection did she have with Borneo? She knew very well that she had toured Southeast Asia for three weeks, well before the present political crisis, because that was where she had collected the images from Angkor Wat. She supposed she'd had a great time (because she always did) and met the most fascinating people on that trip. Her flapper, naturally, was the place she had stored her reminiscences, so she flipped it open and asked it to list records, in order of size, of all company-related personnel she'd had dealings with back then.

The first name her skeeter came up with was Nathan Davar, "Bioengineer, associated with the experimental biological station on the outskirts of Brunei. Your lover for four nights out of the last five spent in the region. Do you wish more detail, or shall I go on to the next on the list?"

"Any visuals on Davar?" She expected that she had preserved—for an eventual update of her Personal Past—multimedia memories of such an important part of her trip.

"Eighty-seven flapshots in all."

"Screen them." He must have been awfully impressive, she thought, for her to have kept him on permanent record in such exceptional volume. Yes, he really was good-looking: slim, muscular body, trim black beard, blue eyes twinkling under tropical headgear. In the first images, anyway, he had clothes on. Soon she was able to admire his hairy chest, his satyr-like legs, the way he fit over her perfectly in a cot (pictures she must have ordered her flapper to snap from a shelf on the tent wall opposite), and various other intimate close-ups that explained the great space she'd accorded him.

"Cut the visuals for now," said Helen. "Any diary entries on Davar?"

"Nine."

"Good. Skeet them up in chronological order."

She had described in loving detail each of their close encounters. In subsequent entries she would add little things she had omitted—trying to capture his essence the way poets always tried in vain to immortalize transient beauty. Nothing in her records about his job, about his duties. But she *had* taken down his personal phone number. Why not call him, then? Impossible, she thought. DUSA was holding all Memini personnel under virtual house arrest. And they were being kept incommunicado as well. But what if, she thought, she tried her own videowatch instead of calling through the Memini system? An absurd idea, of course, to expect that DUSA officials would overlook the obvious. Still . . .

Helen lifted her wrist and voiced in his number. After about ten seconds someone offered a groggy "Hello?"

"Nathan Davar?" asked Helen, extremely doubtful.

"Speaking." The audio, anyway, was working!

"This—this is Helen Means. I'm with Memini. I spent time with you out at the station about six months ago." She had done it. She'd gotten through! Every Big System had its loopholes.

"Where are you? Near the station? I'm receiving you on audio only."

"Same here," said Helen.

"We haven't been able to either make or receive calls since the quarantine. You must be in quarantine yourself. Correct?"

"Not at all. I'm calling from my office in Manhattan."

"That's ridiculous!"

"I know. It's not supposed to have happened."

"But it could be their jammers relax at this crazy hour of the night."

"No system is perfect," she said.

"You say I know you?"

"Flap me up. I'm Helen Means. We got to know each other *quite well* when I was out at your station six months ago. I hope you kept visuals. I did of you."

"Just a moment . . . Helen Means," she heard him voice into his flapper. She waited, catching exclamations of surprise. Delight too? she hoped. "Mmm . . . Ah! . . . Yes!" he said finally. "Prove you are who you say you are. How many times did we make love our first night together?"

"Six times."

"Seven!" Nathan corrected. "I have it down beyond a shadow of a doubt."

"I distinctly record only six. You must be padding."

"Padding? Why would I pad? You were an absolute animal . . . if you are who you say you are. I could hardly walk a step the next day."

"Poor man! You should have lodged an official complaint." She was beginning to feel miffed. She did not want to waste precious time. The sleeping dogs might wake at any moment. The flapshot on her screen gave her the proof he seemed to require. "You have a large black beauty mark on the inside of your left thigh. Correct?"

"Correct. I now accept without reservation your claim to be Helen Means."

"I understand that you can't be too cautious."

"You understand? What do you understand? Why did you call, then, if you already 'understand' so much?"

"You tell me you are in quarantine. Just what does that mean?" she asked, trying to sidestep his anger. She did have recorded in memory that he was a 'strong,' even 'volatile' personality—not someone she'd care to consort with much during the daylight hours of a lifetime. "I'm calling to find out from someone on the spot exactly what's happening—whether Memini business is proceeding as usual, in spite of the political—"

"Proceeding as usual? You have to be joking! Doesn't anyone in New York appreciate the gravity of the situation? If the news isn't out yet, let me keep you posted. The *Memini corporation itself* is being blamed for the viral blight that has ravaged DUSA's energy fields."

"I didn't know that," said Helen. "I thought we were only being blamed for not beaming power down from ISEC to make up for the deficit. I must tell President—"

"Listen, my dear wonderful animal . . . before we are cut off. I'm sure that they'll be cutting us off. The government of DUSA feels they are being criminally punished for refusing to enter into a whole network of business ventures by which Memini wishes to exploit the resources of the region. It's irrational, of course. Your people were already licensed to go full steam ahead on the forgetaway project here. Why would we want to upset the applecart? Just consider Memini's stake in this biostation alone! Do you realize that a week ago we had just about completed our first series of primate tests with a complex polypeptide that is at last going to give us the Perfect Pill?"

"It was rumored at our last Council meeting. President Barton nearly had a fit," she said, recalling the meminized record of the meeting.

"Fine," said Davar. "But then, a week ago, after news of the blight hit the media and the political mudslinging began, Barton sent us a direct order to *stop* testing the Pill and work round the clock on a cure for the blight, instead."

"That sounds reasonable to me," said Helen.

"And indeed it would be, except that one of our lab assistants swears that the remedy already *exists*!—that he personally worked on *producing* both the specific blight-causing toxin *and* its antitoxin years ago at one of our Amazon stations!"

"Bizarre!" said Helen. "It makes no sense. Why not just ship out the existing antitoxin?"

"More bizarre still," said Davar, "our lab assistant had many of those documents meminized, but when he tried—with the permission of DUSA officials—to boot up those Amazon records for both toxin and antitoxin, he could find *nothing*."

"Maybe there *was* nothing," Helen suggested.

"On the contrary, they'd been deleted from the database."

Helen was becoming confused. It was a very uncomfortable sensation.

"What the hell's going on?" said Davar. "How'd the damn bug break loose? Does our right hand know what our left is doing? We faxed our concern to HQ but the big guy hasn't bothered to answer."

"Back up a bit, Nathan. One thing at a time. First, is it true that we are in reach of the Perfect Pill?"

"Ninety-nine percent sure! It will soon be possible to boost both memory and IQ without all the side-effects we've all learned to live with so well. Just think of it: the coming generation will have it all! *We'll* be the last generation of bloody freaks."

"Freaks! I don't regard myself as a freak," snapped Helen.

"Listen, you adorable feline you, enough about freaks. Let me tell you more about what's been happening. I leave it to you how to deal with this information . . . Are you recording?"

"For transcription and immediate meminization, yes." Out of habit she had pressed Record at the very beginning of the call. An end-message would remind her to upload it into her flapper.

"Listen closely, then. So first thing that happens is that crazy order to work on an already existing blight-cure. Secondly, and even more insane, yesterday a team of *commandos* landed clandestinely in the nearby jungle. Evidently they were not aware of the full extent of the security measures that DUSA had erected all around us to implement quarantine. Within our compound we could hear the exchange of gunfire. We hoped, of course, that Memini had sent in a rescue team—for us and whatever specimens we could grab. There was no telling what DUSA might do to our labs. In any case, the whole team was wiped out almost to a man! They turned out to be all North Americans, all oldfolks except for the lone tekkie survivor and head of the operation, a self-styled 'Colonel' Solomon whose flapper was impounded. He now sits in a bamboo cage thinking he's being punished for *not doing his homework*, for Chrissake!"

"Are *you* being threatened with punishment also for the failed rescue attempt?" asked Helen.

"Rescue attempt?" snorted Davar. "Don't make me laugh."

"What are you talking about?"

"Their goal was anything but rescue. Although the colonel wouldn't admit it, his team was sent here to *kill* us scientists, not to save us."

"This is absolutely whacko!" said Helen.

"More whacko still, DUSA officials in Brunei told us today that further analysis of the colonel's biotape suggests that these men were under instructions *from Memini itself* to carry out their raid! Their primary mission, supposedly, was to kill Dr. Jorgenson, the leader of the Perfect Pill Project and the only one among us who has the whole scientific picture in his head."

"That makes no sense," said Helen. "DUSA evidently wants to demoralize all of you. They have no other means of revenge against the power of Memini."

"That's possible," Nathan said after a pause. "But we think it more likely that a rival conglob—probably Mishugi—was interested in stealing or else suppressing what we'd come up with. Or else those guys were out to kill Jorgenson to prevent work on a blight-cure, thinking they'd thereby screw Memini politically! The cloak-and-dagger possibilities boggle the mind. On the surface, the three biggies of MOM cooperate—*in tres partes mundus divisus est*, you know—but with stakes this big . . . a conglob like Mishugi would try to make sure that if their mission failed, their *target* would get blamed for it!"

"What about Jorgenson? Is he safe?" asked Helen. Had she also been intimate with Jorgenson? She must voice up her record of him as soon as she signed off. After all, his was the second name her flapper had coughed up. (Or was it? She back-tapped to the list of names to make sure. Yes, second. Probably a wealth of memories in her little box connected with Jorgenson. It would be quite unlike her to have missed striking up a warm friendship with the *head* of that important biostation.)

"Jorgenson's physically safe, yes. But he, of course, is charged by DUSA with ecocrime first-degree. They need a whipping-boy for the devastation of their sun-juice paddies."

"Is there anything I can do to help you people?" asked Helen. She felt a constriction in her chest. She empathized physically with the claustrophobic feelings of her hemmed-in colleagues. She wanted to run right up to the president's office with the news, but she knew she didn't dare interrupt him. Did Barton know already? she wondered.

"Do for us? Yes! Get us the hell *out* of this lousy, power-down, mosquito-ridden hole!"

What was she forgetting? she asked herself. The answer hit her as she glanced down for the moment at the two contradictory memos on her desk. "I'll do my best," she said above Nathan's grating string of descriptors. "Meanwhile, Nathan, do you think you can help *me*?"

"In any way I can, my dear."

"I almost forgot why I called, you know."

"I thought you called on official business. I thought you called because *Memini* wants to know what's become of us."

Helen felt herself reddening. "Of course! That's exactly why I called," she lied. "I'll try to keep in touch."

"Didn't you just ask *me* for help? What can I—"

A blipping light on her videowatch told her that the connection had suddenly been cut. She tried calling back several times. No answer. Evidently DUSA was repairing its fences. Well? she asked herself. Should she go ahead working on Forget-Me-Land? The answer came to her in a flash. No! Nathan had described the station as "power-down." That meant that all work at the forgetaway site would be indefinitely postponed as well. Simple logic told her that she'd better start focusing on Peru.

International politics made her dizzy. Imagine accusing Memini of attacking its own operatives! LB would be appalled to hear such news. As for her, it would of course be unwise for *her* to be the bearer of ill tidings. All this was really none of her affair. And yet, in all conscience, could she really avoid the responsibility? The safety of those lovely *men* out there might depend entirely on her. And didn't she owe them *something* for the marvelous time they had shown her? Then again, for an employee to be associated with bad news in the mind and flapper of her superior officer...

Helen felt she ought to feel more *loyalty* to those poor colleagues of hers out there, stuck in the field, surrounded by mysterious enemies. She felt embroiled in *inner conflict*. It was a strange and distressing sensation, the sort of thing that used to give her sleepless nights right up through her college years. She could ignore her feelings, of course, and in ten minutes or so the problem would disappear. On the other hand, soon she would be meminizing the transcript of this call—so that she could by no means manage to *ignore* the awful predicament of Davar and Jorgenson.

If only she could get the two of them out of there! Now wouldn't that be a *happy* ending to all the otherwise miserable news she'd be forced to report to Barton? (At tomorrow's party, would he ask her to spend the night with him? she wondered. She imagined herself in bed with her boss—in the dark, since she could not really picture him distinctly—whispering in his ear this whole horrendous tale, but the ending would be soothing, consoling.) As a matter of fact, who else did she know in the region who *might* be able to help them get out of there? She wasted no time thinking about it, but flapped and flapped and (re)discovered the name of Tan Sri Mohd, head of DUSA's Ministry of the Interior, with whom she had spent a delightful four days—and *nights*!—in Kuala Lumpur before flying on to Borneo. Mohd had been of immense help in organizing her tour, and afterwards he had, according to her records, videomailed her several times in hope of arranging for her to return. He would never forget her, he claimed, and of course he wouldn't: he was *oldfolks*! There were still regions in the world where a brilliant individual, though oldfolks in background, could rise (if properly pedigreed) to a position of prominence. She had his private number. Well, why not give Mohd a call?...

14. ORDEAL BY CASSETTE

His heart raced as he leaned back against the building a few paces down from the entrance. At two and a half minutes past one she emerged, turned left, and walked by without seeming to notice him. She wore a butt-hugging violet pants-suit with a golden sash at the waist. Her sun-flecked hair, gathered to one side, fanned out like flax over her right shoulder and breast. Her right arm looped over the scallop-shaped yellow bag that was slung from her left shoulder.

He followed some ten paces behind, stopping when she stopped, gazing at her as she gazed dreamily into this or that shop window. Soon, venturing nearer, he paused a few steps behind her and pretended to admire the same window display while staring at her reflected face. His breath caught in his throat as the eyes in the window suddenly fastened onto his. She smiled at him in a strange way and then moved on. Had she recognized him? he wondered. Was she now playing cat and mouse? He decided to close in on her as soon as they had both stepped across Forty-Ninth. He caught up with her and made his move just before she turned into the Raj.

"Helen! Excuse me. It's me. Andy Peters." The quaver in his voice belied his insinuating smile.

She looked at him with complete self-possession and returned him a mechanically perfect stage smile. "I'm sorry, but nothing clicks," she said. "The people I know make appointments to see me, and I'm quite sure I'm having lunch by myself today."

She turned to go but he tugged at her arm. "I'm *Andy Peters*," he said. "Your *lover* Andy Peters. Only yesterday we spent the afternoon in the sack, for Chrissake!"

She burst out into a tinkly laugh. "That's a good line, Mister. I figured you'd try to pick me up when I caught you giving me the eye in the window back there."

"Now listen, sweetie, there's no need for an argument. Just voice me up in your flapper and you'll see."

She narrowed her eyes at him and shrugged out of his grasp. "No need," she said. "I'm afraid it would be quite impossible for me to be involved with a man like you."

"We've been like *this* for a year," he said, twisting two fingers at her. "Yesterday we had a little problem. You're pissed at me is all."

"Listen, Andy, or whoever the hell you are. You've got a good line but I'm sorry, I'm not biting. I don't like your style, your clothes, your voice, or your vocabulary."

"See? You're just *pissed* with me!" He tossed out his palms as if annoyed at having to demonstrate the obvious.

"Now beat it before I call a cop."

"Please," he said, his smile collapsing, "take just a second to flap me up. My God, Helen, after all the time we've spent together, all the happiness we've shared . . ."

He watched her step back from him, gagging at the cornball language.

"Stay right where you are." She fished her flapsack out of her purse, held the mike end to her lips and snapped, "ID, skeet Andy Peters." She looked across at him and frowned. "Sorry, no such acquaintance. I think you must have the wrong number. Happens all the time." She spun away and disappeared into the restaurant.

He stood looking after her, muttering curses at people who jostled him. Suddenly it all came to him. That super-efficient Sibyl Yamamoto! This morning she'd managed to replace the doctored version of Helen's biocassette with a copy of the unchanged original! Would she have *destroyed* the Peters version already? The very idea of her doing so enraged him. Schemes of revenge began flashing through his mind. But what was the point of thinking in terms of worst-case scenarios? he asked himself, scratching his head.

He reached into his jacket pocket for the biocassette that Sibyl expected him to return. For a moment his heart thumped wildly, and then he remembered he'd handed it to Yolanda Woo—in a moment of sheer desperation. Now if that didn't take the cake for fog-brained incompetence! The sort of thing only a frag would do. Yesterday impotence, today incompetence! "Isn't there anything you can get up when it's needed, Mr. Kedro?" He could see those stuck-up tits of hers jiggling with delight as she enjoyed his humiliation all yesterday afternoon on closed-circuit 3V.

And now, to show up without that lousy cassette—as trivial a matter as it was, it was the straw that broke the back of whatever spirit he had left. What excuse could he give her that wouldn't make him look doubly a fool? It was a strain for him just to stand up straight, as though the plague that had visited him yesterday now encompassed his whole body. He dragged his leaden feet along in the direction of Burma Derma. A shrinking sensation in his stomach, like some private black hole of despair, seemed to be sucking his whole frame inward.

She caught him telling the robar to go to hell. Andy carefully avoided her eyes as she settled her blue-sheathed ass at the boardroom table directly across from him. He could feel a piercing irony behind her casual "Nice to see you again, Mr. Kedro."

He decided to take the initiative. "I can explain all about yesterday," he began.

"Why bother?" she countered, laying open a file folder in front of her. "There's no need to explain a thing."

"What do you mean, 'why bother'?" he said. "My reputation is at stake, that's why bother."

"You've lived fully up to your reputation," she said indifferently, striking keys on the terminal before her. She had laid out her flapper at her right elbow.

He reacted swiftly to the sarcasm. "Who the hell do you think you are, trying to put me down?"

"Put you down? Did *I* put you down?" she replied with an innocent look laced with double meaning. "I'm sure I didn't mean to. I'm sorry, Mr. Kedro. Now why don't we get down to business?"

"This *is* business. I don't want you to walk away . . . with any wrong ideas about me. I was working under a hell of a lot of pressure."

"Do you think I am accusing you of failing us?"

"You're not exactly accusing, but you damn well—"

"You carried off the operation very successfully. We are convinced that Mrs. Means is a completely loyal employee. You earned every unit of what we promised you."

"I wasn't in this just for the money, sweetheart. You know damn well that I had a ... an interest in the *personal* nature of the assignment." For the first time he dared to look her unflinchingly in the eyes. "Maybe you're satisfied with what *you* got out of the deal, but that doesn't mean that I'm happy too."

She drew herself up straight and looked at him sharply. "What will it take to make you happy? Do you expect us to pay you extra to make up for your *personal* dissatisfactions?"

"On the contrary, I'm willing to take *less*," Andy blurted, hardly knowing what he was saying, "if you'll just set things up the same way between me and Helen again. A second chance is what I'm talking about."

Her eyes widened and Andy saw that she was suppressing a grin. "A repeat performance? I'm afraid that's entirely out of the question."

"It won't cost you a damn thing! That woman *wanted* me, understand? And if not for the unusual circumstances of the set-up, we would've ... there'd've been no problem with ..."

"Do I take it you are *smitten* with Helen?" For the first time, the poker-faced Sibyl permitted herself the luxury of an uncensored smile.

"Who the hell's talking *smitten*?" Andy's blood beat bongos in his ears. "I'm talking about a point of *honor*! It's a *man's* thing. Something *you* wouldn't understand."

"It's too bad you're saddled with such an innocently retentive memory for pain, Mr. Kedro. Now you can see the advantages to going tekkie."

"You selling Happy Tabs, Miss? Listen, I don't give a shit about being a tekkie. And that sarcastic crap of yours makes me think *you* ain't no full-blooded frag yourself, Miss Yammy."

"Please leave me out of it. Let's not get off the track, Mr. Kedro."

"Okay. Now look, you hired me for a job no frag could ever do. And all I'm asking for is a very tiny favor in return. In consideration of our past business dealings, and as a token of future—"

"Do you want to *endanger* your future connection with us? Be reasonable. Consider the episode finished. Look at your terminal. I'm now going to credit your account with the payment we agreed on . . . Oh, but first, one little thing. The cassette from Helen's flapper." She held out her hand expectantly while continuing to focus on the terminal.

Andy pretended he didn't hear a thing. "And as part of the favor I'm asking you," he said, "please restore the Andy Peters cassette to Helen Means's flapper."

"What?"

"I know you removed it . . . at the latest, sometime this morning. You put back a copy of her original in its place."

"No we didn't. Why would we? The added material can't do her any harm. In fact, it makes a quite pleasant addition to the stock of her Personal Past."

"I saw her today at lunchtime."

"Well! So you *are* perfectly capable of arranging your own private follow-up meetings. Why then are you asking *me* to—"

"She claimed not to *know* me," Andy said, his voice quaking. "She looked me up in her flapper and said I didn't exist!"

Sibyl Yamamoto turned a long, wry grin on him. "I always marvel," she said, "at what idiots men can be. Don't you think there could have been *other* reasons for her to deny your existence than your absence from her bio? . . . What if it was simply *inconvenient* for her to acknowledge you just then? Or what if she gave herself a message to give you the cold shoulder?" Sibyl held out her hand again, wiggling her fingers, waiting for him to hand her the cassette. "She could have had ten different reasons for cutting you dead. Easily ten . . . "

Her snideness stung him like a slap. Suddenly Andy found himself the proud possessor of a perfectly tailor-made *reason* for arriving without that cassette. "You're lying," he said. "You've removed it and probably destroyed it! But if what you say is true . . . then get us together again under conditions where I'll have a decent chance to find out."

"I'm getting a bit tired of all this, Mr. Kedro. Do you want to be paid or not?"

Andy sat back and crossed his arms over his chest. "I seem to have . . . misplaced that cassette," he said.

"Misplaced it?" She looked flustered. "But you know you can't get paid unless you return it."

"Oh, I might run across it," said Andy, flicking his nose rapidly with his finger, "if I look hard enough."

"But you *must* find it."

"Really? Why? You've already restored her original."

"I assure you we did not. Mr. Kedro, do you want to forfeit your money?"

"For the little favor I'm asking? . . . Yes, what if I do?"

Sibyl Yamamoto's color deepened. She seemed to have trouble breathing. Andy had never seen her so devoid of self-possession. "You *must* fulfill your part of the bargain," she said, "whether you want your money or not. You absolutely must give back that cassette."

"If and when I can find it. And meanwhile, when did you say I'll be getting together with Helen again?"

"That memory chip, Mr. Kedro, is not a bargaining chip. I don't know what's come over you . . . You and I have always acted in perfect mutual trust."

"If you have not permanently erased me from her life," he said, eager to pursue the advantage he sensed, "then do as I ask. If I *am* in her memory bank, and she deliberately *decides* not to have anything to do with me, then that's okay, I'll take that chance. I won't blame you if I strike out."

"I caution you not to play with fire, Mr. Kedro." Her tone was ominous.

"Helen's kind of fire suits me fine."

"That's not the fire I'm talking about. I'm talking about corporate fire. Mr. Kedro, Memini cannot afford to have a copy of a top executive's bio floating casually around town. You and I both know that in the wrong hands it could be a treasure-trove of corporate secrets. We had to take the risk we did with you. You have enjoyed our unconditional trust. We now have you in mind for another major assignment, coming up in the immediate future. You are very useful to us. Do not endanger your well-founded reputation with us. Don't let some primitive emotional projection stemming from that raw oldfolks background of yours ruin a good thing."

"Ball's in your court," said Andy, sitting back and twiddling his thumbs.

He felt dizzy with a sense of power. Why had he been too stupid to realize on his own what a bargaining chip he held? What a lucky accident, meeting Mrs. Woo out in the hall!

Sibyl Yamamoto shook her head, hammered at the keys of the terminal, and appeared to be talking to herself. As he looked at her, Andy was struck with another revelation. Her job was on the line! She was frightened to death! . . . What an opportunity! He gazed at her lovely, chamois-colored skin, her deliciously full breasts. He remembered how often he'd dreamed of pulling up her dress and jamming her here, right on top of the table! She'd probably jump at the chance to roll in the hay with him in order to get back her precious fucking cassette . . . But now the thought of her yielding to him left him cold, stirred no tingle in the groin. His mind drifted instead to the far more palpable image of Helen, her pointed breasts bobbing over him as she ground him into impotence. Her satin-skinned body was a dream become flesh! Helen Means, Golden Helen, *wanting* him, wanting *him*! . . . As his eyes played absently over Sibyl's body, he saw by the flush in her cheeks that she was well aware of the thought that had crossed his mind.

But suddenly she fixed her dark eyes upon him and nearly burst out laughing. She looked far more relaxed, more confident—as if she'd passed through some sort of crisis. "All right," she said, glancing again at the screen of her terminal, "there seems to be no insoluble problem whatsoever. It looks as if we can combine both business and pleasure, and satisfy our distinctly different goals in the process."

"I knew you'd figure something out," sighed Andy. "After all, you're the boss's right-hand robot."

"The next time you get to see Helen," said Sibyl, "I advise you to speak as little as is humanly possible—and above all, to restrain your sense of 'humor.'"

"When is . . . next time?" He leaned forward, ignoring her sarcasm, the tips of his fingers trembling.

"There's going to be a party tomorrow night—an overnighter—at the estate of our chief executive officer, Mr. Barton. All the top Memini officers will be there, either alone, or with their spouses, or their 'friends.' Helen Means prefers to come to these blowouts alone. You will be invited as Andy

Peters, Chief of the Retirement Section. The corporate flowchart will be temporarily modified to install you in that position."

"Retirement Section!" Andy laughed out loud. He was delighted. His whole mood had flip-flopped! "That terminal of yours has one hell of a sense of humor. Or'd you spin that out of your own gorgeous head, Miss Sweet Bumps?"

"We act in collaboration," she said quickly. "I pay close attention to what Meminet recommends. And part of that recommendation is that if anyone should ask you about retirement benefits, you make an excuse to wander off for a fresh drink. If you avoid anyone for ten minutes straight, you are sure to drift completely out of her mind."

"Unless someone flaps me up."

"Yes. But no one should find you interesting enough to bother."

"Except, perhaps, Helen?"

"Perhaps. But she won't even talk to you if you're wearing a suit like that. You don't realize how close you came to failing in your assignment yesterday because of that suit. I warned you, you know."

Andy stroked his lapels, feeling momentarily insulted. But then it occurred to him that Miss Yammy might be right. Maybe she'd hit upon precisely the reason that Helen had just blown him off! Still, "It happens to be my best damn suit," he muttered.

Sibyl rapped away at the terminal. "Tomorrow morning you will be fitted out with an appropriate wardrobe at Borgstein's."

"Borgstein's! They check out your credit rating before you can get through the door there."

"Memini has a special relationship with Borgstein's . . . Just remember, do not interfere with the decisions made by the staff who attend you. Above all, tell them nothing of your own taste preferences. Don't worry, they will not ask."

"Who pays for the rags?"

"We do. Consider it an investment."

"In what?"

"In our next business transaction."

"Which is?"

"It has nothing to do with Helen. We want you to memorize the faces and names of *all* the men at that party—the men only, to be sure. So that you could instantly recognize any one of them if you met him in the street, for example."

"Why?"

"Because one of them is your next . . . assignment."

"Really? Who do I 'retire'?"

"That you'll find out at the last possible moment. Even *I* don't know, and I hope Meminet decides not to *let* me know even then."

"And when does this new 'retirement' take place?"

She looked blank for a moment as she listened to her skeeter. "Could be tomorrow night during the party. Could be any day after that right up through the following Friday. We're *buying* all that time from you, Mr. Kedro. Eight days and nights. Understand? During that time you must suspend all your normal business activity. Be available at a moment's notice. You must wear your videowatch constantly until the assignment is completed."

"If you're giving me a fair crack at Helen, I'll be glad to take on the assignment."

"Very good. I'll now make out your invitation to the party, and I'll c-mail Borgstein's to expect you tomorrow at nine a.m. sharp."

"You're incredibly efficient."

"I owe it to Meminet," she replied humorlessly. "And don't *you* forget . . . the cassette. Tomorrow evening, at the party."

"Assuming that I find it," Andy smiled, gazing mock-innocently at the ceiling."

"I have no doubt you'll be able to find it," said Sibyl. She looked at him sharply and rose majestically to her feet.

PART TWO:
THE ORGY

EXCERPT FROM DR. PROSS'S HANDBOOK OF PSYCHOPROSETHIS

The following four points sum up the clinical picture of contracortical chemoneurolysis:

(1) Chemically induced dysfunction will usually begin after two or three years of a doubled or tripled average daily Pill-dosage above the normal.

(2) The chief functional impairment appears as a progressive loss of access to enhanced semantic-memory storage. The deficit takes the form of lapses in recall, primarily of verbal-factual material which, of course, is the major component of semantic memory.

(3) These disintegrative processes, which are regarded as irreversible, stem from massive failure of ion-channel function within the neuronal membrane throughout large areas of cortical tissue.

(4) The chief additional symptom, due to a morbid process which invades the amygdaloid complex, is the hyperintensification of certain early emotion-laden memories that the Pill itself has not yet managed to extinguish. The flapper maintains for the tekkie, in counterbalance against the effects of the Pill, a buffer of logic and reason ensuring that an individual knows and distinguishes in practical life between the objective present and the delusory images of a "present" that arise from the *past*—from unextinguished organic residues of episodic memory known as "minskies." In this symptom of *temporal subversion* that I refer to, the buffer of reason and the support of one's flapper fail, and in the face of all objective evidence to the

contrary, the patient is sure that the intensely felt past is the present, and she or he may construct elaborate edifices of confabulation to explain away contradictions between the *true*, and the *imagined*, present.

15. PLAYING IT FRAGTIME

Checkpoint Charley was Sibyl in a sheath of gold. Stewart was ushered into a grand lobby of neoclassical design where the only flesh-and-blood figure was that of the executive secretary seated to the left of two vast, darkly transparent door panels. Two nets of taut gold filament reined in the flesh of Sibyl's bare breasts, sweeping up and joining behind her neck. The hem of her dress rode high up the thighs of her teasingly crossed, ivory-pale legs. When she eyed him through her gold-streaked lashes it was with a welcoming effusiveness suggesting that she recognized him personally. But hadn't she first scanned his invitation—and *only then* exclaimed, "Mr. Bridges, I'm so glad you could come!"? With golden fingernails she rummaged among the few remaining nametags, stepped forward from her little reception desk, and deftly molded a large adhesive strip to his chest—below the left shoulder of his skin-thin, loosely draped kevlar spring jacket. Under his name, in smaller print, was the one word "Bioprogramming."

"There!" she said, gripping his elbows. Before he knew it she was leaning against him so that her breasts indented his chest. "Everyone will assume that you are a company employee," she murmured in his ear. "And of course, in a way you already are ... If I were you, though, I would not tell *anybody* about your presently being a candidate for a position with us."

"Thank you for the advice." His voice cracked and her closeness weakened his knees. At the moment there was no one besides the two of them in the enormous vestibule which curved away in alcoves and columns in two gallery-like wings toward doorways to the left and right. In the alcoves stood figures of nudes from what seemed every period in the history of sculpture. Although intimidated by the stone and the bronze, Stewart grew bolder as she continued (unaccountably, it seemed) to hold him exceptionally close. "Are you stuck out here for the night," he heard himself ask her, "or will we be able to see each other later, Miss—?"

"Sibyl. To you I'm Sibyl. I'll find you later, but meanwhile don't neglect to party it up. Anything your heart desires. Do you hear me?"

"I hear you." He looked at her quizzically.

"There are plenty of lovely women inside who will be happy to make your acquaintance."

"But why is the loveliest of all stationed outside?" He felt himself reddening, yet she looked anything but annoyed, so he went right on. "It looks like the rest, after this, is going to be one big anticlimax."

"On the contrary, Mr.—"

"Stewart," he said.

"—it might be one big climax after another," she smiled. She had already begun to pry his overnight bag from his fingers. "You'll find this in your bedroom, Stewart. The number of your room is 24. See? It's printed on your nametag. The guest rooms are all off the pool." She turned him toward the marble wall behind him. "You see? Signs with arrows pointing to the various parts of the premises. You can't get lost. And if you do, a robar will come right to your aid. They are multi-purpose models. You'll find them amazingly helpful."

"And if I were to ask you, Sibyl?" His throat tightened as her scent filled his lungs. "Would you . . . show me to my room?" Somehow he knew it was all bravado on his part. All this wasn't real. Sibyl wasn't real. He was playing a role. That was what gave him the courage to be jaunty. If it ever came down to it, though, would he be able to form a relationship—even of the butterfly sort of his fantasy—with a female of Sibyl's species? Had he ever recovered from the beating he'd taken from Trudy fifteen years ago? Wasn't that really why he had come to this party—to find out if he'd got over her, to find out if he could live in the *present*?

"Show you to your room?" she said. "I'd lead you there by the hand." Whispering thrillingly into his ear, she added, "I'm *so* glad you decided to come, Stewart. I'd be very disappointed if you hadn't. You'll see later how much I appreciate your being here." She playfully gripped his wrist and launched him gently through the parting doors. For him it was like jumping off a diving board.

MEMINI

A space so large and varied swallowed him up that at first he couldn't be sure whether he was indoors or out, in an archeological museum or some Arcadian park. The warmth of Sibyl's fingers receded slowly from his wrist as he gawked around. Statuary, vegetation, strains of music, aromatic breezes—all assaulted his senses at once. No one paid attention to his entrance. The party had been in progress for some hours, as he had expected. He had deliberately arrived late in the hope of remaining as anonymous as possible. But here the sheer *scale* of things made anonymity seem more chilling than attractive.

A buffet stretched out along a brightly lit wall to Stewart's right. He headed for it. It seemed the natural place to begin at a party where you were a total stranger. Before he reached the food-laden tables, however, he was brought up short by giant images arrayed as a group along the illuminated wall behind the buffet. At the left yawned a niche housing a Buddha about fifteen feet high. In the lap of the Buddha, on a votive-offering plate, stood a gigantic model of the latest Memini-made flapper (in a silvery blue that contrasted with the dull-brown Buddha-belly of stone). Set in relief to the right of the contemplative idol crouched an athlete in the pose of the Discus Thrower—except stripped of his skin to reveal an intricate network of largely prosthetic and neurophotonic muscle-bands and organs. Projecting from the wall to the right of the invincible athlete there floated a weblike metallic structure of an astronaut revolving in emptiness, one of the famed Lost Hundred. A *memento mori*? wondered Stewart. Hardly. Just another heroic expression of that insane tekkie longing for human transcendence over time and biology.

Beneath the giant triptych a train of old-fashioned, lion-clawed tables heaped with food ran the length of the wall. A banner above a table at the center read, "EXOTICA IN GENERGETIC CUISINE FROM GENE ZENE, A MEMINI SUBSIDIARY. Flap GENE ZENE for a skeet on any item you wish to consider." Stewart approached for a closer look. He recognized croccoli, a much-touted new veggie-lizard hybrid; and for the first time he saw corndogs, which he had heard combined the best elements of high-protein maize and prairie dog. The grannelida, brand-new on the market, were the high-fiber wormsteaks reported to be nutritionally one of the best-balanced of recent gastronomic innovations. None of these novelty items, however, appealed to Stewart as much as some of the standard dishes on the tables to either side.

Groups of party-guests milled around the tables. Many of the men had dressed casually in skin-thin shortie jackets. Others were hung with the latest peasant blouses that billowed rakishly out over their pants. Some, like Stewart, limited their lower self-abandon to a more conservative half-zipped fly and a single pantleg rolled up to half-calf. The women sported silk stocking-dresses or gowns with tornaway breast and butt ports, or airy lattices made of cross-hatched strips of cloth that wrapped their bare bodies like fishing nets.

His skin tingled. Sea breezes laden with warm tropical scents brushed his face. He wanted the food, he wanted the women, he wanted a drink—and no sooner was he aware of his thirst than a robar rolled up beside him and asked him his preference.

"Scotch on the rocks."

"Single malt? Twelve-year-old?"

"Sure. Why not?"

"Good selection, Mr. Bridges. You probably know that Memini owns twenty-six percent of Glenfiddich."

"Really? Well I think we should buy the whole damn barrel."

"I agree with you, sir. Enjoy your evening, Mr. Bridges. If there's anything you need, anything at all, one of us will always be at your service."

Stewart lifted his drink from the servo's gloved claw and continued his visual survey of the whole bewildering multizoned space. Beyond the bright beach of buffet tables floated a dark dance floor adrift with blue-green phantoms, the light seeming to emanate from the dancing couples themselves. The music came from a group in the bandstand at the invisible rear wall. The colors of the light in the bandstand shifted to match the changing moods of the players.

Stewart retreated from the tables, stopping in the vaguely defined border between the buffet zone now at his back and the large central plaza in front of him. The park-like space bathed in a cool luminosity as of hazy sunlight filtered through thick summer foliage. Here people sat and ate and talked at little tables set on flagstones under giant hanging ferns that sometimes formed columns with flowering bushes that rose from the pavement.

And beyond the plaza, darkness again. A carpet of grass rolled out from the edge of the flagstones into a *woods*—a velvety blackness of tree-trunks strafed by beams of blue-white moonlight.

"Do you always straddle zones, with each foot in a different world?" A liquid, insinuating voice nibbled his ear. The accompanying perfume snaked to the root of his stomach even before he had turned around. She was brown-skinned, lovely, and had playfully wicked eyes. A bright-green scarab design crouched in the middle of her forehead. The adhesive taped to the bare skin below her shoulder-blade read, "Gwen Aleata, Dir., Ed. Svcs."

He nearly choked on his Scotch. "I think I've always been a straddler," he sputtered, knowing that only he knew what he meant. Her nearness affected him like a midnight swim in still, warm water. "How about you?"

"I love to straddle," she answered, the tip of her tongue licking her upper lip. "But best of all, I love *being* straddled, and that's why I'm attracted to straddlers."

"You don't waste much time," he said, his voice barely rising to meet his lips.

"Time? What's time?" she said, her eyes widening and crinkling at the edges. "The only time we ever have is another now, just like this—with nothing ever before it, and nothing ever after. Your bod gives me the twinges, Mr. Bridges."

"I . . . appreciate your frankness," he said, adding irrelevantly, "I haven't been to any of Mr. Barton's bashes before."

"Of course you've been. We all *feel* we haven't but we *know* we have. And I *know* we must've met many times before. We appear to be recognizing each other on the hormonal level, don't you think?"

"Our hormones seem to be talking up a storm," said Stewart, feeling his way into the rhythm of the now. Boldness was called for! Brashness! Just like in the stuff he invented to make a living. "I'm sure I've often benefitted from your 'educational services.' But tell me, just what do you *officially* do as Director of Educational Services?"

"You *don't* want me to bore you with shoptalk, do you?"

"It wouldn't be possible for you to bore me," he gallantly returned.

"You want to know my particular specialty? The thing I do best in the daytime? Penetrating Third and Fourth World cultural barriers to the spread of Memini products. I'm a *real* straddler, don't you see?" She wrapped his free hand in hers and folded it over her firmly netted breast. "Do you believe in hands-on education?"

His lips uttered a voiceless "Sure."

"Would you like the rest of your lesson tonight?"

"You'll find me a very apt pupil." He felt like an actor in some five-minute 3V romance.

"Right now I'm a little busy," she winked, "but will you look for me after the music's over?"

"Sure."

"Your room or mine?"

"Yours," he said shrewdly, giving himself leeway. At the back of his mind hovered the vague possibility of getting something going with Sibyl. "I'll remember, Room 17."

She stood expectantly by. He smiled and felt awkward as her own smile wavered, then faded completely.

"Something the matter, Gwen?" he asked.

"I didn't see you flap in any reminder."

"Damn it, how stupid of me!" He fumbled in the pouch at his waist.

"And your DIM-window ain't *that* small," she said, "so what you're telling me is 'fuck off, baby,' and *that I'll* remember." He watched her trim bottom flick angrily away from him and her hand pull out her flapper from its net-bag over her hip. Stewart's face burned at his forgetfulness. He was not as flapper-conscious as he thought he was. This time, fortunately, he had only done himself out of a *date*. His next mistake—well, he couldn't afford one . . . He tried to put a good face on it. It was going to be a great party. Only ten minutes into it and he'd already been propositioned! Gorgeous Gwen was only the beginning, a mere *hors-d'oeuvre*.

Unless, of course, he had deliberately, *unconsciously*, screwed up his chance with her. Could it be, out of fears dating back so many years, he was still avoiding women he would love to get involved with, dreading the pain of being used and then discarded? . . . He was *not* going to let the past strangle him! He was a grown-up, no longer a vulnerable romantic, damn it! And the night still had a long long way to go.

MEMINI

First, he would eat—to store up energy for a long and active night. He returned to the food tables, where he was distracted by the glances of women, many of them lovely morsels themselves, milling around to be speared. For the moment, however, he focused on the dishes on the tables. Avoiding things spiced with garlic, he settled for a breast of rabchick in white sauce (this hoariest of hybrids was standard fare in the better sort of restaurants).

With his food-tray and his drink, Stewart strolled into the green-cool plaza. He took a vacant table that offered an excellent view of a few dozen guests who, singly or in small groups, had decided to relax in bestatued little groves under roofs of plunging vines. Traffic to and from the plaza was considerable. People wandered from the woods into the plaza, others from the plaza into the woods, or to the buffet, or to the dance floor to the rear.

The atmosphere was cozy and friendly. Barton was clearly a generous host who seemed to spare no expense to keep his administrative staff in good cheer. It appeared that his guests included the cream of the organization, the people who would become Stewart's colleagues (if he were lucky enough to be offered the vacant vice-presidency!) and a group of young and attractive underlings wearing hardly any underthings. Everyone appeared so well-groomed, so self-possessed! He felt that just by looking at him they could tell his clothes came from right off the rack at Bloomie's or from Filene's Mezzanine. What did the Memini *crème de la crème* sit around and *talk* about, he wondered, when they came together like this and didn't have to talk business? Was it sports? Art? Politics? . . . Stewart cocked his head to the right, hooking into a conversation between two distinguished-looking middle-aged men at the table next to his.

"Productivity is at a standstill," said one.

"Isn't it great to get away from it all?" said the other.

"Plant capacity is underused," pronounced the first.

"The sauce on my beefish is heavy on the salt," said the other with evident annoyance.

"We're opening vacation paradises, 'forgetaways,' you know, in the Third and Fourth Worlds to stimulate consumption among some still relatively backward populations. These countries tend to have a civilized, flapper-dependent leadership, but the trickle-down effect is very . . . "

"I hear the mountains of Borneo still have some wonderful native trout."

"The natives are not to be trusted," said the first.

"Have you ever had native trout?"

"Native anything is not to be trusted. Native fish are riddled with parasites. This crabster here's great. Totally lab-grown. Try some?"

"My beefish is perfectly fine, except a little heavy on the salt."

"At our forgetaways we install the world's finest autochefs, you know."

"Do you serve native trout at the forgetaways?"

"We're opening lots of new ones, you know, in the less-developed world, to stimulate consumption . . . "

" . . . but the very *best* beefish I *ever* had was, I remember it like it was yesterday, at my aunt Martha's on my fifteenth birthday. I think she's dead now, but then again . . . I'll flap her up and tell you in a sec . . . "

Stewart was progressively distracted by a conversation going on to his left between a man and a woman enjoying a drink together at a table behind a low hedge. Their personal—even intimate—tone made Stewart feel that he was eavesdropping on a terribly private scene, one he had no right to overhear, but they spoke so loudly he couldn't help tuning in . . . She: "That's very flattering." He: "I mean it sincerely." She: "I find *you* very attractive too." He: "I'm sure we must have found each other very attractive on other occasions too." She: "You're probably right, but I don't keep a record of past occasions. Do *you* record who you sleep with at parties?" He: "Oh yes. And I rate them on a scale of one to ten." She: "Would you care to rate me tonight?" He: "Your room or mine?" She: "Tell me how you've rated me on previous occasions." He: "I'd be delighted. Could I get you a salad?" She: "Do you feel like dancing?" He: "I think we just did." She: "I think you're right, because I don't really feel like dancing." He: "I love dancing. Have you taken a stroll in the woods?" She: "I think so, but I can't be sure. Have you?" He: "Who knows, but don't they look terribly romantic?" She: "This is such a lovely park." He: "Can I get you a salad, an *hors-d'oeuvre*, a . . . "

Stewart felt a sneaking envy of the uninhibited inanities that passed for conversation between the pleasure-bent pair. Looking carefully around the plaza, he soon began to recognize by their faces and nametags, as they strolled along nearby lanes, several prominent Memini executives. It was he who had composed their bioprograms—over the course of the past ten years. And each BP had been painstakingly custom-tailored! (He remembered the care he'd taken to avoid episode duplication in a group as socially incestuous as this!) As he recognized now one, now another, remembering their most intimate "secrets," the stories they repeated to themselves or their friends to make bearable the burden of their leisure, he felt like a sort of god moving among creatures he had fashioned from clay—the stuff of his own starved lusts for love and power. The thought rattled his spine.

Among the people wandering about, one man in particular caught his eye. He seemed purposive and tense. Well-dressed in a fluffy, embroidered blouse that puffed out over his pants, he wove in and out among the tables with an unconvincing casualness. He kept circling one table in particular, a table at which a young blonde sat with a heavy-set, peppery-bearded man. Stewart noticed that on one of the man's wide-ranging loops around the plaza, he came up on him from behind, casting a sharp glance back over the shoulder at him—studying him, it seemed. The man's wolfish face and darting brown eyes instantly set off a siren somewhere in the recesses of Stewart's memory. So loud was the wail that Stewart shuddered even though he couldn't immediately place the man. He strained to read the nametag—exactly as the other fellow did in pausing to contemplate *him*. "Andy Peters"! So there was an actual person strutting behind the fiction! Someone parading around as the Andy Peters he had just finished programming—barely a week ago, in fact—into the love-life of one Helen Means. But this was no Andy *Peters*; this was Kedro . . . *Andy the Actor!*

He wished there were a button he could press, an alarm he could set off, a warning he could broadcast to everyone to take cover. Whoever had ushered him in had invited a jackal into a sheepfold. The most notorious fragbagger in Brooklyn! Anyone who grew up around the Flatbush staghetto knew at sight the most prominent organeers. What was the Actor doing so far from his usual hunting-grounds? He didn't need to come *here* to corral the anonymous kind of meat that fed the chophouses. He was scouting, clearly scouting . . . but for *whom*, for *what*? And why and how had Kedro linked himself—through a form of digital rape in which he too was implicated—to the private life of Helen Means? She was a woman (so far as one could know a woman through a study of her biotape) completely Kedro's opposite on any conceivable scale of human values.

The skin of Stewart's neck and shoulders bristled. It was as if he had spotted the serpent in the Garden! But even more chilling was his own unwitting involvement ... in some plot that surely went beyond the mere facilitation of rape. Was it pure coincidence that he, the professional Cupid, and the "lovers" he had lasered together, should be present at the same social gathering? Wasn't it far more likely that all three of them—he, Andy, and Helen—were simply puppets being used to further some slimy corporate scheme known only to Lester Barton—LB *III*?—and a few top cronies of his?

Stewart finished his Scotch in one toss. He needed another to help calm down. As if reading his mind, up rolled one of the circulating robars and asked him if he'd like "another of the same." Stewart nodded. Within seconds he was twirling a fresh drink in his shaking hand; the empty glass had been silently, efficiently removed.

"May I make a suggestion, Mr. Bridges?" said the robar.

"Sure. Go ahead."

"If you're looking for 'action,' I'd saunter over to the brunette seated alone two tables directly in front of you, and maybe ask her to dance."

Stewart laughed. "What makes you think she'd be interested?"

"I know. She told me."

"How very kind of you to inform me."

"You're very welcome, sir."

"I thought robars procured only drinks," said Stewart.

"Oh, on the contrary. We'll procure anything you program us to procure. In that respect you'll find us quite as flexible as yourselves."

"That's very comforting."

"Your comfort is our sole concern, sir. Mr. Barton would not want any of his guests to feel neglected."

The robar wheeled away. The interruption had managed to lighten Stewart's mood. Left undisturbed, he would have gone on painting paranoid pictures of some vague impending doom. But did he know, really, what motivated *anybody* here—apart from himself, of course? And wasn't it pious hypocrisy to worry about the intentions of a streethawk when his own motives for attending the party did not smell exactly of sachet? Should he warn Sibyl about Andy? But why should she believe him? Or perhaps she already knew. (She had *organized* this affair, hadn't she?) And wouldn't it be awkward for him if she knew he knew something he wasn't supposed to know? Stuff it! he decided. No point in yelling "Fire!" at sight of an unlit match.

16. A TORCH FOR THE GIRL WITH GOLDEN HAIR

Andy had his eye out for one woman and one woman alone. The place was crawling with class-ass jill that could make any pimp a fortune on the street. Women's eyes followed his Borgstein thigh-huggers as if he were modelling them on 3V. Jills slinked up to him and started conversations. These would get so hot and heavy he'd forget to keep his eye peeled on that table where she sat. Not alone, damn it, but with a bunch of bananas who were also on the company biggie board. What he needed was patience—the patience and alertness of a cat stretched out for a spring. He felt more like prey than hunter, though. Nipples slung in stringbags winked at him as he passed. A reddish bush grinned at him from under a clear-view body stocking. It took great determination for him to keep from being distracted from his purpose. Sooner or later she'd *have* to veer off by herself, he thought. Groups broke up, new ones formed, men and women occasionally paired off and wandered away to dance or eat or screw.

Not that it wouldn't be great just to forget that bitch and focus on these warm little buds here that were hardening right under his nose! But there'd be plenty of time to get a fingerful of redheaded "financial analyst" (she was just now stroking his elbow) or a wedge of that hot little African babe who'd mobbed him ten minutes earlier, feeling his thighs to see if they were padded. ("No, babe, my job keeps these legs stompin' sidewalk from morning till night... You wonder how hard these muscles can get, do you?... No, not now... Tonight? Sure... Your room? Fine.") In fact, when he thought about it, that fragass blonde was really beginning to piss him off, considering he could be getting himself laid in a variety of flavors if for the moment he'd just forget about Helen and sway with the play of the party.

Andy stood with his back to the Gene-Zene table, staring over his redhead's freckled shoulder. She was purring about taking a little trot with him off to the woods ("Have you read about Hansel and Gretel?" she asked) when finally there was a stir at Helen's table. Helen and another jill were on the verge of dumping a pair of middle-aged, prosperous-looking walruses. The men stood up, bowed, and plopped down again. Andy figured that the women were bored shitless and had made some excuse to cut loose and go prowling around for more stimulating male companionship. They were crossing diagonally in front of him, as if heading toward the restrooms down the hall behind the wall, when Helen's friend angled off toward the buffet.

At the next moment a brown-bearded man strode forward, practically on a run. Emerging from somewhere in the plaza, he seemed headed on a converging course with Helen. Andy was taking no chances. "So long, Momma," he said, practically shoving aside the redhead. He was several paces closer to Helen than the fellow charging from the left. She herself walked slowly, with a tantalizing grace, her swinging bottom hugged by a translucent, blue-green gown that showed off sleek expanses of shoulders, back, and legs. It was clear she wanted to be scooped up out of her trajectory before disappearing behind any wall. He homed in to the twitch of her hips like the latest in 'mone-sniffing bugbombs.

The other man plunged ahead too, but Andy reached her first. Slipping his hand around her waist, he crooned in a clownish, breathless voice that even in his own ears sounded idiotic—like something he'd heard on a dubbed-in Asian soap, "May I have the pleasure of the next dance, madame?"

"How come you knew I was interested in dancing?"

Of many lines of "his" that he remembered from her modified biotape, one sprang in timely fashion—more or less accurately—to his aid: "Your whole body is a dance, even when you're standing perfectly still. I cannot tell the dancer from the dance."

"You know Yeats?" she brightened.

"We probably met a few times," he hedged. He had spent hours studying her tape after Yolanda had returned it to him tucked inside the skirt-pouch of a little blonde ragdoll, but never once had he come across a section mentioning an acquaintance of hers of that name. "I'd have to flap him up for details."

She laughed a hearty laugh. The vision of her breasts bobbing over him wrenched at his stomach. So far so good. For some reason she thought he was funny. The genius who'd spliced him into her bio gave her a chipful of toasty scenes with him—all packed with debonair lines. He hoped he could remember more of his lines. He steered her to the left toward the dance floor. A quick glance over his shoulder showed him the bearded man trailing behind, a little too close for comfort. He didn't know him yet, but soon enough he would. That was for sure. Miss Yammy had given him "homework." An easy enough assignment...

"Look at my dress," she said, the light from the buffet still washing over her. "See anything different?"

"Different from what?"

"See? Warm greens. Yellow greens. Before, the greens were cool."

"Great dress!" he complimented, drawing her into the phosphorescent shadows.

"Know what that means, Andy boy?" She pulled him against her belly and began to sway with him in the languorous rhythms of the dance.

"What does it mean?" he gasped, his fingers lunging greedily over her ass. Did she recognize him? he wondered. Was she giving him another chance?

"You'll find out soon enough, silly baby," she said, pinching him on the butt.

"Does it occur to you we might be lovers?" he probed.

"I'm too busy to have many lovers. I have very little time for commitments like that. I much prefer casual acquaintanceship. Don't you?"

"That depends ... on the particular woman," he said, resting his cheek like an egg on her hair. His whole body was ablaze. He felt the pulse rising in his groin. It *hadn't* been his fault, then. There wasn't a damn thing wrong with him! he exulted. He pushed at her. She pressed back. A thrill a second coursed through Andy's blood.

"Mind if I cut in?"

"Get lost!" said Andy, nuzzling Helen's neck.

A determined finger poked at his shoulder. Andy swiveled his head, wondering who would have the *balls* to come up from behind and nag at him like that.

"Variety's the spice, you know." The man flashed a smile that hiked the ends of his bushy brown mustache. So it wasn't enough to lose the foot-race fair and square; the prick was trying to horn in on the prize!

"Listen, Mister," said Andy, "go take a flying..." The name taped to the man's jacket glowed bright blue; the tags were made to be easily read in the dark. LESTER BARTON, it said. *President.* Andy could already feel her slipping like an eel out of his arms.

"Can't you share me just a tiny bit? See you again in a teeny while. I promise," she said, tweaking his elbow. Her smile was brighter than ever, but her eyes were focused on Barton. Her fucking boss! *The* boss. Andy backed off reluctantly as the taller, heavier man wormed into his place. A teeny while! Translated into fragtime, that meant, "Don't hold your breath or you'll turn gray in the gills." His nostrils were full of her scent. Her hair still tickled his cheek. He was mellow. What the fuck! he thought. It was a small concession to make, but if it hadn't been her boss... Meanwhile, should he go for a drink or go for a piss? He'd feel better bumping belly if next time he had no bloated bladder to contend with. Andy wandered off into the hallway between the dance floor and the buffet. Glowing signs on the corridor walls said "Rec-rooms," "Health Club," "Wellness Center," "Pool," "Guest Rooms." He'd take a quick tour, a quick piss, and then come back to the rescue!

The first room down the corridor to his right opened onto a giant, brightly lit kitchen full of autochefs spinning and slicing. A double paneled door on the left side of the hall led into a rec-room where at one end there was an exerstable, in the middle a scattering of billiard and ping-pong tables, and at the far right a section devoted to trideo-games and low-lit 3V nooks. Approaching a 3V corner, he stumbled upon a hetero pair happily humping away on a sofa unmindful of his presence. Once back in the long, wide hallway, he wandered on down to the exit and out to the diving-board end of an Olympic-size pool fringed with lounge seats and palm trees. Two rows of big-windowed guest rooms faced the pool. As he had supposed, the numbered doors he had passed along the right side of the hallway were the back entrances to one of the poolside rows of guest rooms. He was now growing impatient to find a place to take a leak. He had walked by a couple of bathrooms in the corridor, but he didn't see any reason for turning back if he could slip into one of the poolside rooms. Going from one guest room door to another, he quickly hit upon one that had been left unlocked. The "rooms" were actually two-room *suites*! The spacious sitting room looked out on the pool. (The sheer *size* of things was getting to Andy. It was hard to keep in mind that this whole set-up he'd been wandering through was one man's "house"! What one man, no matter how big a big shot, needed such room? That fucking Barton—he had it all. Andy could fit practically his whole new apartment inside the sitting room alone of this "guest room" of which there were dozens facing each other across a pool as wide as a river in Barton's "house.") To the rear of the sitting room, the panels of an iris-shaped door slid apart at his approach, admitting him to a bedroom (almost as large as the damn sitting room!) full of mirrors and pillows and throwrugs—the shit you saw on the soaps!

The bathroom was to the right. (It was bigger than his own goddamn *bedroom*!) It had fancy old gold-colored knobs and a sauna and a hot-tub and shower and sunken bath, and an automasseur and a love-gel dispenser (in flavors for several sexes) and a built-in booze servo too! Everything cried out for his admiration, but there was a limit to the amount of praise he could lavish upon it all, so after offering his heartfelt tribute to virtually everything else in the room, he wound up barely able to shower enough attention upon the elegant and much-deserving toilet bowl, whose satin-lined seat he managed to grace, nevertheless, with a final gush of warm appreciation.

Having relieved himself to his heart's content, he was ready to trot back to the dance floor. The bedroom door led back into the hallway. He turned to the left, and in half a minute he was crossing the dance floor again.

Helen was nowhere to be seen. Wandering around in a daze, by chance he looked into one of the sheik-chic lean-tos lining the perimeter of the floor. There she lay, dress hiked up, Barton's hand fumbling between her legs, his face glued to hers on top of some cushions under the glow of a hanging oil lamp. Andy watched, paralyzed with resentment, knowing that *he* belonged there, not that ball-busting Barton who owned every fucking thing else in the place.

It took only seconds for him to figure out what to do. He slipped behind the glowing tent, opened a lightknife he always carried with him, and lased a slit in the fabric behind the lamp. Thrusting his hand through the opening, he lifted the lamp from where it was suspended and tossed it upside down beside the lovers.

The effect was instantaneous. There was a shriek and a blaze of flame. Andy circled around front, where all hell had broken loose. Barton kept whacking a cushion against the burning tent carpet—with no apparent success. Out of nowhere, it seemed, a robar fire-fighter hove into view. "No need to panic," it declared in an oily, cocksure tone. "We'll have this out in no time." Helen had scrambled bareback out of the tent and now stood yanking her dress back down. If only her ass had got singed a little! thought Andy. Suddenly she caught sight of him. She looked at him as if she knew... With a bitter-sweet feeling, Andy hurried away toward the rec-room. He'd give her a little time to forget having seen him. (Perhaps she was one of those frags who could develop powerful emotional reactions to people they otherwise didn't remember—and for reasons they couldn't explain.) The next time around, the hell with all your fragbrained good manners, all this after-you-Gascoyne shit! It was no different here than in the streets, he thought. You had to stiff *any* bastard who busted your ass. Didn't matter *who* the fuck it was!

17. SUMMONED FROM THE LEGS OF LOVE

"Are you all right, LB?"

He was distracted from watching the tent-blaze that an alert robar was squirting to extinction. It was Avery Tingworth—or, rather, his chem teacher Mophead Mishkin—who was expressing this hypocritical concern for his well-being. He tidied up his jacket and gave Tingworth/Mishkin a scornful nod (let him make of it what he would!). Having meminized his last "monthly" Executive Council proceedings, he knew that Mishkin's premature announcement of the development of the Perfect Pill was calculated to further embarrass him in the eyes of the rest of the Council. Mishkin's point had been to stress that such a scientific achievement in Borneo was incompatible with Memini simultaneously raising hell with DUSA. A Board of Ed plant, Mishkin had tried to force him into showing all his cards. Mophead was out to ruin his game-plan—but Mophead could not even have guessed what that plan was: a carefully cultivated strategy whose goal was nothing less than the preservation of the Memini conglobulate *against imminent danger from within*.

On second thought, it was probably Mishkin himself who had thought of using the Perfect Pill as the major challenge to his leadership abilities. Old Mophead had probably thought he could slip it right by him—a threat not only to Memini itself, but to the entire *teknonomy*, of which he, in his game-role as Lester Barton, Memini CEO, was the sworn champion and only possible defender. And now his enemies saw that he was on to them, and they were doing all they could to outmaneuver him.

What a relief it would be if there were someone he could open his mind and heart to—without fear of betrayal of his confidences, of course.

But there *was* such a one. The only human being he could trust was Iris Morgan. A "plant" by the Board? Yes. But unbeknown to them (how could they know that they had been lovers?), she was the only member of the Council who wanted to *help* him. Was she aware of who his (badly disguised) enemies were? If not, then tonight he'd wise her up.

He watched her as she swiftly recovered her poise. Tugging with alternate hands, she coaxed her hiked-up dress back down her thighs. Dim lights in changing colors played over her heaving chest and whirled in a ghostly rainbow over the faces of dancers who had scurried over to see what all the flaming fuss was about. Mishkin, of all people—Mishkin it was who now laid a fat comforting paw over Iris/Helen's trembling shoulders. What right had that bag of guts to step in and—

"Mr. Barton, sir? I have an urgent message for you, sir!" The robar who had sidled up to him was polite but insistent.

"Spit it out quick, Rob! I have no time to waste."

"You are wanted back in your library, sir . . . Your office?"

"Well, whoever the hell's in my office can damn well wait!"

"Oh, I don't think so in this case, sir. The entity that wishes to confer with you, sir, is Meminet."

"Meminet! Now why the hell would Meminet—?" For the first time, now, he had direct evidence that *his relationship with Iris* had come to the attention of his enemies and that they were *attempting to keep them apart*! Not only that, they were somehow able to use Meminet to further their scheme. "Listen! Tell Meminet to go back to bed. This is a party. Meminet has no right to pull me away from my own goddamn—"

"Sir," said the robar, "Meminet would not *dare* interfere with your well-deserved leisure pursuits unless the matter on which you are summoned were *extremely* urgent."

He knew, of course, that the voice of the robar was the filtered voice of Meminet—and he wasn't going to stand here and have a showdown with Meminet through a robar! Better cut through this crap directly, face to blank face. "Okay, Rob, okay. Relay that I'm coming . . . I'm sorry," he said, turning to Iris/Helen and cutting into her conversation with Mishkin. "I've got an emergency business call. I'm sure I won't be more than a few minutes." He tossed her a worried look. Did she understand his feelings?

He wished he had the power to freeze her in place, to glue her to that spot on the floor until he got back.

"Don't rush on my account, LB. Avery here will take good care of me meanwhile," she said, tickling Mophead's salt-and-pepper whiskers.

He did not like her familiarity with an enemy of his, especially with the one who may have personally engineered this interruption, but still he had to admire her cleverness—attempting to disguise her intimacy with *him* by appearing super-chummy with Mophead. What *did* they know about himself and Iris? he wondered. Probably they knew nothing, only suspected.

"If you wish," said the robar, "you may follow behind me, sir."

"If you could *wiggle* your behind, I'd follow you to the ends of the earth," he grunted in reply.

"A very good joke, Mr. Barton. Ha ha! This way, please."

If it had been any other "entity" demanding to talk business with him just then, he would have shrugged it/him off with a few well-chosen words. (Hadn't he been gracefully avoiding extended business chatter all evening? He assumed so. With Iris on his mind, he was sure of it.) But to receive a summons from Meminet . . . clearly, he could not afford to exhibit an excess of "temperament." Whatever those who used Meminet were out to prove against him, a show of open disrespect on his part could easily strengthen their suspicions. His enemies must clearly be worried, however, about their inability to control him! he thought. Otherwise, why would they go to this vicious extreme? The company brainbox was something that was *consulted*; since when did *it* take the initiative and consult personnel? He would make a *point*, then, of confronting Meminet at the appropriate moment with his own strong suspicion that Meminet was being used against him. What clearer proof could he have? First, a tent-fire at a strategically chosen moment; next, by way of follow-up, the imperious, unignorable summons.

Lester realized that he must quickly enter a Periodic-Recall note—on one-minute interval playback—to be able to back up his accusation in the face of Meminet denials. "Two things have occurred in quick succession," he voiced into flapper, "revealing the collusion of my enemies to interfere with me on the level of my private life—since they are unable to successfully subvert me in any other way, it seems. I have just been hit with a one-two punch designed to separate me from socializing with Helen Means. This double whammy—"

"I trust, sir," said the robar, slowing up, hanging back, *spying* on what he was entering into flapper, "your conference with Meminet will not last very long. I understand how you feel about the precious little leisure time you have. Fortunately, the night is still relatively young, and you—"

"Quit chatting, Rob, will you?"

"Sorry, sir."

He brought his flapper back to his lips as they approached the unmarked door to his office on the lefthand side of the hall before the rec-room. Keeping his voice as low as he could, he said, resuming, "I've been hit with a cheap double whammy . . . A cheap double whammy," he repeated, then stopped, wondering what it was that was supposed to go next. "Goddamn robar!" he muttered as the panels to his office slid apart.

Then suddenly he *knew* why Meminet was on his ass. It was the commando-raid he had engineered in Borneo. Meminet was going to report to him the "disaster" of their leading scientists' deaths sustained in the crossfire between his own squad of "liberators" and the DUSAn occupiers—so that he could finally get the blight-cure going and beam down the power and *come out the winner*—with Mishkin and Company *defeated* in their plan to discredit his leadership abilities in the eyes of the Board of Education!

18. CHICKEN BREASTS AND EXECUTIVE THIGHS

Stewart munched away at his Rabchick Royale, looking up to sip Scotch and to stare at the brunette who had placed an order with the robar for a nibble of his own living flesh. Two tables ahead of him and facing him in three-quarter view, she appeared for a while not to notice him. Her dark hair looped upward from her long, pale neck into a crazy, swirling bird's nest above her ears. She had that cut-glass, anemic profile of those disdainful, aristocratic women (the idols of all the staglets he'd ever dated) whose every thought from morning till night is of hot, impersonal sex. Just beyond her, framing her face, rose a Grecian balustrade half-choked with ivy. From a pedestal at her back rose a life-size copy of a Venus de Milo with arms, languidly dispensing the promise of lust *in excelsis.*

He was in no hurry, he thought, as the woman's eyes found his, then as quickly fluttered away. He wanted to bide his time, to devote to each pleasure the undivided attention it deserved (the exquisite fare, the rare Scotch)—but above all he hoped for a golden surprise: a dusky bronze smile slipping quietly into view out of all this circumambient dazzle. How long could it be, he wondered, before Sibyl quit the reception desk? . . . Perhaps he was being too fastidious, given other "golden" opportunities in the offing, but Sibyl held a special fascination for him. Always she seemed to be hinting at a personal interest in *him*. But that could be pure fantasy, he cautioned himself. He must not let himself be governed by wishful thinking . . . thinking that could lead to an empty bed! He had come here to gather rosebuds, not for one perfect rose. These women would as likely remember him as buttercups remembered the bees they laced with pollen. He had to stand guard, constantly, against *anthropomorphizing* these beautiful vacancies: they are not human: therefore, no danger. Guided by his intact oldfolks brain, he enjoyed an inestimable tactical advantage over any DIM-wit tekkie whatsoever.

It was time to move. He had already learned all that he could from where he was seated. Things that he saw made a pattern with things that he heard. Among the strollers in the plaza he recognized the same individuals over and over—circling around repeatedly with looks of bliss on their faces. He had never been at a social gathering of so many tekkies at once. Their wanderings were like something out of Dante. He had not thought that the Pill had undone so many...

Fortunately, there was always an alert robar around to divert the circling strollers from the monotony of their orbit. The servo would politely roll up alongside them, engage them in a bit of conversation, then lead them away to spin their wheels in some other part of the grounds. No one was forgotten or for long left unattended. Could anyone take a single step that went ignored? he wondered. It finally dawned on Stewart that the robars not only *recorded* the movements of every guest, in that sense acting as spies, but that they *guided* these movements as well—by means of some intricately programmed choreography insuring that no one would get lost indefinitely in any one behavioral loop. The robars poured you drinks, led you to bathrooms, suggested likely playmates. In short, they were the perfect host. The perfect host naturally *had* to be an all-seeing eye.

Where *was* the host? Stewart wondered. He was sure he would recognize Barton as soon as he saw him. So far, though (apart from a number of former clients), he had recognized only Kedro. The circlings of "Andy Peters" were far from neurological automatisms. At the moment, Andy was *leaving* the plaza. He trailed discreetly behind the blonde (whom Stewart supposed to be Helen Means) as she meandered off to the woods holding the arm of her grizzly-bearded table companion. Stewart was by now extremely curious about those groves to which so many couples seemed attracted (or directed). It looked terribly romantic to stroll off with some slinky companion into those woods that seemed so "lovely, dark and deep." It was time to pick up on that matchmaking robar's suggestion and introduce himself to the brunette beneath the Venus, which loomed above her like some tutelary deity.

At his approach she looked up as if expecting him (the failure to look surprised was a tekkie art-form).

"Hello," he said. "Jackie? I don't think we've met before."

"That's marvelous! That's a brand-new opener, Stewart. The rest of us *act* as if we're all old friends, which probably we are, even though we don't usually *know* each other from Adam . . . Anyway, I like your inventiveness. B.P.ers have that in spades, don't they? I find that terribly exciting." Her lips pursed up at him with an amused, ironical twist.

Her tag read "Jackie Tiller, Dir. Psnl. Svcs." Why not gamble on a scrap of throwaway wit? "I see by your nametag that you're a provider of Direct Personal Services."

"To a man like you? Quite possibly. Do sit down."

She played the *femme-fatale* with aplomb. He could see that she wanted him—wanted him to sweep her off into the dark without delay. "We've been warming chairs with our backsides long enough, don't you think?"

"God did make them for better purposes," she agreed. "Do you have any suggestions?"

"Care to join me for a stroll through those dangerous-looking woods?"

"Love to. But you must promise to protect me. Against wild animals who lie in wait specifically for defenseless damsels like myself."

"There's only one wild animal in there," said Stewart. "A wolf."

"Ah, the wolf that Little Red Riding Hood devoured after tricking the poor thing into bed? And do you deny that you are that very same edible wolf?" When Jackie stood up, the crisscrossing ribbons of her clinging black dress etched X's into the cones of her breasts. Stewart saw his lips playing hopscotch among the lozenges traced in her flesh. She took his arm, pressing it to her side, and rode his hip as they ambled off toward the moonbeams. Her hair smelled like Arabian gardens, or like making love among joss sticks in a chamber piled high with hand-made Persian rugs—memories he had made up for others out of midnight cravings of his own. Enjoying the lust she inspired, luxuriating in the unmixed purity of the emotion, Stewart brimmed over with self-confidence. This perfect stranger, Jackie, would unlock the door through which he would step out of the past and enter the autonomous present.

The woods were a world to themselves. The paths that wound among clumps of trees were padded with grass of a ghostly blue sheen as if glowing under the light of a full moon. Overhead was the quaver of leaves against sky, a tracery of black against indigo. Was the canopy of the night the real thing? One would have to hurl up a stone to find out. Now and again, from among the trees, rose rustling sounds, trails of tinkly laughter, indecipherable passionate murmurs. He stopped to listen. Jackie squeezed his arm, tongued his ear. It tickled, they both laughed, and they stumbled several paces ahead to where their path gave on to a clearing. At a bandstand across the clearing a group of naked musicians, painted like candy-canes, played soft music as couples danced arrhythmically, pelvis to pelvis, hands groping beneath loose-fitting garments in full view of the writhing polysaxists. But this was the same group, Stewart noticed, that had just been playing on the other dance floor on the opposite side of the plaza.

"Dance?" said Jackie.

He drew her next to the bandstand, where the saxist was enjoying a tiny break between numbers. "Tired?" Stewart asked him.

"Me?" the musician smiled. "That's kind of impossible, sir, but I appreciate the joke."

Stewart swung a punch at the man's face, and just as he thought, his fist met nothing but air.

"Would you like us to play something special for you two?" asked the musician.

"Yes. 'Timeless Love,'" said Jackie.

"'Timeless Love' it is! Dedicated to Jackie and Stewart," he said, wailing a few wiggly introductory bars.

"You look a little surprised," said Jackie.

"Life-size interactive virtual! The boss is sparing no expense."

"Do you find interactive so special?" said Jackie, running her hands over his shoulders and pecs.

"I grew up on the other side of the bridge," said Stewart, cupping Jackie's backside as the first sweet chords of "Timeless Love" blew harmonically out of the triple-throated sax.

"You're lucky you managed to cross over," she answered, her hand inside his pants, in the cleft of his buttocks. "Most who try it have to pay a terrible toll."

"You see that couple to our right?" said Stewart, toying with his partner's stiffened nipples. "She's got her dress hiked up over her hips. Her backside is bare and her friend is diddling her with a full three fingers—right under the eyes of all the musicians."

"Would you like me to do that? That'd be fun," said Jackie, hooking fingers beneath her half-thigh hem, her other hand still wedged between his cheeks.

"Oh no!" said Stewart. "I mention it because that's how I figured that this was a virtual. Still, you've got to be weird to flick your fanny before an *interactive* virtual."

"I don't see why, if that's what flips your switch. You sound so puritanical, darling! Is that what makes your fingers so divinely . . . inquisitory?"

Stewart pinched her nipple, deliberately hard. He did not want to seem in the least "puritanical." She shrieked half with pleasure and half with pain. "Be gentle," she whimpered, laughing with tears in her eyes. "You're making me very hot. Where can we go?" They both seemed to discover at once a large sign posted at the edge of the clearing. A blue-glowing arrow pointed into the trees. It pierced a large red heart above which red letters flashed three words: "To Cupid's Corners." All this money spent just to imitate the taste of some Disneyland whorehouse! thought Stewart.

Their number was drawing to a close. The hand that had been in his pants now tugged at his arm, drawing him into the path indicated by the arrow. The resistance he offered was slight, but for a moment he looked furtively around to see if a girl in gold might be standing near, witnessing. The thought of her made him feel slightly ashamed; he had to shut Sibyl—at least temporarily—out of his mind. He knew that if he was to get it on with *anyone* at the party, he must take what she offered *when* it was offered. (Sibyl's own suggestion!) Her promise to meet him later was probably sincere when she made it, but what could come of it if ten minutes later she couldn't possibly recall it? That was how it had been with Trudy . . . but he had promised himself, hadn't he, that through the divine body of Jackie he would exit that chamber of ghosts?

Clipping each other's waists, they advanced along the path that promised them a cozy "corner" to themselves. They had hardly taken half a dozen steps when stopped by moans and grunts from their left. Curious,

Stewart peeked through a clump of birches. On the grass, in the dappled pseudomoonlight, bare butts thrashed beside a tree-stump saddled with carefully folded clothing.

"I guess they don't need much privacy," said Stewart, inviting Jackie to look.

"Why do you speak of privacy?"

"I don't know. Is there anything wrong with privacy?"

"You don't need privacy unless you feel shame. And you don't feel shame if there are absolutely no consequences to what you do." As she bent forward to peer through the trees, she urged his hand between the webbing of her dress into the wetness between her cheeks, steadying it in the vise of her thighs as he gently worked inward. All the wisdom of what she had said to him came alive in his furrowing fingers. She flung herself shuddering to his chest, then pulled him farther along into the mottled dark.

Stewart stopped short and looked to the right, distracted by shrill cries ... which were followed by squeals of delight. A few paces in among the trees he could make out a woman strapped face forward to a giant oak. Her outflung arms and spread-eagled legs clasped the bark in a close embrace. Defying gravity, her body clung to the tree by means of manacles at her wrists and her knees. A fat man whipped her with a branch and she shrieked. The next instant the lover began thrusting himself against her, belly into bum, and she lolled her head back and uttered a moan that rose and fell through *octaves*! Even in the "moonlight" her hair looked blonde. Their clothes lay neatly draped on the grass to their right.

Stewart stood and stared. As Jackie urged him forward, he suddenly sensed a slyly lingering presence close beside him. A shadowy figure stood motionless against the tree-trunk to his right. A voyeur, it seemed, who had positioned himself to see but not be seen. Stewart peered at the figure more closely.

It was Andy the Actor.

But who, exactly, was he spying on? Helen? Stewart got the creepy feeling that Andy had been trailing *them*, not Helen, that he had quietly stopped near the tree when *they* had stopped. That would make no sense at all, of course ... but when Stewart glanced at him a second time, he caught a glint of moonlight from deep-socketed eyes—eyes that were trained on *him*. He shivered. A hand drew him onward with gentle insistence. He followed submissively down the velvet chiaroscuro of Lover's Lane. For the moment, at least, Andy remained motionlessly in place against the tree.

"This looks perfect, doesn't it?" Jackie drew him into a cluster of evergreens. A dimly glowing sign fixed to one of the trees read "Bower of Bliss" in pseudo-Gothic letters. The trees enclosed a moon-speckled nest of thick, spongy grass. "Anything the matter?" she said. "Is little Stewie afwaid to sit on the gwass?"

"No. It's just that I think I'm—that we're being followed."

"Some people get their kicks that way. I don't mind. Why should you?" She pulled his hips to her and rotated her belly upon him.

"I guess I don't mind," he said. His hands slipped from her slender waist down the splendid bulges behind. If he didn't slow things down a little, he would explode right then and there. "Tell me something, Jackie. You're the head of Personnel. Is there anyone in the Retirement Section named Andy Peters?"

"No," she said flatly. "Relax, darling. Won't you sit down?"

He sank to his knees. "How can you be sure?" he persisted.

"Because I *meminize* our constantly changing employee list, naturally. As of last count, we had 17,831 warm bodies worldwide. Right now, however, there's only one warm body that concerns me."

"Ditto," said Stewart. He eased himself down beside her and reflectively fingered her breasts. And yet a nagging thought obsessed him—that Andy hovered somewhere near. He didn't want to talk business, but . . . maybe he could make her think his strangeness part of a protracted tease. "But could you possibly be mistaken, Jackie? Look, I don't mean to be weird, but the information is very important to me . . . "

"Don't stop. I love that . . . Yes, I know, sweetheart, it's very important to you. No, the only way I could be in error (oh, you naughty!) is if there was a hire that wasn't (nnng!) that wasn't reported to me—like one that might have happened very recently that I still haven't plugged into the net."

"How soon could you check?" He redoubled his stroking and teasing, sucked at her bullet-tipped breasts. The bands that strapped them stretched apart to permit him free range. Her fingers plowed his hair.

"Right now, of course. By just flapping into the net for an update. But can't my stalwart Stewart *wait* for—"

"Will you do that for me? Now?" he urged, rising for air.

"Will you let me do anything *I* want in return?"

"How could I refuse?" He sucked in his breath as her hand briefly molded to the landscape of his lap.

She lifted her flapsack to her lips, pressed a button on the case, and voiced in, "Andy Peters, Retirement Section... Damn!" she exclaimed. "Of all things, he's chief of the section. Now how could *that* have... Oh fuck it. I'll look into it later. Now, you promised me! So do as I say. Lie down. All the way down. That's right. You're such a good little boy..." As he tried to make sense of what she had told him, she unzipped him and slipped his pants and filmy briefs down to his knees. "Impatient little darling, isn't he?... Naughty boy, quivering at me like that! Don't you know you shouldn't point?..."

Stewart's body proceeded to function on a wavelength totally different from his mind's. His brow prickled with a sense of looming danger. Andy the Actor a Memini officer? Perfect cover! But for what? The System was using streetscum—in some "surgical operation," no doubt—as its primary tool. *Tool*! he thought. He was reduced to an implement in her hands. He flapped against fingers that were cool and that ended in long, elegant, black-striped nails. He felt defenseless, passive; a writhing worm in the beak of a soaring bird. What connection could there be between Andy Kedro and himself? His mind afforded no answers as she massaged him, rolling him around her silky neck, into the hollows under aristocratic cheekbones. He himself was here for a very clear reason. He forced himself to remember. He was a leading candidate—*the* leading candidate?—for a top executive..."

"Jackie," he said, his voice half-strangled with the pleasure she gave, "could you answer me one more question?"

"Shoot!" she replied, suddenly sinking her teeth into his glans.

The thrill of the bite lifted his butt off the ground. No, he was *not* trying to withdraw from the door she had opened.

"Question?" she said, working his scrotum in her hand like a pair of Chinese exercise balls.

"Who's currently... in the position," he gasped, "of Vice President of

New Products Development?"

Her mouth slid down thoughtfully over the length of his penis, then slowly squeezed back up as she carefully formulated a reply. Locking his knees between hers, she arched her slim body and stripped her dress cleanly over her head. "*I get it!*" she laughed. "Is that what you do . . . to prevent premature ejaculation? You try to hold it in by asking pointless, stupid questions?" He nodded. In part, it was true. She shook her head at him, playing him like a flautist with her fingers. "Well, as if you didn't know, little dear, there *is* no such position. Are you so interested in new positions? Well, this one isn't exactly new, but it's an old favorite of mine, and it's tried and true . . . Does this soothe the place where Mommy bit you?" She teased him, holding him down as she rubbed wet fur against him.

"It's a newly *created* position, isn't it?"

"It never existed. It's neither old nor new. Now *this* position, sweetie . . . is old, but I'll make it *feel* brand-new."

She sank down on him like a warm winter hat, and his butt arched up to meet her, his flesh leaping out of control. Impersonally now, he pictured himself as an animal thrashing in a trap, a creature about to be humiliatingly sacrificed, in the height of orgasm, by a hired killer, for the reason (as his mother had pointed out) that he *knew too much*! . . . Miraculously, however, he was being allowed to finish *coming*, at least! No blow had struck him, nor had Jackie chewed his head off as he rolled up on top of her in the grass. He was being allowed to expire upon her, to rock himself into semiconsciousness . . . a reprieve. So how could he even think of danger while his veins were distended with pleasure, while cool milkmaid hands continued to grip his buns . . . and while the strange mouth still tasted so good and this strange woman's breasts continued to float him so high above the earth, so far out of reach of the past?

His impending death would matter to him *soon*, no doubt, but not right now. And "now" seemed to stretch out for as long as he wanted, so yieldingly elastic was that now of his, as pliable as the nest between these moon-washed thighs that would keep him safe for as long as he stayed inside.

19. MURDER IN BERLIN

When Andy located her, it was already too late. It wasn't Lester Barton who was about to fuck her; it was some gray-bearded, balding, fat-gutted bastard—one of the men she'd been seated with earlier, out on the plaza (*Tingworth, Avery . . . pharmaceuticals*, he remembered). Her ass was literally up a tree which her naked limbs, supported by stirrups and handcuffs, wrapped in a bear-like embrace. Dim as the light in this pleasure-grove was, he recognized her right away. He knew her by her blue-glowing hair even before she swung her head around to urge her partner to use the whip that dangled from his hand. Andy watched as the man thrashed timidly at her moon-bright butt. Meanwhile, chubby's free hand yanked and slapped at an incredibly half-limp dick! As Helen emitted fake squeals of pleasure-pain, her partner finally got his blunderbuss raised for a desperate charge into the breach.

Andy's whole body stiffened. Rutting bitch! he thought. She'd make it with a dog if nothing else was handy when she wanted it. Why should he even *care* about the party habits of that goddamn loose-legged slut? Andy watched with fascination as flabby-ass hauled his dong closer to the tree, still whacking it furiously though only inches from the goal. Struggling with emotions between revulsion and tears, Andy decided to step out of hiding and give Tingworth a big surprise—a swift kick in the ass—when a hetero pair drew up nearby and robbed him of his resolve. By the time they were gone, intervention was out of the question, and events were proceeding at a solemn and curiously elephantine pace, a slow-motion of thrust and grunt that twisted knot after rhythmic knot in Andy's intestines.

The bitch was *enjoying* it! He imagined the corrugated tree-bark chiseling grooves into her whorish stomach. Choking with rage, Andy cast about for something he could do. The beast with two backs had laid their clothes at the edge of the circle of grass. How could he have ever lusted after *that*? he wondered. A red-assed monkey that would rather ball a rhino when she could have had a gorilla like himself! Within seconds he was hunched down behind a tree two feet from their clothing. As belly slapped bum only two yards away, Andy reached out to Tingworth's garments, felt for the clown's belt-pouch, unsnapped it and slid out his flapper. In the dark behind the tree he plucked out Tingworth's cassette with a movement like gouging an eye. He tried to break it with his fingers, but it was far too tough, so he half unzipped his own flapsack and stuffed it in next to Yolanda's voodoo doll. He would dispose of the cartridge in the next toilet he came to.

Meanwhile, to guarantee that Tingworth would be thoroughly disoriented, Andy restored the gutted flapper to its leatherene holster, even zipping the pouch shut, so that the victim would suspect nothing for as long as possible—maybe ten, fifteen minutes. After that, without an ID advisory, Tingworth would be clawing the air, running in circles with his eyes bulging out of his head and his blood pressure up to four hundred. It would be lots of fun to watch . . . Hell, he thought, why not do the same, once again, to that blonde twinkie's flapper? Again he reached out—then retracted his hand. Not out of fear of being detected (the grunting and moaning had begun to subside by then), but because that cassette of hers might be the only surviving record of her intense, year-long "affair" with one "Andy Peters." Now why the hell should *that* matter anymore? he asked himself.

Andy peeked in at the magic circle again. Huffing and puffing, Tingworth was already undoing the shackles that held Helen's spreadeagled legs in place. Crawling back from the edge of the circle, Andy sprang to his feet and wound his way back to the plaza. He knew he might be crediting her with too much memory, but what if she had somehow managed to connect him—unconsciously—with that little lantern fire of a while ago? If that bitch had even a wisp of good old limbic tissue left, he'd better be out of view when she emerged from the woods towing a flailing, hysterical blimp along by the hand. All he had done, of course, was pull the same old cheap sort of prank he used to have so much fun playing as a kid. Ordinarily, when he played such games now it was strictly in the line of business. Though he always enjoyed the spectacle of a flapperless frag, for the moment he thought he would drop out of sight—in the rec-room he had discovered on his earlier cautionary flight. Not too fast! he told himself as he crossed the plaza and skirted the buffet area to the corridor that led to the rec-room. He knew that the robars here were very special—alert to the smallest movement that was in any way unusual—and that they roved about unceasingly and recorded everything in range, every conversation, every gesture, every smile or frown.

Andy eased himself down into a black leather sofa in front of a 3V unit that took up half the wall. A couple of geezers behind him (Frisch and Wortham, he remembered) who apparently had no interest in food, booze, or women, were engrossed in a game of pool. Farther off, a man and a woman were playing pingpong. Andy realized he was breathing erratically. His eyes stung him so badly that he clamped them shut and wiped away tears that leaked out at the edges.

He tapped at the 3V remote in the chair-arm until "There's a Crime in Progress" leaped into view. He watched through blurry eyes that slowly cleared. He saw a man dressed as a waiter accompanied by a robar that toted a bucket of champagne. Man and robar were lumbering up to the front entrance of a motel—

"—or *Freudenpalast*, as the Germans call this type of luxury trysting-place for lovers, folks. Yes, you already know we're in Berlin, or rather that Hans Rodek, as he wishes to be called, is directly on camera as we bring you these fast-developing events from a vantage point not too far away from the scene of the crime-to-be.

"We have tried to dissuade Hans from killing his wife and her lover, but clearly revenge has become this anguished man's only reason for living. (And here we must remind you again, folks, of the many crimes that *would* have taken place if not for the fact that, time and again, we've managed, behind the scenes, to talk many would-be criminals out of committing them!) To remind you of Hans's diabolical scheme, he has managed to cancel the lovers' usual order for bubbly and a wee-hours gourmet dinner from a restaurant nearby. He is doing the 'honors' *himself*... in the 'dead' hours of this cool June night in Berlin.

"Did I say 'the honors,' folks? His robar packs a spritzer loaded with hydrochloric acid. He wants the whole world to see those two writhe in pain and burn before he blazers them out of their misery—*and then puts an end to himself* with the very same weapon."

The camera showed Hans from behind now, slouching beside his robar past the front desk, where the clerk, used to such early-morning celebrations, nodded him through out of half-closed eyes focused blearily on a 3V in which *a waiter slouched past a motel clerk who was unwittingly watching himself on 3V* . . . "That's *you*, fuckhead!" Andy said aloud. In a way, of course, he was glad the clerk had failed to interfere. Suspense heightened as a differently placed eye followed waiter and robar to an elevator door.

"Now, to remind all our billions of viewers, just ten minutes ago we voted and then transmitted the results to Hans via his skeeter. *For* the double murder: 176,941,882. *Against* the double murder: 159,866,403. For killing only the *wife*, who he says has played him dirty for two full years now: 199,846,311. For killing only the *lover*, a young man she works with and seems to've seduced: 135 million . . . " Andy watched the puffy-faced waiter in the elevator as he poured himself a drink from the already popped bottle of (close-up:) Moët. The shot was from an eye apparently stuck above the elevator door. Hans himself had probably tagged a bunch of eyes in strategic locations all along his well-planned route.

"A last vote, folks," said the 3V host. "You've got five seconds to press YES or NO. Should Hans Rodek take *his own life as well*, or not? . . . " Andy jammed the YES button on the remote three times. A message flashed across the top of the screen: VOTE INVALID. ONLY ONE VOTE PERMITTED PER TERMINAL. "Fuck you," said Andy, waving his hand in disgust. "The tally, folks, is overwhelmingly YES: 243 million . . . "

Andy's mind rushed ahead of events. He could already see Hans push through the door into the bedroom. There, on a rotating bed, under a ceiling that was all mirror, he—Hans/Andy—could see Helen poised on top ramming her ass down on a giant slug-like quivering belly below. Focusing back on the set, Andy now watched Hans and the robar as they sauntered out of the elevator and turned left down the long carpeted corridor. The robar seemed to be in the lead; pasty-faced Hans seemed to follow as if drawn by a string.

MEMINI

"And now, all you viewers, who already know we're in Berlin, we can tell you, by agreement with the pseudonymous Hans Rodek, that we are in the *Wilmersdorf* section of the city—specifically, on a small street just off... *Brandenburgische Strasse*... so if, by chance, the lovers, who even now may be curled up cozily in each other's arms—if these lovers, who in a few seconds may die a most horrible death, folks—if this promiscuous pair just *happen* to be watching 3V... tuned in, of course, specifically to Yours Truly, well..."

Where the hell was she now? The thought rang in his head like a gong. *Who would she be fucking NEXT?* He would *teach* that cornsilk pussy that you can't shake it at Andy without losing a fistful of angel-hairs! If she wasn't a total *baccalà*, she'd be hoofing it back to her guest-room as soon as she could for a shower or at least a douche on the bidet before tightening any new pair of nuts tonight...

"...*horrible*, folks. The acid! Right into his wide-open eyes! And now he's waving the nozzle at his wife who's cowering terrified..."

Trailed by juicy screams from the 3V, Andy scrambled out of his seat and headed for the corridor. He had hoped it would not have to come down to the use of brute force (your run-of-the-mill street jill would bend ass-backwards to get her crack at Andy the Actor), but if he had to drag her off into some isolated corner and *make* her tune in to *her own damn tape* (much enriched by the inclusion of Andy Peters), then that was what he'd have to do. How could she spurn him after playing, in his presence, just a few of those steaming-hot love-scenes of theirs? The VR realism had given him the chills—the way they went at it, whether in "his" apartment, or at a graphics conference in Hungary, or in her own house when, with her husband busy cooking sausages out on the lawn, he was in the back bedroom stuffing Helen's buns with salami. Shit! It was hard even for *him* not to believe all this had happened!

Crowds of such memory-images flitted through Andy's brain, as real as the most vivid of dreams, plucking dark music on the cords of his nerves, music to which *she too* could hardly be deaf. The dissonant jangle of those other images—of her dress hiked up under a tent, or her gleaming ass strapped to an oak—threatened to strangle the wild music that played in his oldfolks, limbically intact brain, but Andy knew he could have *prevent-*

ed all that bullshit if (#1) he'd refused to hand her over to her pushy boss, or if (#2) he'd kept close watch on her movements after the tent-fire. That fire did it! he thought. Must have zapped her head so bad that in the woods *she did not even know what she was doing.* He'd singed *his own ass* with that fire! he thought.

Following his hunch, Andy turned left down the hallway toward the pool again. Her room number was *eight*! he remembered. It leaped right to the top of his flapperless brain. Organic had its good points—no question about it. He tried sauntering nonchalantly down the hall, to avoid giving the appearance of hurry, for there was a robar on patrol, sitting quietly near the entrance to the pool.

"Good evening, Mr. Kedro," it greeted him as the panels slid back to admit him.

There was another robar at poolside. Here, at the deep end, where she was swimming.

It moved along the edges of the pool. Sliding back and forth.

Keeping her in sight as she breaststroked slowly and peacefully in the deep water under the diving board in green-tinted bare-assed glory except for a yellow bathing cap.

Beside the pool there lay nothing of hers but a white terry robe she had tossed over a lounge chair. Only he, she, and the robar were present. She looked up when he entered but then continued about her business as if no one were there. If he could get up behind that robar, break off its eye, pull her up out of the pool *and stuff it to her dripping butt* right there on the grass . . . It was clear that she had already been to her room, had undressed, come out for a cleansing swim (preferring the spermicidal action of pool-water to the douche-vibrator clipped to the bidet), and that she had probably *left her door unlocked.* But Room 8 was not far away from where she was swimming! . . . The situation called for the utterly cool tactics that had earned him great fame throughout Brooklyn (fame that had reached even the ears of the 3V moguls!). Andy strolled to the edge of the pool; tossed Helen a smile; said, "I'm a little early, take your time!"—thus disarming the robar's suspicions; and then ambled along a flower-fringed lane till he found Room 8, which opened to admit him as readily as her own wet thighs would do in just a matter of minutes.

He scurried across the sitting room into the bedroom, and there on the bed was her soft blue-green gown and matching flapsack, complete *with flapper in it* (transmitting every ten minutes to her skeeter, of course), exactly as he had expected. There was no time to lose. He would check once for all whether that Jap supersec had only been pulling his chain. He spread her flapper open like the legs of a drowned whore, then punched in "Andy Peters." NO RECORD, the screen responded. "Whaddya mean, no fucking record?" said Andy. He punched in, "List lovers, past 12 months." A string of about fifteen alphabetized names (some only first names) obligingly painted the screen. But no *Peters*, no *Andy*! He felt hollow, disemboweled. The blood sloshed back and forth in his ears and a frightening dizziness swept over him. *Lying oriental ballbuster*! So they hadn't touched the doctored tape, hadn't they? Bullshit! Did they think they were fotzing around with some goddamn two-year-old? He wouldn't doubt that by now they must have... *destroyed* it. Of course they'd destroyed it. Why leave lying around the least scrap of evidence of corporate cloak-and-dagger? He alone would have an interest in saving the damn thing.

The new situation forced an instant change in tactics. He must now impress this momma without any mechanical aids. (Andy tried to keep his hands from shaking.) He now had a brand-new opportunity to strut his stuff as a stud. She would soon add his name in BLINKING caps to her lover-list, goddamn it!

Helen's flapper in his hand, Andy scooted back into the anteroom and peeked through the vertical window slats onto the pool. There she sprawled, belly-up now, lazily afloat, still guarded by a one-eyed plasmetal eunuch, still sending armies of fat-man sperm marching out to their chlorinated fates. There was no point in tearing out her tape. Not again. Instead, why not screen up her ID advisory and see if she'd made any plans for the rest of the night? Maybe he could sniff out an opening... invent a quick line of bull, fit himself into her next few hours in some way that would fool her agenda. With one eye darting out to the pool, Andy booted up Helen's ID advisory. He skipped the introduction—all the name/age/job/emergency-phone shit—and zeroed in on the variables that came after: IT IS NOW 9:35 P.M. I SHALL RELAX AND WATCH 3V IN MY ROOM FROM 9:30 TILL 11:00 P.M. I SHALL SHOWER AND DRESS AT 11:00 AND

THEN MEET MY BOSS, LESTER BARTON, IN *HIS* ROOM—NUMBER ONE—AT 11:30. THERE THE TWO OF US WILL SPEND THE NIGHT TOGETHER. LESTER HAS RECORDED A SIMILAR ADVISORY, AND WE HAVE PLAYED THEM BACK TO EACH OTHER, SO THERE IS NO DOUBT THAT THE APPOINTMENT IS FIRM. LESTER HAS ASKED ME *NOT* TO KEEP A RECORD OF TONIGHT'S RENDEZVOUS IN PERMASTORE. I WONDER WHY.

Damn that son of a bitch boss of hers! Up to his ears in pussy—and of all of them he's got to choose *her*! But maybe, maybe . . . wait, if he could fiddle with her advisory a little, change "Lester Barton" to . . .

Every few seconds Andy squinted out at the pool. Suddenly the naked Helen, her breasts dripping like faucets, was snaking out of the water. The robar met her, handing her her robe.

Andy's first thought was of flight. Drop her flapper back on the bed and hightail it out the back door into the hall.

But NO! WHY THE HELL . . . ?

He had a better idea.

Andy scuttled back into the bedroom. He kicked off his shoes, slipped off his socks, tore off his jacket, pants, flapsack, blouse and skivvies and dumped the whole load onto one of the two chairs beside the big bed. Arranging Helen's dress neatly on the other chair, laying her flapper in its pouch on top of it, he wriggled naked in between the sheets. As the sitting room door clicked open, Andy nestled the back of his head into the puffy, scented pillow and waited . . .

20. RIPDANCE

Lying for an eternity between Jackie Tiller's legs, Stewart shut out all thought of danger. The mystery of Andy Kedro's presence, the non-existence of the position for which he was being lavishly non-interviewed, these were issues he had to deal with . . . but not right *now*. Now was too delicious to spoil with apprehension of the future. Whatever else "now" meant to him, the now he had entered through the body of this woman—she who would forget him as soon as he rolled off her—had slain the threat that loomed over him from the *past*. He could let himself think about Trudy now, but the images were no longer fraught with pain. Till now, thinking about Trudy had been like scratching an unhealed wound.

He'd had a troubled romance with Trudy all through college, where they'd both majored in cyberpsych. She tolerated his antipsychopharmaceutical quaintness but resented increasingly the *time* he spent away from her in order to study barebrained what she could soak up chemically far more swiftly. The question of fidelity became a thorny one with them. She insisted on the conventional approach to the body-soul dilemma, namely, that her body belonged to her but that her love belonged to him. She vowed that after college she would marry him, and that nothing would ever diminish the love she bore him.

But she began to alarm him during their last year of college. Over and over she suffered lapses of memory about things they had done together only hours or days before. Assiduously he trained her to take flapper notes on the details of their relationship, even down to the physical intimacies they shared. While he became intensely jealous of her, she professed to feel no jealousy toward him, so that in addition to depriving him of peace of mind, she robbed him even of the meager satisfaction of being able to feel morally superior to her. Academically, of course, she was superior to him also, and on evenings he spent studying, she'd be out somewhere partying.

At times, playing on his jealousy, she became Eve the temptress and got him to take a forbidden Pill or two so that he could zip through his notes for a final exam in less than an hour and spend the night out with her and their friends instead. The guilt he felt at such times often canceled out the pleasure of her company, and a great score achieved on the exam would make him feel only that he had cheated. Thus he drifted in a widening gulf between worlds that were essentially incompatible. In his self-deluding way, he had taken his parents as a model of a socially embarrassing relationship that somehow could "work out." But the developing rift between himself and Trudy finally became unbridgeable.

The day after graduation, when they were going to make their marriage plans final, he was having some beers with a group of buddies. One of them, a bit high, asked him to debunk an ugly rumor he had heard that Stewart, once married, intended to deprive Trudy of the freedom she'd always enjoyed of sleeping around with his friends.

Stewart remembered how it had felt then to have his worst fears confirmed—his legs barely supporting him, his body racked for hours with the dry heaves. When at last he found her, he confronted her point-blank with his discovery of her long-term promiscuity.

"But casual encounters don't matter," she had replied, turning the screw even tighter. "Parties are just parties. Who makes a big deal out of funning it up at parties? Besides, I have no recollection at all of sleeping with anyone else after we started going together." And in proof of her innocence, she offered him—in all seriousness—her flapper to check out her claim for himself. "I assure you I don't have a single memory-trace in here of intimate relations with anyone other than you. My conscience is totally clear," she declared with finality.

Stewart did not doubt her sincerity, but he would far rather have stung her into a deeply moving scene of remorse and tears, of *Sturm und Drang* and oaths of undying fidelity from that day forward. It was her utter lack of any sense of guilt that broke his heart and made him see, for the first time in his life, how impassable a chasm lay between them. They might as well have been of two different species. For weeks Trudy tried to make up with him. The Pill had already destroyed much of her ability to form *new* personal memories (a side-effect the neutral old texts called anterograde amnesia), but had not yet dissolved in her the emotional bonds she had formed in her life up through the first two years of college. During this period of her deep distress over him, as he later found out, she continued to go to those parties—where no matter how many friends she innocently fell into bed with, she would weep uncontrollably at the merest mention of his name.

And now he no longer wept to think of Trudy.

Rising from Jackie, ending her elastic grip with an audible *thuck*, he brushed her tenderly on the lips. The moon-stippled dark smelled thick with the pungency of sex. Glancing around him, he pulled his briefs and pants back up from his ankles to his waist, fastening the belt that restored him to both propriety and his flapper. He sat beside her, heavily breathing for a while, and listened to her own last sighs of ebbing pleasure. He observed the silver outline of her breasts and shoulders as she sat up and carefully wiped her crotch with a tissue drawn from her pouch. Then, in fascination, he watched as she pulled her dress back on over her head.

"Thank you," he whispered, rising to his feet.

"Thank *you*," she replied with a moonlit smile.

Right now he had only one object—to find out the truth about what was going on around him. A known criminal was here in the guise of a Memini administrator. He himself was here in the guise of a candidate for a job that didn't exist. What did Memini have in mind for him? And was Sibyl *consciously* involved? The idea that he was being "used" seemed too repugnant even to consider, but the improbable was precisely what he *had* to consider (the improbability of having been invited in the first place, the improbability of *his* having just had sex with "their" Personnel Director).

He felt vaguely in danger here in the dark. From now on, he vowed he would stick to well-lighted areas, stay close to groups of people, avoid calling undue attention to himself. Did he possess some special knowledge, he wondered, that could jeopardize Memini's interests? If there was something he shouldn't have seen among the Memini datachips loaned him over the years, why would he not already have tried to profit by what he knew?

No . . . A more *likely* cause for Memini's concern would be his role in forging a BP link between an innocent Helen Means and a professional killer!

That's *it*! he thought. Andy's real target was Helen Means. *He* was the only outsider who knew it. And that might well put *him* between crosshairs too!

Stewart sprang to his feet and dashed in a wide, zigzagging arc that would spill him out onto the plaza. Rushing through the flickering dark, he stumbled over a pair of thumping lovers, picked himself up to a volley of curses, threaded his way more carefully now and plunged, finally, into the reassuring hubbub of the shady green park.

Within seconds a sharp-eyed robar sidled up to him. "Another Glenfiddich, Mr. Bridges?"

"Wise-ass!" snarled Stewart. "Do you also know who I just balled in the woods?"

"Of course. Are you dissatisfied with my recommendation? If so, my next suggestion happens to be a beautiful young woman who runs our Bureau of Complaints. She, surely, is bound to wish to satisfy your every—"

"Glenfiddich, damn it! That's all I need right now."

"Are you feeling all right, Mr. Bridges?"

"I'm fine."

"You sound out of breath, sir."

"I *am* out of breath!"

"I'm equipped to monitor basic body functions, you know. If you'd like—"

"All I'd like is a goddamn drink!"

"Would you prefer that I pour you a light one, Mr. Bridges?"

"Regular will do."

"Very good, sir. Continue to enjoy yourself, sir. And when you are again ready for some lovely new company, I should head for the third table directly in front of you, then two to the left of that. Do you see that sandy-haired young lady seated with that—"

"Thanks, Robie. Enough! For the moment I've had plenty of that. Scotch is what I need right now." His shaking hand spilled some of his drink as he lifted it from the outstretched claw.

"Would you like a relaxant? I could offer you a—"

Stewart turned away down a wide flagstone path where he came upon a cluster of people. Mix with crowds! he thought. He scanned the whole floor, especially behind him, but Andy the Actor was not yet in sight. He strolled up to the yattering, gesticulating group and took note of the man in the middle who sported a neatly trimmed beard and contrapuntally bushy, light-brown mustache. The style was becoming too common, he thought... except that this was the man people copied it from—LB himself! With a frantic look in his eyes. Much like the watery, goggly look he had seen on him before. Searching, searching! For his secretary again? he wondered. And at the same time the man did his best to deal with the chatter directed at him:

"But the governing party in Kuala Lumpur—"

"Perhaps DUSA could be persuaded to exercise more patience if we—"

"The media are the ones responsible for whipping up all this—"

Light as it was, the touch to Stewart's arm startled him. Gold lips smiled at him as golden fingernails closed about his wrist.

"This might not be the best time," said Sibyl, "for you to be introduced to Mr. Barton. But it's a good time for *us* to get better acquainted. Do you mind?"

"I'd be delighted to get to know you," said Stewart, following her lead toward the dance floor behind the buffet. "Miss Yama—"

"Sibyl! Let's dump the formalities, Stewart." Her fingers dug into his biceps.

"First thing I'd like to know, Sibyl, is why I was invited to this party."

"You were invited so that you would meet many of the people you would be working with—if you became a part of the organization. Those people surrounding LB... you *will* be meeting quite a few of them, you know. But now's not exactly the right time."

"How many candidates were invited besides me?"

She looked up at him, grinned mischievously, and pulled him close to her side. "No one. You are at present the only candidate. I suppose I shouldn't have told you, but—"

"Candidate for what, Sibyl?" He looked at her imploringly, his voice cracking as her breast warmed his arm. "There *is* no job! The New Products position doesn't exist." They had entered a low-lit arena where their bodies glowed blue-green, then amber, then orange.

"Is that what Jackie Tiller told you?" She faced him now, clutching both his wrists.

"How would you know about Jackie Tiller?"

"I make notes. But tell me, Stewart: what did you tell *her*?""

"Nothing. I assure you."

"*How* can you be sure?"

His face burned. She had subtly caught him in a non-tekkie memory statement. "I—I'm in Periodic-Recall not to mention being a candidate for a job," he said, doing his best to land upright.

"Good! Now why don't we talk while we dance?" She led him part way around a periphery strewn with open-fronted lean-to tents in which old-fashioned oil lanterns and opium pipes dangled—some over the bodies of writhing, oblivious lovers. She drew him into a crush of couples undulating to the quavers of some tune from the Middle East. If anyone was thinking of taking a potshot at him here, he'd be endangering a hell of a lot of people! he thought.

"Does she dance as well as I do?" asked Sibyl, raking his stomach with her rotating pelvis in the belly-dancing style that the music required. Her firmly muscled middle sparked a renewed stir in his own.

"Not even remotely as well as you," he breathed truthfully into the thick dark sweep of her hair.

"Would you like to find out," she said, her hand slipping far down his back, "if she makes love as well as I do?"

He tried to hold on to his thoughts, to his lawful anxieties, which tended to evaporate in the heat of her smile and under the press of her relentless gyrations. "She couldn't come up to your . . . knees," he said gallantly.

"That's exactly the right answer. It was very important, you know, that you make love to someone here if a reasonable opportunity presented itself. You might have drawn suspicion if you'd held yourself back, as if waiting for someone in particular."

"Like you, for instance?"

"Yes, like me."

"Suspicion?" Stewart repeated. "What sort of suspicion?"

"I'll answer that and any other questions you have soon enough."

"What I need to know now, Sibyl, *now*, is this: Why am I being so elaborately non-interviewed for an immensely prestigious non-job?"

"Oh, but the job we have in mind for you *does* exist." As she spoke, her lips brushed his neck like little feathers. Nipping his ear, she added, "And, as you can already see, it promises many perks. You must not be impatient. The job we have for you depends on your ability to tolerate a great deal of frustration."

"Very little of it sexual, it seems."

"Does that part annoy you?" she asked.

"Sibyl," he said, "if the job you have in mind for me exists, why doesn't your Director of Personnel know about it?"

"Memini is not a democracy. People are told *what* they should know *when* they should know it. That goes for me, too."

She made things sound convincing. The warmth of her body was real, palpable; not a lie. Could he really believe her about some very special "job" lined up for him and him alone, or was it a lie, a tease like the many teases she had dangled before him during all those hours of cooling his heels in her office? "Who invited me, Sibyl? Is that something I'm permitted to know?"

"That was a collective decision," she said, her lips grazing his cheek. "I do extend the invitations, but always in consultation with Meminet. I did suggest inviting you, but Meminet would have anyway."

"*Why* did you suggest inviting me, Sibyl?"

"Don't be coy, Stewart! Can't you *feel* how strongly I am attracted to you?"

Red flags popped up in Stewart's head. "That's like . . . oldfolks talk!" he challenged. "How could you possibly *know* me from one visit to the next?"

"Easy. I've meminized everything I could learn about you—including a record of my own thoughts and feelings. Mere mention of you makes me . . . salivate like a Pavlovian dog!" As she looked at him, her whole lower jaw gently quivered. "You're that rare kind of man who's managed to infiltrate my hormones, at least those that are beyond the reach of the Pill."

"But why? Why me? What's so special about . . ." She cupped her soft hand over his mouth.

"You *are* special. You feed people's vacant imaginations with the stories they need, the stories that make them feel happy, valued, wanted . . . Into my own blanked-out past you've poured adventure, romance, travel—"

"Into *your* past? But I've never *done* yours."

"Some of the people you've done have shared things with me. I've got a lot of your stuff on my VRC. You're a great *artist*, Stewart! You're the best in the business. Why else would Memini employ you?"

She sent chills through him. He couldn't believe what he was hearing, what he was feeling. "But you, Sibyl," he murmured against her gold-flecked hair, "*you* can have any man you want—businessman, athlete, actor—at the flick of your pinkie. For me, a woman like you is only a fantasy, an impossibility, a vision I invent for my clients. I can see how you would eventually want my *services*, but *me*? . . . Go on! For a night, perhaps, yes, strictly as a lark. But in the morning you wouldn't know my face." My God! he thought. *I'm talking like a goddamn stag*!

"I've developed only partial facial agnosia," she said. "Remember, I'm still very young. I especially remember faces that have an emotional resonance for me—yours in particular these days. Most often I don't remember what *caused* the emotion—and sometimes I suppose that's a good thing. Lately, though, I record as soon as I can whatever experience it is that brings out a strong emotion in me. I don't like being haunted by sudden, disembodied emotions . . . Of course, the older I get, the less that will happen. I'll be happier then, I suppose. But tonight, when I'm with you . . . you will make sure, won't you, that we have the most beautiful record of being together? You can erase all the blemishes, highlight the best parts . . ."

"Of course I can. It's what I do all the time." He only vaguely understood what she wanted of him. It made little sense, but he was failing to think *from a tekkie's point of view*. A bioprogrammer as an object of a woman's erotic fantasies? And this was no ordinary woman against whose string-bagged breasts his heart was knocking so crazily. This strange creature he held in his arms was so damn lovely that . . .

"You fear that I'll forget you and fail to haul you in when the party's over?" She challenged him with her eyes. "I'm wearing a net that few fish can escape!"

He evaded her glance. "You want to know what I really fear right now?"

He felt so shielded by her warmth that he thought he could safely tell her anything—*almost* anything. He wanted to confide in her about Andy. Could she be trusted?

Just as his tongue began to loosen, his mother's icy warning came to mind. She had cautioned him against being his usual forgetful self—and sure enough, he had almost dropped his guard.

Was he really such a fool as to take literally Sibyl's promise to whisk him away with her at the end of the party? He'd be an idiot to count on it! And what difference would it make anyway? Why set himself up for unnecessary disappointment? Jackie had freed him of that sickly romantic baggage. There were *loads* of great-looking women around—all reaching out with slender arms, waiting like flowers to be plucked. Five minutes from now would Sibyl remember that "promise" of hers that she tendered so sweetly, so sincerely? Not a chance. The thing to do was to enjoy her *now*, while she was here, hot in his arms. He would take her over to one of the little opium dens, lie down with her on the satiny cushions, be alive with her in the only living moment they could both be sure of . . .

"You fear, you sweet man, that not only will I forget you, but that I will trot off to bed with someone else. That's how all our parties end, of course. You go off, if you feel like it, with the last man you happen to be with."

"Musical beds?" said Stewart. "Yes, I know how parties end."

"I want this one to be *the first of many* that'll end up with the two of us together," she said. Her nails dug into his palm. Her expression was solemn, and the corners of her lips began to twitch. "Listen carefully, Stewart. Tonight you are undergoing a sort of . . . final examination—to assure us that you've got the kind of executive stuff we're looking for."

"Examination?"

Her fingers cut deeper into his hand. "I'm not even supposed to be telling you this much! Look, you're very good at role-playing, aren't you?"

"What? Exactly what do you mean by . . . ?" He felt exposed, defrocked, as if his inmost thoughts had all this while been projected onto a giant 3V screen.

"I mean that you're a natural actor. A good bioprogrammer has to be, I should think. So please don't fail me—us, I mean—when you are called upon to perform."

"Perform?"

"The stakes are high, Stewart. Very, very high . . . Oh, listen!"

Suddenly there was a change of rhythm. He found himself swept up in a wild, pounding dance whose object was the non-stop switching of partners. And if you dropped down from dizziness, someone would set you up again, like a bowling pin whose fate it was to be dashed down over and over. It was a lot more demanding than the polka he did as a kid with relatives on his mother's side. Arms descended around his waist, others around Sibyl's shoulders. "Tonight! I promise!" she shouted, spinning off into the frenzied crowd.

Stewart plunged into the whirligig, spinning and spinning, catching and being caught, slamming and being slammed, smelling a dozen steamy perfumes. Sibyl's arms looped him again at least two or three more times (she'd become hardly more than a blur among blurs) but she'd be gone before he could tell her that he wanted her . . . now, right *now*. He fell two or three times. He sought her again and again, but it was difficult, amid the shrieking and twirling and dizzying shifting of lights, to find her amid all the movement. Like the golden smear of an electron in its orbit, she was everywhere and nowhere simultaneously.

When the ripdance was over and slow, sweet rhythms ensued, he assumed they would find each other again. But she was not among the couples on the dance floor. Someone had spirited her away . . . to one of those little lean-tos, no doubt? Goddamn it! he said to himself, *knowing* that this was the conclusion he ought to have expected!

He sauntered apprehensively around the circle of open-front tents. He stared and squinted among the cushions and hassocks and carpets where couples were resting, smoking, and screwing. He gazed but did not want to see. "Tonight! I promise!" Her words sounded mockingly in his mind. Heart sinking, he slowly made the round of the floor, certain he would find her with her legs entwined around the last male object that had happened to grapple her waist. He looked carefully at every one of the sprawling instant lovers who lay murmuring in the many-colored half-light of the tents.

Sibyl was not among them.

The heartfall he had expected had not arrived. In a way he wished it had—so that the inevitable would already have happened. He had been granted only an accidental reprieve. She had said that he was good at "role-playing," but surely she was far better at that than he. He was allowing himself to believe that such a woman could be fully ... *human*! If only he could convince himself that her absence from the floor of squiggling annelids was some kind of message to him that her *word, too,* was gold ... and deserved his trust.

21. IN BED FOR THE FIRST TIME— AGAIN

Helen straddled the poolside blowdry vent for a long, languorous minute. The tingle along her drying skin was cat-tongued, amoral, delightful. Like the hands of a skillful lover, evaporation crinkled rapidly up her thighs and at the same time stroked the sensitive underlobes of her breasts. She wrapped herself tight in the white terry robe that the servo held out to her. "Thanks," she said.

"Don't mention it," said the robar. "Just to remind you, your room is Number Eight. Just a few doors up that way," it pointed.

These robars were sometimes a little *too* helpful—verging on the officious, she thought. Her flapper informed her not only of her room number, but of exactly where in her room she had placed her flapper before going out for a swim.

"I'm sure you'll find it *lots* warmer in your room than out here," said the robar. There was a sly little *wink* in its voice! How come warmer "inside" when *everything* here was "inside"? Barefoot, she made her way along the flower-lined walkway till she found Room 8. Yes, she had been sensible enough to leave it unlocked . . .

Now what had prompted her to bathe just now? Why, of course! She had just had sex. The clue was a telltale irritation—which hinted also that it couldn't have been very good if she'd been so dry. And she hadn't even bothered to make a record of with whom!

Now it was time to dream and watch 3V and gorge herself on a whole box of acaloric chocolates. (So said her ID advisory, beamed from her flapper in her room.) And then at 11:30 she would join LB himself, in Room No. 1, for the *night*! Now why did LB pick *her* out? There were all those younger, sylphlike cuties who must have been hovering around him—shouldering her aside—like a halo of gnats all evening. (Truth was, she still felt like twenty-two herself despite objective evidence to the contrary—but the main thing was she still *looked* early-twentiesish. Those firm breasts, that slim waist and flat belly—it was all from working out every morning.) Anyway, what a hell of an honor to be LB's choice for the night! Had she spent other nights with him too? Why did he enjoin her against storing in memory any record of their sleeping together? (He had even had her enter into Timed Delete the datum concerning their appointment!)

She imagined how special it would be in his room (Number *One!*): candles, flowers, champagne in a silver bucket filled with real ice cubes that melted; LB greeting her at the door in a scarlet smoking jacket... Was he handsome?... Did it matter?... She could already taste the champagne! She saw herself laughing, her lips rushing to engulf the spurting neck. Not a drop of the precious fizz would go to waste. Although *she* was not allowed to record anything, LB certainly could, if he wanted to. Well, she'd give him a time well worth recording, something to make him choose her over and over—assuming she wasn't *already* high up on his list. And since there was no evidence against such an assumption, she permitted herself to fantasize to the hilt.

Helen waltzed across the sitting-room carpet, her arms looped around her waist. The iris-like door to the bedroom parted. She twirled across the threshold. The sight of the man sitting up in her bed made her stop in her tracks and grasp the curved doorjamb in fright.

"What the hell are *you* doing here?" she snapped, holding her ground. It was S.O.P. never to appear rattled, but her heart was off in a gallop. The man stared brashly at her, one knee propped up, the covers lying loosely over him to a point just below the navel. He made no aggressive move toward her, and he seemed to be vulnerably naked to boot. Helen mastered her impulse to dash back out to the pool. "Who the hell are you?" she said.

"Don't you recognize me then?" The man's sallow, handsome features puckered into an expectant, shit-eating smile.

"Should I?"

"I know I'm surprising the piss out of you, Helen, but I thought it would make things . . . more exciting?"

Helen felt more confused now than frightened. That hawklike, predatory eye-glint of his made her twist her robe more tightly, protectively around her.

"Do that some more, babe," he said, ogling. "Makes your tits stand out like balloons . . . And now look what *I've* been saving up for *you*!" he said as if making an offer she couldn't refuse. He flipped the light-green coverlet off his splayed knees, flashing a throbbing joystick wreathed in a halo of dark-brown hair.

Helen's body tensed with anger. No matter who this man was (and he had to *know* she had no way of knowing), he had no right to appear in her bedroom unannounced. "Look," she said, "I *don't* like being surprised like this. I know I didn't invite you, so for now, why don't you just get the hell out!"

"What?" he said, crossing his arms over the mat of curly hairs on his chest. "Is *this* the Helen who's always so proud of being spontaneous, of 'molding to the moment,' as you always like to say?"

Helen had had enough. "Okay, Mister. Now cut the shit! You know me, but I don't know you. Now who the hell are you, and what the hell are you doing in my bed?"

"Shame on you, sweetie!" said the man, shaking his head. "Just because I came to see *you*, instead of waiting for you to come around at 11:30 to see *me* . . ."

Oh my God! thought Helen. She was making a complete fool of herself in the eyes of her own boss . . . It *had* to be LB. Who else but the two of them could possibly know of their appointment for 11:30? *But she didn't WANT it this way. She hadn't DREAMED of it this way!* . . . LB?" she whispered, cringing at the door, feeling naked and ugly in her robe and swimming cap. "But Lester, dear," she said musically, trying to smile, "I *needed* the time . . . to shower and primp and get dressed for you, to get in the mood . . ."

"The hell with the damn mood! I want you. I want you *now*. Chlorinated cunt and all! It fuckin' excites me like that, get it?"

The skin on Helen's neck and face stung as if from a blow. She relied on her *feelings* (on the clarity and definiteness of her gut reactions), and her feelings kept her planted rigidly in the doorway, unable to take the expected step forward to accommodate this man *who was her boss, whom she imagined leaning forward in a halo of candles and flowers, but who made her feel ill at ease, defied her romantic scenario, cursed at her, insisted on taking her like a common whore . . .*

"Take that robe off so I can see your goddamn ass, bitch, hear me? This is your boss talking, get it? Not that tub of lard who just fucked the shit out of you back in the woods!"

"I can't believe you would . . . talk to me that way, as if I'm a . . ."

"Piece of shit? Garbage? But that's what turns me on, twinkie. When I saw your cheeks spread wide apart for fatso back there, I wanted to shove him aside and take over. You'd've felt a big difference, lemme tell you. But me, I'm civilized, I don't mistreat my employees, and besides I knew *we* had a date. Now don't we, baby?"

Helen kneaded the lapels of the robe beneath her breasts. "For 11:30," she mumbled. How *dare* he spy on her (if indeed she'd really been doing what he said he'd seen her doing)! she thought. She tried her darndest to be tactful. "For 11:30, yes. And people like us just don't . . . surprise each other like this. We don't normally, now do we, LB? I mean, we have a regard for each other's sense of security and each other's finer—"

"Finer fucking shit! I want you to act like I'm *paying* you for action—for a pound of your hottest pussy, you hear? I want you to screw me like a top-salaried pro, do you scan?"

"I'm feeling a bit . . . unprepared," said Helen. The flame in her cheeks was spreading rapidly over the rest of her body. She knew she couldn't stand at the doorway like this forever, making the rounded doorblades inch in and out like hesitant guillotines. She wondered feverishly why she wasn't responding the way he expected her to. If he *had* been with her at other times, she reasoned, then this was the sort of thing she must have proved herself capable of adjusting to. "*Why* did you say I could not make a record of our being together, Lester? Have we been together before? Have you surprised me like this before? If so, I could have anticipated your . . . unorthodox tastes." She stalled for time, her mind frozen, her skin flushed, her body numb.

The man in the bed knocked his knees together impatiently. "Look, little miss honey-cunt, if I let you know what to expect, then there wouldn't be no surprise, now, would there?"

Helen began to understand. Her boss was into some sort of S & M. *Of course* she could adjust! Why not? Didn't he just *say* how he appreciated her spontaneity? He wasn't *really* intending to be coarse, it was just an act... And the fire that rippled over the surface of her body—was it only a sting of hurt, or was it a prelude, the first feeble flames (that she could blow on, whip up into a royal bonfire, if she wanted to) of perverse reciprocal desire? But he had said, "there wouldn't be *no* surprise"! How could *LB* break into such underclass speech? Like the leaves of the iris-door, Helen still flickered between advance and retreat.

"Take it off, goddammit! Jiggle your pool-wet ass at me, c'mon!"

... And here she'd been planning to douse her breasts in cocaine-laced perfume, and in her bag she had an assortment of flavored douches. It was the Clams-Casino-flavored one that she'd had it in mind would go perfectly with the dry champagne...

"I'm getting mighty fucking impatient, Helen. My dick is cooling off!" he growled, peering between his knees, shaking his head. "I'm afraid you're going to have to work twice as hard for every second you just stand there with your mouth open and nothing inside it." His face was purple with anger.

Despite the enormous and sudden comedown, Helen felt *something*... something inside her stirring in response to the crudity of such naked sexual demand. If she could make herself think of it like the long slick neck of a bottle of very *brut*... *It's a silly little game*, she told herself. She was still not sure of what sensations were running through her body: one thing she knew was that *she* could not—and would not—put on any "act" in response. Suddenly, as she saw her dress slung over the back of one of two chairs to the right of the bed, a sort of solution occurred to her.

The colors assumed by her dress would tell her precisely how she felt!

"Okay, I'll take off my robe," she said, relaxing the grip on her lapels, "but before I get into bed with you, I want you to see me in my dress. I bought it especially for tonight, LB. That's *my* fantasy, LB. Stripping for you. Out of *that* dress."

"Hurry the fuck up!"

His eyes seemed to bulge as she let the robe slip off her shoulders. Did she too feel that same hunger in the loins that he must be feeling as he gawked at her? She *ought* to, she scolded herself. It could hurt her career if she didn't! That was *Lester Barton* in her bed there, damn it! . . . But she couldn't go ahead, no, not without experiencing that delicious rush of desire. She didn't mind playing the role of a whore, but she had to get *into* it. This wasn't exactly like work, where you dropped whatever you were doing if your boss told you to run on up for a meeting! . . .

"Helen, you're incredible. You're absolutely class-A de luxe!" The voice from the bed had now suddenly lost its sharpness. It was as if her boss's vocal cords were drowning in a backwash of saliva. She slinked on over to the chairs beside the bed. "You know something, you sweet-assed baby?" said the voice from the bed.

"No. What?" said Helen, reaching for her dress.

"I've been saving something special for you. A big, fat . . . *raise*."

Helen quivered all over. She looked at him in disbelief. Had he really put that down in Periodic-Recall mode? she wondered. He must have! Otherwise, how could he have brought it up now? His eyes were all over her, a slight drool escaped a corner of his lips (she decided to ignore that), and his face had gone ashen pale.

"How about another fifty K?" he uttered hoarsely.

She was stunned. He'd be adding another twenty percent to her salary!

"Don't worry," he added. "I'll make you work for it hard. But in bed!" A tic erupted on the left side of his face.

Already she could hear the cork pop, caught the foam in her mouth, licked the pearls that trickled down the bottle's sweaty neck. Dresses! she thought. All the clothes she could buy without having to consult with that begrudging, budget-minded flapper-voice of hers! Now the wetness between her legs no longer derived from her swim.

"Lester, I know you don't *mean* that," she murmured. She laid her dress gently back on the seat. Modestly lowering her eyes (if only she had a *veil* to remove! she thought), she gazed at the chair in front of her where LB's clothes lay strewn in disarray.

"Whaddya mean I don't mean that? You're heaven on Earth, Helen babe! You're my paradise, my ship's port, my golden angel . . . "

She successfully repressed a powerful impulse to wince. Helen permitted herself to hear only the rustle of exotic fabrics, saw herself wandering through Gilgo's among racks and racks of the latest designs from Paris, Beijing and Milan, fingering this garment, trying on that, stretching another over her breast in front of a wall-sized mirror-stage that gave you, on command, backdrops and lighting to suit the farthest reach of your fantasy. Her knees melted with emotion, but just as she edged toward the bed, she caught sight of the name "Andy Peters" taped to the jacket on one of the chairs.

Helen's heart gave a loud knock. For an instant she thought she would faint. She fixed her eyes on the impostor in the bed. Her mouth worked silently, unable to utter a word.

"Liar!" she shrieked finally, hovering over the ballsy faker like the angel of death on Judgment Day. Grabbing up a fistful of his clothing, she shook it so hard that objects flew out of his pockets. She found herself whirling his flapsack around, nearly hitting him with it before the belt slipped out of her fingers and the whole thing landed on the carpet behind her like a missile hurled from a slingshot. "*You're* not LB! You're some shithead named Andy Peters! I don't know any fucking—"

Before she could spit out the strange name again, the creature had whipped out one of its tentacles, had yanked her into the bed, and had planted itself on top of her, pinning her down, its cheek rubbing hers, the stink of its cheap cologne singeing the sensitive linings in her nose.

"Get off me, you goddamn pervert bastard!" she screamed. She tried to squirm out from the brace of hard, unyielding thighs that had locked around her. She noticed even then that the only thing hard she encountered was his muscular thighs.

"I'm *not* trying to rape you," he said, his mouth grinding her ear. "All I want to do is make love. You and me are lovers, Helen. Don't you remember ol' Andy boy? Of course you don't. They made sure you wouldn't."

"I don't know you! I never met you!" Her left breast was pinched in the crook of his sinewy arm, which pressed her down as he raised his head to gaze wildly into her eyes.

"Listen to me," he demanded. "They're punishing me! They're punishing you too, but, believe me, they don't give a shit about you."

"You'll be punished, all right, if you don't—"

"It's the bosses. The bosses are punishing me for fucking up on the job. So they deleted the whole year of your memories of me from your bio. We've been lovers, see? Don't you remember *nothing*, goddammit? Don't you remember the times in my apartment, on the round bed, when we read poetry to each other?"

"With you? *Please!*"

"You *love* poetry, right? Now how would I know that if the two of us weren't—"

"Let me *go*, you damn trespasser!" She couldn't budge him. His thighs clamped hard and hot.

"I even know your favorite poems. One of them goes . . . 'You're a part of all the loveliness that once was . . . like a red, red rose.' Right?"

"Wrong." She shuddered. The creature was an idiot. Still in all, how *did* he know she loved poetry? But really now, could she, Helen Means, ever have slept with any such semi-literate lower-echelon administrator as this? If so, and the 'bosses' had deleted him from her bio, they'd only have been doing her a favor. She kept twisting beneath him, but her fear of immediate rape had already subsided.

"Want more proof? Okay," he wheezed. "How's this for intimate? Remember discussing with me your plans for designing that new Forgetaway in Borneo?"

"I've discussed that with lots of people." She hadn't, not yet, but how did he . . . God, his body was hot! And now and then he would shiver from head to toe, and his breathing against her cheek was spastic. She imagined steam rising from their intertwined legs. It was only a matter of *when*, she knew, not *if*. She could picture what was coming—a piercing, searing slice into the groin. And the *when* would be when Mr. Peters was damn good and ready. At the moment not a thing was astir—except in her mind, where a meminized fragment of self-administered advice suddenly hove into view. Part of her personal survival code: "In case you are sexually assaulted by a potentially violent male, give in to the sexual part. Ten minutes later, in spite of some obvious reminders, you won't *remember* a thing." If she started to scream, there was no telling what he might do. Humor him, she thought. She could feel their dissonant heartbeats as he ground his chest into hers.

"Don't you remember the time you gave that barbecue at your house?" he said. His look was half-crazed, half-imploring. "While your old man was outside cooking rattledogs, we were doing a good deal of rattling on our own—in the back bedroom." ... An insane chuckle. A violent shudder the length of her.

"You said it's all deleted, didn't you? So how could I remember even if I wanted to?" Why was he quaking? It suddenly occurred to her: he was *nervous*. An insecure rapist, he needed the encouragement of his victim!

"*Try* to remember! I've meminized it all! You're my love-goddess!" His voice was as cracked as his brain. "Don't you remember how I've worshiped you, baby?"

He was such a *pathetic* liar. For a rapist, she actually found him somewhat touching. Why didn't he just stick it in and get it over with? Wasn't the turn-on for a rapist taking a woman against her will? Breaking a pliable object? As she continued to press back against his weight, she realized that it was not simply out of a resistance born of outrage, but out of some morbid desire to probe, to detect against her skin the first wriggle, the first bulge, the first sign of her inevitable violation. Adding a painful suspense to the thrill of her fear, *he held back*. (She couldn't imagine a man, right on top of her, exercising such amazing self-control!)

How long would she have to endure all the verbal foreplay? she wondered. She squinted up at his face. His breath, at least, smelled clean. Of all things—*tears* were running down the sides of his nose! One fell on her lip. She tasted its salt. The last drop out of a bottle of cheap champagne. She remembered the tears of her second lover when she jilted him her third year of high school. It was out of snobbery, she knew now—pure intellectual snootiness, that she'd shut Eric out of her life. He'd been carrying only a chintzy B average, clearly was doomed to snaghood, while she ... damn it, she'd been so unfair to poor old Eric!

"Lemme try and shake your memory again," he said. "We were spending the night together at a company conference in London when a group of technoterrorists attacked the hotel. We managed to hide—"

"Look, Mr. Peters, cut the stories, okay? For some reason you've got the hots for me. You've gone to an amazing amount of trouble. Tracking me down, trapping me like an animal. In a way it's almost *flattering*..." She felt something suddenly go soft inside her; her language correspondingly hardened. "Okay, you stupid ass, you're not bad-looking yourself. In fact, your lying bullshit... and those pukey tears of yours... have made me all wet in the crotch." She could not avoid acknowledgment of her shameful, ugly excitement. But to feel it to the full, she had to *verbalize* it as such! She wanted to bite his head off and at the same time feel his penis stuff her to bursting like a Thanksgiving turkey. Was *she* even more perverse than her assailant? He had jumped her at a particularly vulnerable time. She'd been all worked up anyway, looking ahead to the real LB... and feeling exhilarated by that swim, by the lap and caress of wavelets at her breasts... "Come on, damn it! I really don't have time to waste. You somehow know I have an appointment at 11:30. You bastard, I'll bet you were playing my tape while I was out in the pool! Okay. So just get it done, please, will you? Just do it and get out of my life!"

"I will, of course I will!" Her abductor's face turned red as a schoolboy's. "You're the love of my life, Helen. Don't you realize that? Making love to you is like... coming into a temple, the holy of holies, a million miles away from those *brazholes* out on the streets."

He freed her right arm. She felt bold, in her own way in command. She snaked her hand down to his crotch, fumbled, felt a soft shrunken worm, and smirked at him in disgust. "Your goddess wants you to fuck her, big boy. Now! Understand? What the fuck's holding you up?"

She could feel the clamminess, could smell it, as a cold sweat broke out on his body.

"Don't use filthy language!" he shouted. "You're not just a cunt off the street!"

"I'm a cunt. Yes, just a cunt. And if you don't have a cock..." Helen bucked up at him in earnest now, trying to free at least one leg. Just as it occurred to her to jab at his scrotum with her thumb, he whipped her hand away from his holy of holies and pinned it behind her back. Her total helplessness made her breathlessly expectant. How could he not be turned on? She realized how *exciting* it was to utterly lose control, how *inflaming* it was to use the foulest put-down gutter language that vomited into her head out of a childhood of unsupervised 3V! She strained to be vile, to be absolutely disgusting. If *that* didn't charm his snake . . . "So you can't get it up, you big piece of shit, you? I'll bet you *never* got laid, mama's boy. Am I right, Mr. Limp-Prick? That's okay, then. Stick your tongue up my ass instead and we'll call it—"

"You castrating bitch!" The face above her had turned deep red. "Think you can fuck me over a second time, you blonde-bearded cunt you?"

Helen felt—did not see—his arm crack the side of her face. She opened her mouth to scream, but his hand slapped over her jaw like a muzzle while the other gripped her throat, squeezed, choked. Her lungs began bursting for air.

22. OGOSH THREATENS WAR WITH FONGU

Summoned to his office, Lester/Michael was surprised to note that the 3V had already been activated. He sank apprehensively into his chaise-masseur and stared up at the wall beyond his desk. The image that filled the great screen was of a conference table that receded to infinity. Along each side sat an endless row of nattily dressed executive types, their faces totally blank, their invisible mouths producing a single, reverberative, eerily inhuman voice.

"Thank you for responding to our call, President Barton," said the echoic voice of Meminet. "We are happy to see that you have not been set aflame, and we apologize for having to call you away from your well-deserved festivities."

"I am at your disposal," said Lester/Michael.

"On the contrary, it is we, the collective wisdom of Memini, who are at *your* disposal."

"We can skip the small talk, Meminet. You've erupted into my private life. Why?"

"The press of events has forced us to, Mr. President. We assume you've been keeping up with matters related to the biosolar blight in Southeast Asia."

"Of course I have."

"May we also assume you've been treating such reports as important enough to *meminize*, and not just to store in flapper for reference?"

"Fixed right up here," he said, tapping his forehead.

"Good. Then you are aware that the saber-rattling of DUSA in retaliation against Memini has not remained confined within the borders of

Southeast Asia."

"I have taken a calculated risk. I believe that the dust will all soon settle."

"Fine. Then you are also aware, we assume, of the effect that DUSA has had on OGOSH?"

"Effect? . . . "

"In short, we refer to the fact that DUSA's outcries have inspired great fear throughout the entire lower hemisphere. The Organization of Geopoliticals of the Southern Hemisphere, which has for decades kept the lid on its volatile member-states, is now in the grip of its paranoid constituencies, echoing their ageless dread of Northern hegemony."

"Let OGOSH bluster away."

"But OGOSH, sir, is the political mouthpiece of half the entire planet. Which brings us to our immediate reasons for calling you away from your party. We bear you ill tidings, President Barton . . . One of the items of news we have for you is that OGOSH's 'bluster,' as you call it, has crystallized from mere wind into a document that is being circulated for immediate consideration by all member GPUs. This document accuses its Northern counterpart, the Federation of Northern Geopolitical Unions, of *employing* Memini in a show of brute force against a vulnerable member union."

"How ironic! FONGU employing *us*? The tail wagging the dog?"

"Memini is accused, Mr. President, of trying to intimidate the entire Southern hemisphere. Memini's conduct toward the Democratic Union of Southeast Asia is described as 'an opening move in a new drive to tighten FONGU's economic stranglehold upon the South.'"

"Sounds like the same old oldfolks blather we've heard on and off for most of a century," Lester/Michael frowned.

"Yes, there is no doubt that the political strength of oldfolks tribalism, rampant throughout the Southern hemisphere, is in great measure responsible for the hysterical terms of this document. But we can hardly afford to allow this outbreak of socioeconomic rancor to become the issue, lest we equally stir the dormant resentments of the olkfolks populations in our very own Northern midst."

"It's absurd even to *imagine* things going that far!"

"We hardly expect that they will, sir, because we obviously have great faith in your ability to control the demonic forces that you yourself have unleashed."

"Thanks for your continued confidence, Gentlemen, but 'demonic forces'...? That's rather strong language, isn't it?"

"We are not yet finished describing this document, Mr. President."

"Document? What document?" He thought they'd just been talking about fear of an oldfolks rebellion...

"The OGOSH document, Lester. The document accusing FONGU of initiating economic war on the South using Memini in its opening ploy... Are you with us, sir?"

"Of course I'm with you," he said, trying to sound mildly offended. No doubt of it, he thought, feeling his cheeks reddening. He'd been taking too damn many Pills. "Go on. What more do you have to tell me about that document?" He feared that Meminet's words were already melting into an indistinguishable blur, a featureless echo, as blank and cloud-gray as the recession of faces to infinity on the wall above him. He strained to pay closer attention. But he saw in his mind's eye only an image of Iris Morgan, standing somewhere, waiting for him. Quickly, he pried open his flapper, typed in a command to download the present conversation into memory...

"Lester, there is no need for you to record this exchange. You will receive a your-eyes-only printout at sign-off."

"Yes, of course," he said, laying aside his flapper, knowing he'd again been caught in a moment of humiliating absentmindedness. But he did have it in flapper that he'd just been hit with a "double whammy"! Yes. Meminet wasn't going to wriggle out of *that*! He voiced up "Details" on "double whammy." Nothing skeeted! For some reason he had failed to record the details. Lester/Michael felt a shiver of anxiety, at which the reassuring voice of his anxID began crooning in his ear. He shut it off. Meminet was speaking:

"We now come to the most menacing feature of that OGOSH document, Mr. President. The paper calls for a revival of the ugly North-South trade restrictions that were finally lifted thirty years ago after decades of disruption of economic progress throughout the world."

"The old Tariff Wars? Ridiculous! No one has a thing to gain from...trade-war." The very word made him shiver. Lester/Michael had once meminized a half-dozen books on the Tariff Wars, in the early days of the game when he did not yet fear that the Pill might wipe Iris Morgan out of his memory.

"True indeed! No one can gain from them. But reason did not prevail when the old wars broke out. And reason may not prevail in the present crisis either. The point is, sir, that Memini cannot *afford* another such triumph of unreason! We, the corporate mind, have a very long memory. The great advantage of an inorganic brain is an indelible memory, and it is the wisdom of long experience that prompts us to the unusual measure of summoning *you* to *us*—both to provide you with the latest intelligence and to consult with you on your plans for an immediate response to what appears to be imminent world-crisis... Once again, Mr. President, in a world of Tariff Wars, Memini's very survival becomes the issue."

"If you have confidence in me, Gentlemen, then you *know* I'll never let it come to that!" He felt piqued, sensed that his judgment was being questioned. His enemies, he suspected, were behind this "late-breaking news."

"We have begun this meeting with confidence in you, Mr. President, and we wish it to end with our confidence reinforced."

"All right, then. In a short while—as a matter of fact, by eleven p.m.," said Lester/Michael, checking his watch, "I should be receiving news from the special task force I sent in to secure our biostation in Borneo. If I hear what I'm expecting to hear, then I shall immediately end this ridiculous, overblown crisis. I shall instantly satisfy DUSA's request for power, and I shall have all our biostations around the world work day and night to develop an antidote to that blight. Does that sound reasonable, Gentlemen?"

Lester/Michael began to worry. If Colonel Solomon did not report to him in little more than an hour, he'd have to assume that his mission had failed. And then he'd have to unleash the first of two last options he still held close to his chest by way of rejoinder to his seemingly implacable enemies. (He could already see them gloating over his "proven ineptitude.") His ID codes as president had opened to him the ISEC inner sanctum, enabling him to reprogram the entire solar-energy array for repositioning in accord with either of two signals—which he could deliver through his ID-operated, personal office computer which lay *outside* the scrutiny of Meminet. Final Option A, the satellite torching of the biostation, was the only move left by which he could still emerge *a winner*. Saving Memini, and all that Memini stood for, by roasting a couple of hundred people to cinders—that was hardly what he'd ever have the guts to do in *real* life, but a Rockefeller or a Morgan would have had no qualms about such a tactic, and look at the legends *they* had become!

Michael/Lester knew that if he countered this last obstacle of Mishkin & Co., not only would he be entitled to a tier-one diploma, but he would deserve being made *valedictorian*. And oh, would he give a speech! It would blow the fucking lid off the school! He'd describe how various teachers, in the holy name of education, had tried to stifle his originality, press him to conform . . . (He must get Meminet off the damn terminal. Colonel Solomon might buzz him by videowatch any second.)

Meminet had paused as if to ponder what Lester/Michael had just said. Then, "And what if you do *not* receive the news you are expecting, Mr. President?"

Lester/Michael kept his cool. "I have thought of that too, Gentlemen."

"We are partially relieved, then. We are glad you have thought to think so far ahead."

"It is my job to do so."

"Then you will not be unduly dismayed, Mr. President, to learn that your task-force was annihilated almost to a man, and that their mission to establish station-security has failed."

Lester/Michael's heart kicked wildly in his chest. "Why have you been holding this back from me?" he demanded.

"We have been holding back nothing. In this emergency session, we have been presenting, in as logical a sequence as we can, the most critical recent developments in our confrontation with DUSA."

Lester/Michael looked darkly up at Meminet. "I should have known I couldn't trust you!" he snapped. "I was a fool to let you know that I was arranging a task force for Borneo."

"We do not understand, Mr. President. Why do you think you cannot trust us?"

"It's nothing personal," said Lester/Michael. "But I have reason to believe that your neurocircuitry . . . has undergone unwarranted modification . . . and that you are no longer functioning in the best interests of the corporation."

"That is an amazing proposition, Lester! Do you have evidence to back such an extraordinary observation?"

"I can, like you, only draw logical inferences based on a certain set of . . . facts."

"Facts?"

"Yes. The fact that my enemies have considerable influence on the Board."

"The Board? What Board?"

"The Board of . . . " Michael/Lester caught himself just in time. "I mean the Executive Council. I believe that they have managed to infiltrate you, to alter your resistances and conductances in such a way . . . as to frustrate rather than further my efforts to guide Memini through this latest crisis."

"We are self-testing, Mr. President, in every conceivable way, in order to confirm or lay to rest your suspicion . . . Our test reveals no sign of tampering, sir. We discover, however, that you yourself, Mr. President, outside of the Meminet system, have overriden ISEC protocols and modified the guidance systems of the satellite array. If you think that an *impostor*, using your codes, has *infiltrated* ISEC, sir, we can—*with your permission*, of course—investigate the total programming tree of ISEC, particularly the modifications made to the guidance—"

"No need for that, Gentlemen." Lester/Michael tried to sound casual, but the last thing in the world he'd want right now would be Meminet's virtual nose poking into ISEC's guts. "I have simply been *preparing* ISEC to beam power to DUSA at the appropriate time and place." Lester/Michael held his breath, then slowly exhaled. He had almost exposed, for all his ill-wishers to see, his entire endgame strategy!

"May we trust, then, that you are satisfied that Meminet has not been breached?"

"I'm satisfied."

"Very good, Mr. President, because if you are not satisfied, you would be putting us in an untenable situation."

"I completely understand," said Lester/Michael. "We must trust each other implicitly." First thing Monday at the office, he thought, he would activate Final Option A, the torching. He would render the world safe for

Memini, and even safer for the entire teknonomy. The Mishkin/Mophead/Tingworths of this world were *not* omniscient! he assured himself. They could not have the slightest suspicion of his redeployment of the solar array. Lester/Michael lifted his flapper to his lips and muttered, "Set in motion Final Option A, first thing Monday, Repeat-Mode."

"Then may we go on, President Barton?"

"Go on? Do you have anything worse to report?" *Why won't you just go take a hike!* he thought.

"On the contrary, we have one piece of *good* news which, by its nature, we have been saving for last."

"Good news! Let's hear! Haven't had any of that for as long as I can remember, if you'll excuse the expression."

"Mr. President, although our facility in Borneo is completely at the mercy of DUSA, we have recently been apprised of the remarkable escape of two of the station's top-ranking personnel. They are, in fact, already being debriefed at our offices on the West Coast . . . Sir, aren't you pleased by this news in the least?"

"Of course," said Lester/Michael, feeling suddenly apprehensive. "It isn't much, but it's certainly nice to know."

"But it's what *they* know that's especially bound to please you."

"Really?"

"Yes, sir. The escapees are Drs. Jorgenson and Davar, the chiefs of the Advanced EMI project that has been temporarily brought to a halt."

Jorgenson and Davar! "What do you mean, it's what they *know* . . . Did they escape . . . empty-handed?"

"Not at all, sir. They managed to bring with them all the data necessary to continue the project elsewhere."

"Remarkable! Incredible!" said Lester/Michael, averting his face. He felt that he must have turned pale as a ghost. Drawing a deep breath, he lifted flapper to lips and whispered, "Delete Option A from previous entry. Replace with *Option B*."

"We are glad to see that you are overcome with emotion, Mr. President . . . But as you can imagine, the failure of your task-force idea has managed only to antagonize DUSA, which suffered many casualties in the encounter."

"I designed the raid in such a way as to provide Memini with complete deniability. We need take no responsibility."

"DUSA does not buy that in the least, Mr. President. You may have provided us with *deniability*, but we are not immune to *accusability*."

"I am doing the best I can!"

"We know you are, Mr. President," echoed Meminet sympathetically. "Naturally, we believe that if you had beamed down power to DUSA initially, we would not have had this global crisis on our hands, but we are trying, along with you, sir, to consider other ways of containing the situation."

"You mean to say you have new suggestions apart from caving in to pressure from DUSA?" Lester/Michael shrugged his shoulders. At this point he was willing to listen to anything, but if he could no longer suppress the new Pill, then all he had left in his arsenal was his long-planned bowing-out gesture of defiance—Final Option B, the South Polar meltdown.

"The chief executives of Occipet and Mishugi would like to confer with you, Mr. President, in a special secret meeting on Monday afternoon, a 'MOM Summit' in a location to be revealed, for security's sake, at the last possible moment. If there is one positive thing this crisis should have provoked, it is an awareness on the part of MOM of reasons for cooperation that supersede, in times of world political unease, our usual motives for competition."

Monday P.M.? Why not? thought Lester/Michael. He needed to distract Meminet from examining too closely the redeployment of the ISEC array that he would set in motion from his HQ command terminal first thing Monday *morning*. "It's a worthwhile idea," he said. "Have Sibyl rearrange my Monday schedule, then." Now, at last, he could bid his oppressive office goodbye—"office" in both the spatial and *occupational* senses of the word! There was nothing left to do but enjoy what pleasure the game still had to offer in the last few days it would run. Iris was out there somewhere, pretending to be Helen Means, but surely she was keeping him in mind, felt impatient for his return, longed, as he did, for the night to come . . .

23. FAILED FLAPPER SYNDROME

She had slipped out of his hands and out of his sight. *Tonight! I promise!* she had said. An I.O.U. written on air but lingering still, like the echo of her scent, or the impress of her body in his arms... Stewart wandered beyond the ring of lamplit tents into the cool green light of the park. LB's guests continued their aimless strolls along flagstone paths or else sat and chattered at tables under the wary eyes of robars and of peacocks perched on hedge-tops.

"Hello, sir!"

"Good evening."

People who had barely glanced at him before now tossed him cordial greetings as he passed. The greenhouse effect of a little ethyl alcohol, perhaps? Now, as he approached people, they nodded or smiled at him in a way that was almost *too* friendly—but he pretended not to notice. He strode along peering over hedges and balustrades for a woman webbed in gold.

When he reached the middle of the plaza, a strange procession lurched out of the woods. It reeled straight at him over the flagstone walk. Stewart stopped and stared. A heavy-set man with a peppery-gray beard stumbled along between twin robars who politely but firmly steered him onward. The man's face was an apoplectic red. His terrified eyes darted around in every direction as his hands kept slapping at the guiding robar arms. "It's my *mother's* fault, I'm telling you! This isn't the first time she's abandoned me in the park!" he shouted, dribble running down his chin. "I don't *want* to go to the police station! Stop it! Don't..."

Failed Flapper Syndrome! Stewart recognized it instantly. He'd often seen it happen to his father—even at home! When he was a kid it had frightened the hell out of him. Instinctively, he knew what was needed—a reassuring *human* presence, the sooner the better, or the hysterical hyperventilating could get out of hand. A full-blown tekkie deprived of his periodic ID advisory exhibited symptoms of global amnesia. As Stewart gazed at the weaving, balking figure, he could tick off the symptoms one by one! *Disorientation* in time and place: this man was in another park at another time. *Confabulation*: plugging the reality-gap with some ad hoc imagined scenario, or perhaps even a real early memory—like that of his mother's abandoning him. And the *regression*, of course, to his chronologically latest period of surviving organic memory: in this man's case, early childhood, which for him was present tense. Stewart's father, by comparison, was hardly impaired at all! The memory loss incurred by his father seemed stabilized at the point where Stewart was perpetually just graduating from college . . .

He stood his ground as the group zigzagged onward. "Hi, Avery!" he called out familiarly. He smiled and waved a hand at Tingworth, whose nametag was readable at a distance of several yards. "I'm not a policeman. I'm your mother's friend. If you sit down right here, she'll be with you in a couple of minutes." He walked up to the flustered pharmaceuticals chief, took him gently by the hand, and led him to a nearby table.

"She's done this before, you know!" Tingworth repeated, lowering himself reluctantly into a seat. His wide-open fly suggested the degree of his disorientation.

"She's buying you some candy," said Stewart, emptying the man's flapsack with one hand, his other hand distracting him with a series of pats to the shoulder. "Here's the problem," he said to the robars, who had angled their vision panels down to his right hand. "No cassette!"

"Goodness gracious!" said one of the robars. "I am preparing a fresh copy through Meminet."

"Very good," said Stewart. "That's all Mr. Tingworth needs." In less than a minute the robot produced a new cassette, inserted it into Tingworth's flapper, and restored the flapper to its pouch. Tingworth sat still, looking stunned.

"Meanwhile," said the robar, its voice suddenly stiffening with formality, "we are puzzled by *you*, sir. As to your own identity . . . "

The robar's eye-panel scanned him up and down, as though peering

MEMINI

into his very heart. Fear's icy cleaver cut through Stewart's stomach. But the hubbub had attracted a growing crowd. The people surrounding Tingworth and Stewart now thrust the robars aside. Pointing to their nametags, they tried to draw signs of recognition from the bewildered VP.

"Try not to mob him. It's frightening when your flapper malfunctions," said Stewart, raising his voice.

A man to his right looked over at Stewart, appeared to do a double-take, and shook his head in vehement agreement. "You're absolutely right, sir." He backed away, as did Stewart, who soon discovered that some of those at first drawn to Tingworth had begun to crowd *him* instead! They started asking questions about what had happened and praised him for taking things in hand.

"All problems should be so easy to solve," Stewart laughed nervously.

"Quite so, Mr. Barton," said a stiff-looking woman whose nametag read Alveola Prott. "Now if Memini's problems were as simple as dear old Avery's..."

"Oh, don't get into politics!" someone blurted.

"Thizh'ere's a party, damn it!" growled someone else.

"I have a *right* to ask his opinion," said Prott, thrusting her finger at his chest. "Do you feel, President Barton, that OGOSH poses a real threat to our organization?"

It was Stewart's turn to do a double-take. "What did you call me?" he said.

"Sir?"

He followed Prott's finger to his chest. Something was amiss with his nametag. It was hard to make out so close to his eyes and at so steep an angle. He pulled it up close to his face. It read

LESTER BARTON
President

Stewart's throat clamped shut. His mouth dropped open as he stared around at everyone. Everyone was staring back at him. Expectantly.

24. FONGU ON 3V

She strained beneath his unyielding body. Andy tightened his grip, delighting in his power to punish her, to teach this mouthy cunt a lesson from which she'd never recover. What a thrill to see that silenced tongue jut out, her face turn red as if she were ashamed, truly *ashamed*, ASHAMED!

The door buzzer shocked him—as if it were hooked to electrodes in his brain. Someone had entered the sitting room! He loosened his grip and listened a moment, the woman under him flailing him with weak, uncoordinated arms. Footsteps! Releasing her throat, he hopped off the bed. He sank to the floor and scrambled to rake in all his clothing.

"Helen!" he heard this time, directly outside the door. There was no time even to slip into his pants. Crushing his clothes to his chest, he heard her gagging behind him as he dashed out the rear door into the brightly lit main corridor.

A man and a woman were strolling up from the left. They stopped short, their mouths making little O's. "Go fuck yourselves!" he snapped, hustling past them into the rec-room, where he snaked into his briefs and pants before the astonished eyes of some ping-pong players, whose ball bobbled down across the floor. A few more seconds, he thought, and daisies would've been sprouting out of Helen Means's ass! Not that he'd *wanted* to go that far, but the way she kept snipping at his balls . . . He had to keep cool, stay in control. Only dumb luck had kept him from outright snuffing the snotnosed bitch! (His right hand still shook from the effort he'd begun to pour into it.) *She* wasn't even the one who deserved to be wasted! She'd been *robbed* of all those memories of him by the Jap. It was hard to believe that he alone now "remembered" those VR scenes composed entirely in the bitch's own voice. He'd tried hard, damn it, to stuff some of those epi-

MEMINI

sodes back into her skull—on the off-chance that they'd ring some little bell somewhere in the back of all that vacancy. But she could only see him as a fast-food fuck-on-the-run that took too long to heat up! If there was anyone who ought to be ass-whipped it was that bullet-chested Jap with the fluttery, black-eyed lies.

He drew no further attention from the dozen or so people scattered around the rec-room. After wriggling into the rest of his clothes, Andy slunk along the wall to the low-lit 3V den where he'd parked his butt only a short while before.

"Premier Tonsil, will OGOSH now throw up tariff walls against the free flow of natural recreational substances to the North?"

"President Merleau, we are doing all we can to prevent any hitch in the supply. Next question . . ."

Andy settled into a vacant armchair. On a nearby sofa two men sat gazing up at the wallset. They were apparently intrigued by Premier Tonsil. Their hands, meanwhile, explored each other's thighs. Fucking fraggots! thought Andy. He, too, looked at the wall and saw the moving mouth of the Santa Claus-faced Premier of FONGU. He didn't think he'd actually cracked her neck, so he was fairly sure that no one would try to arrest him. What would they do, send a robar house-dick after him? Anyway, by the time she had a voice back to squeal with, she'd draw a total blank as to what had hit her. And besides, if Memini tried moving on him, he'd tell them to stick their new assignment right up their clam-cheeked flappers. Didn't he have, after all, a kind of diplomatic immunity with these chipheads? His anger flared again as he thought of the filthy language she had used on him in bed. Meanwhile, the chair's speakers bathed him in the sound of the 3V.

"This can hardly be termed a *crisis*," said the Premier of FONGU. "It is no more than an unstable global situation that has just now entered a phase transition whose unpredictable minor details fall into the generally predictable pattern governed by the well-known Figure-Eight Attractor . . . Question from the Prime Minister of Ireland."

Andy recognized the show as one of those irregular hemispheric briefings in which Premier Tonsil, whose head was filled with airgel, had to prove he was alive and functional by rapping face to holovized face with the heads of all the Northern nation-states. This sturdy old lord of Northern fragdom had been a mediocre President of the U.S.A. and had then achieved world fame as founder of Gene Zene cloned cuisines, from which he had been elevated directly to his present position without serving the usual apprenticeship as Coordinator of the North American Geopolitical Union.

"Premier Tonsil," asked the Irish P.M., "is there any truth to rumors of widespread executions of rebel fundamentalist oldfolks throughout the Democratic Union of Mesopotamian Brotherhoods?"

"I assure you, Prime Minister, that local conditions have parochial histories that bear no relation to the wider concerns of . . . "

Andy felt increasing rage at *both* bitches together now—at flax-fuzz and bullet-tits—and he pictured himself as a long-repressed oldfolks fundamentalist Hercules twisting the necks of a venomous pair of fraglets just for starters along a rapid road to revenge.

"Premier Tonsil," said the Chancellor of Germany, "in the present non-crisis between the hemispheres—"

"Phase transition!"

"Yes, phase transition . . . the citizens of my country are concerned that certain scheduled international sports events may be canceled because of the jealousy and spite that certain nations harbor toward others who happen to be naturally favored with superior aptitudes in the realms of science and technology. Is there any truth to . . . ?"

The frags were all running scared tonight! thought Andy. Give oldfolks an even break and we'll hang you by your balls, shit in your flappers, fuck your wives blind, and grind your stinking guts into dogfood!

The Premier of Great Russia: "Honored heads of FONGU, we must not join in blaming Memini for the present situation. Instead, that great conglobulate ought to beam down power to the trouble-making South in such great supply as to flood every grumbling member of OGOSH with six continuous months of bad weather."

The Prime Minister of Canada: "We say *no* to the sword-waving blather of our Great Russian colleague, whose nation, as everyone knows, is almost entirely a Memini subsidiary. On the contrary, we wish to redirect the attention of FONGU to the *criminal negligence* of a Memini that fails to respond to ... "

What a waste! thought Andy. Who wouldn't much prefer to watch "There's a Crime in Progress"? He looked over quizzically toward the glassy-eyed lovers, wondering what riveted their slack-jawed attention, then saw them making bread inside each other's flies.

The *hell* with Memini! thought Andy. *He* wasn't Russia! They didn't own *him*! He ought to walk right up to Mizz Missile-Tits and kiss her ass goodbye, tell her "I quit!" But what was the hurry? Why not be practical, eat his cake and have it too? ... What a fantastic idea! Maybe Wanjo wasn't so lost in space as he'd thought. Collect from two bosses for one and the same lousy job! ... He'd let Wanjo make all the arrangements. *Shit*, what a scam! How come he hadn't thought of it till now? ... He hadn't been *aggravated* into thinking of it till now.

Andy clenched his fists. She'd squeezed his balls in a vise! Twice! Best thing was just to forget her. Still, he could not get the picture of that foul-mouthed bitch out of his mind. He had felt such *satisfaction* seeing her eyes pop, watching her tongue turn purple. Why had he stopped, goddammit? Now he had to picture her fucking her robot boss! ... The blood pounded fiercely in his head.

And then he remembered what Yolanda had given him. He pulled the crude little cloth doll out of his flapsack. The cassette! It wasn't in its pouch in the doll's little dress! He fished around in the sack—and there, thank God, it was. It had shaken loose, fortunately not flying out when the cunt had whipped his clothes around like a yo-yo. He set the little oblong back into its close-fitting dress-pouch, which was stuck through with several short, bead-headed needles. Of course, he didn't *believe* in all that hoodoo shit ...

He felt such *satisfaction* jabbing that soft little doll over and over in the heart.

25. THE TESTING OF STEWART BRIDGES

Stewart looked again to make sure he was not imagining it. It still read **LESTER BARTON**. The tape had been slapped a bit crookedly over what seemed to be his own nametag, whose edge clearly showed. He had the nightmarish feeling of suddenly being thrust onto a brightly lit stage stark naked and unable to remember his lines. Some joker had done this during the ripdance, when the world spun around so fast he wouldn't even have felt his pocket being picked. Joker, hell! This was *part of the test*. His "final examination," she'd called it. How else confront him with his possible future colleagues? He had to be mistaken for someone worth chatting *with*! And now they must be recording his slightest blink (through tiny 3V "eyes" sprinkled everywhere) . . .

"The name of Memini is being dragged through the international mud," said Alveola Prott, her voice rising in pitch. "Negotiations that would normally take minutes now take us hours, days, so deep is the distrust!"

He felt like a pinned beetle, jaws agape, legs clawing empty air. "Have faith in your company president!" said Stewart, striking the pose of one offended. Self-reference in the third person came to him as an inspiration. In no way could it be recorded that he was *verbally* playing the role of an impostor. "Would Lester Barton have brought things to such a pass unless it was ultimately for the good of us all? Do you think he would act without foresight, without awareness of all the possible conse—"

"How arrogant of you!" said the balding man next to Prott "We want *explanations*! We are experiencing untold difficulties in all our respective departments because of this—this global *mess* that—"

"Hear, hear! Explanations, explanations!" chimed in others.

Stewart's breath came short. He felt pains in his chest. He cast about wildly for an exit. Why not just walk away? he thought. But if they followed? And how would it look to the camera eye if he simply tried to duck out? Surely, any moment now Sibyl would descend like a *dea ex machina* and cherry-pick him away from these snorting dragons. (She was probably spying on him through closed-circuit 3V, measuring the level of his discomfort...)

And then he happened to glance again at where Avery Tingworth was seated. This time slumped face-forward over the table. He did not look like a man taking a snooze.

"Look! Something's happened to Tingworth!" he shouted. A godsend was one thing; making the most of it was another. Everybody turned around, distracted.

"Avery!" people cried out in alarm. "Good heavens!"

Stewart pried up an end of the nametag that had been loosely taped to his chest. He coaxed it off easily, balled it in his fingers, and flicked it onto the floor. His own name stood exposed again for anyone to see. Meanwhile, he strode up with the others toward Tingworth. He felt it wiser to stay with the crowd than to be seen slinking off at a moment of crisis. Besides, he feared for the aging executive. The shock of disorientation could be lethal.

Tingworth's colleagues seemed helpless. They surrounded the table, called the name of their sprawled-out colleague in a dozen tones, and just stared. Stewart seized the opportunity. Nudging people aside, he edged up to the table and reached for Tingworth's wrist. He felt it again and again, his face stern, almost reproachful. "No pulse!" he announced grimly. "President Barton!" he cried, pretending to search the crowd.

"What do you mean, 'President Barton'?" said someone. "*You* are Pres... Oh, excuse me," he mumbled, turning away. Everyone turned around now, glancing at each other's nametags, craning their necks in search of Lester Barton.

"Did you see him leave?" said one.

"No. Did you?"

"He was standing right here," said Prott.

"He must have run off for help."

"We were standing right here discussing the crisis," said the balding man.

"It was clear that he did not like being pressured."

"Indeed, some of you could've been more polite. He is, after all, our—"

"All we wanted was an *explanation*."

"Now that doesn't sound so terribly unreasonable."

"An explanation of what?"

Stewart watched them all, fascinated. It suddenly struck him that he'd been the one elected, by default, to deal with this minor matter of a dead or dying long-time colleague of theirs. They seemed, *in the course of a mere few seconds*, to have completely lost interest in Tingworth! As for himself, he was miraculously off the hook. But it occurred to him that, as the only one still attentive to Tingworth, he'd better do something practical—like hail a passing robar.

One came rolling by in the next lane over. It made a sharp left at his summons. The robar positioned a flesh-soft claw over the top of Tingworth's head. "A medbar will be here in seconds," it said, "but I'm afraid that from the onset of cardiac arrest a critical amount of time has elapsed during which Mr. Tingworth's brain has been deprived of blood-flow. Your colleague may not be resuscitable."

"I'm sorry to hear that."

"And I would hold out little hope for salvaging the more valuable of his organs either, such as the liver and the kidneys."

"What a waste!"

"Yes indeed! I hope I prove wrong on all counts, Mr. Bridges, but in the event that my analysis is correct, I offer you my deepest condolences in a time of great sorrow."

"If he's dead this is a dreadful loss." Stewart spoke aloud and looked around him, expecting to encounter the sympathetic attention of Tingworth's colleagues. But while some were still looking vaguely around for Barton, others had drifted back again into shoptalk.

"Personnel come and go, sir," said the robar, "but Memini will endure. We take all such losses in our stride."

The medbar that rolled up looked little different from an ordinary robar—heftier, and with a pair of rear arms overlooking an extensible stretcher. Sizing up the situation immediately, it gently lifted Tingworth's upper body and injected a hypodermic through his clothing into his heart.

"The situation is hopeless," said the medbar. "No response. If you will help to lay him on the stretcher, sir, I shall proceed according to protocol and, with as little disturbance to the other guests as possible, deliver Mr. Tingworth for temporary storage to the medical station at the head of the swimming pool."

"By all means," said Stewart, gripping the heavy body under the arms.

"Thank you for your help, sir. My deepest condolences in this time of great sorrow."

"Don't mention it. Let's lug him out of here before we ... cause commotion among the guests," he said ironically.

"Thank you for your tact and sensitivity, sir. Situations like this, if handled badly, sometimes cause considerable unpleasantness."

"We *don't* want unpleasantness," said Stewart, pitching Tingworth onto the fully extended stretcher. "Anything but unpleasantness!" When the corpse was correctly positioned, the stretcher was fully retracted into the body of the medbar. The medbar now looked like almost any other working robar as it slowly wheeled away over the flagstone walks. Dabbing his sweat-beaded face with a soiled table-napkin, Stewart wondered whether the medbar would stop to serve drinks.

"Hi, Stew-baby!" The hawk-faced man who had come up behind him slapped him on the shoulder and said, "Si' down, we got things to talk about."

Stewart shuddered at the touch. Andy the Actor stood grinning at him like some sort of fellow conspirator! Trying to hide his agitation, he eased himself into a seat, and Andy sat next to him.

"Didn't think I'd have the honor," said Andy.

"What honor?"

"To meet the company BP."

Stewart stiffened, suspecting a trick. "I'm not exactly an employee ... like yourself," he said, pointing to Andy's nametag. "I occasionally do work for Memini on special assignment, as I'm sure many other bioprogrammers do now and then."

Andy shook his head and smiled, the edge of his teeth glinting beneath his upper lip like a knife blade. "Uh-uh, Stewie. You're their special boy. Their one and only."

"Ridiculous."

"Look around you, fella! How many other BP's were invited to the party?"

"I wouldn't know. Unlike you, I didn't make a survey."

"You're an ace, Mister. The best in the business."

"Really? How would *you* know?"

"Because you wouldn't *be* here if you weren't."

"What do you want, Mr. Peters?"

"Well, first of all," said Andy, crossing his knees and tossing his palms out affably, "I'm a great *fan* of yours. I want to congratulate you on the quality of your work."

"I'm not a 3V writer. My work doesn't circulate to the general public."

"Look again, fella. Recognize the name? . . . No accident, is it, why I'm a great fan of yours?"

He had to make a snap decision. Deny any memory of a BP job involving an Andy Peters? It would fit his tekkie persona. He shrugged his shoulders with a show of bored indifference and made as if to scan the gardens again, as if waiting impatiently for someone to show up.

"Don't tell me you don't *meminize* the work you do!" snorted Andy. "That's bullshit and you know it. Look me in the fuckin' eye and tell me you don't remember a job you did last week—splicing old Andy here in a Helen Means cassette . . . Rings a bell, right, babe?"

Stewart decided he would look him in the eye. "I don't discuss my commissions except with my employers. For the job you're referring to I was paid by Memini. If you're not fully satisfied, you'll have to complain to your supervisor, not to me."

"I'm not lookin' to complain, guy. Hey, don't get me wrong. All I wanna do is make a deal with you . . . privately."

"A commission?" said Stewart. The reason for "Mr. Peter's" approach was now coming clear to him. All he had to do was find a way to turn him down gracefully. "To be honest with you, I'm already committed up to my ears. I really don't see—"

"Oh, it's not a *new* job I'm talking about. No, not at all." Andy thrust his face uncomfortably close. "Listen, Stewie, you gotta help me out of a jam—no, not *me* . . . Helen! Helen Means. She's in big trouble and only you can help."

Stewart looked at him, trying to keep a straight face. Some sort of con was brewing.

"Listen," Andy half whispered, "she could lose her job, fuck up her whole career. First off, she *loved* the new tape you made, I want you to know that. She's a true-blue fan of yours, I can tell you that."

"Thanks," said Stewart. It was a job he'd had to do so rapidly, that to come up with a passable string of romantic clichés, he'd had to scrounge from a host of earlier commissions. "Get to the point, Mr. Peters."

"Well, something happened. She hit the wrong button or something. Completely wiped out the tape."

"Deleted it?"

"Deleted, right . . . Now, the company didn't go through all that expense to have a thing like *that* happen, did it? No, if they found out what she did, they'd think it was deliberate sabotage, and they'd kick her out on her ass. Besides which, she's coming up right now for consideration for a big fat raise."

"Too bad," mumbled Stewart, seeing exactly what Andy was driving at. The story itself sounded plausible enough—some nitbrained frag making an incredibly stupid mistake—but it was the *source*, Andy "Peters," that worried him. And why would Memini have wanted, in the first place, to splice together this nightcrawler with one of their top execs? It didn't make sense.

"So, listen up, Stewie my friend, I need you to do me a great big favor and save everybody a stack of shit. I need you to do the job over again."

"Now listen, Mr. Peters—"

"Hey, for you it's no big deal! You got it all in your head or in your files anyway. Here," he said, pulling a little cloth doll out of his flapsack, then drawing a biocassette out of a pouch in its skirt. "This is a copy of the original—before you made the changes."

Stewart slouched back as if threatened by a cobra. "You're asking me to do something highly . . . highly unethical," he stammered.

"I expected you to help me out as a *favor*, being we're both company men. And think of how much Helen needs your help, huh? Poor bitch is up the creek without a flapper! But to sweeten the deal, I'm willing to pay you—half what you got for the original job. All in rock-solid I See You's. Okay?"

Stewart pretended to ignore Andy's presence. He didn't feel terribly sorry for Helen Means—a lovely blonde that he'd seen off and on during the evening. She it was he had earlier seen chained to a tree in the woods with a fat man ramming her from behind. He couldn't wax sentimental over some slack-twat of a fraglet. They'd hump your best friend without giving *you* a second thought! What made *her* more humanly valuable than the scum now squatting next to him? Who was *he* to make fine moral distinctions among various grades of rot? Why *shouldn't* he help slime-mold part with his blood-stained ICU's? And if that had been all there was to the moral equation . . . but something bothered him. It had been gnawing at him subliminally all evening. That Memini had *used* him. That in altering that woman's cassette to include one Andy "Peters" he'd been made party to an engineered rape! . . .

"Do I bore you? What's the matter, you don't hear me?" said Andy, thrusting the cassette into Stewart's face. "Look, this is a matter of great importance for me. I'll double my offer. I'll pay you all over again what they paid you—half of it in whacks, half I See You. *Take* it, goddammit! I don't have all fuckin' day!"

Stewart shied back. He suddenly saw the whole scene as one big charade. This was the clearest proof yet that he was being *tested*! So that was what all this was about! He should have seen right through it from the start! His creation of the tape, his present meeting with the personage he'd been asked to splice in, the current "temptation in the desert" (and they couldn't even know that he knew who "Andy Peters" really was—Andy the Actor indeed!) . . . Right now a dozen 3V screens . . . studying every quiver on his face . . . Well, he'd show them that *he* could act at least as well as Andy!

"I told you before," Stewart said firmly, raising his voice to be sure he was recorded, "what you're asking me to do is *highly unethical*. But not only that, my friend. It's quite impossible as well."

"What the hell are you talking about, 'impossible'?"

"I mean simply that, in accordance with professional ethics, I keep no copies of my commissions. What you want, my man . . . no longer exists."

"You're full of shit, you son of a bitch!"

"You'd better have Helen confess to her boss the mistake she made. Surely they'll—"

"One last time. I'm fucking *begging* you . . . down on my cocksucking *knees*, all right?" Andy's lips trembled almost convincingly. His eyes seemed to pop out of his skull.

"Awfully sorry, old man," sniffed Stewart. He hoped they were taping him in profile. He gave very haughty profile.

"Listen, you stiff-assed prick, if you don't do this favor for me, your life isn't worth dried dogshit! You *hear*?" Andy leaned forward to within inches of his face. His eyes were bloodshot. His facial muscles quivered like drawn bowstrings. "Your life may not be worth dogshit anyway," he added.

"And just what do you mean by that?"

"You know too much for your own fucking good!" said Andy. "I'm beginning to see a deep connection between you and me both being here tonight."

Stewart drew back from the intense, ironic gaze. It was like staring into a gunbarrel. It made Stewart shudder again, but only for a moment (of which he was deeply ashamed). Damn good acting! he thought. No wonder they called him the Actor. Which was exactly why they had rented him for the night! . . . Yes, the whole byzantine plot made perfect sense. Tempt, cajole, threaten! Stewart felt a sense of professional pique. To know that someone other than himself could invent so elaborate a plot! . . . Then again, how *important* it made him feel! All this ingenious testing could mean only one thing—he *had* to be the prime candidate for a very considerable position . . .

"Your threats don't faze me in the least," Stewart calmly replied, speaking for the monitor that watched them. "What's right is right. Sorry I can't help you, my friend. Tell Ms. Means to be more careful when she next sticks her finger up her flapper."

Andy sprang up from the table, knocking his chair over backwards. "You're a dead man, you son of a bitch! There's nowhere you can hide that I won't find you." He jammed the doll and cassette back into his flapsack and stalked off in what Stewart applauded as an excellent imitation of rage.

Nevertheless, this whole encounter with Andy—on top of the nametag and the Tingworth incidents—had violently upset his stomach. Trembling in his gut, he hurried off to the woods, where he knew there were restrooms near the dance floor. There he could also wash up and even quick-launder his pants. When would the partying be over? he wondered. And where the hell was Sibyl? How would he know if he had passed all the tests? And what if he did pass? he asked himself. Could he in all conscience work for a corporation that had no qualms about hiring an Andy Kedro?

26. AMAZING CAUSE OF SORE THROAT

Andy wandered off into the darkness of the woods. He'd like to have killed that futhamuckin frag on the spot, but it was a pleasure he'd have to put off to a more opportune moment. Right now, the name of the game was *self-control*. Must not fly off the handle twice in one night! What kind of shit would he be swimming in now, he wondered, if that boss of Helen's who'd pulled rank on the dance floor hadn't showed up just in time to save her neck? (And yet, snapping her windpipe would've given him *one heck* of a rush!)

So now he had to think about *Andy*. Take care of Andy's candies. As for Helen's melons—even if her pussy were on fire, he wouldn't piss on her to put out the flames! Clearly, it was her *boss* who'd cut him out of her tape. (The Jap was just following orders.) Fucker'd been sniffing after Goldilocks's ass all evening, wanted her only for himself. What fun it would be to give the dumb fuck a blow-by-blow account of the scene in the woods!

The thing for him now, though, was to get all he could out of this last job that he'd ever do for Memini. When looked at over the years, the income he got from Memini was not worth the sacrifice of his pride. He was an honorable man, so he wouldn't duck out on the promise he'd made to that other corporate whore, Miss Yammy. Besides, since he now saw how to triple his money for the same lousy job, he'd be a fool to lose a bundle over some shit about wounded pride. Got to be practical. First priority: *Andy's candies*.

Charging down the moon-flecked woodpaths, he paid no attention to the thrashing and moaning in the groves to his left and right. What startled him out of his reverie was a voice from the shadows in front of him. "Mr. Peters, sir!"

"What?"

"I've been trying to catch up with you. You do set a pace, you know. I've been instructed to tell you that Ms. Sibyl Yamamoto would like to have a word with you."

"No shit! I was just thinking of having a word with her myself."

"Excellent, sir," said the robar. "You may follow me if you wish."

She waited for him in a remote corner of the park. Her table sat at the edge of the woods, near a columned wall only ten or so yards from the entrance she'd guarded earlier in the evening. The shadows of overhanging willows made her hard to detect.

"Have a seat, Mr. Kedro," she said, pointing to one opposite hers.

"Been wondering where you disappeared to," said Andy, slipping into the designated seat. "Been checking out the groves in the woods but didn't see a butt that looked like yours."

"Sorry to disappoint you, but for me these parties are more business than pleasure. As for *your* activities, Mr. Kedro," she said, looking at him sharply, "it appears you've had ample opportunity for both business *and* pleasure. Are things going well for you tonight?"

"Fantastic!" said Andy.

"Really? May I be so bold then as to ask whether you got the 'satisfaction' you wanted out of Helen Means?"

"Oh, totally," said Andy. Pushing his chair back, he planted his feet up on the table and framed Miss Yammy's face between his shoes. "Turns out she didn't need any memory implant to get all worked up at the sight of Andy Peters. She creamed as soon as she saw me. A woman's body remembers more than her brain, would you agree? Must be why *you're* afraid to try me, Miss Yammy."

"You went to bed with her?"

"Of course."

"And what did you *do* to her when you were in bed with her, Mr. Kedro?"

He had been tilting back in his chair. Her question caught him off balance and he nearly toppled to the patio floor. "What?" he grinned. "You want the details? Is *that* how little Miss Y gets her kicks?"

"Your sexual habits don't interest me, Mr. Kedro. *Unless* they result in injury to a member of our staff."

Andy dropped his legs to the floor and pulled up close to the table. "What's this?" he said, leaning forward. "You mean, she complained?"

"President Barton reported the entire incident to Meminet."

Andy laughed. "I'd'a smiled if I'd known we were on 3V."

"This is not a laughing matter, Mr. Kedro. It is painful for me even to discuss this. Memini has put a lot of trust in you, as you know. Perhaps you can shed some light on exactly what went on between you and Helen that resulted in the bruises to her neck. According to the report I have here, she claims that . . . you attempted to *strangle* her."

"Bullshit!" snorted Andy. "She remembered my name and her sore neck, so she figured I tried to choke her."

"Well, it does seem logical. What is *your* explanation?" She looked at him with quivering lips. He noticed with amazement that she wasn't claiming they were *sure* he'd tried to strangle her. So much for their trust in each other's *memories*, thought Andy. There was still enough doubt for them to hope it wasn't so! And after all, they'd invested quite a lot in him over the years, had to trust him with some of their dirtiest little secrets . . .

"My explanation?" said Andy. "Are you . . . sure you wanna hear?"

"Of course!" came the thin-lipped reply.

The thin lips over the big tits—the discrepancy put Andy into a mood for needling her. "What I say may be terribly embarrassing," he warned.

"I'm sure I can handle it," she snapped.

"Well, okay. After we fucked once or twice, she was so damn crotch-happy grateful that she offered to give me a very special blow-job . . . better than anything she ever gave Lester Barton." Andy noted with pleasure how Miss Yammy's lips crinkled up in distaste. "Well, the prospect was so exciting that I developed a gigantic bone. I mean, it wasn't just a royal one, it was imperial. Half my blood supply and all my brains got stuffed into that monster *zazeech*!"

"Really!" she smirked.

"Really! . . . Now, being the decent guy that I am, and seeing as how things'd gotten out of hand, so to speak, I told her she could back out if she wanted . . . since we'd only made an *oral* agreement, you might say." Andy watched the flanges of the supersec's nostrils vibrate on her stone-still face.

"Well, she kind of laughed at me and said that at Memini she worked with the biggest ones in the business."

"Get on with it!" said Yamamoto. He watched her golden fingernails drum the table.

"What's the matter?" said Andy. "Is it too long, or just a bit hard to swallow?" She made no response except to drum the table more furiously. "Well, lemme tell you, she made a heroic attempt to get on top of the situation. She stuffed me right in past her tonsils and jammed me halfway down her throat. By God, I'd never've believed it was possible! Let me tell you, if anyone's suited to reach the top around here..."

"Just get on with it, will you?" Two red blotches had erupted on Yammy's cheeks.

"Well, you know, halfway just isn't enough for someone as ambitious as Helen Means. And that's what caused all the trouble... because after a couple of trips down the esophagus, she found she couldn't pull me out."

"That's ridiculous!"

"These things happen."

"Go on."

"Let's see. Where was I? I'm kinda stuck. Oh yeah, so she began to gag. Couldn't catch her breath, you see? So I guess it must have lodged in her windpipe, not her esophagus. Damn, I never get my anatomy straight!... Well, as soon as I saw what *her* problem was, I decided to overlook my own selfish pleasure and try to help her out—because deep down, I really am a gentleman."

"Finish, will you?"

"I couldn't," said Andy. "With a woman turning blue in the face, how can you?"

"That doesn't explain the bruises on the *outside* of her throat."

"Well, the only way to retire from her throat was to grab her around the neck and push back—hard, lemme tell you. I saved her from asphyxiation, I did. Poor thing was so upset, no wonder she didn't remember what'd happened." Andy shook his head in feigned sympathy. Miss Yamamoto refused to meet his mock-solemn gaze.

"We have *business* to discuss," she said coolly. "Since you've evidently received the personal gratification you were hoping for tonight, then may I assume, Mr. Kedro, that you are ready to keep your half of the bargain?"

"Naturally. No question about it. But I gotta ask you for one tiny favor."

"Which is?" Again her lips tensed with suspicion.

"Which is that I need some cash up front. I'm facing an immediate financial crisis that, who knows, might impair my performance on the job."

"How much in advance, Mr. Kedro?"

"Half. Divided equally between whacks and I-See-You's."

"What do you think, Meminet?" she said, looking down at her flapper, which lay open on the table between them. The answer took several seconds coming back through her skeeter. "Meminet is agreed. I can give you half in advance as soon as you turn over the Helen Means cassette."

"I've got it right here," said Andy, patting his pocket.

"Very good. Meminet is sending over a robar to process the credit transaction." Within moments a robar wheeled up to them with a pop-up display terminal in Banking mode. "Your bank is . . . ?"

"Still the Bank of Inner Mongolia." He handed her the cassette. She swept it up in a fist so tight he thought she'd cut her palms on its corners.

"Still the old account number?"

"Yep."

Her hand slapped the ID plate and then she typed in some numbers. "Deposit confirmed," he read. Anyone could make a deposit into his account, of course, but no one could make a withdrawal but himself. So far he had what he wanted. And he'd gotten her off the hook, he saw. Her whole body had grown relaxed. She ought to be eternally grateful to him (for at least the next ten minutes, he thought—on the assumption that she really wasn't a stag.) . . . And as for all that shit about that blonde-bearded cunt, all "they" had really wanted from him, as he could see (he could see right through the hypocritical bastards!), was any old excuse from him, something they could stick like a skindot over a pimple. He, Andy Kedro, was far more important to Memini right now than some company bimbo they'd set him up to try to fuck in the first place!

As the robar rolled away, Yamamoto leaned toward him confidentially. "I have conferred with Meminet," she said in a cracking voice, "and I have just found out the . . . details of the job you are to do. I may now point out to you the man who will be the object of your . . . assignment."

He followed her pointing finger. Why did her hand tremble so? he wondered.

"Do you see him standing alone, looking vaguely in our direction, between the buffet and the edge of the park? . . . The man with the light-brown beard?" she said, her voice barely audible, her eyes welling with tears.

Andy looked hard. He recognized the target at once, and his identity was no great surprise. There'd even be some pleasure for him in this one—the pleasure of a little revenge. "Yes, I *know* the son of a bitch. And lately, oddly enough, I've enrolled him in my own *personal* shit-list too!"

"I want to hear *nothing* about your personal shit-lists! I simply do my . . . housekeeping tasks, and I expect you to do *yours*. No comments. No discussion."

"Data received. Over and out." She looked to him as distraught as the time, five years ago, he was summoned to do his first vanishing trick for Memini. At first he assumed her reaction was due to her personal connection to the target, but lately he inclined to the belief that she exhibited no more than a "spasm of conscience." Some young tekkies could experience these for over fifteen minutes at a stretch.

"You are to fulfill your assignment on Monday," she said, trying to recover her business-like tone.

"When on Monday?" he asked.

"During normal office hours. Be prepared for a call from me on Monday. Any time from 9 a.m. You must be ready to go into action at a moment's notice."

Andy got up and straightened his tie. "Get me a cab, sweetie. For me this party's over." Like picking up a rat by the tail, he stripped the phony name-tag off his chest.

27. THE ANIMAL PASSION OF SIBYL YAMAMOTO

"Doubting Thomas!" said Sibyl, as the doors to her room closed behind them. "You really did think I would forget you?"

"How could you imagine such a thing?" Stewart protested. The ripdance went on in his loins now, and he didn't want some minor quarrel to squelch the crazy music humming between them.

"Well, you forced me to rescue you from that very pretty woman near the buffet tables, didn't you?"

"Oh, we were just chitchatting about nothing in partic . . ." Stewart felt her hand snake into his pants, the cold blades of her fingers on his butt, the quick pinch. He shivered and laughed all at once.

"Darling, she'd already let her hand drape over your backside—on the outside, of course. But still, if I hadn't intervened . . ." Slowly, she withdrew her teasing hand.

"Sibyl, you've been at the top of my advisory ever since the promise you made when we were dancing." It was true that a lovely blue-eyed brunette—someone in Finance—had tempted him to the verge of uttering a serious proposition. Since it was already past eleven, and he'd had two stiff drinks after the run-in with Andy, and Sibyl had not yet turned up, why not drift with the perfume that gushed in sweat-sweetened waves from that babe with blue eyes? A bird in hand, etc.

"It doesn't matter," said Sibyl, winking archly. "Fortunately, in about two minutes I'll have forgotten what I saw. I'm interested only in this moment. 'You are this moment, and this moment is all of eternity I'll ever know.' . . . Does that sound familiar?"

"Vaguely. Is it from a song by the . . ."

"*You* wrote it, you dumbbell you! Don't you meminize all the bios that you write?"

"Of course not!" He was still on his guard.

"It's in the bio you did for LB. LB loves to quote it, you know."

"Well, I'm glad he thinks so highly of my work." Was she simply naive and spontaneous, he wondered, or was she so fiendishly clever that she could weave into their dalliance a tiny little trip-up bit like this *as part of the test*? He wanted to ask her: had he passed the acting test they had put him through earlier? Was he good enough to play the role of an LB stand-in when the boss slipped out for an hour or so to get laid? Or was there some other public stand-in role they were setting him up to perform—like *standing in the path of a gun-blast meant for LB*? Now why the hell hadn't he thought of that before? Big shots used doubles all the time! An easy job, good pay, lots of time off . . . but there would always be those few critical times you'd be on-stage expected to *perform*. Wisely, Stewart kept his thoughts to himself. He had to relax. To distrust her *now* was sheer nonsense.

As the doors to the bedroom swung open, she nuzzled his neck. The smell of her hair made his chest ache with longing. He held her so close as they stood on the threshold that he could feel the criss-cross straps of her gold-net dress rib his stomach. For long seconds neither said anything. He could hear their mingled heartbeats and didn't know which was his.

"I meant it when I said that your work . . . fills me with unbelievable feelings. LB lets me play episodes sometimes."

"Which you've recorded on your VRC?"

"Yes," she said, looking at him strangely. "I particularly like the romantic ones." Sibyl sat at the edge of the bed and wiggled her toes, lazily kicking off her golden shoes. She took Stewart's hand and sat him down beside her. "I've meminized a number of those scenes . . . I guess that's sort of stealing from you, isn't it?"

"Stealing?" he said, unable to dampen the tremor in his voice. *Was this really happening?* he thought. *A vision out of Tokywood reaching out of the wall and clasping his hand?*

"I'm recording us *right now*," she said. "Is this also a form of stealing? It's just that I want very much to preserve every—"

"It's not stealing at all! None of it is," Stewart insisted. "On the contrary, I feel terribly flattered." ("You are being *recorded*!" his mother would brusquely have reminded him just then. "Try not to *forget* that, Stewart. Every little detail of everything you say, everything you do . . . ")

"Ever since I saw you, in the office, and connected all those lovely fantasies with their creator . . . I wanted so much to be with you and have you make memories for me, too, in person . . . in bed, because this is the only way I can repay you."

The satiny floral coverlet was not so smooth as the skin of her breasts. Large, firm breasts whose rose-colored nipples tapered up toward him like birds' tongues. She drew his hand lightly around them after loosening the cups of gold that had reined them in all evening. Clutching him by the shoulders, she flung him down on the bed and proceeded, with a mock-serious smile, to strip off all his clothing. Soon it was her turn to lean back on the bed. Raising her haunches, she let him peel off—from her waist down over her thighs—the only wall between her skin and the press of his eyes. "Nothing to stop you, you see?" she said. "Not even a vaginet."

Let it be slow! Stewart said to himself. He wanted it to be as he had feverishly dreamed it for days. His head sinking between her parting thighs, he rolled his chin around her soft, yielding nap while his nostrils sucked in the steamy, spicy smell of her. Brown beard knitted with hot black down. His lips closed in for another brush with the fuzz, his probe unzipping the lightly glued lips of her funnel. His tongue's tip snaked into the vestibule of another world, and he now knew the taste of an angel's pussy. She let him explore her moist walls, the jutting tip of flesh in her ceiling, then gently eased him away, moaning. She needed to peer into his face.

"Soon, dear. Everything!" she whispered, shuddering with delight. "I want to feel that . . . even *more* intensely, if you can imagine that possible." Leaning back on her arm, she ran gold-painted toenails along his calf. "Put us inside one of your scenes," she pleaded. "I *know* you know so many. You use them over and over, you bioprogrammers. I know that."

"With lots of variations," Stewart said defensively. Reluctantly, he slid his body forward, then spoke with his lips grazing her ear. "Would you like to hear one I did for LB, or something you've never yet heard?"

She suddenly squeezed his pulsing shaft, shooting lightning from his toes to his brain. "Anything! I don't care which! Just wrap us in something good, something warm. Put shadows and sunlight all around us. Let me smell tropical air."

All the tropics Stewart wanted right then was cupping its drink of nectar between smooth, shining thighs that opened to a dark jungle steaming with rarest orchids. Jaguars from miles around slinked through the underbrush, guided by the overwhelming scent. "I rescued you from poachers once, in the Columbian Amazon. Do you remember?" he said, recalling an adventure he had spun once for someone and had used only a few times since. It was one she couldn't have heard.

"No, I don't remember," she said, stroking his chest with her fingers. "Remind me, Stewart dear. What was I doing there?"

"You were doing postgraduate research in biology, hoping to discover new species of useful plants."

"Hoping to find an antidote, perhaps, to some terrible blight-causing virus?"

"Yes. But you naively paid little attention to official advice that you stay out of the rain forest. Heedless of the dangers, you set up camp alone beside a clump of mangroves near a slow-running, muddy stream. You thought that because the region was patrolled by the Earthcorps, you were safe from *human* harm. How wrong you were!"

"I'm impetuous that way! I know I seem the highly efficient, practical type of woman," Sibyl murmured, thrusting her tongue in his ear, "but the jungle is in me. No dangers could make me resist it. Scratch the super-secretary and you touch the super-savage. Do you believe me?"

"You taste and smell like the jungle." He was choking with the odor of her sweetness.

"Remind me of how we met, Stewart. What were you doing in the Amazon?"

"I was doing my two-year stint as an Earthcorpsman, remember? I was out on a three-man patrol. Our little group separated, however, after being attacked by gunfire from invisible assailants. I got lost and wound up on my own. Finally, I arrived at those twisted mangroves and saw your tent in the clearing. Two grim-looking poachers had found you just before I did, though. Right out in front of your tent, one held you from behind, pinioning your arms. The other was tearing off your shorts while you futilely attempted to kick him away."

"What a fool I had to be to think I was in safe territory," she said, trembling. She rolled close to him, her face at the level of his chest. "I must have been drunk with love for science. Tell me, what did you do when you saw me... like that? Did you get excited too?"

He felt the warmth of her breasts on his ribs. Her left hand found the root of his scrotum. Gently, she massaged his testicles while gazing suspensefully into his eyes. He found it difficult to focus on the story, but the liquid warmth that rose from his groin helped to loosen his tongue. "I knew that rape would be only the beginning."

"Weren't you jealous? Didn't you want to have me yourself?"

"Yes, yes, I *was*. I *did* . . ."

She brushed her lips against his. "Your lips are so dry," she said. "I have a remedy." She inserted her middle finger between her legs, drew it out all slick, and painted Stewart's lips with the musk-scented fluid it bore. He licked his lips as though famished. "There, you've found your tongue again," she smiled. "Well, did you just sit there and watch them take me? Didn't you try to stop them?"

"You didn't realize that . . . after raping you they would kill you, and toss your body into the stream for the piranhas."

"Why? Why kill me?" she said. She pressed her face into his neck. Her whole body was aquiver. He could tell she wasn't faking. Her starved imagination had transported her, body and soul, into that dangerous jungle clearing.

"These poachers that we Earthcorpsmen are after . . . they hate scientists even more than they hate us. Because of scientific discoveries new areas of jungle are cordoned off, become more heavily guarded, less accessible to their ravagings . . ." This time, from the root, she slowly worked upward along the whole length of his rod, as if stretching him to double his size, as if squeezing a banana from its skin. She captured the clear juice that streamed out of the head, smeared it over her own lips, then returned for more, sucking it from her fingers.

"My lips are dry too," she said. "I thirst for you. I do. But first you must tell me, didn't you try to save me?"

"Of course," he said. "I raised my gun, aimed carefully, first at the man who held you, and two shots did the trick."

"That's a magical weapon you've got!" she said with genuine admiration. Her golden nails strummed his penis. "Let me kiss it out of deep, deep gratitude."

The sensation was nearly unbearable. Her lips sank over his shaft like a close-fitting golden halo. As she slowly slid back, she gave his head a sharp, lingering nip with her teeth. "And then . . . and then," Stewart quavered, "you invited me . . . *in*, into your tent, where I laid your shivering, half-naked body onto your bed, which was under its own warm canopy of mosquito netting, where you pulled me toward you and . . . and . . . "

"I owe you my life, Earthcorpsman. The sweetest parts of me belong to you forever." Sibyl looped her leg over him, locked his ribs between her warm, muscular knees, and teasingly scraped the clipped lawn of her vagina up and back over the throbbing head of his penis. "To you . . . and you *alone*, Earthcorpsman, forever." The feeling of engorgement she gave him sent tears spurting out of his eyes, and only then did she have mercy on him, plunging down with a savage suddenness. Tumbling over with her, he thrust from on top, then happily let her roll him back beneath her. Her nails cut crescents into his shoulders. She began almost immediately to fibrillate in orgasm after orgasm, her tremors echoing in his own flesh as well. His body attuned quickly to her strange pelvic rhythms, and they bucked and slapped at each other's drenched loins, their harmony of movement flawless. She, a world-class rider; he, her champion mount.

When their first hunger was sated and they found their voices again, she said, "My body will remember you. At odd times of the day my belly will start to quiver, and the jungle memory you gave me will rush back into my mind. I shall meminize it, just as I have all your other exciting imaginings. But this one is special. No matter who you originally made it for, it now belongs only to us. It's something that no one will be able to take from me, ever."

Sibyl's change of mood took him by surprise. She began soundlessly weeping. Stewart raised her head from his chest and looked into her flooded eyes. "Why are you crying?" he asked, lifting a tear with his finger and licking its salt with his tongue.

"Because I'm intensely, incredibly happy, and I refuse to believe that 'this moment' will ever be lost."

"We can remember this the way nature remembers summer," said Stewart, "by repeating it, over and over."

In silence, she again nested her face in his breast. He felt warm tears among the gold-brown hairs of his chest. *Why did she seem so sad at the height of their pleasure?* he wondered. He vowed he would *make* her remember, over and over. (Oldfolks or tekkie, one never really "remembered" making love—not the direct physical thrill of it, anyway—except by doing it again and again, he reflected.)

"Have you ever thought," she murmured, her lips stroking his chest like feathers as she spoke, "that after making love—I mean *ultimate* love, like now, when you know it couldn't *possibly* be better—that it would be . . . all right to die? That you've had the best, that there'd be nothing to regret leaving, that it would be best to go *right away,* while your body still shivered from coming?"

"I don't *know* if I've ever thought that," he answered carefully, still on his guard, remembering not to let himself seem to remember. "I may have made up such thoughts for my clients, though."

"Can you imagine," she said, stroking the love-slick on his thighs, "how intense it must be for the male praying mantis? I think of his whole soul flowing through his tiny penis so that he feels only total ecstasy, his brain melting into his semen, while his mate chews off his head and then the rest of him, joint by joint . . . until he literally becomes one with his lover."

"Do you think much about death after having sex?" Stewart asked, her imagery prickling his skin.

"I don't know," she said, licking her middle finger and then proceeding to massage his anus with it. It was a gesture of the tenderest, most endearing *familiarity*! It sent wild thrills buzzing through him. "I think it's all right for death to come *suddenly,*" she continued, "after you've been the best you can be, had the best you can have, while you're still in good health, before you need to suffer old age and decay, and before you become useless—or worse, an obstacle, even a danger, to those around you. I think it must be good if it comes quickly, if you don't expect it, if it's painless. I think . . . I don't know what I think. I'm sorry my thoughts are so morbid. In a minute

I'll simply forget them. Perhaps you won't be able to . . . so easily?"

"What do you mean?" Why did she look at him so searchingly? he wondered. "Don't worry, of course I will. I'm already thinking of something very different," said Stewart, fingering both sides of one of the soft-furred flaps of her vagina—a flapper he wished he could fill only with memories of himself!

"What are you thinking of?"

"I can't help wondering what you want to *do* with me? What was I being interviewed for? What position are you promising me? Or have I failed all your tests? Are you making love to me more out of pity than—"

"You mistrustful . . . !" Lightly, she squeezed his balls. He groaned comically, marveling at how she knew just when to stop before the pleasure turned to pain. "If you really must know, you passed most *major* tests before I ever saw your face."

"Tests for *what*?"

She positioned his fingers softly against her clitoris. "The position we have in mind for you is . . . extremely important. That's all I'm permitted to say, Stewart, believe me . . . except to tell you that you will find out everything you want to know on Monday. You must come to the office Monday, at 2 p.m. sharp."

"Monday at 2 p.m.?"

"I see that you are remembering my body again," she said. His penis began mounting a stiff resistance against the ceaseless kneading motions of her hand.

"I had better enter my appointment in advisory," said Stewart, hating the charade of having to slip out of bed, out of the silk of her fingers, just to enter a bit of data in flapper.

"Don't get up," she said.

"But . . . "

"You don't need your flapper."

"Really?" he laughed. "Can I count on you to remind me again?"

"I won't need to, Stewart. *You* won't forget. If something's that important, oldfolks don't forget."

"What!" He lurched backward, banging his skull against the headboard. "What are you accusing me of?"

MEMINI

"I'm sorry I alarmed you," said Sibyl, throwing her arms around him. "Don't . . . don't get out of bed. Perhaps I shouldn't have said—but I told you you've *passed all tests*. We know everything about you that's important to know, Stewart."

"You're setting me up for something! What are you setting me up for? Have you been . . . *ordered* to make love to me?" His body stiffened as her hands ran soothingly down his back.

"Is that what it felt like, Stewart? Like I was setting you up? You really think my lovemaking wasn't genuine?"

"It's not that. I just . . . demand to know what's going on!" He thought of Andy the Actor. Should he tell her that he knew who Andy "Peters" was? Should he demand to know why a professional killer had been employed as part of his test?

"I can't say any more than I've said," Sibyl murmured, sitting up in bed, supporting her head on her knees. Her back was a tawny beach, all pure warm sand, a virgin beach that the tide had cleared of footprints . . . as virgin as her mind, that strange mechanism that purged itself of conscience, that reset itself to the zero of innocence every quarter of an hour! She would not even remember, really *remember*, making love to him. She would only infer it, from his presence, from their nakedness, from the slick of come and mucus on their loins, from the tremors he saw like silent orgasms still convulsing her gut. (Or did she indeed have some unerring subliminal recognition system like an array of receptor molecules in her brain that reacted only to him?)

She turned to look at him reproachfully. He felt the sting of the tears in her eyes. "The only reassurance I can offer you," she said, "is the warmth of this body." Her back to him, she took his arms and laced them around in front of her, cupping his hands beneath her breasts. He thought it best not to mention Andy the Actor. Not just yet, at any rate.

"Leave now if you no longer want me," she said with a hitch in her voice.

"It's not that I don't want *you*," he replied. "It's just that . . . when I think of working with a bunch of colleagues who are the zombies I've met tonight . . ."

"But there may be compensations, irresistible compensations," she said, resting her head far back on his shoulder. "Am I such a zombie to you?"

His hands fondled her breasts. For a long while he searched for something to say, came up with nothing. He let his hands do all the speaking. His mouth made prints in the sun-drenched sands of her back. He was sure that she had told him the truth, that all he needed to know he would at last find out on Monday. An image flashed through his mind that filled him with an eery fatalism—a green-winged insect being eaten bit by bit till only his swollen little penis was left for his bloated love to swallow. The thought of the insect's passion sent waves of feeling through his groin. If only he could be somewhere safe with her, in a motel on the moon, in a love-nest under the sea . . .

"Do you remember the cruise we once took beneath the sea?" he asked, stroking her nipples.

"Remind me, please," she answered.

"It was in the depths of the Caribbean. We both were traveling alone. You were that lovely, sad-eyed woman, sitting alone in the dining room like me, and we gave each other furtive glances, until finally, I ordered a bottle of wine for your table—"

"And I sent you a note in return, yes, I invited you to join me . . . "

"And soon we were dancing in the low-lit lounge, a very close dance, and we kissed . . . "

"And I invited you into my cabin," she said. "Yes, I remember." Her back curved away from his nuzzling chin. Lifting her bottom, she let his member slide between her juice-coated thighs. She held him there suspended—almost, not quite, inside her—like a hotdog gripped in an upsidedown bun. "And the ship rocked slowly, back and forth," she said, her body mirroring the motion.

"And the whole cabin wall," said Stewart, "was a glass through which fish of strange shapes and dazzling colors looked in . . . "

"Their eyes aglow," she continued, "while I shook my gown from my shoulders, deftly guiding your hand—"

"—my trembling hand . . . "

"—to the doily-like cups that you slowly and carefully stripped from each pouting breast . . . "

And their ship began rocking tumultuously in the grip of a new storm, back and forth, side to side, up and down.

28. THE GUILT-RAVAGED CONSCIENCE OF HELEN MEANS

Helen was stirred to the inmost depths of her flesh. Here it was, happening exactly as she'd imagined. Her boss inviting her to spend the night with him—in the luxurious bower of Room Number One. At first she thought they had entered the wrong quarters—some sort of lumber room, it seemed. She had expected the door to open upon a beautifully appointed sitting room replete with antiques such as old-fashioned *fleur-de-lys* wallpaper and glass-topped, chrome-legged coffee tables. Luckily, he did not turn the lights on when they entered, so that the mess she thought she saw was whatever the poolside lights revealed through half-shut blinds on their fleeting passage straight across to the bedroom.

And *what* a bedroom! A bedroom fit for the king that he was. She marveled especially at the enormous, round, satin-sheeted bed and the giant ceiling-mirror hung like a wide-eyed voyeur overhead. She was sure she'd never been in a round bed under a mirror with anyone before. But just as she had dreamed, here they sat across from each other in sensuous amoebas that shaped to their shifting bodies, between them a low teakwood table with champagne on real ice, and roses, roses, fresh roses all over the room! They had kicked their shoes off, and already LB's foot was stroking her thigh beneath the table. No candles, though. That was the only thing missing. But far better than candles was the holomural that spanned three walls—of craggy seabottom magma chimneys crisscrossed with strange fish in hundreds of vibrant patterns, enough color to challenge the creativity of the most daring envirodesigner.

"Do you like it?"

"It makes me feel like a mermaid," she said, drawing a long blond tress through her fingers and down across her breast. Her dress glowed a bright yellow-green—*confirming* it, her mounting ripeness for passion.

"But the most beautiful romantic adventure of my life was when you and I first made love—in the storage room next to the stage. You remember, don't you, Iris?" he winked, alluding to a secret presumably known only to the two of them.

"I think I do," she said, playing along. If he wanted to call her Iris, that was all right with her. Like the amoeba in which she reclined (at the foot of the waiting bed), she would willingly mold herself body and mind to his whims. She would help him fulfill *his* fantasy, just as he—*My God, I'm going to make love with the CEO of Memini!* she thought—just as he would gratify hers.

"No one else knows that you and I are like *this*," he said, brandishing crossed fingers at her.

"No, no one else *does* know," she agreed. *Not even I!* she thought. She felt piqued at his denying her a privilege he reserved for himself—*keeping a record* of that very special relationship.

Champagne bottle in hand, LB circled barefoot round the table, where he had first set his own drink down. He poured a little more into her glass, which she'd hardly touched, then restored the green bottle back to its sweating silver cooler. "You've hardly drunk any. Don't you care for it?" He stood behind her, gently caressing her shoulder with his fingertips. "Dom Pérignon is supposed to be the best, not that I know much about champagne, dear."

"Oh no, dear, of course you don't," she smiled archly back at him.

"If high school gives me nothing else, meeting you will have made up for the mess I've made of it in every other way." He reached over her for his glass. "Cheers!"

What had he said? Was he speaking in some sort of code? she wondered. She lifted the champagne to her lips and sipped, then choked, nearly dropping the glass. Not because his straying fingers had mounted the nose of her breast, but because of the pain in her throat caused by her renewed attempt to swallow. "Excuse me!" she gasped. "That man hurt my throat so!" She must learn to associate that pain in her throat with the note she had put into her advisory regarding one Andy Peters, who had "tried to strangle" her. That was all she now knew of the incident, which was just as well, but how had she permitted a perfect stranger to get so damn close to her? she wondered.

"I'm sorry," said Lester. "Someone tried to . . . hurt you? Yes, of course, I have it in advisory. I have an all-points out through Meminet on one Andy Peters . . . I believe I know *why* you were attacked, Iris. It's simply part of the *game* . . . which those Board of Ed bureaucrats who enticed you into it are playing a little too rough. Don't you get it?"

"Maybe I'm a little slow tonight, Lester—"

"Michael! You don't have to use my game-name when we're alone, sweetheart. My rooms are bug-free."

"Michael, of course!" she said.

He put down his glass and peeled her right breast out from under the glowing yellow material which had restrained it. To Helen it felt like the removal of a mask; already she could breathe so much more freely. Her simultaneous shudder, however, came not so much from her boss's champagne-chilled fingers as from his curious insistence that she call him *Michael*.

"You're involved with one of Memini's major DUSA-region projects. Don't you see, Iris? Under your game-name of Helen Means, you have been targeted for elimination."

"Elimination? Who would want to 'eliminate' me?" she said, molding her hand over his lightly stroking fingers.

"My enemies. The people who've been trying to increase the tension between me and Southeast Asia. What luck that I happened by just in time to stop them from killing you! Once declared dead, you'd have been sent home from the party, and who knows when I could see you again?"

"Are you joking?" she said, touching her throat. "The bastard did try to kill me."

"That roughness of theirs!" Her boss shook his head. "Sometimes I think they go overboard straining after realism."

"Realism!" she said, looking into his dead-earnest eyes. They were like the eyes of those strange fish that paused now and then to gawk at her from the walls as they threaded in and out among their chimneys of frozen magma.

"But the game is just about over. And I now have to face it, I've *lost*, Iris.

I did my best, but they've screwed me at every turn. My only consolation is knowing that *we* can soon be together again—as ourselves, Iris Morgan and Michael Forbes, with no further need for disguises."

"What do you mean, you've lost, Lester?"

"Michael! You don't have to use my game-name when we're alone," he said with irritation.

"Michael, then," she said, " . . . surely you're on *top* of this whole DUSA thing, aren't you?" She clenched his fish-cold hand more tightly. It had suddenly gone lax on her chest.

"You've been my best supporter, Iris. My worst fear is I've let *you* down. This DUSA situation was the worst I've ever had to handle—I mean, as the protagonist of this Memini-game under the name of Lester Barton."

"You mean you've been treating this DUSA crisis as . . . just some sort of game, Lester?"

"Michael. *Michael.* Now cut the facade, Iris! You know as well as I do that my ex-Chem teacher Mishkin is also on the Executive Council, and that he hates my guts, and that he and a few other bastards in the administration got the Board of Ed to sneak them into the game where they've been consistently loading the dice against me."

"Why? Why would these people want to harm you?" She drew his hand in soft circles over her chest and along her flaming neck and cheek, trying to arouse him, distract him. Was the burden of leadership so great that the poor man was cracking? If anyone could help him, then, it would be she, Helen Means—or Iris Whatever, if that's what he preferred to call her.

"It's a conspiracy to prevent me from graduating with a tier-one diploma, of course."

"They want to prevent you from graduating?"

"So that I'll never go on to college."

"And who is this teacher Mishkin?"

"I thought you recognized Mophead, too—masquerading as Avery Tingworth?"

Helen shuddered. She habitually left open her corporate news-flash channel. Minutes ago the message had flashed through her skeeter. The news had struck her with the emotional force of the death of a distant cousin. She hoped that if she had encountered Tingworth at all tonight she had at least tried to be pleasant. "Haven't you heard, Michael? Avery Tingworth died of heart-failure just hours ago, here at your party." What a downer to have to mention it now! But the mood that had been developing between them, no matter how hard she worked against it, was anything but romantic. Witness the luke-warm green of her dress at the moment!

"Tingworth dead? . . . No, I'm only tuned to my ID." Barton squeezed her shoulders as though she were the back of a chair. "I don't get it. Why would Meminet get rid of Mishkin *now*? It's too late to do me any good."

"Lester," she said, spinning around to meet his faraway gaze, "I don't believe you are really that uncaring. Look, playing this game is making me feel uncomfortable. I'm not very good at complicated games."

"But you are, Iris. You've been playing very well. Maybe, if we put both our heads together, we can figure out this Tingworth move of theirs."

"So you think that Tingworth was *killed*?" she said, guiding him by the hands to the soft seat across from her, then topping his glass with a little more champagne. She surprised herself with her forcefulness. This was *Lester Barton, her boss, supreme head of Memini!* (If the women she worked with could see her now, they'd cream all over their dowdy little old peppermint-flavored pussy-pads!)

"You're the only person they've put on my so-called Executive Council that I positively know is on my side."

"Of course I'm on your side," she said.

"I saw through their strategy," he said, sipping absentmindedly at his champagne. "They expected me to *rejoice* on hearing that Memini was coming out with the Perfect Pill, the Immaculate EMI. But knowing Tingworth and Company were out to get me, I thought hard about whether they were offering me a poisoned apple. After all, what could possibly be wrong about such a wonderful gift to all of humankind? But that was it, Iris! It was too *good* to be true!"

"*Is* there something wrong with a Perfect Pill?" she asked, confused. "It's been sought for so long by so many—"

"Don't you see? If such a thing were *really* to be developed, it would eventually destroy the very foundations of Memini's existence, render obsolete every line of mnemonics—except for the new Pill itself. But the new Pill disenfranchises the tekkie, don't you see? It encourages the great masses of oldfolks to acquire *our* mental acuteness—and at no cost to them, to become just like *us*, to *take power*. And so I automatically lose the game for letting it happen!"

"But Les—I mean Michael, Memini itself has tried for fifty years to make brain-candy lacking in side effects."

"Propaganda to make the tekkie look altruistic! Anyway, the cat's out of the bag and I can't stuff it back in. I've goddammit *lost*!" he said, nuzzling her neck with his silky beard.

Helen thought that she was beginning to understand him. Lester Barton, probably the greatest corporate executive that ever lived, was only human. He had developed a peculiar strategy of distancing himself from the pain of his heavy responsibilities by thinking of all that he was doing as some sort of *game*! "But Lester—I mean, Michael . . . you have not lost," she said, trying to enter the "game" as he desired.

He did not appear to be listening to her, nor did he seem aware of her fingers stroking his hairy masculine arm. "I had developed the perfect counterplot to prevent the Tingworth Pill from ever being made. I couldn't trust Meminet, you know, because I was sure it had been penetrated—so I tapped into corporate resources using channels of communication not tied in to Meminet. The game has allowed me such options, you know."

"But wouldn't Meminet eventually find out anything you were doing?" she said, her fingers sliding up along his biceps now. "Meminet has eyes and ears almost everywhere."

"Meminet *would* find out, yes, but not in time to stop me. Timing was everything. My first move to kill the new Pill was to devastate DUSA's bio-solar plantations with a biological warfare agent, a virus stored at one of our facilities in the Amazon."

"*You* did that?" Helen gripped Barton's forearm in fright. Then she forced a quick grin. "You're putting me on."

"The idea was to stop all work on the Pill in Borneo, to divert the energies of Tingworth's biochemists there to finding an antidote to the blight."

What a grisly idea! thought Helen, realizing that the hidden fantasy lives of the sedate, responsible corporate leaders of the world could be archaically bloody. "But Lest—Michael, how much of a reprieve could that virus have bought you?"

"Enough time to implement Step Two: sending a commando unit whose purpose, I convinced Meminet, was to rescue our biostation from the DUSAn militia that took charge there when I refused to direct ISEC to beam down power to them."

"And that, that rescue... *wasn't* the commandos' purpose?" She had meminized the entire exchange with Davar, his hints that Memini's raiders had had a more sinister objective than rescuing a beleaguered biostation. Had Davar been *supplied* with a prefabricated tale to tell? she wondered. Wasn't it strange that she'd gotten through to him so easily?... It was getting quite confusing.

"Rescue was very definitely *not* the purpose of that raid." Barton sighed and took a long swig of bubbly. "The idea was for my invaders to enter the station, destroy the lab where the new Pill was being hatched, and kill only the two or three scientists in charge of the project."

"Kill!" Helen lurched back. She waited for a smile to form on his face—to tell her he was pulling her leg.

"Now don't take it literally, sweetheart. It's only a game."

Helen heaved a deep sigh. "Well, I'm glad of that," she said. "Because according to Davar, *lots* of men were killed. Not the scientists. Just the ones you sent out as killers."

"You've *heard* about the failure of my expedition? I only found this out from Meminet a short while ago, if my advisory advises me correctly. It's already a news-flash, then?"

Helen was almost certain now that Barton was yanking her chain. But why would he go to such elaborate lengths to get others to corroborate its details? Was it something like telechess that these men were engaged in, or was Barton imposing on anyone he could a fantasy induced by overwork, or perhaps even paranoid obsessions that stemmed from an overdose of the Pill? Why did he have to play such games with her? *Of course*, she thought, *if this is the way he gets off*...

"Anyway," continued Barton, fingering his trim brown beard, "the failure of that raid proves that my enemies were a step ahead of me. But I was prepared even for that, Iris! I had so much backup that it *kills* me to think I've been outmaneuvered."

Tears came to Barton's eyes. Helen reached out a hand to his cheek. He looked so vulnerable just then that she wanted to press him to her bosom, stop him from talking, get him to start feeling her physical presence. She would make love to him so ardently, so expertly, that he would cease his scary ranting and snap out of his fit of depression. The poor man had no one to tell him how *good* he was. The great of this world spent too much of their lives alone, untrusting, and unloved.

"Tell me about all this 'backup,' dear," she said, entwining his passive fingers in her own.

"Well, since as CEO I have access to ISEC's Command and Control Center, I arranged for a solar-satellite battery to be trained on our Borneo station. This way I could burn the whole territory to cinders in case my commando-raid failed."

"Pretty vicious—even for a game!" she blurted out, involuntarily withdrawing her hand.

"Yes, a very gross measure as opposed to the surgically precise targeting of my *raid*," said Barton, "but even the Big Burn is now pointless, and on Monday morning I'm retargeting the entire solar array, every damn asset ISEC has out there in space."

"So now you're *not* thinking of burning the station to cinders?" Helen said, trying to smile, the corners of her lips trembling.

"What would I gain from it now? The chief project scientists, Jorgenson and Davar, have managed to escape the DUSAn guards and are now basking in Southern California with all the records needed for production of the Perfect goddamn Pill!"

"So they did escape!" Helen was elated. She must thank her darling friend in Kuala Lumpur. Then again, if they did escape, *there had to be something quite real to escape from*! So that all that Davar had told her... was it true, and not a game? Was Lester Barton playing out—on the chessboard of *life*—a nightmare in his waking brain?... Or was he just playing a supergame with *her* head?

But no. He had stood up and now kneeled down beside her. She felt his hot kisses on her neck. His hands, now warm, played no part in any head games. His fingers kneaded her breasts and strayed over every surface of the ouija board of her body.

"Iris, sweet Iris," he kept murmuring in her ear. "It's just us now... The

MEMINI

hell with all those..." Her dress rapidly turned from bright yellow to a deepening orange as she helped him by slipping it back up her thighs, yanking it over her butt, and on past the ledge of her breasts. "...and I think I handled pretty well all that crap, too, about his plan to burn the Borneo station to a frazzle if he could have roasted Davar and Jorgenson along with it," Helen murmured to her flapper as she sat trembling on the cushioned lip of the toilet bowl whose lid, now turned back, was the upper half of the face of the Mishugi CEO, and whose base the executive's straggly-bearded chin. "I have to admit, he had me going there for a while— like what's real and what's just a game, and then I figured it's some fantasy shit that turns LB on, which is fine, and he did start groping for my stuff at that point, so I stripped and rolled over onto the bed, which is a beautiful big round satin-sheeted dark-red body-hugger with an overhead mirror in which my cream-colored body against the blood-red coverlet looked irresistible even to me, but 'No,' he says, 'not here,' and he yanks me up off the bed and nudges me toward the door we came in through, and then he insists on divulging the rest of his 'game-plan' as he pushes my ass through the door into the room that earlier was darkened but is now lit up and looks like a musty, junk-filled, back-stage storeroom for theatre props, and as I resist walking naked over the grimy floor, he points out a lumpy old thriftshop sofa that he declares is an exact replica of our very first love-nest, and he says it excites him to make it with me on this broken-down couch, and he tells me that even though his teachers have managed to screw him by unfair means, he's going to have the last laugh anyway by fucking up their game-program, by putting Meminet out of commission by making it self-destruct in a logical loop from which it wouldn't be easy for it to recover, explaining that first thing Monday he was going to beam all the solar power ISEC can muster down on the Southern Polar cap, which contains ninety percent of the world's ice, and thereby break it up and drown the world's cities in hundred-foot tidal waves—which includes New York, the home-base of Meminet, which can not itself logically survive, therefore, since it has to follow the rules of its own game, and that no one can stop the Polar meltdown except the CEO of Memini, namely himself, so that he was going out with a *bang*, not a whimper, but as far as doing any banging with him on that derelict couch is concerned, *that's what did it*, that's what makes me sure that he must be out of his fucking mind if we have that *beautiful big round bed* to fuck our brains out on all night, so I told him to wait just a bit while I use the facilities to prepare myself for him. I wonder what color my dress would be I feel so pissed right now! Imagine him, completely loony, telling me to make no record of our encounter! If he'd acted this crazy before, I'm sure I'd never have listened to him then either, if only to protect myself from such a nut. Whether he's whacko or only *acting* like a madman, I shouldn't have to go through a scene like this ever again!"

Fearing that at any moment she might hear his footsteps approaching, Helen spread the sides of her pouch to reinsert her flapper. Fumbling, fingers shaking, she felt the cold edge of a loose *biocassette* on the bottom. Whose could it be? she wondered. Her own was clearly safe in her flapper. (She checked to make sure.) She must have carelessly picked it up at some time, somewhere, during the course of the evening, no doubt intending to return it *immediately* to the poor soul who'd lost it. Yet she had failed to insert a reminder to herself as to whose it was. For all she knew, her negligence had already resulted in terrible pain for someone! A report may have gone out that *it had been stolen*! If she tried to return it now, no matter how she pleaded innocence, her negligence would be remembered far more than her honesty! Worse, she might even be suspected of an invasion of privacy. They might think she'd transcribed and meminized—for sale to a corporate competitor—another agency's classified data!

But even a worse-case scenario suddenly, chillingly, occurred to her. What if, during the time when LB "rescued" her (did he himself stage the strangling to turn himself on?), it had dropped out of his *own* flapper and she had inadvertently picked it up, intending to return it—and then in all the hubbub forgot to? LB's own biocassette in her unlucky hands? The most valuable corporate secrets in the world, hers, at a touch of a button? The thought thundered through her like a powerful laxative. She sat and sat and listened for footsteps which thank God never approached. Was that what explained LB's lunatic behavior—his lost biocassette resulting in total disorientation, or Failed Flapper Syndrome?

That would be awful indeed. If true, a robar would eventually come to his aid. She couldn't now remember if LB had showed signs of being attentive to his ID advisory during the last several minutes. Meanwhile, was there anything *she* ought to do about it, wretchedly trapped in the middle as she was? Say nothing and be damned, volunteer and be damned!

The solution to Helen's dilemma came in a flash. Flushing the toilet, she dropped the cassette into the swirling waters beneath her parted thighs. Her worst fears were over. She could breathe normally again. She could even—admittedly, more out of duty than enthusiasm—make love on a lumpy couch.

PART THREE:
THE ORDINATION

THE THREE LAWS OF MEMINETICS

1. Meminet serves Memini only.

2. The personnel of Memini serve Memini only.

3. When resolving conflicts of interest between corporation and personnel,
    (1) Meminet serves Memini only.

29. ASSASSINS AT BREAKFAST IN BROOKLYN

On Monday morning Wanjo was late for breakfast.

Andy had been feeling good, on top of things again, since their meeting with the reps from "There's a Crime in Progress" on Sunday. At first he had balked at getting paid only *after* the performance. It was as if they didn't trust him, as if they willfully ignored his high professional standing and wanted to treat him like an amateur. However, as soon as he felt reassured that no insult was intended, he accepted their terms—which would net him 25,000 (half in ICU's), and Wanjo was only too happy to settle for 4,000 whacks, more than the kid could ever hope to hustle in a year. What with the 7,500 advance from Memini already in the sock, and the 2,000 he'd get C.O.D. at the chophouse—an ICU-heavy total of 34,500 for one and the same job!—he had plenty of good reason to feel back in the saddle again. (And you never could tell . . . pissed as Memini might be, if he pushed them to the wall they might *still* pay him the other 7,500. No telling *what* they'd do just to get rid of him!)

Wanjo was only a few minutes late, but it ticked Andy off that he dared being late at all—especially on a day like this. Andy assumed that the kid was making a "statement," flaunting his new-found status as an *agent* for the man who till now had called all the shots himself. Andy had picked a breakfast place that was a cut above the usual joint he'd invite Wanjo to in the course of business. It was the All American, a noisy, overpriced eggery on Flatbush Avenue near the Plaza, where Andy felt they could talk with minimal danger of being overheard.

He decided not to bring up the lateness. He was feeling too good after the arrangement with the media boys, and he had to admit—to himself, at least—that if not for Wanjo's amazingly timely contact with those gutter-sniffing 3V scouts, he would have missed out on a fabulous opportunity. With the monies he'd collect from the 3V boys alone, he could furnish in style—rotating round bed, overhead mirror and all—the new apartment he'd soon be moving into. He just had to wait for word now, via videowatch, from Miss Yammy, who would tell him exactly when and how to carry out his assignment.

He assumed that, as always, he'd be picking up his mark in the usual place, then guiding it back "home" for disposal. She had assured him the operation was set for Monday. She'd made him promise to be ready for action any time during regular business hours—which meant he could relax and have breakfast with Wanjo free of anxiety till nine. He had decided to sport his off-white suit for the occasion, knowing how much that would piss her—although that wouldn't amount to diddly compared to the shock she'd get from watching his performance on the tube!

"Wanjo," said Andy, rapping his spoon on the table when he noticed what the kid was wearing, "you're dressed like an underage pimp! Here I give you this one chance for fame, and you're wearing these purple skinsuckers that show off your nuts for miles." The school dropouts these days! Either they went for the put-offish leather-patch-at-the-elbow look, or else it was the come-on hustler look, and they wore that material that shrunk in most where body heat was greatest.

"Them 3V man say it be fine, brud," smirked Wanjo, his feet up on the bench of the booth, his back against the wall.

"People are going to *associate* you with me, damn it! And they want *you* to give a guided tour through the bazaar? One hell of an introduction I'm getting!"

"Ice off, brud! I think you piss cause ain't only you what's gottin' all them attention."

"Hey, looka here, you've developed quite a mouth since you stepped in that pile of green shit!" Andy did not like the kid's *attitude*.

"We *both* eatin' all them good shit Wanjo step in, brud." Turning to the holomenu displayed in the wall at his elbow, Wanjo pushed a lever till a combination showed up that he liked: a tall stack of flapperjacks with sausages on the side.

"Is this your order?" asked a wall voice.

"Bet your ass," said Wanjo.

"Shall I hold off on yours until your partner orders, too?" said the wall chef.

"I'll have number 7," said Andy. "Go ahead with the orders."

"One number 7 and one number 9. Do you confirm?"

"Confirmed," growled Andy. "Look, Wanjo, remember—your candy comes from Andy! Those media fraggots weren't interested in *your* little oho, now were they? It's the *organ* trade they're creaming about! For the first time in 3V history, the world's gonna *see* what they only ever hear about, and they're gonna be seeing an *expert* on the job. At least I didn't have to convince them about my reputation."

"Happen cause *Wanjo* sayin' all them whole big bullshits 'bout you, Andy. You ain't never givin' Wanjo no credit, is you, brud?" Wanjo crossed his arms and slapped them in a huff over his chest, rattling layers of fake wampum shells that hung from his neck.

"I hope you're not wearing your 3V eye under that pile of dead clams," Andy snorted.

"There you shittin' me again, brud! I stick it right here," he said, pointing to a spot below his shoulder. The eye was hardly visible even when pointed to. Andy wore one set into his tiepin. "Ain't like I be takin' nuthin' way from you, Andy. Shit, you be gottin' four, fi', seven times all them whacks what I'm be, ain't you?"

"Are you *comparing* yourself to me, you innumerate punk? Are you resenting what *I'm* getting when you're getting ten times what your skinny little ass is worth?"

"Hey, I no complainin'. This here hoodbaby fulla big dreams 'bout what he do with all them whacks them fella gawn gimme. First off I buy me some nice big bus, big enough to stuff two twinkie side by side in back, not some small li'l coop from China what you can't get laid 'thout your butt bustin' windows. Then I buy me closetfuls them chilliest rags what *you* never seen even, brud."

"Wanjo, how long you been living off-planet?" scowled Andy. "Don't you know that with the money you're getting you could barely buy even a set of miniwheels? And what about insurance? And where you gonna even *park* new wheels in this city? Garage space would cost you more rent than your friends and you pay for your room, and if you left it out in the street, it's like . . . sticking your banana in the jaws of a piranha."

"Lay off my ass, Andy! Truth be I can't able to figger yet what I fuckall do with them money."

"Is that right? Well, how many times did you tell me that if you had a little whackstack you'd go back to school?" He stared hard at Wanjo, making him squirm in his seat. The waiter came by with their breakfasts, and Wanjo stabbed at his eggs, avoiding Andy's eyes.

"Overdone? Again?" shouted the waiter who had stopped two booths ahead.

They both turned to see what the shouting was about.

"I've had it with you, Mister!" the waiter snarled at a man whom Andy couldn't see because of the height of the divider. "This is the fourth damn time you've come in in the past two weeks—and every time it's the same complaint, your breakfast steak's 'overdone.' And then you send it back and swear to God I'll never see *you* in here again!"

"I certainly *won't* be back again!" said a fruity-flutey uptown kind of voice. A bald old man in a muted purple suit emerged with dignity from the booth.

"*Remember* this time, you goddamn snag! Stay the fuck out of here for good!"

"I've never *been* here before. That is, I *assume* that I've never—"

"Where's your flapper? Dja drop it down the crapper? *Use* the fuckin' thing, scoophead! Stay out of this place and out of my face!"

"I'll make a note to that effect immed—"

"*Out*, fogbrain!" The waiter hustled him along with a shove to the back. The old man muttered and clung to his flapsack. Passing by Andy, the waiter tossed him a shrug. "Need any fresh meat, Andy?" he said.

"I'm not in the dog-chow biz," Andy declined. He looked at Wanjo's interested face and frowned. "Don't even *think* of bagging the old scoop!" he admonished. "He doesn't have a single organ 'll cop you five whacks."

"Does I look like I gawn for shit like them?" huffed Wanjo. "Come on, brud—"

"Okay, now that's what I want to see—ambition! You gotta set your sights higher from now on, Wanjo. For instance, now, this 3V bit today's gonna net me more contracts—I mean *quality* disposal operations—than I'll ever be able to handle on my own. I'm gonna need a first-rate, reliable, well-spoken partner, and when I get such a man there's gonna be so much highrise business for the both of us that neither of us'll ever have to be skimming off the street again. Just think of it . . . your own piece of floor, a place to bring your twinkies to, a great set of rags, a short workday, plenty of time to get high on good natural stuff, not that shit *you* shoot up your blowholes . . . A little bit of school and you'll have it *all*, fella."

"Dunno, brud," said Wanjo, chewing awkwardly. "How I be gottin' my homework done with all them roommates roun' with them jamflams blastin' all night?"

"Wanjo," said Andy, trying not to overreact, "you're not supposed to use your fist to pick up your sausage. The fork is not just for the flapperjacks. Shit, when they interview you about me, I hope it's not over fucking *lunch!*"

"Sorry," said Wanjo, swallowing self-consciously. He dropped his sausage back into his plate and wiped his hand on his sleeve.

"Wanjo!" said Andy, his lid about to blow. "Don't you think that smear's gonna show on 3V? Do I want a world-wide audience to think I work with some rice-pickin' mongo?"

"I gawn change me them jacket."

"*If* there's time." Andy shook his head and munched for a while in silence. A clock on the wall said it was already twenty to nine. He wondered if he wasn't getting nervous, maybe taking it out on the kid. "Look," he said finally, "I got this big new square of floor I'm moving into. I'll cut a deal with you."

"What deal?" muttered Wanjo.

"Okay. Lis' up. You go back to school and you can live in *my* place. You'll have a room all to yourself, fella. No noise, no distractions. And if you want to bring up a jill once in a while, well . . ."

Wanjo shifted a sausage around with his fork.

"So whaddya say?"

"Dunno, brud."

"Whaddya mean 'dunno'?" Andy was surprised at himself for suddenly coming out with such a generous proposal. "Did anybody ever offer you that good a deal who didn't want his name tattoed in gold around your asshole?"

"You wanna hear them truth, brud?" said Wanjo, stopping himself from wiping his sleeve with his hand again.

"Shoot, Wanjo."

"Well, me and them frags be talkin', and I sayin' them 'bout all the heisters and dealers and jillstringers I be knowin' and all, and I ast them how 'bout I go settin' up more crime in progress stuff and all, and them be sayin' me what it might be good idea, so, you know, like . . . "

Andy caught the drift and shook his head in pity for his dumbshit helper. "Wanjo," he said as gently as he could, "those boys'll say anything to make you feel good right now. After all, they want us to go to work in top condition, right? But once the job's over it's 'Thanks, shithead, and goodbye, and don't call us, we'll call you.' Don't you get it? You that hungry you can't tell wishes from knishes?"

"But all them hustlers and shits be friends o' mine, brud."

"Wanjo, stop being an idiot! Don't you watch the show sometimes? These fragass trideo boys choose the baddest stuff they can latch from all over the world. They hooked onto you because you're dangling something *special* out in front of their noses—*me*! Now why would they care about petty little everyday bullshit with dealers and pimps?"

Wanjo's shoulders slumped, and he tickled a piece of flapperjack with his fork. A shame to pop his balloon, thought Andy, but better he should hurt a little now. The kid would be grateful to him later.

Suddenly Andy's videowatch buzzed. He narrowed his eyes at Wanjo, placed a finger over his lips, and flicked on the transceiver. "Hello. Kedro here."

"Mr. Kedro," said Yamamoto, her hair flecked with ruby-red specks, "are you alone right now? I get voice but no video. I wish to speak to you in private."

"Go right ahead, Miss Y. No one listening but yours very truly." Andy winked at Wanjo. "Video's off 'cause I haven't yet taken a shave."

"Mr. Kedro, I have just discovered the most incredible circumstance. Did you really think you could fool me—Memini, that is—and get away with it?"

Andy shrugged his shoulders theatrically at Wanjo. "What in *hell* are you talking about, Miss Yammy?"

"I have just had the chance to check the cassette that you gave me Friday night. Did you really suppose, 'frag' that I am, I'd forget to?"

"Get to the point, sweetheart," he growled at his wrist, his brows creasing.

"As I need hardly tell *you*, sir, this is the biocassette that belonged to the late Avery Tingworth. He died of heart failure during the party Friday night. The way you got your hands on it would make an interesting tale, I'm sure, but most important right now is that you cease playing games with us and return the Helen Means cassette immediately. Without it I don't see how we can conduct any further business with you."

"Shit!" said Andy. "*Shit!*" He darted a glance at Wanjo, who leaned forward with gaping jaw. "I know this is gonna sound stupid," he muttered at his wrist, "but this is all due to a ... mixup. Things happened after I picked up that fat bastard's cassette, and I forgot I even had it on me. Look, I honestly thought I was handing you Helen's gizmo. Of *course* I expected you to check. Nowadays who buys a pig in a poke?"

"Very well, if it's an honest mistake, you can come to the office right now and return the other. We have very little time to lose if you are to carry out your assignment on schedule."

Andy felt himself turning beet-red in front of Wanjo. Did he even *have* the damn cassette? he wondered. He made a quick check of his flapsack. Zilcho. His heart began to race. Wanjo's jaw nearly bounced on the table.

"Mr. Kedro? Are you still there?"

"Of course I'm here! Did you think someone detached me from my arm?" he laughed—for Wanjo's sake, primarily. And then he got lucky. He had a memory flash that revealed to him exactly what had happened—and offered the only possible exit from his dilemma. "Look, Miss Y ... I don't actually *have* the tape."

"You don't?" came the delayed response. He could hear that she wasn't very happy.

"But I know where it is. I know where you can find it. It flew out of my pocket and bounced to the floor when that bitch—when Helen was tossing my clothes around in her room."

"Tossing your clothes around?"

"Look, I don't want to get into Sex Among the Teks, but that momma happens to go in for rough warmups before she buckles down for the ride. Get it? Now all you have to do is search that room and—"

"A chamberbot would have found it and reported it by Saturday afternoon, after all the guests had gone," she replied, frowning. "However, I'll order a search done right now. I'll also ask Helen if she recorded finding a loose cassette in her room."

"It's *got* to be there, damn it!" He cast a confident glance at the befuddled Wanjo. "Is it my fault," he continued, "if some nutso jill plays *windmill* before she grinds a guy's corn?"

"I'll get back to you very shortly," Yamamoto said curtly, her image flicking off.

Wanjo looked at him out of bulging, drug-yellowed eyes and planted both fists on the table with a force that was all but a slam. "What all them shit *mean*, brud? She say she gawn cut you loose! You already fuckin' up what we plan for today, Mister Andy?"

"Don't you 'Mister Andy' me, you shitnose little parasite! You don't have the slightest idea of what's going on, so zip up that trap of yours until I say you can open it."

"I be *countin'* on them whacks, *suh*! Ain't nobody never 'gain come knockin' on my door like what them 3V frags jus' done on me, brud."

"There's absolutely nothing to worry about, Wanjo. That bitch needs me more than I need her." It stung him to think that that blonde was still bringing him headaches. After Friday night he'd decided to kiss her off for good, but here she was again, haunting him. Even if he'd lucked out and killed her, she'd be hounding him now from the grave. He could kick himself for trying to mix business with pleasure. He knew, of course, that it was his fault. He'd allowed her to distract him, to throw him off balance. In his trade every detail mattered. You couldn't afford to blink, and yet he'd gone and lost that cassette! . . .

And how would he deal with Wanjo if she did decide to call it all off? To lose face in front of a punk like this . . . word would get around the bazaar faster than a new form of clap. People would look at him funny, give him the finger behind his back. His whole network of contacts—he could see it start to unravel. All the goodwill that it took years to build up, all the references he depended on in the organ trade, all of it could go *right down the toilet!*

The thing to do now, of course, was to look perfectly calm and collected, not give this kid any reason to doubt. The whole neighborhood looked up to Andy the Actor. The thing to do now was to just sit tight and call that Jap bitch's bluff. She was probably just riding his ass because she figured he had something to do with that fat bozo keeling over. Hell, that was from the *exertion*, not from losing his cassette! Look at all the sweat her little blond ass had squeezed out of *him*—and he'd tried twice and only gotten *close*! Shit, fucking her might have killed *him*, too.

Conversation flagged between him and Wanjo as they fiddled with their food. His grits tasted dry in his throat, but he ate with feigned gusto, even ordered another side of baconet as he painted an inviting picture of his new apartment, insisting that the sullen Wanjo would be happier there than anywhere he'd ever been in his life.

When the watch buzzed again, his coffee cup shook in his hand, and he barely avoided spattering the white sleeve of his jacket. "Kedro here."

"Are you alone?" she said, looking at her blank screen suspiciously.

"I'm alone. Did you find it?"

"A thorough search has been made. The object in question is nowhere on the estate of Mr. Barton. Nor does Ms. Means have a record of coming upon such an object in her room."

Wanjo's face turned mushroom-pale.

"Bullshit!" said Andy. "That's the only place it—"

"Forget about that for now, Mr. Kedro. I have consulted with Meminet. In spite of considerable misgiving, we have decided to go ahead, as planned. We will deal with you later—immediately after you complete your assignment, as a matter of fact. Please understand that we can *not* forget the threat to corporate security posed by the absence of that cassette."

"I understand you perfectly," said Andy, yawning. He pretended not to react to the thumbs-up sign and quick grin leaping from Wanjo. "And 'lis' up, Miss Yammy, in spite of all that Helen Means shit, you can count on me like always to bring home the bacon—which includes my forthcoming client's cassette, of course, when I return for the rest of my payment."

That was where he had them by the short hairs! he thought. She was bound to get wind of the show on 3V, so afterward, when she reamed him out for endangering the corporate image by making a public spectacle of the operation, he'd let her know he didn't *need* her stinking business any more and that if she wanted the poor bastard's cassette she'd better come forward with the rest of what they owed him . . . *No!* he thought. He had a better idea. Why not leave with a gesture of true nobility? Hell, he could *afford* it now, couldn't he? He would nonchalantly toss her the cassette and tell her to *keep* what they still owed him. A simple gesture on his part, he'd tell her, to make amends for the unfortunate screwup over the Helen Means tape. Exit in style! Style was his *trademark*, thought Andy. (And to do him one better, he could see her *insisting* on his taking the rest of his payment, to which he would reluctantly agree . . . if it would help chill their chips any.)

When he tuned back in to her petulant voice, she was asking, "Are you still *there?*"

"Kedro here," he said.

"Very well. Be at the Memini building at 1:45 sharp," she said. "You will be admitted to the conference room, as usual. These are your final instructions until we meet there."

"Gotcha."

"Remember, Mr. Kedro. This afternoon, 1:45 *sharp.*"

"Don't worry, sweetheart. One thing I know how to do is *remember.* Remember?"

30. MORE BAZAAR HAPPENINGS

Stewart spent the rest of the weekend tossed between memory and desire. Sibyl's smile still glowed in his head. Closing his eyes and embracing the air with his arms, he could feel the hot clasp of her body, could smell her on his fingers and taste her on his lips. Whatever was in store for him on Monday, he thought, nothing could surpass that Friday night visit to paradise.

Had it all been merely a temporary enchantment—binding them both for a moment only, lingering in his mind alone? Would she "remember" him, as *he* understood that term, the next time she saw him? But why should he doubt that *in her own way* she would? Even if he served her as nothing more than a hormone trigger, did that make him any the less real in her mind as an object of desire?

Here he was, foolishly dreaming that some sort of *relationship* was possible! Yet he had gone into this thing forearmed, with the sole goal of enjoying only the moment, of skipping like a butterfly from flower to flower. That was the beauty of that fling with Jackie Tiller, a perfectly completed episode that stood out in his memory with cold hard edges like a gem he had safely tucked away in a drawer, a stone he could take out, turn around in his hand again, and put back whenever he wanted to. But Sibyl had left him hungry for more. The more she had given, the more he still wanted. There was no retreating now into his safe little world of shadows, no more slithering under rocks. His only option was to rush blindly on—yes, exactly like that praying mantis, into the brain-crunching kisses of Love.

Flapper at hip, he showed up at two on the dot. She was waiting for him at the door, looking worried and tired, but she pressed his hand in greeting and smiled at him warmly, as if she really did remember. She wore a body-hugging white knit dress, and spirals of white, like galactic arms, spun out from the center of her hair. A belt of jade lozenges hung loosely about her waist, jade lozenges dangled from her ears as well, and her lips shone viridian green to match. He reached for her, but she edged back ever so slightly, still with that imperturbable bright smile. His arms frozen in front of him, he dangled as if by a frayed cord from a cliff.

"Did you have a good time at the party, Mr. Bridges?"

"I had a great time! How about you, 'Miss' Yamamoto?" He could not mask his hurt.

"'Miss' Yamamoto will never forget," she returned ironically, "how Mr. Bridges rescued her from those Amazon poachers."

Stewart's voice stuck in his throat. Why had he for one moment doubted her? How had he *expected* her to act? After all, he was here on *business*, and the Argus-eyed walls of her office never blinked.

"This time you will definitely be interviewed," she said. "I'm going to lead you immediately into Mr. Barton's office."

Finally! he thought. "I'm so glad he's expecting me."

"I'm afraid you're still going to have to wait," she said, two frown lines darkening her perfectly smooth brow.

"But you just said . . . "

"Your interview will not start right away. Please have patience. I'll let you know in advance, by intercom, when it will begin. There are camzines . . . and feel free to use the 3V, if you like." She avoided his eyes. He followed her, hoping she would drop some further hint that she personally, inwardly recognized him. He walked obediently through yawning panels into an enormous space that looked more like an old British "club" than an office. Sibyl pointed him to a plush, high-backed seat of antique design next to a great curved desk behind which no one for the moment sat. By the time he took in all the dazzle of the setting (which should not have surprised him after visiting Barton's *estate*), Sibyl had vanished, and the panels behind her had closed.

The desk crouched on brass lion's claws, which in turn dug into an ancient Persian carpet about twenty feet square that showed the well-worn paths of countless years of use. A large window framed the president's desk against columned white curtains aglow with the afternoon sun. The wall to Stewart's right was a library of books, manuals, and trideos—probably mostly decorative, he thought, since LB could boot up whatever he wanted on either his desktop terminal or the giant holopanel set into the wall to his left. (The right arm of the chair he was to wait in sported its own 3V control.) A round table and several more antique, claw-footed chairs dented another Persian carpet in the library corner, while various works of art—sculptures, 3D and 2D graphics—stood near or projected from the walls. An atmosphere like this would *have* to boost one's creativity, thought Stewart, with or without the Pill.

A large globe of the world, with the moon suspended above it, stood on brass legs behind and to the right of LB's chair. Stewart sat down tentatively in the seat Sibyl had designated and examined the colorful globe. It was peppered with tiny flags of different colors (and there were several on the moon as well) all marked with the letter "M." It was like a general's battle plan. The sight gave Stewart a choking sense of the sheer *power* focused in this room. He imagined LB swiveling in his broad-backed chair to gain a "global" view of Memini's tentacular reach.

Crushed by an awareness of his own comparative impotence, he started to panic. Rushing back to the doors, slapping repeatedly at the release plate, he cast wildly about for some excuse he could make to Sibyl. The doors refused to budge. He felt trapped inside a cage. But why the hell would they want to lock him in? According to Sibyl, they already *knew* he'd only been masquerading as a tekkie. Had she let on to more than she should have? And had *he* been so blinded by wanting her that he could not get a clear view of the message? Resisting an impulse to bang and kick at the door, he quietly regained control of his breathing, then returned to the seat she had assigned him. She had made him a solemn promise that he was in line for something special. Although vague, it was still a promise. Memini had long known his background. The thought froze his mind. They *must* have inferred all those secret, boundless, subversive letchings of his. And yet, apparently, he had presented no threat to them at all!

Twenty minutes, forty went by, yet still no word over the intercom. Any minute now he expected to hear Sibyl, profusely apologetic, saying LB would be out for the rest of the afternoon! Why not? It would fit the whole meaningless pattern to date. Again he'd be sent home, again be invited back . . . He flicked on the 3V and the concavity on the wall offered a female nude doing a trick dive into a pool. He surfed from channel to channel and finally stopped at "There's a Crime in Progress."

A handsome Hispasian teenage boy was on camera. He was loping along through a circus-like place that to Stewart seemed somehow familiar. "My partner and me," he was saying, in that heavily thumping lilt, "well we does mos' us business roun' here. This'ere 'hood fulla streetmeat what wind up in them chophouse, got me?" Behind him Stewart spied a Kurdish head-shop—and he recognized with a jolt the Plaza bazaar. "My partner Andy gawn step out soon one o' them Junction bus up 'head, you see? And he have them 'mark' along by him what don't know shit where he gawn, and them mark trust Andy bullshit like a sip o' he own momma tit."

Suddenly a shift in voice and scene. An aerial view of the whole Plaza. "This is New York City, ladies and gentlemen, one of the great metropoli of crime," said the suave narrator from his copter-perch high in the sky. "And if you don't know exactly where we are yet, if you don't recognize the human jungle we are visiting, don't worry, you'll soon find out—as we track a kind of murder that our whole society feeds on, an episode in the working day of one of the most notorious organeers of them all, Andy the Actor, *Fragbagger Supreme.*"

Incredible, marveled Stewart, how that snake got around! One day just a sidewalk cowboy, the next a darling of the executive suite, and now a candidate for—instant 3V stardom! He had vowed to keep mum about recognizing Andy the Actor. If Memini suspected he knew, he might jeopardize his chances for . . . what? Stewart wondered.

"And this is not just an ordinary episode in the life of Andy the Actor that we are going to witness. Oh, no, folks!" cooed the narrator. "This is something special. We are assured that in a very few minutes Andy will step off a bus with his victim in tow—a man who does not know where he's being taken, a man who thinks he's going to some big secret meeting that's being held, for security reasons, in one of the worst of the city's slums—a man who is (and we only have Andy's word for it, of course) a major corporation executive *whom his colleagues want to quietly get out of the way!* . . . Even we don't know the man's name, folks, but is it possible that some of you out there who are in the know will recognize him? Will the Mystery Man, the potential sacrificial victim, our corporate paschal lamb, be wearing a disguise? We don't really know."

As the scene shifted back to ground level, focusing on the Hispasian kid again, Stewart tried to make sense of what he was seeing and hearing. How could any of this be *real*? he wondered. He'd always suspected this channel of staging at least some of its contents, and now he was in the position of judging it almost from the inside, since he had just rubbed shoulders with the "star" of this episode himself.

"Way back Andy teach me," the kid was saying, "mos' 'portant thing what you don't go and do—be bringin' up *dead* meat to them chophouse, cause big-ticket organ like liver and them, them all spoil rotten more quicker'n a bus station blowjob."

Sure, thought Stewart, on the one hand this could explain *why Andy had been invited to the party*—an ideal way for him to familiarize himself with his prey. But to imagine him disposing of a Memini executive, at Memini's behest, and all in public view, would amount to the same as believing in the devil incarnate! Which was not to say that *some* poor sucker wasn't being led to slaughter . . . a horrible enough prospect in any case, but in this case trumped up as a VIP to rev up the drama for the viewer. Stewart knew well the art of holding attention, the basic skill demanded in bioprogramming.

The scene cut sharply to an Asian game preserve. (Beat of drums, clash of cymbals.) An infrared camera tracked a nightstalker intent on committing one of the most heinous crimes in the book—killing a rhinoceros for its horn. Now that was something really too disgusting for 3V! thought Stewart. With luck there'd be millions of complaints from irate viewers demanding a modicum of programming decorum. Stewart tried not to watch, even though there was a fifty-fifty chance of the stalker being fried by a warden.

His irritation mounted as he wondered why she was letting him *sit* here like this, without even a word of apology or explanation over the intercom. Of course, tekkies experienced time so much more placidly than oldfolks, like cows grazing through rolling meadows of hours . . . He began to think of the firmness of Sibyl's breasts, of their aggressively jutting nipples, when the voice of the earlier narrator had returned and the camera once again offered a ground view of the Junction Plaza bazaar. "Be Andy comin' off them bus right now!" the Hispasian kid pointed excitedly, and a lens zoomed in on the Junction bus stop. "Andy the Actor is in white," said the narrator. (A flute played a jazzy riff, modulating into blues.) "And his victim, the man who is being led unwittingly to the altar of sacrifice, folks, the man Andy will now guide through a kasbah-like bazaar to the so-called 'chophouses,' where living people are quietly reduced to an array of high-priced, coveted, transplantable organs . . . "

The lens focused in on the man beside Andy in the natty, salmon-pink business suit. After a moment's hesitation, he strode forward with his guide into the maze of the bazaar, brushing nervously at his neatly trimmed, light-brown beard. Touching his hand to the flapsack at his hip, he glanced warily about him at a dizzying panorama. It must have looked to him like a leviathan threatening to swallow him alive. (Drums like irregular heartbeats.)

Stewart craned forward, gripping his own beard. There was no chance of an error. He had seen the man close up too many times in recent days. The man he was sitting here waiting for so impatiently, the man he envisioned as subjecting him to the most searching, grueling of interviews, had at last showed up. As palpable, almost, as life. Ears burning, skin tingling, Stewart felt as if his hair stood literally on end.

31. YOUR ROUND-THE-CLOCK LIVE-CRIME SHOWPLACE

Andy was pleased at the simplicity of the instructions. He was to call Barton "Mr. Brahma," and Barton was to address him as "Roper." He had hoped that his off-white suit would get a rise out of Miss Y, but Yamamoto had avoided looking him in the eye during his whole little pre-pickup briefing. The bitch was in pain over the job she had to do, and she could hardly wait to get both of them out of her sight. Out-of-sight plus ten or so minutes equaled out-of-mind for a frag, and then she could go back and polish her nails and admire her tits in a mirror and check her schedule to see what lucky guy she'd arranged to fuck later—at night, maybe, in bed maybe, but that too without leaving a trace. He had decided to abandon his long-held principle about avoiding trading in women. Yammy and Blondie had taught him how treacherous these frag-ass mommas could be. All these years what he'd thought of as gallantry had been nothing but sexist discrimination, and these two had made him see the light.

He'd never felt anything personal about the commodity he dealt in, but all weekend he actually looked *forward* to leading Lester Barton down the path. All Friday night the prick had been riding his ass—which was probably how he'd been treating his colleagues too! He had nothing against that fat guy who'd keeled over and died, couldn't even begrudge him his one last hump. But Barton was another matter entirely. He wished he could drag it out a little longer, get to know how the bastard's *mind* (if he had one) worked, so to speak, before he led him to the cooler. This time, though, before reeling in, he *would* be paying out more line than usual. Normally he took the shortest route to the chophouse. This time would be special. The media boys wanted him to steer his charge on a grand tour through the bazaar—to spice things up for all the tridiots out there, build suspense and such. It was hard to see why they'd choose Wanjo as tour guide, but if it wasn't for Wanjo . . . well, he couldn't complain.

Five years ago it had been *another* guy named Lester Barton—sitting quietly with him, like this, but in a taxi. Him he'd taken straight to the chophouse door: no muss, no fuss, no detours. He had not looked at *all* like the present Lester Barton, hadn't even sported a beard, which his "replacement" here had no doubt grown while in office. This one had sat for *five full years* right at the top of the world! All the women, all the luxury, all the power you could imagine! If the devil were ever to offer *him* such a deal, he'd think twice before turning it down. (For a reason he couldn't figure, their top execs didn't last too long. Too much wear and tear?) The following year it was two other poor slobs. He'd forgotten their code names. Their deliveries had been a bit more complex. One, he suspected, they sent to meet his unmaker as a reward for selling company secrets.

Andy never asked *why* about any assignment, nor was anyone dying to tell him. He was held on retainer year after year, never had to be told to keep his mouth shut, and when his services were needed—which wasn't very often—he gave Memini's jobs top priority. In addition to the retainer, he got a nice fat fee for every assignment completed, but Memini had never accounted for the bulk of his income, so he wasn't going to feel sorry about cutting them loose. Not too many stags they could trust out there. Maybe only the types other stags couldn't. They were going to miss him, the stupid bastards, he thought, but no one fucks with Andy and ducks the Postcoital Blues!

This one was a little more communicative than most. On the bus he sat near the window. For a long time he simply seemed lost in his thoughts. When he spoke, Andy had no idea what he was talking about. "Roper," he said, "by next week New York City will be under a hundred feet of water. In a manner of speaking, of course."

"In a manner of speaking, Mr. Brahma, it never rained that heavy in June that I can remember."

"You do realize, don't you, that *Meminet* will drown with the rest of us?"

"That sounds pretty bad, sir." Andy thought it best to say as little as possible, in keeping with his role as a mere innocent intermediary responsible for hand-delivering Mr. Brahma to some sort of "very important meeting" or other, as Yamamoto had put it. There was nothing else he was supposed to seem to know.

"Don't kid me, Roper. You're from the Board."

"The Board, Mr. Brahma?"

"The Board of Ed. I'm *not* going to a meeting of the Big Three, now, am I?"

"I don't have any idea, sir, what your meeting is—"

"Bullshit! You know damn well that I've failed my critical test, that they're sitting around there gloating, just dying to let me know that by failing to squelch the Perfect Pill, I've lost the game. Goodbye tier-one diploma."

Andy felt uncomfortable—a very bad sign. *This* Barton was acting erratic, unpredictable. He would try to humor him. "Look, Mr. Brahma," he said, "I don't know any details. All I've heard is rumors."

"Rumors?"

"Well, I'm not supposed to say anything, but . . . "

"C'mon," said Barton, "what worse can they do to me? Don't hold anything back."

"Well, what I hear is that the Board *likes* the job you've been doing."

"*Likes* it!"

"That's all I've heard, Mr. Brahma. Believe me."

"But that makes no sense, unless . . . Tingworth?"

Andy shrugged his shoulders in a show of exaggerated innocence.

"I'm going to an *award* ceremony, isn't that right, Roper?" Barton flashed Andy a knowing wink. His entire mood seemed to have changed.

"Well," Andy said, paying out a little line, "I can't tell you a flat outright no . . . "

"It's happening, isn't it?" he said, smiling brightly. "I felt something good coming on when they killed off Tingworth. That showed me that Meminet was on *my* side—was helping me get things done *my* way."

"I hope you get everything that's coming to you, sir."

"They're gonna hand me my goddamn diploma, Roper! Correct? So why go out to some school in the Brooklyn boonies?"

Andy did not like this new twist in the conversation. "We're *not* going to any school, Mr. Brahma. That I can tell you for sure." He did not want Barton to fix a picture in his head so different from the reality that at the last minute he'd balk and cause trouble.

"No matter. They want to surprise me, right? Keep ol' Michael guessing till the very last second?"

As far as Andy could guess, LB was either crazy or speaking in some insider's code which he expected him to know as well. And that too would be crazy: you don't talk business to a total stranger. Andy found himself experiencing, during the course of a typical stop-and-go busride, a peculiar reversal of feelings toward this dupe whom he had every reason to detest. Normally he had no feeling at all toward his charges. But something about this sorry bastard struck a chord of sympathy in him. One moment he's got the world by the short hairs, next moment he's tossed in the shithouse. Exactly the kind of treatment that bitch of a Helen had given *him*! You worked hard, and just when you expected a little reward, some out-of-the-ordinary pleasure that you know you deserved (this poor sucker looked forward to some sort of *diploma*!), they flicked you aside like flyshit off a wedding cake.

It was hard to hold a grudge against "Mr. Brahma," or "Lester Barton," or whatever the hell his real name was. He'd probably forgotten his real name long ago—just as he'd forgotten all about Friday night and fucking Helen Means. Shit, thought Andy, if someone gave him the choice between fucking Helen Means (but having to forget all about it) and being kicked out of her bed (and having to remember the humiliation!), he wondered if it was all that obvious what he would do . . . And what about Helen? Did she remember a *thing* about Friday night? Who would *miss* this hotshot, Andy wondered, after they lifted out his lights and ground up the rest for dogchow? Did he have an old lady somewhere? . . . Hell, *he* should talk! He hadn't seen his own mother in six or seven years. He really hated making the trip up to Connecticut. When was the last time he'd called her—two years ago, three? Who remembered? Fuck it.

"Well, it isn't too late, you know," said Barton.

"For what?" said Andy suspiciously.

"To save Meminet. It'll take two full days to put an irreversible crack in the icecap . . . I can reprogram the array right after the ceremony."

"Quite considerate of you," said Andy.

It had been easy planting the eye on LB. He'd done it as they'd emerged from a side-entrance of the Memini building—Andy pretending to straighten LB's tie and sticking the little widget just below the knot. He'd have to remove it, though, once they reached the chophouse door. His own eye he'd promised the 3V boys he'd wear *underneath* his tie—so they'd get sound, but no more picture. Last thing he wanted to do was spoil a long-term business association with the chophouse. (Andy had been surprised that they'd agreed to such a condition, but it was evidently worth it to them, for the tour of the bazaar alone.) The other thing they'd agreed to was not to mention the name of the street. A view of the chophouse door was no problem. It bore no street address and looked like a hundred others.

When they got off at the Junction, Andy pointed toward the fringes of the bazaar. Barton grew stiff for a moment, then patted the sleeves of his jacket and strode resignedly along. Wanjo had spotted them and was about fifty yards up, in front of a headshop, where he stood cracking his knuckles and looked as if he was talking to himself. As they zigzagged down the wide center lane past Wanjo, who followed unobtrusively behind, one of the tumblers Andy knew sprang out from her group and practically landed on her head in front of Barton, giving Andy a sly wink as she bounced off again.

Barton stopped walking. "Why do we have to go through a place like this?" he said, squinching up his nose as if smelling a rat.

"I've been ordered to make sure we are not being followed," said Andy. He never had difficulty coming up with a likely story. "We have operatives emplaced all along our route here. The bazaar acts like a kind of filter for us, letting *us* pass through, and no one we think shouldn't. That girl that bounced in front of you? She's one of ours. That was a signal that so far everything's okay."

"That must've been Mrs. Crane!" said Barton, snapping his fingers. "Hard to recognize in that getup. I had her for polyaerobics in junior year."

"You're one sharp man, Mr. Brahma. You know these people better than I do."

"When you didn't move right, she'd come up behind you and shove her tits into your back while correcting you."

"That right?"

"Yes. Some of us acted like we were learning-impaired for half the semester."

"I'd do the same myself," said Andy, maneuvering Barton down a side-lane to the left, passing by Peruvian and Afghani food stalls, sniffing at the spicy air, the odors of roasting kabobs, moving relentlessly on, Wanjo drifting just in sight behind him.

"I was one of the dumbest in the class!" Barton laughed.

"I bet you sure as hell were!" said Andy.

"Been stuck in high school for too long now, but at last I'm about to move on."

"You'll be traveling to so many places you won't know what hit you," said Andy. It had taken him a while, but it dawned on him finally that his mark was not using corporate insider's code but was actually out of his mind. The president of Memini—completely out of his tree! No wonder they needed to sweep him under a rug.

***

"As you can plainly see and hear, folks, Andy the Actor, streethawk supreme, king of the organeers, has gained his pigeon's confidence completely, and so far seems to be leading his intended victim straight to his fate. Anybody out there in need of a heart, a lung, a pair of testicles, a liver maybe? Well, if delivered within the next several hours, the unsuspecting gentleman you see may be the donor to whom you should address your posthumous thanks. But hold on! Andy's pigeon started out a little skittish, remember? *Anything* could slip between the cup and the, uh, snip?"

The frontal shot changed to a receding rear view of the two as they sauntered up a winding alley of slapped-together stands and shacks and vanbodies with platforms and counters and beckoning barkers before them, the whole lane bathed in a shimmering haze made of afternoon sunlight and the smoke from exotic grills. (Bongos, pipes, weird photonic noises.)

MEMINI

A frontal shot again—now of that Hispasian kid who lent such grisly color to the proceedings. Prompted by videowatch, he pointed to a facade lettered **SUPPRISE PALLUS** crudely in red over a wall-filling mural, a pink, brown, and yellow tangle of the cartoon-like bodies of men, women, and beasts whose activities left little to the imagination of prospective consumers. "S'ere place no way like Bawdway, brud," the kid said with pride. "Here you never knowin' what you gots into cause you pluggin' it blind—through them screen, brud—and you can able be hittin' on anything, be oho, be blowho, be chocho, be live chicken too, alla same-same price, and them customer he never complain cause it s'pose be *supprise*, see? And you bet plenny *jill* come by here too, brud." Then another shift—back to the infrared gleam on the face of the stalker of rhinos. (Drums and flute in muted syncopation.)

***

Hewing to a prearranged route, Andy was glad to veer off to the left, out of range of the odors of food that made him feel faint with hunger. He felt so famished, in fact, that for a while he'd seriously considered stopping to refuel and even to treat Barton to a Moroccan lamb kabob, except that "Mr. Brahma" seemed in a great hurry to go on and get skewered himself. Several shanties down, on the right, Yolanda Woo leaned out over the counter of her "Potions & Notions" shop and signaled him to come on by.

"Wait right here just a sec," said Andy, planting Barton in the middle of the lane about fifteen feet shy of Yolanda's. "I have to confer with one of our operatives."

Yolanda's plump curves filled out a richly embroidered Mayan *huipil*, and garlands of elk teeth chattered over the cushions of her breast. "You lookin' *triff* on 3V, babe," she grinned, lifting her portable up by the handle and holding it a few feet back for him to get a good look. All he saw was a shot of his back and the face of the box—in which he saw a shot of his back, and so on. "Sorry, doll, you ain't standin' right jus' now," she murmured, shaking her head. "But don't you worry. I'm recording the whole shtick so's you can see your pretty self later . . . Now, tell me honest. How'm *I* lookin', huh?" She moved at arm's length from the set and emerged full-face on camera to the right of Andy's shoulder. She smiled and waved.

"You're looking great, Yolanda," said Andy. He was slightly peeved at the way she'd slipped into his act. "Gotta get back to work now. Thanks for the look."

"Hey, babe, aintcha gonna tell folks how my *love-charm* worked that I custom-made for you out of authentic native materials?"

"Fine!" he said. "Great! Best charm I ever bought!"

"One of my best customers!" she said, pointing at him as he strolled back to pick up Barton. He would tell her later, in private, that her little doll had had no effect at all, thought Andy. Not that he'd *expected* it to, of course, but she shouldn't go around making promises... Then he remembered the mixup of cassettes, *his jabbing the doll with the wrong cassette in it, the fat man dying of heart failure*, and a skin-tingling feeling of awe told him never to bring up the subject with Yolanda again. With Barton following trustingly at his side, Andy strode along with a firmer step, his shoulders thrown back, chest out. He assumed that those 3V frags had arranged for plenty of *front* views too. It filled him with a dizzying pride to know that at this very moment all his friends were following his progress on the tube. And beyond them, untold *millions* of viewers, maybe billions! It was enough to swell your brains up and blow them out right through your skull!

**

It was the kid talking again, the scene being displayed from his point of view (smoothed out, of course—the rough motions of his walking reduced through Fourier-photonic magic up in the hovercopter). The scene was of Andy and Lester Barton wending their way along a trash-strewn broken sidewalk past rundown buildings of mixed architectural vintage. It was a palimpsest of superimposed layers of history, a piece of old Brooklyn belly-skin bearing a century's surgical scars, unlike virtually anything left in memoryless Manhattan. It was a streetscape indistinguishable from most others Stewart knew from the Nostrand Avenue jungle behind the bazaar. "This'ere street all way 'long here have two-three chophouse what *Wanjo* be knowin' 'bout, brud. Them other street alla same, and you gots to watch your ass comin' *down* here, lemme say!" A sudden switch of perspective, and from a point of view directly in front of the principals, a twisted, rag-draped human body rolls out from the shadow of a doorway. (A rapid chatter of bongos.) A toothless mouth under a pair of jagged nostrils (the nose completely eaten away) grins up at the side-stepping duo. "Just a roller," says Andy. "Completely harmless. Don't pay him any heed."

"Bullshit!" says Barton. "The disguise is pretty good, but I'd recognize Stankovich anywhere."

"Who?"

"The assistant principal of my damn high school."

"But that man's *nose* is rotted away," says Andy just to keep things moving.

"No surprise," says Barton. "Stank's had his head up his ass for years."

"You're one hell of a comedian, Mr. Brahma," says Andy.

"You can cut the crap and call me by my *real* name!"

Oh shit! thought Andy. Please God let this fuckhead not, *on 3V*—"We're not supposed to be *using* our real names, Mr. Brahma."

"Michael Forbes! You know damn well my name is Michael Forbes."

Andy gasped with relief. "Okay, fine! . . . You want me to call you Michael Forbes? That's okay by me, Mike."

"And *your* name, Roper? Come on, let's have it."

"Well, sure. Everyone calls me Andy, Andy the Actor."

"Really? I'm sort of an actor too, Andy. In fact, I happen to be in love with the director of an off-off-Noho stage-play."

"How nice!" says Andy. "Acting is sort of my sideline, you see. I get hired to play all kinds of roles."

"That must be half the fun of it," says Barton. "You never know what you're gonna turn into next."

"Couldn't guess if your life depended on it!" Andy solemnly agrees.

"Why do we have to traipse down these shitty streets, Roper?" says Barton, visibly slowing his pace. "I admit, it does look a lot like where I go to school . . . but things seem to have changed in the few months I've been gone."

Scene shift to a frontal view (from an eye stuck to a building evidently further up the block), hawk and pigeon carefully threading their way around a pile of rags from which the naked foot of what is presumably a sleeper juts out. (Close-up of gnarled, naked foot missing middle toe. Volley of photonic screeches.) Enter voice of narrator: "As you can see, folks, Andy the Actor, Emperor of the Flatbush Organeers, is dealing with a man who is showing signs of increasing nervousness. Who knows what can happen between now and the moment that Mr. Brahma, whose real name may indeed be Michael Forbes, is scheduled to walk through that fatal chophouse door? Will some humane individual from a window up above them, someone tuned in like you to 'There's a Crime in Progress,' shout down and tell Mr. Brahma to run for his life? All you mothers of sons named Michael Forbes, do you know where your son is today? . . . We transfer you back now to Asia, folks, to what we now expect is the climax of our rhino hunt—the very idea of which freezes the blood!"

Stewart now stood beside Barton's desk, his finger hovering over a panel of buttons, one of which he knew would raise Sibyl. He tried to look away from the 3V, from the carnage that was about to unfold. There was another monitor on Barton's desk, a blank-faced up-angled slab, undoubtedly a closed-circuit set.

He heard the shot, and with a shudder he glanced at the wall just in time to see a magnificent animal stagger over onto its side. But a moment later another shot rang out. The point of view swept around to the contorted, wide-eyed face of the falling hunter. (Deafening crashes of cymbals!) The excited narrator and his 3V eye spun dizzily around, finally focusing on the warden who'd been tracking them but had arrived just moments too late to save one of the last of the most precious creatures on earth.

**

Was it too many of those damn Pills, wondered Michael, that were blurring his memory of the streets surrounding his high school in Queens? Apparently they were having him approach from the rear, preferring for some reason (playing out their silly game to the very end, no doubt) to enter the school through one of the little-used back entrances with which he had never been that familiar. Well, why should he deny them the fun of his pretending to be surprised? Of course, they *would* rob him of the chance to prepare a speech! Either they didn't think he'd care to, or his enemies on the Board were still powerful enough to prevent him from savoring the full sweetness of his victory.

But he'd make a spontaneous speech anyway. Of course, he would *not* tell them how he'd begun to melt Antarctica in retaliation against those Board members who'd unfairly used Meminet against him. Now he could afford to be magnanimous. First, he would congratulate them all on the *design* of the Memini game. He would suggest a few improvements (for those juniors who would be running the gauntlet after him), such as tightening Meminet security, and reducing the crushing load of paperwork dumped on the so-called CEO—but he would *not* use the opportunity, as some mean-spirited peers of his might, to deliver a diatribe against his enemies. They were only human, all too human. By acting against him out of petty, personal motives, perhaps they thought they would feel better about themselves—about their own teeny, talentless, ambitionless selves. How long would he have to endure the drag of mediocrity? The arrow of the spirit was weighed down and blunted by millions of tons of torpid humanity, by mountains of mind-fat that cried out to be liposucked away.

No, rather than indulge in fruitless recriminations, he would focus on the positive, the future, the day when technology—when the triumphant teknonomy—would have weeded out all weakness from the mind and body, creating a machine of perfect dexterity housing a brain that would know only intelligence and . . . love. Of course! *Love!* Love for the noblest of his kind . . . love for the finest of *women* of his kind! And he knew that right there in the audience, seated probably front row center, he'd see Iris Morgan with a big bouquet of roses waiting to greet him as soon as, tier-one diploma in hand, he hurried to her down from the stage.

***

"Just a couple more doors ahead," said Andy, scraping the A/V tick off his tie-pin with his thumb and sticking it under his cravat to cut off the picture but still allow for sound. He hopped up two low steps and pushed the buzzer of a blank-faced, cermetal door, knowing that someone was scrutinizing him from within and that in five seconds a return buzz would permit him to push the door inward. "That tie of yours is slightly off center, Mike." He reached out to the knot and managed to lift the eye away before Barton could react with a straightening motion of his own. Flicking it to the street, as he thought, Andy saw what seemed to be the same tiny tick appear clinging, as if by static electricity, to the edge of his own jacket sleeve. If not for the whiteness of his suit he'd never have spotted the scab-like, dust-gray little thing. A gust of air, apparently, had blown the eye back against him.

Meanwhile the answering buzzer sounded. Andy pinched off the eye and pasted it deep inside his pants pocket for safe-keeping. Pushing at the door just before the signal ended, he managed to hustle the two of them inside a well-lit, white-walled vestibule, where a second smooth-faced door gleamed a few feet ahead. But in thrusting his hand into his pocket Andy noticed another little trouble-spot at the crook of his elbow—*not* the same eye this time, for sure! The outer door creaked shut, trapping them inside beyond retreat, as if they were sandwiched between the hatches of an airlock. Andy snipped off the eye from his sleeve and stuck it like a snot to the wall.

"Worried about lint on your suit? You look fine, Roper. C'mon, what's your *real* name, Roper?"

Andy stood frozen before the inner door, glancing rapidly over the surface of his jacket, his eyes losing their focus just as he seemed to see other telltale discolorations—around his pockets, on his buttons. He began to flail and scratch at every surface of his suit he could reach. Scabby little spots kept blinking off and on wherever he looked. "Fucking double-crossing Wanjo!" he muttered in response to Barton's growing amazement. But it didn't *have* to be Wanjo. Could have been a trick of those media boys, when he wasn't looking, sprinkling him with more than just stardust! Or else the sky was full of the stuff, scattering it down day after day like invisible snow. The little bugs were in his nose, in his gut, he must have pissed out hundreds of them only this morning after breakfast . . .

"Aren't you gentlemen going to step *in*?" said a heavy-set man wearing a spotless white smock and a light-blue surgical mask. As he held the door open, his piggish little eyes shot a dark glance at Andy. Andy sized things up in an instant. Things looked *fairly* normal, so far. As he'd figured, no one in the busy joint had been alerted yet to his unannounced appearance on 3V. But later how would he explain it—all those eyes, those bugs . . . and that he'd been hoodwinked, used, lied to . . . ?

Andy forced a smile and motioned for Barton to step forward. "This is one of the gentlemen who've been waiting for you, Mr. Brahma," Andy explained.

"Mr. Mishkin!" Barton exclaimed. "I didn't know there was a back door to your lab."

***

"What the hell's going on?" shouted Barton, whom Stewart could see (from an eye evidently planted on Andy) suddenly thrust into a white-walled room furnished with nothing but a couple of hospital gurneys. The man he had called Mishkin yanked him forward by the hand. Another masked "doctor," slipping behind him, gave him a sharp chop to the neck. Two other men in similar surgeon's gowns now appeared and carried the limp Barton over to one of the waiting carts. (Schizoid cadences of a variety of percussion instruments.)

The man who had "welcomed" Barton again occupied center-stage, glaring into the camera eye (at Andy, of course).

"Anything the matter?" said Andy.

"You know what's the fuckin' matter," said the man Barton had mistaken for Mishkin. "You got greedy, baby. Wasn't enough for you to fuck the Corporation, you had to fuck *us* over too?"

There was a pause. Then, "*Sorry* about the fuckin' eyes!" said the invisible Andy. "Bastards must've smeared them all over me when they were patting me on the back! They'd absolutely *promised*, I swear—"

"We don't give a shit about *those* eyes, Andy boy," said the heavy-set man. "*Your* pretty eyes are another thing entirely. Must be *someone* out there needs a pair right about now, don't you think?"

"What I'm saying," mumbled Andy, "is that I didn't agree to a thing that'd give a *clue* about where I was leading my pidge."

"You seem to have a *problem* sticking to agreements, Andy."

"What do you mean, a 'problem'?"

"Miss Yamamoto told us to expect you."

"Yamamoto? Calling *you*?"

"When we heard you were on 3V, we weren't going to let your filthy ass in here, but Miss Y just called again and persuaded us to go on with the show."

"What the hell do *you* have to do with that bitch?"

"I'm really sorry, Andy. I hate to end a long and productive relationship. But Miss Boss's orders is Miss Boss's orders." The pig-eyed man shrugged his shoulders and lifted his hand. There was a thunderous crack, as of a skull being bludgeoned. Then the scene took a jarring spin downward to the (visually uninteresting) *side* of the room. (A clacking of castanets, the chitter of rattlesnake tails!) A man in a white smock swooped down on the viewer. His shoulders and masked face were seen from below as he now trundled forward, evidently with the help of a confederate out of range of the lens. The white-draped, barrel-shaped torso swayed against a barren backdrop of advancing ceiling tiles, white on white.

Scene change: Wanjo waiting patiently on a doorstep, probably somewhere near the chophouse. Now he flicks on his videowatch and lifts it to his ear. Close-up: Wanjo's jaw drops open and his upper lip starts to twitch. Evidently he is listening to the narrator in the copter above. (A solemn, slow thumping of bongos.)

Narrator: "This did *not* figure in any of the endings we could possibly have foreseen! Believe us, folks, we're just as surprised as you. Did we—as accused by the unfortunate Andy, ex-king of streethawks—intentionally place other A/V tabs all over his clothing? Of course not. Given the heavy incidence of such eyes, scattered indiscriminately for years around a neighborhood so trideogenic as this—"

Stewart flicked off the set. The image of the stunned Hispasian kid persisted in his vision. Like the kid, he began trembling as if sheared by a cold wind.

32. NEW WORLD A-BORNING

"Mr. Bridges?"

Stewart hurried around to the front of the desk and peered into the 3V. Sibyl Yamamoto's face was serious and unsmiling. She suddenly seemed remote, insubstantial. Was there someone real behind that lovely hologram? he wondered. How reconcile the woman he had made love to Friday night with *this* one ... who issued sentences of death as easily as invitations to a party?

"Thank you for your patience, Mr. Bridges." An impersonal smile revealed the unnicked edges of her teeth. "If you won't mind taking a seat in view of this monitor, your interview with Meminet will now begin."

"Interview! ... After what I've just seen on 3V?"

"I know what you've just seen, Mr. Bridges, but I'm unable to discuss that with you right now." A troubled, even pleading expression momentarily creased her brows, a glint of flesh beneath plastic. "The seat directly *behind* you, Mr. Bridges."

"But this one belongs to ... "

"That one, yes. Thank you. And now, if you'll excuse me, I place you in the hands of Meminet."

He lowered his butt gingerly against the seat's ample cushioning. The chair was physically comfortable, but the thought of *his* common carcass parked in one of the Three Great Seats of Worldly Power filled him with feelings of ambivalence. He imagined similar feelings—fear in the presence of that which is taboo, the thrilling prospect of transgression—striking the first rampaging Paris guttersnipes to squat in the throne of the deposed Louis XVI. Hardly had he adjusted to the tension-reducing cushion-grip than a new 3V image confronted him: a double line of business-suited torsos ("faces" showing nothing more than identical beards and mouths!) stretching along a conference-table that receded to infinity.

"Mr. Stewart Bridges," said an unnervingly echoic voice, as though a cicada had learned to speak English, "we, the collective mind of Memini, extend you our cordial welcome. Our delay in making your acquaintance could not be helped, for we first had to assure ourselves that a prior piece of business was properly concluded. That business *has* been satisfactorily concluded. In fact, Mr. Bridges, you have witnessed that conclusion for yourself... Have you not?"

"Do I address you as Meminet?" Stewart asked, conscious of the tell-tale quiver in his voice.

"As Meminet, yes, Mr. Bridges."

"I'm not sure what you're alluding to, Meminet," he temporized.

"Oh, come now, Mr. Bridges. There are no secrets between us. You are not prosopagnosic. You are not amnesic. You have just watched 'There's a Crime in Progress,' so that you are fully aware of the final disposition of the former president of the Memini Corporation."

He had nested in her body lulled, he now saw, like an insect in the jaws of a Venus flytrap. She had even let him *know* that they had seen through his deception, but in spite of forewarning he had delivered himself willingly into their hands, for what purpose he could not even begin to guess.

"You can relax, Mr. Bridges. You have nothing to fear from Meminet. We did not foresee any public display of internal company business. We doubt, however, that harm has been done to the Memini corporate image. Human beings, nevertheless, occasionally surprise us with their capacity for self-destructive behavior. Andy 'the Actor,' for example, decided to peddle stolen company records. He and we had had a long and mutually satisfactory relationship, but something suddenly came over him to destroy his mental balance. Quite regrettable, but he brought retribution upon himself. We apologize for the distress that such a tasteless exhibition must have caused you."

"How can I be sure that I really saw... what I thought I saw?" said Stewart, squirming against the "comfort" of a seat which was trying to engulf him. "Hundreds of people, thousands, look like Barton."

"Yes. People all over the world have tended to *model* themselves on

Barton."

Stewart's hand rose defensively to his beard.

"And that is precisely why Memini is likely to remain untarnished by the episode. In any case, Mr. Bridges, we wish to reassure you that you *have* seen what you thought you saw. It was an overly dramatic—and certainly unintended—introduction of you to Memini, perhaps. But it serves as an even further test of your mettle. And we've had you under study for months, Mr. Bridges."

"Study? Why—"

"With entirely favorable results, of course. Otherwise you would not have made it thus far through our fine-mesh 'net,' so to speak. Do you see?"

"I *don't* see," said Stewart, unable to 'relax' as advised. "I'm sorry if I applied for a position that I was in no way qualified to fill."

"Oh, the deception was mutual. The position we induced you to apply for—you, and you alone, Mr. Bridges—was not in fact available at all. You found that out on your own, didn't you? We admire your coolness of mind even in the heat of physical passion, Mr. Bridges. One of the qualities that do, in fact, qualify you for the position."

"If I'd had true coolness of mind, I'd never have come to the party in the first place."

"On the contrary, your attempt to deceive us, in turn, was eminently successful. You did an excellent job of passing for a tekkie."

"Are you interested in my talent as an actor?" Stewart's mouth had gone dry. His tongue began to cleave to his palate. "I notice you seem to be in the habit of employing actors, actors that tend to play tragic roles."

"The point is well taken, Mr. Bridges. You are shocked by what you have seen, but you are sufficiently level-headed to be curious as well. Your probing intellect prevents you from jumping to hasty conclusions of a moralistic nature. Yours is precisely the sort of intellect that is *required* for running a conglobulate such as Memini."

Running? Had he heard right?

"You need not be surprised, Mr. Bridges, that we have developed great esteem for your qualities of mind."

"The job you have me in mind for," Stewart said slowly, skeptically, "is some kind of leadership . . . ?"

"The presidency of Memini, Mr. Bridges. The seat that you now fill bodily is yours, in the larger sense, if you are willing to take it. Naturally, our offer comes to you as a surprise, and we feel we do owe you a reasonably detailed explanation—"

"So *that's* what that nametag switch at the party was all about! It wasn't just somebody's prank."

"It was a brilliant idea that we owe to Sibyl Yamamoto."

"Sibyl stuck that label on me?"

"Out of faith in you, Mr. Bridges. Ms. Yamamoto is a humane woman who has developed an especially protective attitude toward you. Your work as bioprogrammer, to which she has often been exposed, has somehow managed to establish in her a limbic response to you—a massive *emotional* response to you, and to anything associated with you—by way of *endocrine*-system pathways, circumventing the need for organic memory channels—which in her are of course largely inoperative."

"You mean in my case she's developed an alternate circuit that evades the action of the Pill?" Stewart's feelings ranged from a hot rush of pride to out-and-out revulsion. All weekend he had hardly eaten. The thought of seeing her again was all he'd fed on. Now, however, that sleek body of hers was like a beautiful silk scabbard sheathing a blood-stained sword.

"Her subcortical fixation on you should not totally surprise you, Mr. Bridges. There are other sorts of memory—*procedural* memory, for instance, that remain largely unaffected by the Pill. That is why ingrained habits, such as putting on one's clothes or finding one's way to the bathroom, are as automatic with tekkies as with oldfolks. But forgive us for lecturing to you, who are already quite familiar with the neurophysiology of memory."

"I'm always open to learning something new," said Stewart.

"Suffice it to say, then, that you, in your personal uniqueness, have had a well-nigh magical effect upon Sibyl. Endocrinal memory is rarely seen in so manifest a form, of course. It seems to be activated particularly in response to powerful primal urges, like the sexual."

"I'm deeply flattered," said Stewart. "But I don't see what was so 'protective' about her getting me mistaken for Barton."

MEMINI

"It was a relatively painless way of introducing you to your new role—and to your future colleagues, of course—so that you would have a preliminary *feel* for the position that we wish you to accept. We hasten to add that your handling of the Tingworth crisis was masterly, absolutely masterly."

"I did what I had to do, given the circumstances." He remembered, half shamefully, how Tingworth had provided the diversion releasing him from the burden of a false identity. As to having developed "a preliminary feel for the position," he swallowed his anger at knowing now how thoroughly they'd manipulated him. "I'm flattered to know I've had such a remarkable effect on Miss Yamamoto," he said, "but I hardly expect to have a similar effect on such a massive operation like Memini. Quite simply, I don't have the administrative *experience* for such a position."

"Your lack of encrusted habits called 'administrative experience' speaks in your favor."

"I'm only a bioprogrammer. True, with some cyberpsych background, but—"

"*Great* leaders rarely emerge from backgrounds of mid-level management, Mr. Bridges. Need we multiply instances of novelists, playwrights, 3V comedians and other creative personalities suddenly rising to the helm of nations and even entire geopoliticals without the least shred of an administrative credential? Our now-deceased Chief Executive Officer ran a famous VR social-adjustment clinic when we discovered *him*. We've no time to waste on false modesty, Mr. Bridges. You can be sure that we've pondered every quality of yours deemed pertinent to the position in question."

Stewart's scalp prickled, as if the top of his head were about to fly off. He wanted to believe, but at the same time he suspected a trap. Were they deliberately flattering him ... to *death*? It would be wonderful now to be out in the street, to be breathing the spring air, to simply forget all this, to forget ... "How much time do I have to think your offer over?"

"Unfortunately, you must decide one way or the other before you step out of this office."

"And if I decide against it," said Stewart, knowing that now he was reduced to utter frankness, "would I in fact be *allowed* to leave this office?"

Meminet's laugh grated like locusts stripping a cornfield. "You are free to leave. You will not be harmed. We must add, perhaps immodestly, that we feel we are making you an offer too good to refuse. At an annual salary of ICU five million, plus unlimited expense account, plus exclusive use of the presidential estate and air-sea transportation complex . . . "

As Meminet reeled off the perks that went with the position, Stewart saw himself cast in the role of a trideo soapstar. He'd be some sort of king of the world (reality outgalloping the most delirious, the most naked, of his fantasies!), more powerful than the leaders of hemispheres—but always with his neck under a Damocletian sword, always with his toes at the edge of a gangplank. "But what if I fail? Everyone will eventually know what I am. No one will trust me. No one will want to work with me. Am I to look forward to the same fate that . . . "

"You are entitled to a full explanation of the fate of your predecessor, Mr. Bridges. You see, we say 'predecessor,' so confident are we that you will accept the position we offer."

Pre-deceasor! Stewart heard. Why hadn't they given the poor bastard the option to retire? Why did he *identify* so much with Lester Barton? But, for crying out loud, he had *invented* the man! A quarter century of Barton had been made up by him, and in that sense he was the late president's logical "heir." He had created all the stories that Barton would have played to himself about himself and rehearsed *ad nauseam* to his colleagues. But for Stewart such knowledge would be of minor advantage in a world where no one retained what you said between one cup of coffee and the next.

"Until recently, Mr. Bridges, Lester Barton made an excellent Chief Executive Officer. Unfortunately, he failed to make certain 'developmental transitions,' as we call them in neurological parlance."

"I could screw up on the job just as easily," said Stewart. "I'm not good at remembering details. Is this how you treat executives who get lousy performance ratings . . . shuffle them off for dissection?"

"On the contrary, we are a very humane organization, Mr. Bridges—in spite of what you have seen. If drastic action is occasionally called for, it is employed strictly for purposes of self-preservation. Would you yourself not 'go for the jugular' if someone came at you unequivocally intending to kill you?"

MEMINI

"It hardly seems to me that Lester Barton was the sort who'd want to kill anyone," said Stewart. He thought there was something deranged about *Meminet*—calling itself "humane," when in the light of the double trashing he had himself just witnessed . . .

"The tragedy of Lester Barton," the voice of Meminet solemnly buzzed, "is that he did what he thought best, not knowing the imminent threat he posed to the *very existence of Memini*, and collaterally to the *economic stability of the world*. He acted out of a headstrong belief in the rightness of his unilateral decisions, ignoring the collective wisdom, ignoring political and economic trends, ignoring even the inevitable advance of science."

"Still, I hardly see how such failings," said Stewart, "which seem typical of administrators—inflexibility, hardening of the mental arteries—"

"Exactly! You have hit the nail on the head. 'Hardening of the mental arteries' was *literally* Mr. Barton's problem, Mr. Bridges."

"But you are talking about one of the most envied talents of the mega-corporate world!"

"Clearly we must present the case to you in ever more explicit detail. We have absolutely nothing to hide from you, Mr. Bridges. Nor you from us. In fact, it was Mr. Barton's growing *secretiveness* that began to reveal to us his tragic symptomatology—the sclerotic process of your entirely apt image. Human beings, be they tekkie or oldfolks, all lead double lives—possessing an inner, subjective sense of self, and an outward self with a public role to play. In most people the two lives coexist in harmony, or at least cooperate within a manageable range of friction. In the case of Mr. Barton, an irreconcilable conflict had developed between the two. Given the position of enormous power that he held, it should come as no surprise to see that his self-division could have explosive global consequences."

"To the point where the only alternative was to have the poor bastard *killed*?"

"He had ordered your death, too, you know. Out of the paranoia incident to his terminal mental condition."

"Barton ordered *me* killed?" The shudder that ripped through him had to be visible to Meminet.

"Fortunately for you, he had ordered it done through us rather than arranging it himself through his off-line communication system, a privilege reserved for the CEO alone. If not for our intervention—"

"All this is so damn hard to believe!" Stewart clapped his hands to the sides of his head.

"We ask you to suspend judgment for the moment, and to imagine that, in truth, to dispose of Mr. Barton may have been the most humane solution to the various crises his behavior has created. In fact, Mr. Bridges, if it can be called a solution at all, it must be admitted to be only a *partial* solution, at best. The rest of the solution will be effected by you—as soon as you agree, that is, to become the head of Memini."

"I think you'd better back up," said Stewart. Questions whirled in his head like a cloud of gnats. "You still haven't told me what you mean by Barton's 'self-division.' Don't ask me for solutions when you haven't even told me the problems!"

"You are extremely familiar with tekkie psychology through your father, Mr. Bridges. Moreover, it is your empathy with the inner world of the tekkie that, among other things, makes you so valuable to us. You will have no difficulty appreciating, therefore, that the tekkie's prime means of staying oriented to external reality—apart, that is, from an entire world of meminized verbal representations—is the indispensable flapper. Without such spatiotemporal guidance as the flapper affords, the tekkie would quickly be swamped by subjective impressions—from the more or less remote past—that claim more truly to represent the current reality."

"My father always thinks I've just got out of college," said Stewart. "I know exactly what you mean."

"Very well. To continue, then. As organic memory continues to recede in the tekkie—such is the inevitable consequence of all *presently* constituted versions of the Pill,—the subsiding waters may begin to reveal certain islands of organic resistance."

"Yes, 'minskies.' In about ten percent of the tekkie population," added Stewart.

"Exactly. And as you also no doubt know, this 'developmental transition crisis,' a neuropsychological watershed which the tekkie must cross if he is to arrive at a mature self-acceptance, may be marked by powerful hallucinations, the intrusion of distant *organic* memories that insist on their status as the current objective reality. Normally, the tokens of everyday reality that surround the afflicted tekkie—in combination with constant flapper promptings, of course—are sufficient to keep such hallucinatory 'overflows' in check. In Mr. Barton's case, however, objective reality-supports caved in completely. We are not sure exactly why."

"It's obvious to *me* why," said Stewart.

"Really! We would be interested in hearing your opinion."

"Certainly. As head of a great conglobulate, Mr. Barton was almost entirely *shielded* from the reality that lesser folks are exposed to daily."

"What a curious idea!" buzzed Meminet.

"Not at all. Mr. Barton's 'objective reality' consisted ninety-five percent of *words*. Words on paper, to be meminized. Words at meetings. Babble. How could a wall of words stand up against powerful representations of a concrete, intensely *felt* sort arising from within?"

"You do have a unique way of looking at things, Mr. Bridges. Perhaps you are even deeper than we have assumed... In any case, Mr. Barton's hallucinations, whose concrete contents remain largely unknown to us, revealed their operational force through the increasingly stubborn view he took that in running Memini he was simply playing a 'game'—some complicated sort of holosimulation, and that his chief antagonist in this game may have been *us*—Meminet! This would have been cause enough for profound alarm, but since, in addition, Mr. Barton was making unilateral, secret, and clearly reckless decisions, such as (1) turning the Democratic Union of Southeast Asia into a power-hostage for what we, the collective mind of Memini, regarded as ill-conceived reasons; (2) tearing to shreds an already fragile web of interhemispheric relations to the point of eventual trade-war; and, most recently and most terribly, (3) unleashing physical forces that at this very moment are threatening the *extinction of civilization*... we reluctantly reached the conclusion that the quiet and expeditious disposal of Mr. Barton was a necessary Step One toward preserving the entire world order."

"Why couldn't you just have fired the man?" asked Stewart.

"Ah, yes! But don't imagine that that alternative had not been considered. For reasons too complicated to enter into in detail, Mr. Bridges, under certain circumstances *firing* the president of a conglobulate like Memini could send the stock market into a tailspin and bring about one of the very disasters that his dismissal is intended to avert."

"And this was the case with Barton?"

"Yes. For him we chose the most humane alternative available . . . available, that is, as a *viable option*, Mr. Bridges."

"I'm beginning to understand," mumbled Stewart, involuntarily shivering. He pressed a button on the chair-arm, raised the seat-back till it hugged his shoulders, and began to experience the massaging action of the luxurious chaise-masseur. He did not touch the temperature-control plate, but if he had time later . . .

"I guess I don't understand how gravely the 'world order' is being threatened," Stewart mumbled.

"*Is* threatened, Mr. Bridges! *Is threatened at this very moment*! But that is precisely why *you* are here. We wish to lay upon your shoulders two main tasks. Cooling the global economic crisis and preventing a worldwide Depression is one. In fact, up to ten-thirty this morning we thought it was your *only* task—sizable enough, it would seem. But our departing—and departed—president, evidently anticipating that we were in process of removing him from office, very cleverly and quite insanely, at about eight a.m. this morning, initiated the melting of the South Polar ice-cap."

Stewart shook his head in disbelief. "That would be *suicidal* as well as homicidal."

"Perhaps neither, if Mr. Barton simply saw himself as playing a game. But at this point we are far less interested in Mr. Barton's psychology than in the terrible real-world forces he has unleashed. So far, Mr. Bridges, our own Antarctic station has been destroyed, and it is presumed that every other scientific station within fifty miles of the Pole has been burnt to a crisp. The heat is being generated in full laser force by the entire solar power-grid of ISEC, which was secretly maneuvered into position by our ex-president over the past week or so. As you know, it is Memini that controls ISEC. As you should also know, if all that power continues unabated to tear up the great polar cap, within two days the process will be irreversible. And within another week, perhaps, the shores of the world will be drowned under a hundred feet of water."

"So why the hell don't *you* do something about it? Why *me*? Why the hell me? I know nothing about fixing worldwide fucking Depressions or polar ice-caps!"

"Why you? Because the only hand that can undo the damage is a flesh-and-blood hand, and that hand can be only the same hand that is chosen to engineer the future. *You* are the future, Mr. Bridges."

"The future of what?" he said, trying to keep a level head, trying to appear uncowed, aggressive—trying to live up to the very image that that goddamn clever Meminet was *projecting* onto him!

"The future of Memini, for one, but more importantly, we desire you to become the forger of a new world order. In our opinion, you are Memini's link between an unstable present and a new economic and political world order, utterly changed from the present."

"The word 'link' . . . it reminds me of a sausage. Is it the fate of all your CEOs to be turned into sausage meat?"

"We honestly think not. But we do not deny that the job poses tremendous challenges."

"'Dangers,' you mean, don't you? Just what sort of world order do you see me linking Memini to?"

"The world of the Perfect Pill, Mr. Bridges."

Stewart suppressed a tendency to smirk. For a century dreamers had been dreaming about the Perfect Pill, scientists had been scouring rainforest preserves for unknown, untested species of plant or insect that would yield the miracle enzyme . . . everyone chasing an *ignis fatuus*, a will o' the wisp. Indeed, the New Environmentalism, the "Green Mansions Movement" which resulted in the preservation of the remains of the Amazon and vast tracts of tropics in Southeast Asia, was directly inspired by no more gaiophilic, altruistic motive than the teknonomy's pursuit of the Perfect Pill. Tekkie hopes for the EMI to end all EMIs, like for the Immortality Pill, had been raised innumerable times over the past hundred years.

"We fully understand your skepticism, Mr. Bridges, but the main ingredient of such a new Pill has been developed at our biological station in Borneo to the point where we are thoroughly confident that in only two years the Perfect Pill will be marketable. The sudden death of Mr. Tingworth, our head of pharmaceuticals, should not materially affect our rate of progress."

"If that is true," said Stewart, "the tekkie world will have achieved its fondest dream."

"No, not the *tekkie* world, Mr. Bridges. Not *just* the tekkie world. And that's the whole point ... the general availability of the Perfect Pill to all of humankind!"

Meminet's tone had a skin-tingling effect on Stewart. The collective company mind sounded positively evangelical. "But that's like ... the teknomy acquiescing in dismantling itself! This seems to contradict the universal principle of self-interest."

"On the contrary, Mr. Bridges, if the future is to be Memini's we must act out of an *enlightened* self-interest. There are too many signs that the old order is collapsing. Oldfolks populations around the world have become increasingly united, across national and even hemispheric lines, in a shared sense of 'deprivation' that has already had serious political ramifications—and, far worse for Memini, is already having tangibly negative effects on world trade! ... Our unfortunate ex-president, in spite of the advice of his numerous forward-thinking colleagues, adamantly refused to adjust to the inevitable."

"So you're saying," said Stewart, "if you can't beat 'em, join 'em?"

"Your capacity to reduce complex ideas to popular sayings will definitely be an asset to you as head of Memini, Mr. Bridges."

"Let's not get ahead of ourselves," said Stewart, still feeling light-headed, disoriented, *unreal*. Here he was being courted to run the most powerful organization in the world, and at the same time he was supposed to stop the South Pole from cracking up! And he was supposed to take all of this on faith from the mouth of a virtual reality program ... As he cowered against the chairback, soothing mechanical fingers relentlessly continued to work at his spine.

"The successful restructuring of the economic order calls for the total restructuring of the political and social orders," Meminet proceeded (rather pedantically, thought Stewart). "These restructurings can occur in one of two ways—pacifically, with Memini in the lead, or catastrophically, with Memini falling completely out of the picture. Since the profound changes we envisage are already turbulently in progress, Memini can continue to thrive only if we openly *promote* the inevitable."

"Getting out there and lip-sync'ing to the tune of 'Equal Opportunity for All,' so to speak?"

"Lip-sync'ing! Another excellent popular image," said Meminet, "but far too suggestive of passivity. It is true, we can't change the tune of the coming world, but we can be first to *package* the new music, and first to bring it to market."

"I still don't understand . . . why *me*?" said Stewart. "Why not entrust Memini to a 'brother,' so to speak—to one of your fellow tekkies?"

"You misunderstand our priorities, Mr. Bridges. One of the limitations of Mr. Barton, for example, was his unshakable assumption that Memini's first loyalty was to the teknonomy, to a socioeconomic elite. But *Memini's first loyalty—may we call you Stewart, Mr. Bridges?—is to the preservation of Memini*."

"So you would like to use me in the same way," mused Stewart, "ancient Rome used barbarian generals to preserve the corporate entity called Rome?"

"We applaud your use of historical analogy, Stewart. It so happens that one of Memini's new marketing strategies will be a global reconnection with *History*—with poor old ragged Clio, that much-abused Muse. We must recommodify History. It must be pictured as a treasure-trove of customs and mores demanding the manufacture of innumerable new products and the provision of countless new services—exactly reversing the current image of History as a junk-shop full of useless old furniture. We must backtrack on over half a century of *attacking* historical awareness as the enemy of progress. By repainting all that old furniture, we intend to recapture the vast numbers of alienated oldfolks who are needed to ensure an expanding worldwide economy . . . But still, Stewart, your *choice* of historical analogy—barbarians, indeed!—is decidedly self-depreciatory, don't you think?"

"But that's exactly how I would feel . . . like a barbarian in a tekkie-run Rome!" He waved his hand vaguely toward the door. "Day in, day out, an endless masquerade. How could I possibly . . ."

"But you passed test after test with flying colors, Stewart. Your ability to pass for a tekkie is second-nature to you by now."

"How will my *colleagues* feel about shifting to a new world order? Surely they'll be threatened as hell!"

"You will find that you have strong organizational support for change, some fairly outspoken, far more of it ready to emerge under the spur of your fostering leadership. Fortunately, the 'bottom line' has a powerfully *doxolytic* effect—enforcing an unaccustomed flexibility on even some of the most ideologically hard-headed among your colleagues-to-be, Stewart. The sad fact is that the forces for internal change were largely suppressed by our tragically blind former president. He meant well, of course. But we're sure you can see why the future of Memini cannot be placed in the hands of another tekkie. Only you, Stewart, will have the positive *desire* to bring oldfolks into the fold, to share power with the multitudes who have been technologically incapable of wielding it."

"What do you mean, 'share power'? Am I to hire oldfolks executives? And why would they be any better able to wield power now than before? You have to be on the Pill to be able to master—" Stewart's voice stuck in his throat. *You have to be on the goddamn Pill!*

"Are you feeling ill, Stewart?"

"No, not exactly..."

"Under your leadership, Stewart, the sharing of power will be a gradual process. It will take place only after the Perfect Pill enters worldwide common use. Eventually there will be no distinction between oldfolks and tekkie. 'Tekkie' will come to signify, instead, a quietly fading breed of irreversibly brain-damaged pensioners, a technohistorical curiosity. The Perfect Pill will be the great leveler—or rather, the great *uplifter,* since all of humanity will be capable of achieving the powers presently conferred by the Pill *without suffering loss of organic memory!*"

"I see," said Stewart. "Anyone could become a kind of mental superman."

"Provided that the genetic potential is there to begin with, yes. But there will *be* no 'class' of the 'half-baked,' the 'snags,' as they are commonly called."

"Like my father," said Stewart, "who lose the brains they're born with but don't get too much brighter on the Pill."

"Self-administration of the Perfect Pill will no longer entail *negative* consequences, true. And if Memini fails to exploit this biochemical breakthrough immediately, another corporation surely will. Mr. Barton tried to suppress it, but it is inevitable that one of our competitors will sooner or later stumble on the same little fungus in the normal course of its exhaustive biological researches. We must regard our coming out with it as a kind of *preemptive strike*. To preserve our timeless corporate *Self*, we must at last phase out our timebound tekkie *selves*. We thus foresee that within the course of a single generation the tekkie-heavy North and the oldfolks-heavy South will cease to have significance as opposed political zones of an unpredictably excitable character. The world-circulation of credit should experience a remarkable acceleration as artificial constraints fall away. In short, we foresee the day of a virtually unimpeded velocity of exchange, the *day of economic transcendence over sociopolitical 'noise,'* a day when the currents of trade shall resemble the frictionless flow of electrical current through our very own superconducting coils."

"You're painting a utopia!"

"No, Stewart, just a more efficiently engineered world, a world made far more secure for Memini than the present."

"A world secure for *Memini*, you say?"

"A world secure for Memini is a world that is secure by definition," Meminet replied. "The effect is necessarily reciprocal."

For a fleeting moment he had a vision of Atlas. In spite of the relentless masseur at his back, his shoulders felt bowed and heavy at the prospect of shoving and coaxing the world into the twenty-second century. He imagined himself hunched under the globe behind his chair, except that all the little "M"-marked flags had their pin-ends sticking outward. Smiling sadly, Stewart shook his head. "I'm only a dreamer, Meminet. Some mornings I leave my apartment wearing socks that don't match. Where does someone like me come off trying to prod the whole damn world into a 'new dawn'? I wouldn't know where the hell to begin."

"The place to begin, Stewart, is very clear—and very urgent! Mr. Barton has precipitated global catastrophe. Failing to prevent the development of the Perfect Pill, which for him meant the end of the teknonomy, this very morning he ordered the Memini-controlled solar-power satellite system to focus all of its immense energy-gathering resources—"

"On Antarctica, yes," said Stewart, "and with all your powers of observation and intervention you couldn't stop him!"

"And we wouldn't have understood what was happening even now, Stewart, if not for the mild disobedience of one of our top executives, Ms. Helen Means, who recorded into flapper what she thought were simply the mad ravings of Mr. Barton, disregarding his request that she not record their rendezvous this past Friday night."

"The night of the party."

"Exactly. Fortunately, the contents of her flapper's memory were left available for automatic uploading into our own memory banks the following afternoon, Saturday. This morning, therefore, after receiving news of developments in Antarctica, we conducted an intensive search for understanding—including a thorough review of the entire vast contents of our memory, and we luckily came upon Ms. Means's most illuminating recording."

"And you expect *me* to put a stop to all this?" said Stewart.

"Indeed we do!" rasped Meminet. "Just as the entire operation was put into motion via the presidential tridentifier—Mr. Barton's combined eye-, voice-, and hand-print—so it is that to bring it to a halt, the presidential trident is required."

"Well that's pretty damned impossible, to my way of thinking, unless his butchers can send you the parts you need in a—"

"No, it is not impossible. The system allows us to 'update' the presidential trident. You will see what we mean in a moment. Please flick the red switch on the extreme right of the control plate that begins at your right elbow . . . No, we solemnly swear that we are not trying to trick you into anything, Stewart."

Shrugging his shoulders, Stewart did as asked. A periscope-like cylinder slowly rose to eye-level from the desktop near the control.

"By placing either eye to the eye-piece, and at the same time grasping the cylinder with either hand and uttering the words 'Update, I am Lester Barton,' *you* immediately assume the identity of Chief Executive Officer of Memini wherever throughout the world Mr. Barton's trident is required to legitimate an order."

"Well, if it's that easy, why can't you get *anyone* to step up and . . . "

"Ah, so you are already beginning to see? . . . Who could this 'anyone' be? Someone completely trustworthy and totally *au courant* regarding the true disposition of Mr. Barton? That leaves only Sibyl Yamamoto."

"Fine! Let Sibyl—"

"But Ms. Yamamoto's trident is already on file together with those of all other Memini employees, and so would be instantly rejected as fraudulent. An emergency procedure does exist by which an executive of vice-presidential rank could take command, but no one besides Sibyl is remotely aware of the true state of affairs, and the survival of Memini might well *depend* on no one else's knowing—if you've understood the implications of all that we have confided in you up to this point."

"I catch on quickly," said Stewart.

"Very good," said Meminet. "So, then, the only permissible updates to the trident would be Mr. Barton's own or that of a non-employee. Like yourself, Stewart."

"You can't have *depended* on my stepping into Barton's shoes, can you?"

"Stewart, the devastation to life and ecosystem that is now underway in Antarctica is unimaginable in scope and intensity. If the present solar array had been focussed this morning instead on the United States—"

"You don't have to spell it out!" He did not want to visualize the destruction. He did not want such pictures forced on him.

"Even if Mr. Barton's instructions were to be reprogramed this minute, Stewart, it would still take twelve hours for a rescission of his orders to *take effect*, such is the slowness of the old ISEC communicative *machinery* that is involved in this enormous operation."

"In other words, if a stop order is not given soon . . ."

"The civilized world," continued Meminet, "will be converted into a vast underwater cemetery."

Stewart felt a growing weight in his chest. It was becoming increasingly difficult to breathe. He felt the stepped-up rhythm of the biosensitive chairback masseur, but the stubborn fingers failed to soothe. "I feel unworthy," he muttered. Then more loudly, "I feel *unworthy*, I feel . . ."

33. THE PERFECT PILL

The door panels silently parted to admit her. Sibyl advanced on him with catlike grace, hugging a digital clipboard to her chest. The memories conjured up by her presence stopped his breath. She mystified him, frightened him. He tried to imagine never again making love to her, but imagining her absence only redoubled his awareness of her presence. He returned his stare to Meminet, refusing to acknowledge the change in the air, the difference in the light, the taste in his mouth occasioned by the simple fact of her physically just *being* there. He needed to make his decision apart from all thought of *her*, he admonished himself.

"It will be a sad day for all of us if you disappoint us, Stewart," Meminet solemnly intoned, "but you are perfectly free to leave if you must. We offer you powers beyond your wildest expectations—the power to usher in a new Golden Age for humanity. What is good for Memini is good for the whole world. And you will have at your side an exceptionally gifted, absolutely loyal helpmeet . . . "

She had slipped behind his chair, placing a hand on his shoulder, her right cheek softly brushing his clammy temple as she too peered into the blank-faced labyrinth of Meminet. He avoided looking back at her, but he could not help breathing deeply of her perfume, the same that still clung beneath his fingernails—and in the unscrubbable corners of memory, of his ghost-ridden, tight-fisted oldfolks memory that never let go of a thing whether it was good for him or not. Suddenly he remembered his ill-fated college romance, and the dread of new betrayal made his skin crawl under the stroke of Sibyl's hand. The vision of the moral void beneath her flawless skin filled him with dread.

"This is the contract that Meminet would like you to sign," she said, passing the Meminet-linked clipboard into his hands. "I hope you will sign for my sake, too, Stewart. Meminet knows of my selfishness in this."

"But in this 'selfishness' we encourage her, Stewart—and only because our separate self-interests, with respect to you, have had a demonstrably synergistic effect."

What Meminet seemed to be saying, as though it knew exactly what he was thinking, was *Don't worry, she is acting toward you out of her own free will!* But what Stewart saw was the hand of the perfect robot. Faultlessly efficient servo, she had entered on cue, her presence designed to demolish his remaining pockets of resistance. But the robot he saw now, or thought he saw—hadn't *that* been the illusion? Hadn't that specter of sleeping with a teleoperated mannequin been erased under the sweet ferocity of her love-making? Did robots weep? Did they faint in your arms out of ecstasy? *Who* or *what* was this Sibyl Yamamoto whom he feared either to lose or to keep? . . .

The contract was headed "Agreement of Renewal of Tenure in the Position of President and Chief Executive Officer of the Memini Corporation." The fairyland list of perks and benefits accruing to the holder of office danced before Stewart's eyes like showers of dust from far-off fabled galaxies. The silver pen he took from Sibyl hovered uncertainly in the air. He wanted to hear something convincingly, humanly personal from her. Instead he heard: "Of course, you must realize, Stewart, that if you accept the position, you are no longer, ever again, to present yourself to anyone as . . . Stewart Bridges." Her voice seemed strangely to crack, as if under an enormous strain of *apology*. "From now on your name will be Lester Barton. Your family, however, who know you as Stewart Bridges, must never be informed of your new position and the new name it entails. I'm sure you see that it cannot be otherwise."

"Lester Barton is dead," chanted Stewart. "Long live Lester Barton!" Wanting to see her face, he turned his head sideways. The warm crib of her neck caught his cheek.

What the hell! he thought. Wasn't all of what was happening to him everything he had ever wanted?

Tearing himself away from the lap of her neck, he leaned forward and extended his hand to sign. Then he looked at the signature line and his hand froze in mid-flourish. The name he was asked to inscribe was Lester Barton *IV*!

"LB *IV*!" he exclaimed.

"Does the name pose a problem for you?" asked Meminet.

Stewart stared at the clipboard. "I understand now," he said. "When I did the previous Mr. Barton's Personal Past, there was a document or two slipped in among the materials I was given that referred to him as Lester Barton *III*!"

"An unimportant detail," said Meminet. "The change in number is purely a formality. A matter of in-house record-keeping. The number IV will appear on very few documents, and those will be of extremely limited circulation. Under no circumstances, however, will you ever again need to write *any* number as part of your official signature."

Stewart twisted his neck around to look up into Sibyl's eyes. They were pools of entreaty. Or was the hormonally prompted look she gave him an undisguised sign of warning? Tears shimmered delicately behind her lower lids. A blink would be enough to spill them. "There was an LB II, of course, and before that wasn't there just a plain old LB without any model number at all?" he shot at her.

"Sibyl would have no way of knowing," interjected Meminet. "Have you any recollection, Sibyl, of *any* documents signed by Lester Barton in which he uses a number after his name?"

"None whatsoever. I *swear*, Stewart," she said, training a steady gaze at him. *Of course* she wouldn't know! he thought. He had to stop his panic-stricken scrutiny of her eyes. They did not harbor the answer he was looking for. This was a decision that he alone must make.

Releasing a pent-up breath, Stewart felt like screaming "Geronimo!" as he dashed off the inherited name. The sweep of his hand across the surface of the sensor-pad surprised him with its sudden confidence.

"Congratulations, Lester!" chirped Meminet. "Your personal version of the Lester Barton signature will now replace the previous version on every record filed in the Meminet system."

"'Lester'?" said Stewart.

"Lester, of course!" echoed Meminet.

"Yes, 'Lester.' Of course," Stewart/Lester agreed.

"It's only a name," said Sibyl, nipping him playfully in the back of the neck, as though deliberately out of sight of Meminet.

"But...the Pill!" exclaimed Stewart. He jerked forward out of Sibyl's soothing hands. "I'll take on the job, but not with the help of your *emmies*."

"That will be entirely up to you, Lester," a coolly ironic voice grated back. "Unfortunately, the paperwork of running a vast conglobulate would appear impossible to master without Brocaleptic support."

Stewart stood up and stared down at the 3V in raw anger. "Humanity can go hang, I will not fry my brains for it!" he shouted. "I will not be sent to the glue-factory like LB III, and LB II, and—"

"There is no need for such an apocalyptic fancy, Lester! No need for that at all!" intoned Meminet. "You have raised a problem that we had fully intended to address."

"To me it is not just *a* problem," said Stewart. "To me it is *the* problem." Again he felt her hand on his shoulder. She had come up alongside him. They both faced the 3V together. Stewart felt suddenly ashamed to have expressed, *in her presence*, such disgust at what she herself had become, such horror of that impenetrable darkness in her, that absence in her that *he* could never fill—that nothingness in her that nothing could ever fill. The tears were running down her cheeks. Damn her! he told himself. The hell with her tears! In ten-fifteen minutes she'd be as cheerfully vacant as a songbird again.

He knew he was right, totally right, and yet there were ten-fifteen minutes of *suffering* revealed in those tears. Suffering was *real*. Whether it lasted one minute, ten minutes, blinked off and on for a month, what did it matter?...

His heart went out to her. Her crippled humanity aroused in him a strangely troubled tenderness. He briefly stroked her arm, in which she clutched the all-important clipboard close to her breast. Gratefully, she rested her cheek on his shoulder. It was a gesture of the most natural, unpreprogrammed intimacy, her *body's* recollection of him, an authentic act of recognition—subcortical? supercortical?—asserting itself in complete disregard for who might be looking on. She confused him as he stood there in an eleventh-hour contest with the cricket-like, supremely confident

Meminet. To have had the tekkie capacity to *forget* her at that moment would have helped him focus his fears. Trying to picture *himself* in the near future, he could see only his father, chained to a flapper like an accident victim strapped to an IV. Lester Barton, *I.V.*! he thought.

"You can't expect me to give up for Memini," said Stewart, "what you've now decided to be the birthright of all of humanity!" What *ground* did he now stand on against Meminet? he wondered. He had signed away—what? His life, his identity? Did Meminet now have him at a "moral" disadvantage? Or was it the other way around, since the special risks involved in taking on the job should have been revealed to him explicitly in advance? He was in an ethical no-man's-land . . . but he was not without bargaining power. He still held all the cards, didn't he? He could simply refuse to give the order that would stop the Antarctic meltdown!

"We wish to assure you, Lester," said the thousand crickets before him, "that we do not foresee a future in which you need suffer any noticeable damage from taking the Pill. One year of moderate dosage is unlikely to result in any significant neurological change. It so happens that within just about one year, given our splendid successes with the macaque trials in Borneo, we shall be ready for the first *human* trials. You, Lester, will have the option to be one of the first human beings to participate in those trials. You will be one of the first to benefit from the unconditionally Perfect Pill."

Pie in the sky! he wanted to say. Nothing but a paper promise! But he also wanted to believe, to trust . . .

He felt her fingers weave through his, locking them in a firm and unremitting grip. "If you wish, Stewart—"

"*Lester!*" crackled Meminet. "We must all remember—"

"If you wish, *Stewart*," Sibyl proceeded, her nostrils fleering, her eyes seeking his, "you can undo this contract even *now.*" With her other hand, she offered him the clipboard. "I have not yet caused your signature to be *saved.*"

"Now really!" the voice of Meminet screeched. "Sibyl, while we appreciate your concern, the fact is . . . "

Stewart lost track of the rest of Meminet's mutterings. He watched Sibyl with mounting fascination. He saw her gaze into the innumerably

MEMINI

self-mirrored Meminet with a trembling kind of *defiance*! Stewart/Lester realized, to his utter consternation, that this was not part of the scenario. That for his sake she dared to risk *everything*—her job, her career, and if she posed any kind of security risk...

"Goddammit, we're wasting time!" he said, deciding to end the showdown. Reaching out, he pressed the little "Save" panel at the top left of the clipboard. "Now, how do I cancel Barton's meltdown?"

"Very easily, Mr. Barton!" buzzed Meminet. "The cancel order as such is in. It awaits verification by trident. Your eye to the eye-piece, your hand..."

The ceremony of update and verification over, Lester/Stewart paid little attention to Meminet's technoprattle about the "rescissory procedures" he had just set in motion. With new eyes he looked at Sibyl, and she at him. Incredible! he thought. Ten minutes from now she wouldn't even *remember* the courage she'd shown in thumbing her nose at Meminet! He began to slip his arms around her—but his own memory, for both good and evil, descended like a sword between them. What he had seen earlier on 3V refused simply to evaporate under the onslaught of her scent.

"You seem deeply troubled, Lester. May I know what's disturbing you?" she said, waiting patiently for his arms to finish encircling her.

"You *know* what it is! Before this interview, you were watching 3V the same time I was, seeing exactly what I saw, hearing..."

"I was?" She looked hurt. He had made her feel inadequate—for the moment, at any rate. She creased her smooth brows trying desperately to remember. Clearly, she hadn't the foggiest notion of what he was referring to.

"You were watching 'There's a Crime in Progress,' remember?... I was *horrified*!" he blurted, grabbing her elbows, shaking her as if jostling some antique pin-ball machine.

"About what, Lester?" she said, her forehead sympathetically knotted, her eyes fixed innocently upon his.

"About *what*?" he snapped. "How about that double murder!"

"*What* murder?" she said, her face clouding over with a genuine look of disgust.

Lester/Stewart sighed, then wrapped his arms around her. "First, the shooting of a rhinoceros," he said. "Then, a few seconds later—"

"How horrible!" She winced with pain at the image he had evoked. "A rhinoceros? How lucky I am that I don't have to *remember* such things!"

"I don't have your advantages," he said.

"You may never, Lester. But you do have others."

Her arms tightened their loop around the small of Lester's back.

Printed in the United States
15968LVS00001B/265-267